THE STONE WIFE

Books by Peter Lovesey

THE STONE WIFE

A PETER DIAMOND INVESTIGATION

Peter Lovesey

Published by
Soho Press, Inc.
853 Broadway
New York, NY 10003

Library of Congress Cataloging-in-Publication Data

Lovesey, Peter.
The stone wife : a Peter Diamond investigation / Peter Lovesey.

ISBN 978-1-61695-566-3
eISBN 978-1-61695-394-2

1. Diamond, Peter (Fictitious character)—Fiction.
2. Police—England—Bath—Fiction. 3. Bath (England)—Fiction. I. Title.
PR6062.O86S76 2013
823'.914—dc23
2013019794

Printed in the United States of America

10 9 8 7 6 5 4 3 2 1

THE STONE WIFE

1

"Will somebody start me at five hundred?"

A card with a number was raised near the front.

"Thank you. Five-fifty. Six hundred. Six-fifty. Seven. Seven-fifty at the back. Eight."

The bidding was keen by West Country standards. Morton's auction house in Bath was used to lots being knocked down almost at once. This had a sense of energy, even though the faces were giving nothing away.

"A thousand."

Four or five local antique dealers were still interested and Denis Doggart, the auctioneer, needed the help of his assistants to keep track of the small movements that signified bids.

"Two thousand. Two thousand two. Four on my left. Six. Eight. I have three thousand on the phone."

Heads turned. Not everyone in the room had realised bids were being phoned in. This wasn't a sale of impressionist paintings at Sotheby's. It was only the regular quarterly disposal of bits brought in to the Bath office for valuation, many of them bric-a-brac or tat.

Doggart was unfazed. He had been told to expect two telephone bidders from New York and Tokyo.

"At three thousand."

The man who had appeared to be pushing hardest shook his head. He'd reached his limit. But others were still in. The price mounted steadily, way past the valuation figure.

"At five thousand pounds."

A stifled gasp came from the back where some onlookers had gathered.

The remaining bidders were regulars at auctions all over the West Country, except one, a dark-haired man in a cream coloured linen jacket and white shirt with a red bow tie. This stranger, more than anyone, was driving the sale. A spark of determination had kindled in his blue eyes. But who the hell was he? He'd obviously registered and been given the paddle bearing his number. He'd shown no interest in any of the hundred and twenty-eight lots that had gone before.

Doggart believed he recognised the man. He would have liked to check with his clerk to learn the name, but controlling the auction demanded total concentration.

After five thousand, the bidding would be stepped up by increments of five hundred pounds.

And was, with no sign of anyone faltering. Each fresh bid from the local dealers was immediately topped by the visitor.

"Ten thousand in the front."

Bow Tie Man was in it to win it.

At last came a pause.

"All done?"

Far from it. A new bidder raised his card, Sturgess, a London dealer, who only made the trip to Bath when the catalogue contained something exceptional.

Unfazed, Bow Tie topped the bid.

The interest from Japan and America had ended somewhere between five and ten thousand. Sturgess and the mystery man could settle this between them. And now their bids were coming in with the pendulum precision auctioneers love.

"At twenty thousand pounds, then."

Who wears a bow tie these days? A few doctors and academics. The occasional eccentric. Certain auctioneers.

After a moment's consideration, Sturgess nodded for twenty-two thousand.

No hesitation in the response.

"Twenty-four thousand from the gentleman in the front. Are we there yet? A unique item of excellent provenance."

A new, aggressive voice broke in: "Nobody move."

The shock in the room was unimaginable. When an auctioneer is at work, his voice, and his alone, is all anyone expects to hear. The bidding is silent. An utterance from anyone else is an outrage.

If "Nobody move" was an order, it was not obeyed. After the collective jerk of surprise, all heads turned to see who had spoken.

A larger shock awaited. The speaker was wearing a black balaclava mask that covered his face. He was holding a handgun. He must have been standing all the time against the wall within ten feet of the auctioneer. He'd slipped on the mask and produced the gun and spoken his two words while all the attention was on the bidders.

Denis Doggart, on his rostrum, was supposed to be directing the show. He turned his head and said, "What's this about?"

"Shut up," The masked man said. "Everyone stay right where you are and nobody will get hurt."

Doggart said, "This is intolerable."

"I told you to shut it."

If any doubt remained how serious the situation was, it evaporated when two more masked men with guns entered the saleroom from the door facing the rostrum. They marched up the aisle that was kept clear for safety reasons and took a grip on the handle of the wooden dolly supporting lot 129, the object currently under the hammer.

This was too much for the bidder with the red bow tie. "You can't steal that," he said in a shrill, appalled voice. "Get away."

"Shut up, mister," the first gunman said. "Get on with it," he told his companions.

"It's under auction. I made the last bid. No one is taking it."

"Let them be, sir," the auctioneer said. "They're armed."

"They're not having it. It's too precious." Bow Tie was up from his chair and striding towards the men starting to shift the heavy burden. "Get your hands off."

The steady build-up of adrenalin during the auction must have given him extra courage, blind, foolhardy anger at the crime being committed in front of everyone. He was a slight, middle-aged man, no match for the crooks except in strength of will. He grabbed the sleeve of the nearest and succeeded in tugging his hand away from the dolly.

The gunman swung around. He had the automatic in his right hand. He levelled it and squeezed the trigger.

The report echoed through the auction room, deafening everyone.

The force of the bullet sent Bow Tie Man crashing against a walnut table stacked with china. He hit the ground at the same time as a mass of cups, saucers and plates. Pandemonium followed, screams and shouts, some people diving for cover, others heading for the door.

The would-be thieves panicked like everyone else. Any thoughts of stealing lot 129 were abandoned without a word passing among them. All three dashed for the exit, stepping over their wounded victim.

A silver delivery van was waiting in the street outside with rear door open and a ramp in place. Two of the crooks dived in and hoisted the ramp aboard and the third slammed the door, dashed to the front and climbed in. The driver, obviously primed for the getaway, had the wheels in motion before the door closed. With a screech of rubber on tarmac, the getaway vehicle rounded the tight corners of Queen Square and was gone.

Inside the auction room, fumes of cordite hung in the air. People were kneeling beside the victim, wanting to assist, but a man shot through the belly needs more than first aid. Blood had seeped through his clothes and dribbled from his mouth. He had turned as grey as the lump of stone he'd been bidding for.

"Who is he?"

"No idea."

"Doesn't anyone know who the poor guy is?"

"He was bidding. He must have signed in."

"Good point. We can check."

"Someone better phone the police."

"I already did," Doggart said, stepping down from his rostrum. "They're on their way and so is the ambulance."

"Looks like he needs an undertaker's van, not an ambulance."

From saleroom to crime scene: a swift, harsh transformation. A forensics team was already at work in a cordoned area among the array of antique glass, silver and furniture.

There is only so much information you can get from looking at a shot corpse. Peter Diamond, Bath's head of CID, had seen all he wanted, moved past and was taking more interest in lot 129. "Someone was killed for *this*?"

"Crazy," Detective Sergeant Ingeborg Smith agreed. "As a motive for murder, this tops everything."

"Topped him, for sure." He passed his fingertips along the chipped surface. "It's not even in good condition."

"It's antique," Ingeborg said and added before realising he wasn't being serious, "There are going to be signs of wear."

"As I say when I look in my shaving mirror each morning."

"Don't."

"Why would anyone want such a thing? It's not decorative. Would you give it house room?"

"Speaking personally, no, but people were bidding good money for it."

"Did you find out how much?"

"Twenty-four thousand and rising."

"Twenty-four grand?" Diamond said on a high note that startled the CSI team behind him. "For this?"

The object in front of them, standing on a wooden dolly, was a slab of carved stone about one metre in length, half a metre wide and as thick as a mattress. Whoever had lifted it on was probably nursing a back strain.

"Can you make out what it is?"

"Isn't it supposed to be someone on horseback?" Ingeborg said.

"Looks to me like a bunch of bananas."

The face of the slab had been worked by a sculptor at some time in the remote past and most of the detail had long since been eroded. Thanks to the build-up of centuries of grime in the chiselled areas you could conceivably make out the outline of a horse and rider. If so, the horse had thick legs, which was no bad thing. Either the sculptor's sense of proportion was faulty or the person in the saddle was an XXL.

"Does the writing give any clues?" Diamond asked.

Along the base was some damaged lettering: " N AMB RE ES Y SHE SAT."

Ingeborg shook her head. "The last two words are all I can make out. I suppose they tell us the rider is female."

He eyed the carving again. "You could have fooled me."

"The auction catalogue may throw some light. There must be some about."

He nodded. "See if you can find one while I have a word with the pathologist."

Bertram Sealy in his blue zip-suit was squatting in a mass of broken china beside the body and speaking into an audio recorder. He put up his hand as Diamond approached. "Don't come any closer with your big feet."

Diamond let go of the do-not-cross tape as if he had never intended to creep under it. "I'm not new to this. First impressions?"

"No great loss," the pathologist said.

There was a pause. "That's callous even by your standards."

"Bits of a tea service, cheap 1950s willow pattern. The table may take some repairing, but they're clever, these restorers. It will take something off the value, even so."

There is an unwritten law that the professionals hide their emotions, and black humour often comes to the rescue. Sealy's laborious efforts always put an extra strain on his dealings with Diamond. "I was asking about the victim."

"Him? He's beyond repair."

"I can see that. What's your opinion?"

"I'm not a ballistics man."

"And you're not here because a few cups and saucers got broken."

"Single shot to the abdomen seems to have killed him. The witnesses say he died in a short time, so it must have hit a vital organ. You don't expect one bullet to the body to kill someone outright. In the skull, yes. In the belly, hardly ever."

"Bad luck, then?"

"Not at all," Sealy said. "I just told you it was quick. Could have been slow and painful. That's what I would call bad luck."

Diamond should have saved his breath. Whatever was said to Sealy got corrected. A sure sign of insecurity.

"You're going to tell me you'll find out more when you open him up."

"And you can have a ringside seat."

Diamond didn't answer. He'd long ago stopped attending autopsies.

"Or will you send your deputy as usual?" Sealy added with a sly smile.

"There are more important matters to attend to in a murder enquiry," Diamond said with dignity. "I'm better employed in the incident room than watching you pick over the entrails." With that, he turned away to see where Ingeborg was.

She was waving the auction catalogue as she approached. "Found it, guv. *Lot 129. Relief sculpture, medieval, depicting a bunch of bananas.*"

The joke wouldn't have been worthy of Sealy.

"Pull the other one, Ingeborg."

"What it really says is that it's a figure on horseback believed to be the Wife of Bath."

"You're serious now?"

"Chaucer."

He didn't respond. Memories from way back stirred in his brain, of struggling through a dog-eared school textbook much defaced by notes of uncertain reliability from previous users.

Like most of his classmates, he'd survived with the secret aid the English master turned a blind eye to, a translation into modern verse even an eleven-year-old could understand.

Ingeborg took his silence for ignorance. "*The Canterbury Tales.*"

"Remarkable as it may seem to you, I once went to grammar school and passed an exam on Chaucer," Diamond said. "Does it tell us any more?"

She read from the catalogue: "*The inscription is damaged, but is almost certainly line 469 of the General Prologue to* The Canterbury Tales*: 'Upon an amblere esily she sat.'* What's an amblere?"

He sniffed and looked away. "Can't remember everything I was taught."

She stooped to examine the stone. "The words do seem to fit. If it's a quote from the poem, then I begin to understand the interest." She read some more from the catalogue: "*Formerly in the collection of William Stradling of Chilton Priory, Somerset antiquarian.*"

"A medieval carving of the Wife of Bath must be a rarity," he said. "I still can't see why someone had to be killed for it."

"Especially as the killers left it behind," Ingeborg said.

"Botched job. They panicked when the shot was fired. The whole idea of hijacking a block of stone strikes me as daft."

"It's not any old block of stone, guv."

"But you can't pick it up and run with it."

"It was on wheels," Ingeborg said, trying to be patient with him. "If they'd succeeded, we might have said they were master criminals. It was audacious. It involved planning—the masks, the firearms and the van. If there was any security, they cracked it. No one was prepared for three masked men interrupting the auction."

"No one was prepared for a fatal shooting. It was never in the script. The victim's actions weren't predictable."

She nodded. "As you say, he must have got shot because he created a moment of panic. Everyone was supposed to respect the guns and let the robbers get away. I would have. Wouldn't you?"

"Every time," Diamond said, looking down at the stone, "but then I can't think why I'd want to own this. He must have wanted it badly. We need to discover what made it such a desired object."

"I've bought things at auctions," Ingeborg said. "The pressure builds, even at the low levels I was involved in. When the bidding is in the thousands it must be heartbreaking to see a bunch of crooks about to walk off with the prize."

"What were you buying?"

Ingeborg reddened. "Shoes. Designer shoes."

Diamond decided to speak to the auctioneer, whose name was on a card still displayed on the front of the rostrum: Mr. Denis Doggart. He'd been pointed out when they arrived, a stocky figure in a red corduroy jacket doing his best to cope with the crowd outside the entrance. After their contact details had been taken by the police the bidders had all been asked to quit the building. They weren't going far. Most were dealers who had no intention of leaving Bath without their booty.

Doggart was now with his clerk checking the computer record of who had been there.

"This is a situation I've never encountered before," he said when Diamond went over.

"Pleased to hear it," Diamond said.

"We're not a war zone. We're country auctioneers. Most of what we offer is pretty small beer. Security isn't usually an issue."

"Meaning what? You don't have any?"

Doggart clicked his tongue and drew an angry breath. The reputation of Morton's obviously mattered to him. "There's always someone here. We had two people in the entrance issuing paddles and taking names."

"Paddles?" Diamond frowned, thinking about canoeing.

"Cards with numbers on them. They raise them when they bid."

"Does everyone get a paddle, then?"

"Serious buyers. Everyone intending to bid. All the dealers, certainly."

"Can other people get in—without a paddle?"

Doggart shrugged. "It's open to all."

"I expect you recognise most of them."

He hesitated, as if it was a trick question. "The regulars, anyway."

"Did you know the robbers?"

Doggart took a sharp breath between his teeth. "Certainly not."

"So, did you notice them as newcomers before the incident happened?"

"No chance of that. I'm fully occupied looking for bids—watching for numbers, basically. I don't have the luxury of checking every face in the room."

"After they interrupted the auction you must have got a look at them."

"They were masked. Balaclavas with holes for eyes. I haven't a clue who they were."

"They couldn't have arrived wearing balaclavas."

"The main man must have pulled his on a moment before he spoke. The others came in after he'd drawn the gun."

"You didn't recognise the voice?"

"I don't know if you're familiar with auctions, inspector."

"Superintendent."

"The bidding is silent. I'm the only one who speaks."

"Yes, I got that much," Diamond said. "It's all done with paddles. But he spoke."

"I said I've no idea who he was."

"Do you recall anything about him, what he was wearing, what he looked like?"

"About your height."

"A bit above average, then."

"But slimmer, quite a lot slimmer."

Diamond didn't take it personally. He'd heard worse.

"Black T-shirts and blue jeans," Doggart added. "All three were dressed the same."

"And they all carried guns?"

"Yes, the one who fired the shot was one of the pair who came in after. A young man, going by the way he moved."

"Did you get a look at the guns?"

"Revolvers, all of them."

"You're sure of that."

"I know what a revolver looks like."

"What about the victim? Is he a dealer?"

"Not to my knowledge. It's the first time I've seen him here."

"You must have his name from the list of bidders."

"We do. We already checked and it's Gildersleeve."

Diamond turned to Ingeborg. "Did you get that? See what you can find out." He glanced back at lot 129 before asking Doggart, "Was the Wife of Bath the main attraction today?"

The auctioneer nodded. "Certainly there was a lot of interest. We circulated dealers in advance and there were telephone bidders from America and Japan. As it turned out, the bidding went considerably higher than our valuation."

"Is that unusual?"

"A piece such as this is a challenge. You don't have anything to compare it with. We settled on three thousand and evidently underestimated the value. Mr. Gildersleeve got into competition with a London dealer and things were getting exciting when the interruption came."

"At twenty-four thousand, I heard."

"Yes. When the bids outstrip the valuation by as much as that, there's an element of embarrassment I can't deny. Did we miss something that certain people in the know discovered? In the trade we call that kind of item a sleeper. Our reputation as experts is called into question."

"Twenty-four grand sounds a good whack to me for a carving you can hardly recognise," Diamond said. "I suppose it was the link to Chaucer that pushed up the bidding."

"Yes, and the provenance. The piece was once in the collection of an early nineteenth-century antiquarian called William Stradling who made it his mission to rescue bits of masonry at risk of destruction from modernisers. There was a campaign of so-called restoration going on in the early eighteen hundreds and Stradling's home at Chilton Polden became a refuge for fragments that would otherwise have been destroyed or discarded. The tablet was listed as one of his finds, so we know it can't be a modern fake."

"A fake?" Diamond's eyes widened. "Faking never crossed my mind."

"It happens all the time. We're trained to watch out for it. Reputations can be ruined if you get taken in."

"Difficult to fake a block of old stone."

"But well worth it if the artist does a good job. They're still artists, even if the work is fraudulent."

"But this, you say, must be genuine?"

Doggart nodded. "The provenance. Stradling knew what he was doing. His pieces came from centuries-old buildings."

"You knew there would be a lot of interest?"

"It's always difficult to predict, but as I told you we had plenty of enquiries."

Diamond gave the matter some thought. There was more to this auction business than he'd first appreciated. "Anyone keen enough to bid would want to see the thing ahead of the auction, I expect."

"Anyone able to get here. We're open for viewing six days a week."

"I'm thinking one or more of the gunmen may have come here to case the place, posing as a possible buyer."

"Conceivably." Doggart plainly didn't enjoy the suggestion.

"We'll need to talk to your staff."

"That shouldn't be a problem."

"They would have been hired thugs—the crooks, I mean, not your staff. We can assume they were acting for someone else, someone with a good eye for an antique sculpture."

"Not necessarily."

"Why not?"

"It's not a Dresden shepherdess," Doggart said.

"Come again."

"A unique item such as this is difficult to classify and even more difficult to dispose of."

"I get you now. Like trying to unload the *Mona Lisa.*"

The auctioneer wasn't impressed with Diamond's example. "One of the Elgin marbles might be a better comparison."

"True," Diamond said. "Unique and a bugger to move. Who would have dreamed up something like this?"

"Don't ask me," Doggart said.

"You're in the trade. Better placed than I am."

"I can't think of anyone."

Ingeborg had been busy with what Diamond liked to call her pocket computer. "This sounds as if it could be the dead man, a John Gildersleeve, author of a book called *Chaucer: The Bawdy Tales.*"

"I hope we're not getting into something my mother wouldn't have approved of," Diamond said with a wink at Doggart. "How did you find this out?"

"Googled the name."

"You Googled Gildersleeve." He turned back to Doggart, who was more his age. "Sounds like something out of *The Goon Show.*"

"Professor of Medieval English Literature at Reading University," Ingeborg added, still using her iPhone. "Here's a picture of him."

Modern technology regularly ambushed Peter Diamond, but he tried not to show it. He glanced at the tiny head and shoulders photo. "That's the victim, I'll grant you. Now it's falling into place. He must have lectured on Chaucer. Not surprising he was a bidder."

"As an expert, he may well have been consulted when the piece was identified earlier this year," Doggart said. "Until then, it was a miscellaneous stone tablet of the medieval period of no particular interest. It was in storage in the Bridgwater museum for at least half a century. The story is that one of the staff took another look one day and worked out what the lettering was and where the quote came from. Some Chaucer experts confirmed that he was right. The museum committee had a meeting. Some were in favour of keeping the thing, but the majority voted to cash in on the discovery and do a modest upgrade of the museum. They had their exhibits crowded into a few Victorian showcases. So the piece was put up for auction."

"The news must have travelled fast in academic circles," Ingeborg said.

"We publicised it quite widely," Doggart said. "It got into *The Times* and *History Today,* which would explain the telephone bidding. America and Japan are quickly onto anything like this. Even so, I couldn't see it making much over three thousand. It's a mystery to me why the bidding went so high."

"The bigger mystery is why Professor Gildersleeve took on the gunmen," Diamond said. "That wasn't the act of an intelligent man."

"I warned him from the rostrum not to get involved," Doggart said. "He took no notice. He was very agitated."

"We'll look into his motives."

"Was the Wife of Bath a bawdy character?" Ingeborg asked. Neither man answered.

"I'm thinking about the professor's book," she said. "He'd written about the bawdy tales."

"All I can recall about the lady is that she'd been married several times," Diamond said. "I suppose you'd call her a woman of the world. I don't remember anything bawdy, as you call it. My school would have made sure we didn't get to read stuff likely to corrupt our pure young minds."

"'The Miller's Tale' is the rude one," Doggart said.

Diamond grinned. "Now you mention it, yes, I do have a memory of that. A copy was passed round, but not in class."

"Your young minds weren't so pure after all," Ingeborg said.

"I was being ironical. I bet you read it at school."

"That's beside the point," she said, giving nothing away. "We're dealing with the Wife of Bath here, not the miller."

"One thing of immediate concern is what happens next about the tablet," Doggart said. "Clearly someone will stop at nothing to acquire it. I can't see the owners wanting it back in the Bridgwater museum and we can't keep it on the premises here, with the risk of a break-in."

"That's all right," Diamond said. "It's evidence. We'll get

it shifted to the nick. I'll send a van and some fit young coppers. But I'll let you know when to expect them. These villains are well capable of impersonating the police to get what they want."

"This much is certain," he told Ingeborg when they were far enough away from Doggart. "It's an organised crime—or was meant to be, anyway. We must get the local pond life under the spotlight. Use all our snouts to see if there's word of a failed job that ended with a shooting."

"You want me to handle that?"

"Not at this point. There's something more urgent."

"What's that?"

"Don't look so suspicious. I'll get reinforcements."

"What for, exactly?"

"Freeing me up to work out what the hell was going on."

"Okay," she said in a tone that left him in no doubt she'd expected a better answer.

But Diamond was off on his own track. "I need to look at it from the angle of the victim, try to find out why he was so keen to buy the tablet, as Doggart calls it. I find this fascinating. What's so special about a beaten-up chunk of old stone you can hardly recognise as anything at all?"

"He's dead. He can't tell us."

"We can question the other bidder, the London dealer who was pushing the professor all the way."

She nodded. This was a point she'd missed.

"Who was he?" Diamond asked.

"His name is Sturgess. Came down from London."

"Still about?"

"Most of the bidders are, waiting to collect their purchases."

"Did Sturgess bid for anything else?"

"I'd better find out. He could be gone by now."

She left to check and was soon back.

"Sturgess is still here, but I don't think you'll get much from him."

"Try me. Did you say I'll see him now?"

"Yes, and he said you'll be wasting your time."

"He's got something to hide, then," Diamond said. "Bring him in."

She hesitated. "What about all the other bidders?"

"Are they outside as well?"

"Well, yes. I'm thinking someone in that auction must have got a good look at the first gunman before he put his mask on. People were standing pretty close. We're going to need statements from everyone who was present."

"Thanks, Ingeborg," he said. "You're a mind-reader."

3

Sturgess, the dealer from London, began in a lofty tone that irritated Diamond straight away. "I hope the police are competent to deal with this. John Gildersleeve was a leading authority on Chaucer."

"He's a dead man."

"That doesn't alter anything."

"It altered him. He's not the leading authority on anything now."

Sturgess gritted his teeth, obviously more used to dealing with connoisseurs than smart-mouthed policemen. "I'm saying the reason for his death may have to do with his field of expertise."

"It was murder, whichever way you look at it. That's my field of expertise."

"But one needs to know what the motive might have been."

"Which is why I'm interviewing you, Mr. Sturgess."

"I'm not a Chaucer expert."

"You're not?"

A shake of the head.

"You knew enough to bid well above the valuation. Were you acting for someone else?"

"Certainly. My firm wouldn't bid at that level without instructions."

"Who from?"

"No comment."

Diamond blinked in surprise.

Sturgess raised his chin defiantly. "Wild horses wouldn't drag the name from me. Client confidentiality."

"I don't think I'm getting through to you," Diamond said. "Do you see what's going on across the room? That's a forensic pathologist examining a murder victim. I'm the chief investigating officer and you're a witness. Don't talk to me about client confidentiality."

"The name isn't relevant, anyway," Sturgess said.

"I'll be the judge of that. I could do you for withholding information."

"I won't be bullied."

Diamond took that as a challenge. "Were you hoping to return to London tonight?"

Sturgess turned pale. "You wouldn't detain me?"

"Tonight, tomorrow and next week if necessary. Don't look so alarmed. We allow you to contact your solicitor." Threats have to carry conviction and Diamond issued this unlikely one as coolly as if he was stating the time of day.

There was an immediate change of tone. "Officer, I'd better explain. I've no wish to put myself on the wrong side of the law. It's just that our whole business is founded on good faith, respecting the confidence of clients. To reveal the name of a potential buyer would be ruinous to our reputation. It might mean losing not merely the account in question, but numbers of others when they learn that trust has been broken."

"So who is it?" Diamond said.

"Weren't you listening? I'm not at liberty to say."

"Carry on like this, my friend, and you won't be at liberty, full stop."

The man was shaken, but he wasn't about to cough. "I don't see why you need to know it."

"That's pretty obvious, I would have thought," Diamond said, his patience exhausted. "There were two bidders left in this auction and one was murdered. The survivor has some explaining to do."

"But the people who killed him weren't bidding."

"We don't know who they were acting for."

"Can't you take my word as a gentleman that it's impossible for my client to have been involved?"

Diamond shook his head.

"This is beyond a joke," Sturgess said. "May I make a phone call?"

"To tip off your client?"

This was received with an icy stare. "To my office, to explain the impossible position I find myself in."

"Go ahead. I'll be listening." He could see this nonsense going on indefinitely, and he reckoned Sturgess was a minor player.

Whoever was on the other end of the call took some convincing, but Sturgess was a man in a fix, explaining that he was facing arrest, with all the damage that would do to the good name of the firm. Finally, he switched off, pulled at his tie as if it was strangling him, and said, "This must be in the strictest confidence."

Diamond waited.

Sturgess glanced to right and left before saying in little more than a whisper, "I was bidding on behalf of . . ." He mouthed the words.

"Come again."

As if he was in breach of the Official Secrets Act, he put his mouth within six inches of Diamond's ear and said, "The British Museum."

A moment was needed to absorb this. "Yes?" Diamond said.

"Yes."

"I hadn't thought of them."

"Now do you see my difficulty?"

"I suppose they would have an interest."

"Please keep your voice down. If it got out, all manner of complications would arise."

"But the sale didn't take place."

"We still represent them. And the tablet may come up for sale again."

"Not for some time, it won't."

"We wouldn't want to alert the other great museums of the world. And we wouldn't want to be pushed to some exorbitant price by someone acting for the seller. Or the auction house."

"Does that happen?"

"It's not unknown in the provinces. They call it bouncing a bid against the wall. They artificially inflate the bidding."

"On the assumption that someone will go higher?"

"Or has unlimited resources."

"How much would the British Museum have gone to?"

The eyes opened wide in shock. "I'm absolutely not authorised to tell you."

This time Diamond didn't press. He'd asked out of curiosity, no more. "But you would have won eventually?"

"I assume so."

Diamond was deflated. He'd begun to believe all the secrecy was about shielding some sinister Mr. Big, an oil-rich Russian with mafia connections, or an African dictator with blood money to bury in objects of art. "So what can you tell me about Professor Gildersleeve? Would he have been bidding on his own account?"

"I can't say for certain, but from his whole demeanour I gathered this was a personal matter, as if he was on some sort of mission to own the tablet. It became so obvious that I almost felt guilty topping his bids. He couldn't have known he was up against one of the great institutions of the world."

"And do you know of any other parties with an interest?"

"Obviously America and Japan, who were bidding by phone, but they stopped at ten thousand."

"I mean was there any hint of other interest before the auction?"

"I heard of none, but the sale was widely publicised in academic circles."

"Were you tipped off that Gildersleeve was a bidder?"

"No."

"You seem to know all about him."

"Only by reputation. I did my homework before coming here. When they identified him as the man who was shot, I recognised the name. He's the author of several books on Chaucer."

"Could he have been bidding for some rival museum?"

"I doubt it. My firm belief is that his interest was personal, which is why he challenged the gunmen."

"Makes sense," Diamond said. "Did you get a good look at them?"

"No more than anyone else."

"Did you notice the one who first produced the gun?"

"I was far too caught up in the auction to notice anyone except Professor Gildersleeve. Your attention is all on the rival bidder and the auctioneer."

Understandable. Diamond glanced across the room, his thoughts moving on. He'd got what he needed from Sturgess. "Unless there's something else you can tell me, I have no further questions."

Sturgess didn't need any more encouragement to move off fast.

Diamond called Bath Central and asked if there was any progress tracking the getaway van. A world-weary voice told him nothing had been reported and without a registration number or even the make, he shouldn't get his hopes up. They couldn't do hard stops on all the silver vans across the city. Maybe if it had been stolen they would find it abandoned later. Professional robbers generally arrange for a car change along the escape route.

All down to CID, then, he told himself. What's new?

In the far corner of the auction room, several of the team were at work interviewing witnesses. They had commandeered some elegant chairs and small tables that could have been Chippendale or Sheraton for all he knew. DI John Leaman and DC Paul Gilbert had joined Ingeborg and appeared to be getting through at a good rate.

He went over.

"Any description worth having?" he asked Ingeborg when she'd finished with her latest.

"Zilch so far, guv," she told him. "Everyone remembers what the villains were wearing and not much else."

"The balaclavas."

"And the T-shirts and jeans."

He stood with arms folded, listening to the latest witness. Ingeborg was good at this, cutting through any useless prattle to get to the real point of the interview and doing it with charm and precision. But she wasn't getting much for her efforts.

It was Paul Gilbert who summoned Diamond by tilting the chair away from the table and saying, "Guv, I think you should hear this."

His witness was a small, sharp-featured woman in her fifties with hair streaked red and green and makeup that was meant to tone but hadn't.

"This is Miss, em . . ." Gilbert paused to look at his notes.

"It doesn't matter a hoot," the woman said. "Everyone calls me the glass lady."

"Alice Topham," Gilbert read out. "From Brighton."

"Long way to come," Diamond said.

"I go to all the sales," Miss Topham said. "There's always glass worth buying. Some of the best lots still hadn't been reached when the interruption came. I suppose I'll have to wait for another day. But I want it on record that I was the successful bidder for the Jubilee Commemoration dish. In all this chaos, things could easily go astray."

"Tell Mr. Diamond what you were saying about the man who stopped the auction," Gilbert said.

"Him?" she said with distaste. "It was my bad luck to be right behind him. He was annoying me because he wouldn't keep still, blocking my view. Twitchy, checking his pockets. You don't want movement in an auction. All I could see half the time was the back of his neck. This was before he pulled the mask over his head."

Gilbert prompted her again. "But what did you tell me about it?"

"The hairline was uneven. Some kind of scar had stopped it from growing normally."

"This is helpful," Diamond said. "Was there a shape to the scar?"

"It was roughly circular and concave, like a little crater on the moon, if you follow me. I expect he'd had a carbuncle removed at one time."

"How big?"

"No more than that." She made a shape with her thumb and forefinger about the size of a penny. "Most people wouldn't notice, but I have an eye for detail. It's my business, you see."

"Do you remember anything else about him?"

"I only had the back view."

"Try to remember."

"Now you're asking. The hair was dark and straight and starting to go grey, quite long, almost covering his ears, but I could see where the lobes should have been. There weren't any. I'm always wary of men without lobes. There's an old superstition that murderers have no ear lobes."

"He wasn't the killer. He didn't fire the shot," Gilbert said.

"He's one of the gang, so he's just as culpable," the glass lady said and turned to Diamond for support. "Isn't that so?"

"We could charge him, yes. What about the others?"

"I couldn't see their ears under the balaclavas, could I? They came in wearing them."

"I was interested to know if you spotted any other detail."

She shook her head. "As soon as they appeared, I ducked behind that harpsichord over there."

"You go to all the sales, you said. Have you ever seen anything like the lump of stone they were after?"

"Anything and everything," she said.

"Stone objects?"

"Bird baths, statues, even a headstone once. If it's old, it has a value and a price. Personally, I only buy glass. It's prettier and easier to get home. Have you finished with me, because I'd like to pick up my dish and get on the road?"

"We may contact you later to identify the scar if we make an arrest."

"I hope you will, and soon. I'd like to see them locked away for the rest of their undeserving lives."

She went off in search of the auctioneer. Diamond watched the red and green streaks until they were lost to view behind an oak sideboard. "This is shaping up as one of the wackiest cases I've been involved in," he said to Paul Gilbert. "The Wife of Bath. A glass lady. A gunman with a moon crater on the back of his neck. A guy afraid to speak the name of the British Museum. What next?"

4

No one was under any illusion that the three hitmen were Chaucer scholars. Everything pointed to professionals, even though the job had been botched. But finding them wouldn't be easy. Basically, the only description Diamond had was that the first robber had longish dark hair, a scar on the back of his neck and no ear lobes.

"This will be tough," he warned the team at the first briefing. "I don't need to tell you snouts go silent when the crime is murder. We'll try. We bloody have to. But we may need a better way."

"*Crimewatch*?" Paul Gilbert said, ever eager to contribute.

Everyone except Gilbert saw the glint in the boss's eyes that said *Crimewatch* was a non-starter, but the youngest, greenest member of CID pressed on. "It would make great television, reconstructing the auction."

"No question."

"It's a massive audience."

Diamond was patient with him. "But there's only so much information Joe Public can provide. We interviewed everyone who was there."

"All we'd end up with," Ingeborg added, "would be a list of suspicious characters from other auctions."

"A thousand other auctions," John Leaman said.

"A few hundred, anyway," Ingeborg said.

Gilbert's shoulders sank. "It was only a thought."

"Don't take it personally," Diamond said. "I'm always open to suggestions."

A few looks were exchanged. Everyone else in the team had been cut to shreds at some point in the past for coming up with a half-baked idea.

"The way I look at it," Leaman said, "we don't just want to find the three who held up the auction. We're looking for the guy who hired them."

"Too right we are."

"Whoever he is," Keith Halliwell said, "he's not a happy bunny."

Gilbert returned to the fray like a boxer bouncing off the ropes. "What was he hoping to get out of it? Even if the hold-up had succeeded, all he'd end up with would be a lump of stone."

"An antique lump of stone," Ingeborg said in a measured, bored voice, "linked to one of the most famous poems in the language and valued at over twenty grand by the British Museum."

Everyone except Gilbert felt the force of the putdown.

John Leaman repeated his mantra: "We need to find the guy behind all this."

"Agreed," Diamond said. "So who would have an interest in acquiring a carving of the Wife of Bath?"

"Another museum?" Gilbert said.

"Get real," Halliwell said. "Museums don't hire armed robbers."

"Some nutty professor, then."

"Another? We already have one and he's dead."

"Well, it has to be some weirdo."

"There's a question that always comes up when a well-known work of art is stolen, and we need to ask it, too," Ingeborg said. "Why do they do it?"

"To sell on to a third party?" Halliwell said.

"Or demand a ransom?" Leaman said.

"An insurance scam?" Gilbert said.

"Was the stone insured? I doubt it," Leaman said.

"Never mind," Diamond said. "This is good. Brainstorming. Keep it rolling."

"The best scheme I ever heard of was the *Mona Lisa* theft from the Louvre," Leaman said.

Gilbert screwed up his face. "Is this a joke?"

"No. It's a fact."

"When was this?"

"About a hundred years ago," Ingeborg said. "It couldn't happen these days."

"It was still the cleverest art scam there's ever been," Leaman said. "The main thief was an Italian glazier who helped construct the protective glass box it was housed in, so he knew exactly how to beat the security. This heist was three years in the planning. They stole other works from the Louvre before they went for the big one. The glazier went in with two accomplices dressed in workmen's clothes on a day the gallery was closed for cleaning, hid in a storeroom and walked out next morning with the painting."

Ingeborg shrugged. "The cleverest ever? I dispute that. Anyway, it wouldn't be possible in the twenty-first century with modern security."

"But do you know the motive?" Leaman said. "That was the brilliant part."

"Give it to us, then," Ingeborg said in a bored voice, well used to being trumped by the team know-all.

"The whole thing was masterminded by a crook called Valfierno who'd worked out this method. He'd used it before in Argentina and Mexico. He would hire an insider—in this case, the glazier—to steal the original. News of the theft would get into the papers. Then—this is the brilliant part—he would sell copies to rich collectors who believed they were buying the real thing. They were clever forgeries painted by his accomplice, a skilful artist called Chaudron. In the two years the Leonardo was missing, Valfierno sold six *Mona Lisa* forgeries to rich American collectors at three hundred thousand dollars a go. Big money in 1911. The fall guys each believed they secretly owned the most famous painting in the world."

"How was it detected?" Gilbert asked.

"All this time the glazier had kept the original rolled up under his bed. Stupidly he tried to cash in by offering it to an art dealer in Florence. He was caught and jailed and the painting was returned to the Louvre, putting an end to Valfierno's clever scam. They could have gone on indefinitely selling fake *Mona Lisa*s to rich mugs."

"There's always a reckoning," Ingeborg said.

"Not in the art world, there isn't," Diamond said. "Fewer than ten percent of art thefts are ever detected."

"We're on a loser, then," Leaman said.

You didn't say that kind of thing in Diamond's CID meetings.

There was an uncomfortable silence before the main man said, "I'm going to take the last remark as a joke. A few minutes ago you were all supplying theories. Come on." He snapped his fingers.

Leaman said, "I thought my *Mona Lisa* story was a good example."

"It can't teach us much about the present case. They'd be hard pushed to sell forgeries of the *Wife of Bath*."

"The theft of the *Stone of Scone* was closer to what we're talking about," Halliwell said.

"Stone of what?" Gilbert said.

"Before your time. And mine, come to that. The ancient coronation stone nicked from Westminster Abbey in the 1950s."

"Political," Ingeborg said. "That was all about Scottish nationalism."

"The practical problem of shifting a bloody great rock was the same."

"True. But there the resemblance ends."

"So, what's your theory?" Halliwell asked Ingeborg.

"It's about single-minded people, collectors, who covet great works of art. They don't want them in public galleries being enjoyed by everyone. They want the thrill of having the stuff all to themselves. Thousands of precious artefacts have been stolen over the years and never recovered. They can't be sold on. They're too well known. Van Goghs, Picassos and Rembrandts. It's possible our mystery man is a secret hoarder."

"With an Aladdin's cave piled high with stolen treasures?" Leaman said with a curl of the lip.

"Doesn't matter where he stores it. Collector's mania is a recognised condition."

"You think he has a stack of stone carvings at home?"

She sighed and spread her hands. "Listen, guys, all I'm suggesting is that we focus our investigation on the brains behind this operation."

"Ingeborg is right," Diamond said, before anyone else chipped in. "The paymaster is our main target. We'll investigate everyone with a conceivable interest in acquiring the stone."

"Excuse me," Leaman said.

"What's up?" Diamond said.

"That was my suggestion."

"What was?"

"You said Ingeborg is right about investigating the paymaster."

"It's bloody obvious, isn't it?" Ingeborg said to him. "I didn't think we were reduced to scoring points off each other." But she'd just scored a good one off him.

It was clear to Diamond that the brainstorming was at an end. Nothing more would emerge while they were sniping at each other. He liked his team and valued them, but bright people tend to think their opinions should carry the day. "This doesn't mean we let the gunmen go free. I'm thinking one or more of us may need to go undercover."

Conversation ceased while they all considered their options.

When Keith Halliwell spoke, it was to say, "High risk."

Diamond didn't say a word.

Halliwell was supposed to be Diamond's back-up, the senior man. "There's a fine line between getting on the inside and aiding and abetting. We all know about certain high profile cases where the officer concerned got too involved. The law doesn't take kindly to cops bending the rules."

Diamond knew he should have discussed this first with Keith. The man was speaking sense. But it was still a cause for anger that his deputy's first reaction had been so negative. "You've made your point," he said, tight-lipped. "Whoever takes this on will need to be ultra careful."

They wouldn't be queuing up to volunteer.

"Anyone wants to speak to me, I'll be in my office."

What followed was to become a classic "I was there" episode to be endured at the time, cherished in the memory and relayed to generations of CID officers who came after. Diamond stepped into his office and closed the door. Actually "slammed" would be a better word. Immediately came an almighty thump followed by the sound of glass shattering and a roar of mingled pain and outrage giving way to a passage of swearing the like of which had not been heard in Manvers Street in twenty years. Then silence.

There was no rush to assist.

Consciences were being examined. Everyone could picture the scene inside. They should have seen it coming and warned the boss. He'd stumbled, staggered, made a grab for the only thing within reach and brought his computer screen crashing down with him.

Diamond had tripped over the *Wife of Bath*.

Earlier that morning six fit young policemen in a van had transported the stone from the auction room to the police station in Manvers Street. As an exhibit, it should by rights have gone into the evidence store in the basement, but the sergeant in charge had baulked. He'd insisted the thing was too heavy to take off its dolly and carry downstairs. The PCs who had shifted it were only too pleased to wheel it into Diamond's office. Just inside the door.

Ingeborg said, "We can't just sit here. Someone's got to go in."

All eyes turned to Halliwell, the senior man.

The responsibility couldn't be shirked. Halliwell rose, crossed the room and opened up.

He found the big man still conscious, sitting on the floor, picking bits of broken circuitry and glass from his clothes.

No words are adequate in a situation like this.

"You okay, guv?"

"Does it look like it?"

"Can I help you up?"

"Which idiot is responsible for this?"

Halliwell tried his best to explain the problem the removal team had faced. Diamond didn't seem to be listening.

By now some of the others had joined Halliwell in the doorway. Leaman asked, "Are you injured, guv?" As the keeno in CID, he'd long ago been made the first aid man. Everyone had the training, but Leaman had the bandages. "Are you bleeding?"

"Bleeding mad. Why didn't anyone warn me?"

"We were about to. You were too fast for us," Halliwell said. "You opened the door and went straight in."

"Isn't that what people do when they enter a room?"

No one answered.

"You had at least twenty minutes to warn me."

"We were brainstorming."

"Brainstorming be buggered. I could have ended up in hospital. Someone give me a hand."

With Halliwell's assistance, he hauled himself upright, making a sound like wind chimes as bits of the smashed screen hit the floor. Glass was distributed widely in all directions.

"I'm bruised all over."

Instead of offering sympathy, Leaman said, "You need an immediate shower and a change of clothes."

"Why? I'm not incontinent."

"The VDU."

Abbreviations had always been Diamond's blind spot. His features twitched. "WHAT are you trying to tell me now?"

"You need hosing down. Most of the parts in that visual display unit are highly toxic. Mercury in the circuit boards, lead in the cathode ray tube and chromium protecting the hard surfaces. If any of that gets into your system, I can't answer for the consequences."

"It's too bloody late to answer for the consequences. That's what I'm hopping mad about."

Leaman refused to be silenced. His authority in this emergency overrode rank, discipline, everything. At any rate, that's what they'd told him on the training course. "And you're not to use your office again until it's been completely decontaminated."

"Get lost."

"That's an order."

"*What* did you say?"

"If you happen to remember," Leaman said through clenched teeth, "you appointed me the health and safety rep as well as the first aid man. What I say goes."

The only shower was in the custody suite and the only change of clothes was the cornflower blue paper suit normally used for suspects and victims whose clothes were taken for forensic examination. Diamond emerged some time later looking like a visitor from another planet, but free of contamination. At this low point in his life he had nowhere to hide. The *Wife of Bath* was now in sole occupation of his office. A block of weathered stone had reduced him to this.

Leaman was a credit to health and safety. He had locked the door to Diamond's office and pinned crime scene tape across it. The top and bottom were sealed with wet tissues. He'd contacted the fire service. Their decontamination squad would go in overnight and remove all traces of the toxins.

From the CID room Diamond phoned his friend and sometime lover, Paloma Kean. Everyone could hear his end of the conversation. He couldn't ask them to empty the room and he wasn't going to step outside where other people would see him in the paper suit.

"Me," he said to Paloma. "Got a big favour to ask. Any chance you could call at my house in the next hour and collect a set of clothes for me?"

Fortunately Paloma worked from her home in Lyncombe, running her business supplying antique artwork for costume designers. From what was said next she must have asked what had happened. A reasonable question.

He said, "I'd rather not discuss it over the phone."

Pause, for another question.

"Everything," he said. "Shoes, socks, pants. Picture me naked and you won't go wrong."

The team was enjoying this. They all had their heads down, but some of them were shaking uncontrollably.

"In the bedroom, most of it. I'd better warn you. It's not all that tidy."

He glanced over his shoulder.

"If you can't find the underwear, don't worry. I could manage without on this occasion, until I get home, that is."

Behind him, Ingeborg was in tears of mirth. Paul Gilbert had covered his face and was emitting a muffled cooing sound like a pigeon.

"In a black plastic sack would be best," Diamond said, "preferably knotted at the top and labelled personal, with my name. You could hand it in at the front desk and tell them it's urgent. I'll call you tonight and give you the whole sorry story."

The paper suit wasn't made for warmth. Temporarily positioned close to a radiator, he had time to reflect while waiting for his clothes to arrive. "The fire service, you said? They'd better treat the place with respect. I don't want anything destroyed. I've got personal things in there, the photo of my wife, my coffee mug, my cactus."

"Not sure about the cactus," Leaman said, still exerting his authority. "It may have to go."

"It's on the filing cabinet, well out of range."

"Plants absorb things from the air. It could wilt."

"I brought that cactus with me from London. I had it when I was in the Met."

"Difficult to clean."

Keith Halliwell said, "We may need to have a whip round and get you a replacement. The least we could do, really."

Ingeborg said, "There's one good thing about this."

"What's that?" Diamond asked.

"The *Wife of Bath* will benefit. A good cleaning can only improve her."

5

Paloma treated Peter Diamond to a superintendent-sized ham and pineapple pizza and several beers at her house the same evening and listened in sympathy. She offered to smear arnica ointment on his bruises, but he was quick to thank her and say the soreness was just a memory now. He didn't want her getting the idea he was too damaged to go to bed with her. She'd learned about the shooting and said it was hard to understand how people could get so violent. From all she'd read in the papers, Professor Gildersleeve had been respected in academic circles.

"Yes, it's hard to understand," he said. "If he'd stayed calm he'd still be alive. He lost his cool when the robbers tried to grab the piece of so-called sculpture he was bidding for. Obviously he'd set his heart on buying it."

"What's it like?"

"The *Wife of Bath*? Unappealing."

"There speaks the man who tripped over her."

"Truly. It's a chunk of dirty old limestone with some carving you can barely make out. A figure on horseback and some broken lettering underneath that they say identifies her."

"And now she's sitting in your office?"

"She's taken it over."

"Smart gal, not moving until her case is solved."

His jaw jutted. "We'll see about that."

"Better not let it get personal, Peter."

"Don't you worry about that. My feet are firmly on the ground."

A ripple of laughter greeted the second statement and presently he remembered why and joined in the amusement.

"Like her or not," he said, trying to sound impartial, "my job is to find out more. If I'm going to understand the professor's reaction I'll need to brush up on my Chaucer."

Paloma rose from her armchair and looked along her shelves of books.

"Don't tell me you have a copy."

"I once did the costumes for a revival of the musical."

"A Wife of Bath musical?" he said in disbelief.

"*The Canterbury Tales.* You must have seen it."

"Theatre-going isn't my thing, if you remember."

"Gotcha," she said, picking out a paperback and handing it to him. "This is the Nevill Coghill modern English version, much easier to follow than Chaucer's original. Coghill also wrote the lyrics for the show. He was an Oxford professor."

He opened the book at random and read a few lines. "I recognise this. We used it at school. Even a peasant like me can follow it."

"Keep it. I doubt if I'll need it again. The musical was a romp, quite naughty by the standards of the time, not long after censorship ended. Before that, everything had to be vetted by the Lord Chamberlain's office."

"Naughty in what way?"

"Simulated sex, four-letter words."

"Which ones?"

"Read your translation. They used three or four of the tales in the show, including the Wife of Bath's. It's about one of King Arthur's knights—a right bastard he is—who rapes an innocent girl and is condemned to death. But the queen, who should have known better in my opinion, asks for him to be spared and sends him on a quest for a year and a day to discover what it is that women most desire."

"Some quest."

"I can see how your mind is working and you're wrong. Actually the tale itself isn't as bawdy as some of the others."

"More of a tease, then?"

"Yes, basically it's the frog prince story. After much travelling and asking for help, the knight finds an ugly old woman who makes him promise to marry her if she gives him the answer to the question. He's desperate by now and agrees. Then he returns to court and tells the queen the answer and wins his pardon, but of course the old crone insists on the marriage."

"And he does the decent thing?"

"Without much grace. In bed the first night he calls her loathsome. For this she gives him a dreadfully long lecture on the meaning of gentility that seems to wear him down. Eventually she offers terms. Either she'll stay ugly and be an obedient wife or she'll become young and beautiful and he can take his chance on what happens. He's so beaten down by now that he says it's her choice. She's pleased. Basically, she's now the boss and asks him to kiss her, whereupon she magically turns into a young beauty."

"And what was the answer?"

"What do women most desire?" She widened her eyes. "If you haven't discovered by now, I'm surprised."

"The same as what men most desire?"

She shook her head.

"Shoes?"

"Actually, no. Women want sovereignty over their men."

"Girl power?"

"It sounds modern, but it goes back to the medieval notion of courtly love, the noble man devoted to his lady and willing to suffer all manner of trials and tribulations even to approach her."

"Worship from afar?"

"Something like that. She is perfection and he perpetually desires her and performs deeds of valour in a vain attempt to win her favour."

"Story of my life," Diamond said.

"Come off it. Even in Chaucer's story, the bloke has his way with her at the end."

"With the pretty one?"

"Yes—and wouldn't you know it?—instead of insisting on running the marriage her way, she promises, basically, to love, honour and obey. End of story—as written by a bloke."

"But is she happy?"

"Supposedly, but it's not true to the code of courtly love. The woman is supposed to be unattainable."

"If they were, men would give up and watch football."

"Very likely," Paloma said. "Another beer?"

"Depends."

"On what?"

"On whether I'm to stay the night."

"There you go," she said. "Twenty-first century man. Where did I go wrong?"

He was thinking of something else. "The Wife of Bath. I wonder why Chaucer picked Bath, rather than any other town. Is that explained in the poem?"

"Not that I recall."

"Was he from around here?"

Paloma shook her head. "Far as I recall, the family were Ipswich people and he was born in London."

"So she could have been the Wife of Ipswich."

Paloma sighed, and it wasn't a sigh of admiration.

"But why Bath?" Diamond said. "A random choice?"

She shook her head. "No, there's good evidence that he knew this part of the world. First, he says she was 'of beside Bath.' Chaucer used words carefully. There was a city wall from Roman times and there were suburbs beyond the walls to the north and south even in the fourteenth century. It's believed he must have known about these to have placed her there."

"She may even have lived in Weston, where I do."

"Or much closer. St. Michael's church and Broad Street were outside the walls. So was Milsom Street. We think of this area as central now, but it was outside the northern limit."

"The slums?"

She shrugged. "I expect there was snobbery about who the real citizens were and who came from the other side. And that's not the only bit of local knowledge Chaucer used. The local source of wealth was the wool trade and when you read the Prologue, as I'm sure you will, you'll see that

Alison—that's the wife's name—was an expert weaver. She surpassed the cloth-makers of France and made all her own clothes, which were beautifully spun. So she's a Bathonian by residence and occupation."

"You know a lot about this."

"I had to, for the costumes. I could tell you more about what she wore than you'll ever want to know."

"Yet you still say Chaucer didn't live in Bath?"

"That wouldn't stop him knowing the place. People like him, in the service of the king, travelled more than you might suppose. He spent time in France and Italy, so Bath wasn't any distance at all."

His thoughts were already moving on. "The carving is a West Country piece, apparently, in the local stone. I wonder if it's a relic from one of Bath's medieval buildings."

"Could be. There aren't many left apart from churches."

"The carving wouldn't be from a church. You can't call the Wife of Bath a religious subject."

"She was on a pilgrimage," Paloma pointed out.

"True."

"A pious woman. Worldly and down-to-earth, but God-fearing."

"But she was fiction. Would a church want a piece of carving that wasn't a Bible story? If it's fourteenth century, as they seem to think, the church authorities would have to be very open-minded to adopt a character from a modern poem, a fruity one, too."

"Put like that, you may be right," Paloma said. "The carving could have been part of a private dwelling. I don't know of any in Bath that are old enough. But some fragments of stone from old houses will have survived."

"I'm thinking Gildersleeve knew something we don't, something that ramped up the value."

"Maybe he discovered where it came from."

"Some old guy in Chilton Polden owned it in the eighteen hundreds, but I don't think anyone knows its history before that."

"Provenance is hugely important in the buying and selling of works of art. And you said the British Museum was bidding, so they must have done some research of their own and decided it was worth a bit."

"Yes, I'll be speaking to them."

"And obviously the robbers were also well informed."

"Or whoever hired them."

Paloma was looking thoughtful. "Have you examined the back and sides of your lump of stone?"

"What for?"

"Mortar—to see if there's any evidence it was once attached to a building."

He liked that. "When I'm allowed back in my own office, that's the first thing I'll check. I can picture it built in, maybe with other carvings from the poem."

"A frieze? But do you know of any other pieces that survived?"

"None that I've heard of. I'm no expert."

"You will be before you're through."

He nodded. "I'm already working on it. Do I get that other beer?"

"In a mo." She got up. "Or should it be 'In a mo, sire?'"

"The 'sire' sounds good to me."

"Let's have some courtly grovelling, then, and we'll see."

He decided as he opened the can that it was a good thing no one in CID had ever heard Peter Diamond spoken to like that.

Next morning he made a detour to Weston to feed the cat. Raffles had been his late wife's cat and always treated him with disdain after being left alone for the night. They say animals aren't capable of judging people's conduct, but this old tabby could give him a guilt complex with one look and a flick of the tail. He was relieved to leave the house and drive in to work.

Manvers Street, the home of Bath police, was definitely "beside Bath," on the wrong side of the walls. In all his time there, Diamond had never had reason to think about the original layout of the city, but this morning it dawned on him that the Roman heart of the place had once been enclosed by Upper Borough Walls to the north and Lower Borough Walls to the south; street names he'd heard a thousand times without ever realising the significance.

For all its tawdry appearance, a block of lemon-yellow reconstituted stone masquerading as the real thing, the sixties-built police station was where he made his living, and he was comfortable there. Recently he'd been troubled by the Headquarter's decision to site the custody suite in Keynsham. He could foresee Manvers Street becoming a ghost station. He had long since given up on the decisions coming out of Portishead, known to the lower ranks as ASDA, the Avon & Somerset Dream Academy.

No negative thinking this morning, he told himself. There's a killer at liberty and it's my job to find him.

He marched in and greeted the team. It was always good to see the place transformed with the trappings of an incident room: display boards, crime scene photos, extra phones, more civilian staff. The fire service had done their work and he could get into his office—or so he briefly believed. All traces of the shattered VDU, as Leaman had called it, had been removed, but the *Wife of Bath* on her dolly had not, and she remained a hazard. Worse, the room reeked of ammonia or some chemical. Having stepped inside, he came straight out again, forced to slum it with the rest of the team.

He parked himself temporarily at Keith Halliwell's vacant desk. There was plenty to catch up on. John Leaman with his brain-numbing efficiency had been looking through CCTV footage from a camera in Queen Square in the hope of spotting the silver getaway van. The one-way system round the square meant that there was not much interference in the view of traffic. The imaging was good and the registration numbers showed up well.

"This could be our best chance, guv," Leaman told him. "I've recorded seventeen sightings of silver vans in the two-hour slot."

"Where's this camera located?"

He pointed to the map on the whiteboard. "Top corner, where it links with Queen Square Place and Charlotte Street."

Diamond spotted the snag straight away. "The auction rooms are on the other side of the square, so this would be the second possible exit."

Leaman reddened. "Actually the third. They could have escaped down Barton Street. But if I was driving a getaway van, this is the way I'd go, heading straight out of the city."

Diamond wasn't persuaded. Professional criminals would surely have taken note of where the cameras were sited. "Better trace the owners, then."

"Do you want me to run the film for you?"

"Of seventeen silver vans? No thanks, John. I'm sure you missed nothing. Why is this desk empty? Where's Keith?"

"At the autopsy."

"Right you are." He wished he'd remembered. It was well known in CID that Halliwell regularly got the grisly job that should, by rights, have been the top man's. All Diamond could offer as an excuse was that he expected little of interest to emerge from the mortuary. Everyone knew how Gildersleeve had met his death and there was small likelihood that the dissected corpse would yield more information about the killer. Ballistics would specify the bullet used and maybe the type of weapon, and that was it. In a shooting such as this, forensic science was about as helpful as clairvoyancy. The CSI team were unlikely to have recovered any DNA, fingerprints, shoeprints, stray hairs or specks of blood other than those of the victim.

"Has anyone talked yet?" he turned in his chair and asked Ingeborg. He was damned sure the case wouldn't be cracked without outside help.

"It's early days, guv."

"That's a negative?"

"Well, yes. Making contact can't be rushed."

She was right. Meetings with informants generally happened over a few beers at a time and place of their choosing. They couldn't risk being seen with a detective.

Diamond felt his arm touched lightly. He looked up at Paul Gilbert.

"Guv, could I have a word?"

"Go ahead."

"It's personal."

"I see. We can go outside."

Normally he would have used the office.

The corridor was crowded with uniformed officers just out of their morning briefing. He took the young DC out of the building and across the street to a coffee shop.

"Something up?" he asked when they'd been served and had found a table well away from anyone else.

"No, guv. It's this. You said yesterday you might need someone to go undercover and find out who fired the shot. I want to volunteer."

"Really?" He was taken by surprise. "That's good to hear. Thanks." Pity he couldn't have sounded more enthusiastic. Gilbert wasn't remotely right for the job. The lad had performed well in some tough situations, but this was a totally different assignment calling for guile and coolness under pressure.

"Is that a yes?"

"I'm going to keep it in mind," he said. "The situation hasn't yet arisen. I'm bound to say you're the least experienced member of the team, even if you're one of the keenest. For one thing this will be bloody dangerous and for another it's walking a tightrope. Whoever does it needs to get in with the pond life without dirtying his hands."

"With all due respect, guv, I'm up for it."

"Right. You've made yourself clear."

Gilbert appeared to sense the barrier coming down. "I've been attached to CID for four years now. I'm not the rookie I was when you took me on for the hangman case."

"As long ago as that, was it? Time flies."

"I'll be perfect for this because my face isn't all that well known locally. Some of the others will be known to the gangs."

"Did someone put you up to this?"

Gilbert coloured a little and shook his head. "It's my own idea."

And he had to be believed. He spoke the truth, which was the quality that barred him from the job.

"I want to get more sand in my boots."

"You what?"

"Sand in my boots. Experience."

"Odd turn of phrase for a young guy."

The blush became more obvious. "It's something my mum says."

"So your mum's been getting at you, has she? You're still living at home?"

"Can't afford a place of my own. It's expensive round here. On a sergeant's wage I could manage it, but I won't get the stripes for years and years at the rate I'm going. They still ask me to fetch tea for them."

"You're out of uniform. Plenty would swap with you."

"I know. But mum keeps on—"

Diamond tensed. "Have you talked at home about this case?"

"Christ, no. I wouldn't do that," Gilbert said with such a start that he slopped his coffee. "It's an ongoing gripe of hers. She says I've got no ambition."

"I expect she's as keen as you are to see you in your own place. What does your dad say?"

"He died when I was eleven. An operation that went wrong. There's just the two of us."

Diamond had a rush of sympathy. He could see it all now. "Your mum wants the best for you. It's understandable. But you can be sure she'd miss you if you moved out."

"I don't think so. She's got a boyfriend."

He'd *thought* he could see it all. The pressure on young Gilbert wasn't what he'd imagined. "All I can say is this. In CID, opportunities present themselves sometimes when you least expect them. You may not be right for one job, but there's always another in the offing."

Gilbert nodded. He couldn't hide the disappointment.

"It's good that you spoke to me," Diamond said. "Your mum's wrong about you not having ambition. We'd better drink up and get back to the job."

Keith Halliwell was back from the autopsy and biting into a doughnut, unaffected by what he had witnessed. He stood beside his desk uncertain how to deal with the large cuckoo in occupation. After yesterday there was still tension between them—not so much over Diamond's pratfall as the fact that Halliwell had spoken out about the suggestion to send someone undercover.

Diamond showed no sign of moving. "What's the story?"

"The professor was unlucky. The bullet severed the aorta. That's the main artery that supplies blood from the heart to the rest of the body."

"Not much doubt about that, then."

"But he probably wouldn't have lived much longer anyway. When Dr. Sealy opened the brain he found a tumour the size of a plum. The medical records made no mention of it. I'm wondering if that helps to explain Gildersleeve's behaviour at the auction."

"Erratic, you mean? Taking on the gunmen? Possible, I suppose. On the other hand, you'd expect people to get hyped up when the bidding is going on. We don't know enough about this guy and what drove him. Want to come with me to Reading and find out?"

6

"Someone has to go undercover," Diamond said as they headed north to join the motorway.

"You said." Halliwell took a glance in the mirror as if he needed to check who was following. Out of favour for challenging the idea when the boss had first put it to the team, he had no wish to be drawn into an argument that could last the rest of the journey.

"It's bloody obvious."

"If you say so." There's no escape when you're at the wheel and your passenger wants to thrust his opinion on you.

But the force of the last utterance struck home. Bloody obvious? Was it possible Diamond wanted *him* to be the fall guy?

"I see it as an opportunity," Diamond said. "If I wasn't running the show, I'd take it on myself. Somebody has to."

Halliwell stared at the road ahead. He knew better than to show a scintilla of interest after such a statement.

Then Diamond surprised him by saying, "I've had an offer already."

"Oh?"

"Not my number one choice."

"You don't say?" The response sounded feeble even to the man who made it.

"I might as well tell you. Young Gilbert."

"Good lad."

"Up to a point, but . . ."

A long pause. Clearly Diamond wasn't going to complete the statement. He could play this game for as long as both men were strapped into their car seats. The pressure on Halliwell was unrelenting.

"But what?"

"It's not a risk I'm willing to take," Diamond said. "However . . ."

Halliwell waited yet again, flogging his brain for cast-iron reasons to reject what was coming.

". . . he did make one telling point. He's not known to the local godfathers."

"Very true." This could be a lifeline. "You and I have tangled with too many of them, guv. We'd never get away with it."

"Not in a million years."

Mightily relieved that he seemed to be off the hook, Halliwell asked, "Who were you thinking of—John? He's more of a backroom man."

"Leaman? Too inflexible. He has qualities, certainly. Great in the office beavering away, but I can't see him rubbing shoulders with crooks."

"Ingeborg?"

This time Diamond's silence was as good as a nod.

"She's the only one I can think of," Halliwell said with more confidence. "More streetwise than Leaman, for sure."

"But she hasn't volunteered. I was hoping she might. I'm not going to pressgang anyone into something as dangerous as this."

"She's bright enough to carry it off," Halliwell said. "I don't think she's known to any of the mob. The only one she met was Soldier Nuttall and we put him away last year."

"What's going on in her life these days? Is she in a relationship?"

"If she is, she hasn't spoken about it. Blokes come and go, I think. She lives alone, doesn't she?"

"A year ago, she would have been the first to volunteer. She's more cagey since she got to sergeant. Doesn't need to impress, I suppose."

"I can sound her out if you like," Halliwell said. "See what's holding her back."

"Would you?"

■ ■ ■

They ignored the first sign on the M4. Driving anywhere near the centre of Reading is enough to reduce even long-serving policemen to quivering wrecks. Five miles further along the motorway, just when you think you've overshot, the next exit brings you without much hassle to the campus at Whiteknights Park, southeast of the town. It wasn't long before they were seated in the office of the lecturer put up by the university as the colleague Gildersleeve had known best.

"Unfortunate name," Diamond commented to Halliwell while they waited for Dr. Poke to finish a seminar.

"I've heard worse."

"There was a story at police college about a new instructor on his first day. The old hands on the staff had already looked at the intake and handpicked his class to embarrass him when he first called the register. As far as I remember, it went Adcock, Allcock, Badcock, Balls. At that point he lost control and fled the room."

Diamond had barely finished the story when Dr. Poke entered his office, a short man with a shock of fine, flame-red hair in a bouffant extravagance. "Don't get up, gentlemen," he said in a voice that could only be described as precious. "I'm Archie Poke. I gather you're here to enquire about the unfortunate John Gildersleeve, late of this parish."

Diamond wasn't new to academics. There were plenty in Bath. In their own surroundings their status gave them an air of importance not easily blown away—and their desire to impress could be useful when you wanted inside information. He identified himself and Halliwell. "The professor was a close colleague of yours, I was told."

"Depends what you mean by close," Poke said with a sharp glance. "We had adjoining offices with the same entrance, but that wasn't our doing. They removed his name from the door only this morning. All his things are still in there."

"We'll look inside presently, in that case. Is this the Chaucer suite, then? Are you another expert?"

"Not to the extent Gildersleeve was. The Anglo-Saxon language is my specialty, but I do some lecturing in Middle English to take up the slack in the timetable." He made it sound like slumming.

"Did you know about his trip to Bath for the auction?"

"Everyone in the senior common room knew. He made no secret of his ambition to—how shall I put it?—possess the *Wife of Bath*." There was a twitch of the lips in case the visitors had missed the innuendo.

"Put it any way you like," Diamond said. "Was he bidding on behalf of the university? Do you have a museum here?"

Poke raked a hand through the spectacular hair. "I'm not Gildersleeve's spokesman, you know. I was asked to meet you because I saw more of him than anyone else. From all I can gather, his interest was entirely selfish. Quite where he intended to keep the lady he coveted so much, he didn't ever say. She's substantial, I was told."

"He'd have a job carrying her upstairs. So he was bidding with his own money?"

"His wife's, more likely. She's comfortably well off. I can't imagine any bank would have given him a loan."

"Is there any way he could have sold the carving on? He'd bid twenty-four thousand when the gunmen arrived."

Each time Poke shook his head, the locks sprang out like solar flares. "I don't think he had the slightest intention of making a profit. Owning her was the prize. From the way he was boring us all with his raptures about the wretched thing, he would have bought her at any price."

"What exactly was he saying?"

"How miraculous it was that this amazing relic had been sitting in a small town museum for donkey's years and no one had appreciated its importance. You'd think it was Tutankhamun's tomb."

"But it wasn't his discovery, was it?"

Dr. Poke laughed. "You're right. The credit for that went to some sharp-eyed fellow who was working at the museum and is probably blissfully unaware of the curse of the *Wife of Bath*."

"The *what?*" Diamond felt a creeping sensation down his spine.

"Do I have to explain everything? A clumsy attempt at wit. Another allusion to Tutankhamun."

"Okay." Mostly reassured, Diamond said, "I still can't understand why this lump of stone was so important to him."

"Possibly he knew something the rest of us didn't."

"Such as?"

"A connection to Chaucer himself. It's old enough."

"Is there any chance of that?"

This was greeted with an indrawn, cynical laugh. "I can't imagine how one would find out after so long."

"What sort of connection?"

Dr. Poke gave a shrug. Having raised this hare, he didn't want to run with it.

Diamond refused to let it rest. "Is much known about Chaucer's life?"

"Considerably more than we know about Shakespeare's. He had a public profile. Diplomat, justice of the peace, customs officer, member of parliament, clerk of the king's works. The poetry was only a sideline. I can't help wondering how he fitted in the time."

"When did he write *The Canterbury Tales?*"

"Towards the end of his life. It was a hugely ambitious project that was not even a quarter finished when he died in 1400. He makes clear in the prologue that each of the pilgrims was to tell four tales, two on the journey to Canterbury and two on the return, making about a hundred and twenty in all."

"How many did he write?"

"Twenty-odd that we know about—and some of those are incomplete. The tales we have aren't even in Chaucer's hand. Nothing has survived that shows us how he worked. They are all copies by fifteenth-century scribes, up to eighty of them, but it's generally agreed that two manuscripts are the earliest and most reliable, one now in the National Library of Wales and the other in the Huntington Library in San Marino, California."

"Professor Gildersleeve was an expert on all this?"

"No question of that. He'd written some of the standard commentaries. I expect he visualised the *Wife of Bath* gracing the cover of his next volume."

"She's no Gwyneth Paltrow."

Light-hearted comments from anyone else passed Dr. Poke by. "But the finding of this unknown likeness would guarantee good publicity, especially as it seems to have been carved in the fourteenth century. The international press make hay with a story like this. Hardly a year passes without some report of a new Shakespeare play or an undiscovered portrait of Jane Austen. Why shouldn't the father of English poetry get his share of the limelight?"

"Why shouldn't Professor Gildersleeve?"

Dr. Poke got the gist of that remark and appreciated it with a scythe-like smile. He wasn't without envy.

"So you seriously believe it was a sound investment for him?"

"He acted as if it was. As you just pointed out, he was willing to put up twenty-four thousand of his wife's money."

"Were they very well off?"

"Monica came into millions when she divorced. I thought you'd met her. She travelled to Bath to identify him."

Halliwell cleared his throat. "I should have told you, guv. She was at the mortuary first thing this morning, doing the ID before the autopsy."

Diamond's eyes rolled upwards. The drive from Bath had been a perfect opportunity to mention this. He wondered if Halliwell was losing his grip. He'd never known him so silent. "Did you speak to her?"

"No, guv. She'd come and gone."

"A resourceful woman," Dr. Poke said. "Her second marriage. John's first."

"How long were they together?"

Dr. Poke said primly, "Only the lady herself could tell you and I doubt whether she will."

"Why?"

"They had what used to be known as an adulterous relationship for some time—I would say at least two years—before she obtained her divorce. They only tied the knot last autumn."

"We'll need to speak to her."

"That shouldn't be a problem. She's staying in Bath with her sister, getting over the shock. It sounds as if you have her contact details."

A glance towards Halliwell confirmed this much. "I presume Monica will tell us why the professor put such a high value on the carving."

"I wouldn't count on it."

"If it was her money he was bidding with, she must have wanted a say in the deal."

Poke released a long sigh, as if in despair at how little these so-called detectives knew. "It was a trifling amount to Monica. She brought a fortune to the marriage. Her ex is a property developer who floated his company on the stock exchange and trousered millions. She made sure she got her legal entitlement when they divorced."

The high bidding at the auction was more understandable now. "Have you spoken to Monica since the shooting?"

"I sent a sympathy card." Said without any sympathy at all.

"Is her ex-husband still about?"

"Bernie Wefers? He's everywhere."

Diamond blinked at that.

Poke said, as if to a dull first-year unlikely to make it to the second, "You see his name on boards all over the south of England. He's been scarring the green belt with his afford-able housing for years."

Diamond recalled seeing the surname.

"Was the professor popular with his colleagues here?"

"Popularity isn't a concept we're familiar with. The faculty of Arts, Humanities and Social Science is not a working man's social club. We're academics. He wasn't overtly disliked, if that's what you're asking."

"Eccentric?"

"Come now, we're not all like that. I'd call him colourless."

"But capable of excitement?"

"Admittedly, going by what happened at the auction, but it didn't manifest itself in his professional life. It was obvious to all of us that the prospect of acquiring the *Wife of Bath* lit some kind of fuse. I've seen it with other people. A cloistered existence can be very dull. We need the occasional pick-me-up."

"Was he sure the piece was genuine?"

"Supremely confident. They're reputable auctioneers, aren't they? And he wasn't the only one prepared to bid high." He hesitated. "Don't tell me it's actually a fake. That would turn a tragedy into a fiasco."

"It's real," Diamond said. "I tripped over the damn thing in my office yesterday and you can take it from me it isn't polystyrene. It's solid Bath stone."

"Fitting."

"Why?"

"The Wife of Bath in Bath stone." From the look Dr. Poke gave Diamond, this conversation had become a pain.

"Got you," Diamond said, unperturbed. "Let's explore that. We know Chaucer got around a bit. Did he ever live in the West Country?"

"He may have done, but it's far from certain. I can't give chapter and verse without checking the textbooks."

"Let's do it now. There'll be some in the professor's office, won't there? You said you'd show us."

"Did not," Poke said. "You announced that you'd be taking a look. It's not for me to invite you into a colleague's office, even if he's dead."

"I can't be bothered with the niceties. We're on an investigation."

The office next door was similar in layout to Poke's, but with more evidence of its user, with poster-size maps of medieval Britain and Europe and behind the desk a small framed print of a figure on horseback reproduced from some medieval manuscript.

"Geoffrey Chaucer," Poke said with a flick of the coiffure. "The Ellesmere portrait, from the manuscript I mentioned, now in California."

"Either the horses were small in those days or the artists were piss-poor at proportion," Diamond said. "This is like the poor old nag in the *Wife of Bath* sculpture, no bigger than a large dog."

"A miniature pony?" Halliwell suggested.

"The figure of the poet is exaggerated to give him status," Poke said. "It's a good likeness."

"How do you know? You didn't meet him."

Dr. Poke was unamused. He reserved his smiles for his own wit. "It's one of several portraits in existence. The National Portrait Gallery has another, an oil painting on a panel, a standing figure, without the horse, and there are at least two others in manuscripts."

Diamond stepped closer to the picture. Chaucer was wearing some kind of head dress. Sharp brown eyes, a straight nose with a strong bridge and a moustache and beard trimmed at the edges to leave the side of his face clear of whiskers. A modern face, intelligent and with a sense of destiny. *If you want to know more about me,* the poet seemed to be saying, *you'll have to work harder than this. I don't give up my secrets easily.*

"I can assure you, gentlemen," Poke added, "that John Gildersleeve knew what Chaucer looked like. He was the leading authority in this country and probably the world on portraits of the poet. A few years ago he was asked by the National Portrait Gallery to authenticate a newly discovered drawing said to have been of Chaucer. They were proposing to buy it for some ridiculous amount. He was able to demonstrate that it was of the poet's son, Thomas, and thus saved the gallery a great deal of money."

"I hope they rewarded him."

"I've no idea. He didn't discuss it with me, but the story was in the national press. The man trying to sell the drawing had some hard things to say. His own reputation as an art dealer was seriously dented."

"I'm surprised Professor Gildersleeve didn't discuss it with you. You obviously know about these things."

"We only spoke when it was absolutely necessary."

The notion of these two academics obliged to work closely together, yet unwilling to communicate, was puzzling Diamond. Pure chemistry—or had there been some issue between them?

Halliwell said in an awed tone from in front of a wall of books, "Do you think the professor read all of these?"

"Some people still possess books," Dr. Poke said. His own collection was pathetic by comparison. "Others store them electronically."

"And others nick them from the library," Diamond said, taking one down and confirming what he'd suspected from the lettering on the spine by opening it at a date-sheet headed Reading Public Library. It was a life of Chaucer by an American. He thumbed through the pages and found a chronology of the significant events in Chaucer's life. "This may be helpful." But presently he said, "Three pages of dates and places and not a mention of the West Country."

"We can't expect to strike gold the first time," Halliwell said.

"How true," Poke said. He selected a book and turned to the index with obvious confidence of finding what he was looking for.

Diamond went over to the desk and switched on the computer. He was no expert, but he knew the basics these days and after the condescending remark about e-books he intended to demonstrate that he wasn't out of the Stone Age.

"Should you be doing that?" Poke asked. "It seems disrespectful."

"He isn't going to object," Diamond said. "We'll be taking it with us, anyway."

He accessed the emails. A check of the inbox revealed little of interest. It seemed to be monopolised by online booksellers.

"Found it," Poke said, looking up from the book in his hand. "Towards the end of his life Chaucer was named as deputy forester of Petherton Park in Somerset."

"*Forester?*"

"Deputy. I expect it was a sinecure," Poke said. "A way of thanking him for services rendered to the king. He completed diplomatic missions to France and Italy and he was a senior civil servant, the clerk of the king's works, with responsibility for the construction and repair of numerous buildings, including all the royal palaces."

"The Bernie Wefers of his day."

Poke wasn't amused. "Hardly. In case you were wondering, I doubt very much whether the clerk of the king's works practised tree surgery as well." He raised a finger. "It's come back to me now. Some years ago, John Gildersleeve spent a whole summer down there under canvas with a group of students on an abortive excavation of a house said to have been owned by Chaucer."

"Abortive?"

"They found absolutely nothing. He became a laughing stock. I doubt if he ever got over it."

"This might explain why he got so excited when the *Wife of Bath* came up for sale."

"A vindication of his wasted summer?" Poke said. "That's not outside the realms of possibility."

"Have you heard of Petherton Park?" Diamond asked Halliwell. "I'm damned if I have."

"There's a small town called North Petherton on the A38, south of Bridgwater."

"The same place, but there's no certainty Chaucer ever went there," Poke said with a clear desire to undermine them as well as his former colleague. "He was living in London at the end of his life."

Diamond ignored him and spoke to Halliwell. "How far south of Bridgwater?"

"Only two or three miles. Strange that the *Wife of Bath* should end up in the museum there."

"Correction," Diamond said. "She ended up in my office."

"There's something else about the place," Poke said, pressing a hand to his forehead. "Something far more interesting. It'll come to me presently."

"Petherton Park?"

"North Petherton. I'm trying to think. It has associations with Anglo-Saxon studies. Would it be the church, I wonder?

No, I have it now." He clasped his hands in triumph. "North Petherton is where one of the great Anglo-Saxon treasures was found—the Alfred Jewel, a spectacular piece from the ninth century, unearthed by a ploughman over three hundred years ago, filigreed gold enclosing a highly polished piece of clear rock crystal, now in the Ashmolean at Oxford. The lettering round the side provides evidence that it was made for King Alfred."

"All I know about Alfred is that he burnt the cakes."

Dr. Poke's tongue clicked in contempt. "Supposedly at Athelney, where he took refuge from the Vikings. Such stories must be treated with reserve. However, Athelney is a mere four miles from North Petherton. This is my period. I can tell you a lot about Alfred."

"We'll pass on that, unless it ties in with Chaucer," Diamond said.

"Hardly. Chaucer came five hundred years later."

Halliwell spoke up. "Well, what if the jewel was presented to Chaucer in thanks for all the services he performed for the king? It may have been a gift from the royal family."

"And then he loses the thing?" Diamond said. "Unlikely. I think we can safely forget about the Alfred Jewel. I'm interested in the link with Chaucer. It's safe to say Professor Gildersleeve thought there was good evidence, even if he failed to find it."

"We can make a search online," Halliwell said.

Seated in front of the computer, Diamond could hardly refuse. Never comfortable with technology, he grasped the mouse and stared at the screen.

Halliwell said, "It's one of the icons at the bottom."

"I know, I know." He found the Google icon and typed in PETHERTON PARK.

"Put in Chaucer's name while you're at it," Dr. Poke said. "See what you get."

Up came a welter of results. The one that caught Diamond's attention was towards the bottom of the screen. In bold blue letters: CHAUCER CLOSE, NORTH PETHERTON.

"Promising."

The other two moved to his side to look. He pointed to the name and immediately the list of websites was replaced by an estate agent's website with a list of houses.

"How did that happen?"

"It's touch-sensitive," Poke said.

"You see?" Halliwell touched the screen and restored the list of hits. "But this is good news. North Petherton must be the right place."

"I wouldn't get too excited. We've got a Chaucer Close in Reading," Poke said.

"There's a Chaucer Road in Bath," Diamond said.

Halliwell leaned over Diamond and brought up a map that showed the location of North Petherton. "Well, I wasn't wrong about where it is, just down the road from Bridgwater."

"I saw another hit mentioning Petherton Park," Diamond said.

They returned to it and Halliwell was proved correct. Petherton Park, North Petherton, was, indeed, a one-time forest, and Geoffrey Chaucer had been the deputy forester from 1391. After his death in 1400, his son, Thomas, had succeeded him with the title of forester and had lived in the Park House in Park House Field, currently known as Parker's Field.

"This is getting better," Diamond said. "We have a house." He was starting to enjoy the hunt for evidence. He could even see some pleasure in using the internet.

"It tells us the son lived there," Poke said, "not necessarily the father."

"But we now know that being the forester was more than— what was your word?"

"A sinecure."

"Yes, Thomas Chaucer must have taken the job seriously, so why shouldn't his father have lived in Petherton Park before him? Nothing says he did, but nothing says he didn't. And if there was a house, it wouldn't be remarkable if somewhere in the structure they commemorated *The Canterbury Tales* with a piece of sculpture. Does Park House still exist?"

"You're an optimist," Poke said. "Just as poor Gildersleeve was."

Notes from a website called British History Online revealed that Park House had been in place as early as 1336 and may have been renamed The Lodge about 1400. Most of it was dismantled during Queen Elizabeth's reign.

"Pieces may have been preserved," Halliwell said, "particularly anything associated with Chaucer himself."

"All of this is tenuous, to say the least," Poke said.

Diamond nodded. "But at the end of the day, I have a chunk of masonry in my office that no one disputes is the *Wife of Bath*. And she must have come from somewhere."

With the computer and other items from Professor Gildersleeve's office stacked into the boot of Halliwell's car, the two detectives drove home. They agreed on one thing: Dr. Poke was a jealous man as well as a pompous twit.

"He thought he should have been the professor," Halliwell said.

"With Gildersleeve dead, he may get his wish," Diamond said. "But in case you're about to say it gives him a motive for murder, let's keep a grip on what really happened. The professor was shot because he tried to take on the hold-up men. Everyone who was there agrees on that. The mystery is why he was so possessive about the *Wife of Bath*."

"And who hired the robbers."

"Exactly. I can't picture Dr. Poke staging a hold-up himself, even if he thought it would upset his rival to this extent."

"He'd be obvious, with a voice like his, and that hair."

"They were wearing balaclavas, remember."

"Well, he isn't the gun-toting type," Halliwell said.

"Agreed. But I didn't ask him where he was on the day of the auction. Slipped up, there."

"I wouldn't lose any sleep over that, guv."

"One thing he said gave me a bit of a turn. About the curse of the *Wife of Bath*. I'm sharing an office with her."

"He was on about Tutankhamun's curse, the old story about

people dying during the excavations, supposedly because they disturbed the tomb. Load of balls dreamed up to sell newspapers."

They checked in at the incident room at the end of the afternoon and found an email printout from the CSI team. Diamond read it, frowning, and jerked back in disbelief.

"Something the matter?" Halliwell asked.

He handed the paper across. "The bullet that killed the professor was more than fifty years old. It was a thirty-eight calibre designed to be used with a Webley Mark IV revolver."

Halliwell looked it through. "That's a name from the past. Webley. The army were using them as standard sidearms in the war."

"Both wars."

"Long time ago. It says here the Mark IV remained in service until 1963."

"When sexual intercourse began."

From Halliwell's dropjaw reaction, it was obvious he missed the reference.

In a lofty tone, Diamond said, "The Larkin poem. Do I have to quote the lines? And you thought I was just a Chaucer expert."

Halliwell was lost for words.

"Don't look like that. Let's stay with guns. You're going to ask me how they can tell it was fired from a Webley and not some other weapon."

Now Halliwell grinned. "No I'm not. It's the striations."

Diamond was impressed. He knew the basics, but he had never bothered much with the terminology.

"The grooves on the side of the bullet," Halliwell went on. "All the makes have their own pattern so that when the bullet passes through the barrel it gets marked. You'll find six grooves when it was fired from a Colt and seven with a Webley. A Colt has a left-hand twist and a Webley a right. Now, a Browning—"

"Enough said," Diamond interrupted the lecture. "It was

a Webley. If ballistics are convinced, so am I. My point was that this is an out-of-date weapon."

Halliwell nodded. "But it doesn't have to be the latest model. If it works, it can kill. Obviously this one did. In a way it's fitting that an obsolete firearm was used at an antiques auction. At least it wasn't a duelling pistol."

"Does it tell us anything about the hitmen?"

"Only that they didn't have state-of-the-art guns."

"Cut-price hitmen."

"They messed up badly, that's true."

"The email goes on about making a check of the records. It's not going to be a licensed gun, is it?"

"Definitely not," Halliwell said. "But there are still plenty of old Webleys knocking around. Thousands of servicemen never handed them in. I expect what they mean is that they're comparing the, em'—pause for a smile—'striations with ammunition recovered from other firearms incidents. We may discover the gun was fired in some other raid."

"We could use some help like that. But let's not get our hopes up. It may have been sitting in someone's sock drawer since 1963."

7

One of the items they had brought back in Halliwell's car was John Gildersleeve's book, *Chaucer: The Bawdy Tales*. Diamond took it home to read. A spot of bawdiness would go down well, and he might get a clue as to why the *Wife of Bath* was worth at least twenty-four grand to the professor. His chance to impress the academic world? Or was the man obsessed, in thrall to one of Chaucer's best known creations? As a policeman who had seen a lot in his time, Diamond couldn't accept that the weather-beaten piece of stone had anything remarkable about it. He wasn't impressed. The experience of being evicted from his own office had left him only with negative thoughts, a suspicion that this thing was trouble. If nothing else, the book ought to act as a corrective.

In his small house in Weston, with Raffles perched on the arm of the chair—and purring—he turned to the chapter entitled "As Help Me God, I Was a Lusty Oon: The Much-Married Wife of Bath." It was not the hot stuff he expected. It opened with a statement that this would be a "deconstructive study of certain assumptions, avoiding the twin snares of reductivity and indeterminacy." Even Raffles turned his head away in disappointment. Two pages in, Raffles was yawning. Diamond dropped the book on the floor and reached for the modern English version of *The Canterbury Tales* Paloma had given him.

Generations of schoolchildren had reason to be grateful to Nevill Coghill and now so was Peter Diamond. Here was the Wife in language he could understand and enjoy, with some mild bawdiness thrown in regarding her "chamber of Venus," the pleasures of love-making and the demands she made in bed. Fair enough, he thought, this isn't roll-in-the-aisles stuff, but it does the job with style and zip, written in rhyming verse that apparently uses the same metre as the original.

The General Prologue gave him some background. Alison was a bold-faced, healthy-looking character who queened it over all the other women in her parish, insisting on being first to make the offering in church and furious if anyone challenged her right.

This he found easy to believe.

She spun her own clothes and dressed on Sundays in a flowing cloak, red, tight-gartered stockings and tightly laced shoes, and a hat as large as a shield and weighing as much as ten pounds. He could understand Paloma's delight in dressing an actress like that. Upon her amblere—which he discovered was an ambling horse—the wife was a much-travelled pilgrim. Impressively for a fourteenth century woman, she'd been to Jerusalem three times and other religious sites in France and Italy. She was chatty and quick to laugh, displaying a gap in her teeth which was said to be a sure sign of a lustful nature.

Cue the five husbands.

He turned to the Wife of Bath's Prologue for her own account—and what an extraordinary piece of self-justification it was, running to thousands of words. After wading through all the Biblical arguments for serial marriage (King Solomon's thousand wives among them), he learned that three of the husbands had been good, the others bad. The first three—the good ones—were rich and old, but were given a hard time once they married her, required to be energetic lovers and regularly scolded and put in the wrong, accused of being drunk and unfaithful, 'innocent as they were'. Presumably they died of exhaustion.

Husband number four, a younger man, made the mistake of having a mistress. The wife got her own back by 'frying him in his own grease' and flirting with others, making him jealous. When she returned from her pilgrimage to Jerusalem, he died and she was glad to see him buried.

She was still a lively forty when she married for the fifth time—to a handsome twenty-year-old called John, whom she had been 'toying and dallying' with while husband four was in London during Lent. 'I think I loved him best, I'll tell no lie.' She'd been turned on by the sight of his sturdy legs at her latest husband's funeral. They married inside a month and she handed over all the land and property she'd inherited from the earlier marriages. But there was an early crisis. With lamentable want of tact for a newlywed, Johnny made it his habit to read to her about the misdeeds of all the wicked women of history from Eve onwards. One evening Alison was so enraged by this that she grabbed the book and ripped three pages from it and hit him in the face, causing him to fall back into the fire. He got up and struck her so hard that she became permanently deaf. But she made him pay dearly. At first she alarmed him by pretending she was at the point of death. He begged her to forgive him and promised never to hit her again. For good measure she smacked his face a second time and said they were now even. But she'd won the prize of sovereignty. She made him burn the book. In future she ruled the roost in the marriage. She became kindness personified, faithful and loving, and so, she insisted, was Johnny.

Diamond's reading was done. He couldn't say he was enchanted by Alison, but her spirit was undeniable. She had come alive for him, a recognizable human being from seven centuries ago. Anyone reading her life history would warm to the robust humour and her brand of feminism. Whatever you thought about her, she wasn't repressed. You had to feel sorry for the men in her life.

Reading about her had helped him by sharpening and enlivening the impression of the character he remembered faintly from his schooldays. Without doubt she was the leading lady in *The Canterbury Tales* and it was possible to understand how she must have figured strongly in the thoughts of John Gildersleeve, whose entire career was founded on Chaucer's work. Alison would have been very real to him. The chance to possess the stone carving had obviously excited him. And so Gildersleeve had become one more man to fall under the influence of the Wife of Bath, one more who ultimately perished.

Job done, his eyelids getting heavier, Diamond became as drowsy as the cat. Images of a stout, gap-toothed woman in an enormous hat drifted into his brain. She was sitting in his chair at Manvers Street leading a case conference, her red-shoed feet on the desk. Her amblere was tethered to the radiator, feeding from a nosebag, and no one seemed bothered by it.

He was next aware of the cat's claws pricking his thighs. The doorbell was ringing. Raffles, startled, had just leapt from his lap. Clearly they had both been dozing. How long, he was unsure.

He heaved himself out of the chair and jammed his feet into the flip-flops he wore around the house. He still ached from the fall in his office the day before. He shuffled to the door, muttering about people who came calling in the evening. If it was a local politician he'd tell them what they could do with their policies.

Ingeborg was standing there, hands open in apology. This wasn't her usual confident manner.

"I know I should have phoned, guv."

"You'd better come in. Something the matter?"

"No, I just thought this is the best way to see you away from the office."

"Coffee?"

"No, thanks."

He showed her into the living room. Raffles had already returned to the warm armchair and was staring at Ingeborg in the way only a cat can, daring her to eject him. She chose another chair.

And so did Diamond.

"What's on your mind?"

"Am I right in thinking you'd like me to go undercover?"

"Someone been talking to you?" he said, thinking Halliwell must already have called her at home.

She shook her head. "I'm the obvious candidate, aren't I? You only have to look at the rest of the team."

He shifted in the chair, unsure where this was leading.

"But you haven't actually asked me."

"It's a dangerous job," he said. "I'd rather have a volunteer. I'm not ordering anyone to take it on."

"You definitely need one of us to get among the hard men."

He was fully awake now, alert to what she was saying. "That's true. They're hard men, all right. Professionals. Admittedly they made a hash of the robbery, but they were carrying guns. We must find out who put them up to it."

"But who are they?" Ingeborg said.

"Inge, you know as well as I do that there's only one gang in our manor capable of mounting an armed hold-up. In Bristol there are three or four. If I were planning a crime here I wouldn't hire the local mob. I'd bring in some of the Bristol boys."

"I totally agree," she said. "And it puts one of my doubts to rest. Anyone from here trying to cosy up to the Bath lot runs the risk of being recognised."

"What are your other doubts?"

She sighed. This was clearly difficult for her. "Whoever takes it on has to face up to what happens if some situation arises."

"Situation?"

"Law-breaking."

"I get you. How are you going to deal with it if they commit another crime?"

"Not just me. Anyone. If it comes to court and the under-cover cop is found to have aided and abetted, he or she is as guilty as the perpetrators."

The "he or she" meant he couldn't yet count on her.

"It's a grey area, I admit," he said. "That's why I want some-one who can think on their feet. My own feeling is that the law would take a lenient view."

"If the cop doesn't actually fire a shot?"

"But it doesn't have to come to that. We're interested in a killing already committed. It's about getting their confidence."

"Yes, but that could mean joining in some other heist. They'll look for the recruit to show loyalty and they'll be suspicious of anyone who doesn't."

Diamond hesitated, searching for the right words. There was an obvious point here, but how could he say it without offending her? "The gang culture is macho, Inge. They're unlikely to want a woman at the sharp end of a crime. You may not like it, but that's the real world."

"So?"

"There are other ways of getting on the inside."

The look in her eyes wasn't promising. "Go on."

"Using your natural assets."

She held up a warning finger. "I knew it would come to that. I draw the line at shagging the bastards."

"For God's sake, I wouldn't expect you to. You're well capable of chatting up a guy without going the whole way."

She glanced across the room at the book he'd dropped face up on the floor. "Is that where you've been getting your ideas?"

Chaucer: The Bawdy Tales. The Wife of Bath again, muscling in.

"Christ, no. It's unreadable. I gave up after a couple of pages." He leaned forward. "Listen, Inge. You've done journalism. You've gone after stories. Basically, that's what this is."

"With one important difference," she said, unimpressed. "The people I was hounding knew I was press. This is another game altogether."

"It's why we don't wear uniforms."

"That's one thing. Trying to pass ourselves off as crooks is another."

"I'm not doing very well, am I?" he said.

"Guv, I didn't come here expecting to be persuaded," Ingeborg said. "I can make up my own mind and I will, but not right now. I wanted you to front up with me and I suppose you have. I was uncomfortable with nothing being said.

At least we know where we stand now. If you ordered me to take this on, I would."

"I won't insist," he said. "It's too dangerous."

She stood up, preparing to leave. "All the others would find out, of course. It would be no use telling them I was on leave."

"We can trust them."

"The civilian staff?"

"We have to."

She walked to the door. "I'll sleep on it and let you know."

He got up to show her out, put his foot on Gildersleeve's book and skidded forward, arms flailing, almost falling over. "Bloody hell, not again."

Ingeborg turned. "You all right?"

"I'm starting to feel jinxed."

She smiled. "She's fiction, you know."

"And I was almost history."

In the morning plenty seemed to be happening in the incident room. Leaman was running through the CCTV tapes of silver vans, Ingeborg checking statements she'd taken from the antique dealers at the auction, Gilbert searching the files for evidence of armed robberies in Bath and Bristol and Halliwell on the phone to the CSI team chasing results of their findings at the crime scene. Even John Wigfull, the press liaison man, was there, wanting to know when he could issue an update for the media. Interest from the press was growing, he said. *The Mirror* had asked if they could get a new picture of the *Wife of Bath* with Detective Superintendent Diamond.

"Stuff that," Diamond said. "I'm not posing with her."

"She's the story, she's your case and she's in your office already," Wigfull said, obviously prepared for a skirmish. "It's a done deal."

"It isn't. We don't allow the press in here."

"We can't move her out."

"Tell me about it."

"So will you make an exception and cooperate for once?"

"Get lost, John." They had a history, these two.

"Be reasonable. The only picture they've got is the one from the catalogue. They need something more dramatic."

"Like me standing over it with a magnifying glass? You're out of your tiny mind."

"How about Ingeborg, then? Give them some glamour."

"Hang about," Ingeborg called from across the room. "I heard that."

"It's give and take," Wigfull said. "There are plenty of times when we need their help."

Diamond wasn't having it. Ingeborg in the national press would blow her cover before she started. "Listen up, John. If they need a picture, you can have one taken by a police photographer and the only shot they're getting is a close-up of the stone. No one will be posing for them. Get that clear."

In truth, there wasn't any progress, for all the show of activity. He wasn't expecting much. The drama of the killing in the auction room had been a gift to the media, but as a case to investigate, it was a brute. A failed heist and an unintended killing by masked men didn't give much to work on.

The only good thing this morning was that he could use his office again. He stepped inside—gingerly.

She was still in occupation, of course. His cactus had turned an unhealthy colour and was leaning over, but the *Wife of Bath* had received a makeover from the fire service. The result was as good as a stone-cleaning firm could have achieved. She and her amblere were better defined and improved in colour. Fresh from reading the poem, he could see the curve of the jowls, the fleshiness of the face under the substantial hat. She was starting to come alive. She looked well capable of turning her head and giving him the gap-toothed grin.

Idiot, he thought. What's getting into you?

He turned his back on her and stepped the other way round his desk and sat down. She wasn't in view from here. He could turn his thoughts to other things. They hadn't yet replaced the computer, but he didn't feel deprived. Why, he now had space for pens and paper and his picture of Steph, his late wife. Everything must have been stuffed away before they started the decontamination.

His phone started ringing, but where was it? Fairly close to hand, for sure. He tried two drawers before tracking it to the bottom one. They'd tucked it away when they were clearing the fumes.

The switchboard said they had a caller for him, a Monica Gildersleeve.

The professor's wife.

"Put her on," he said, while numerous possibilities jostled in his brain.

The voice was on a low register and would have sounded sexy in any other situation. "You're the officer on my husband's case, I believe. I've been trying to reach you."

"Thank you for calling, Mrs. Gildersleeve," he said. "I've been out of the office. Please accept my condolences."

"It's so sudden," she said. "I find it hard to believe."

"I know what it's like to lose someone close. We're still at the early stages, but we're doing all we can."

"We were married only a few months. So you haven't yet found the people who shot him?"

"No, ma'am."

"They gunned him down in full view of everyone at the auction."

"Correct, but they were in masks and nobody got the number of their escape vehicle. Are you speaking from Bath?"

"I'm staying for a day or two with my sister Erica in Camden Crescent. I don't feel comfortable in the Reading house. I'd like to speak to you about certain things you ought to know, things I can't say over the phone. I'm worried."

If he'd had antennae, they would have twitched. "I can call as soon as you want."

"Not here," she said, lowering her voice. "Walls have ears. Do you know Hedgemead Park below the crescent?"

"Quite well."

"The gazebo near the entrance?"

"With the curved seat?"

"Let's meet there, say, at eleven. I'll be in a black leather coat and purple scarf."

"I'll find you."

He'd once heard another version of the proverb she'd used: fields have eyes and woods have ears. Parks have both, he reckoned, but he guessed the sister was the problem.

He passed the next twenty minutes restoring his office to the shambles that made it his own. Then he put on his hat and stepped through the CID room. "Meeting someone. Shouldn't be long."

"If you ask me, he isn't comfortable in there," John Leaman said when the big man was out of earshot.

Hedgemead Park, on a strip of land topped by Camden Crescent and sloping steeply to London Road, was created out of a disaster. It was once occupied by two hundred and seventy-one Georgian houses known as Somerset Buildings, but whoever surveyed the site had been seriously at fault. The first landslips started in the 1860s and continued intermittently until June of 1881, when a hundred and thirty dwellings collapsed or were damaged beyond repair. With typical Victorian resource, the city fathers cleared the rubble, shored up the terrain, planted extensively and converted it into a pleasure ground with bandstand, water fountain and boundary railings. The former name of Edgemead was too suggestive of more slippage, so someone had the bright idea of adding the "H." It was all about presentation in those days and it hasn't changed.

The octagonal gazebo close to the south entrance was a good viewpoint and a useful place to meet. The lady was already there when Diamond arrived. Short, slight and dressed in the sombre colours she'd described, she looked him over with dark, intelligent eyes before confirming her name and offering her hand.

"Sorry you had trouble getting through to me," he said. "Actually I was in Reading."

"At the university?"

"Why don't we sit and talk here?"

She glanced right and left as if making certain her sister hadn't followed her. "If you like, then. Who did you see at Reading?"

"Dr. Poke."

The edges of her mouth turned down. "He wouldn't have been John's choice or mine. They didn't get on."

"Why was that?"

"Differences of approach, for one thing. Archie Poke is a linguist, while John adored the literature."

"*The Canterbury Tales?*"

"And much else. He was a great champion of everything Chaucer wrote, poor darling. The man was alive for him. To hear him speak, you could almost believe they'd met. The poetry really excited him."

Hardly the impression Diamond had got from Gildersleeve's book, but this wasn't the time to say so. "That's one way he differed from Dr. Poke, then. And the other thing?"

"Oh?"

"You said 'for one thing,' so there must be another."

"Only that John occupied the chair of Old English and had no plans to move on. I think he hoped to get a knighthood eventually. People do, for long service in high office. Archie Poke would have had to leave Reading to get a professorship. There aren't many openings in semantics unless you're willing to go abroad."

"A block on his promotion prospects?"

She shrugged. She didn't need to labour the point.

But he was glad he'd asked. This could be crucial. Ambition is a strong motivating force and can easily lead to malice. What if the shooting hadn't been over the *Wife of Bath*, but over Dr. Poke's career prospects? Could he have hired the gunmen to kill his rival at the auction?

"Do you think Poke will get to be the professor now?"

"It's on the cards. He's the senior man in the department. He's been there nearly twenty years."

"Longer than your husband?"

"At least as long. But you can't believe—"

"May we talk about the auction?" Diamond interrupted her.

"I wasn't there."

"But you knew he was going?"

"Of course."

"And did you know he was prepared to bid so high?"

"He was fired up," she said, and flapped her hand in a gesture that showed she didn't care how high the bidding went. "He'd set his heart on that wretched carving. Believe me, he meant to have it."

"Did he already have other sculptures?"

"No, but put yourself in his place. This was a link with Chaucer. He'd have loved to possess a medieval manuscript, but they're all in museums."

"When you say it was a link, I recall Dr. Poke saying something similar, but there's no proof, is there?"

"The sculpture is fourteenth century, isn't it?"

"They say it is."

"That's when Chaucer was alive. A carving of one of his main characters. It's well possible the poet himself took an interest, don't you think?"

"I don't know how we'd find out."

"Chaucer's family are known to have lived in the Bridgwater area at one time."

"Petherton Park," Diamond said.

"Why ask me if you know about it already?"

He felt chastened. For the newly bereaved, she had a sharp side. "I'm no expert," he told her. "I'm picking up bits of information where I can. I'm sure you know masses more than I do. Did he discuss the sale with you?"

"He tried and I did my best to sound interested. After all, this was a major part of his professional life. And of course he'd gone through the false dawn of the dig."

"Tell me about that."

"Haven't you heard? About twelve years ago he led a dig at North Petherton, a joint effort with the history department, trying to locate the Chaucer house, a wonderful project for his students. The university have spent many years excavating the Roman town at Silchester, so they know what they're doing. The geophysics showed them the site of a substantial building in a place called Parker's Field, where the Chaucers were believed to have lived. The dig lasted right through the long summer vacation. They exposed the foundations, but found nothing more than a few fragments of pottery. It was a huge disappointment to John, like when you hear about an Egyptologist entering a tomb and finding the robbers got there first."

"Could that have happened?"

"What—someone plundering the site? Impossible. They were living there in tents. Any disturbance would have been obvious. He told me the excavation was extremely well supervised."

"I meant before they even got there."

She shook her head.

"What was he hoping to find?" Diamond asked. "Books and papers wouldn't have survived."

"No, but other objects sometimes get discovered. Things more personal than shards of pottery, like combs, buckles, brooches, pins, shoes, even. Anyway, they gave up when the summer ended and the farmer insisted they filled in the holes in the ground."

"So there's nothing to see any more?"

"I believe it's back to being a field now. John never went back. The entire experience was deeply depressing. Some of the students became bored and unruly."

"In what way?"

"One had a supply of cannabis with him and encouraged the others to smoke when they were supposed to be digging. It led to more than one confrontation. The students claimed it was their summer vacation and this was recreation, but John insisted it was a university project and he couldn't condone the use of drugs. He was dean of the faculty at the time, with responsibility for discipline. He felt he was undermined."

"Not a happy camp, then?"

She gave a sad smile. "Not for John. Later, the same lad was reported to him for selling cannabis on the university premises and he was sent down, a wretched postscript to the whole expedition." Monica's voice switched to a more optimistic note. "So perhaps you can understand the excitement after all this time when the *Wife of Bath* piece came up for auction. He was convinced it must have come originally from the site and after all the time and effort he'd invested he didn't want anyone else to get his hands on it."

"It had been around a long time, hadn't it? The auctioneers said it was in someone else's collection before the museum acquired it."

"William Stradling of Chilton Polden. John told me all about that. Old Stradling was a magpie who amassed this huge collection and built a folly to house it. There's no doubt that the carving was one of his pieces and he may have connected it with Chaucer, but nobody else did until recent times. It was catalogued as a much eroded medieval figure on horseback with fragments of lettering along the base—or some such. When the Stradling collection was dispersed after his death it ended up in a small museum at Bridgwater and wasn't considered well enough preserved to display. So it was put into storage for a hundred and fifty years."

"She won't have enjoyed that."

A gleam of recognition shone from Monica Gildersleeve's eyes. "You're talking just like he did—as if she's a real person. I wasn't going to say this in case you thought him odd, but he said he was going to *rescue* her at the auction." She smiled for the first time. "In fact, he went on so much about her that I was starting to wonder if he preferred her to me."

Diamond grinned, too, encouraged that other people had been lured into treating the carving as more than just a slab of limestone. "Have you seen her? She's seven hundred years old and shows it."

"I've seen the picture in the catalogue."

"She's in my office now, an item of evidence. She won't leave until justice is done."

"I approve of that." She looked away at the view across the trees towards the city.

"When we spoke on the phone, you said there were things you wanted to tell me," he prompted her. "Things that worry you."

"It's personal," she said, continuing to stare into the distance.

He waited.

She seemed to need to psych herself up. "I don't even know if I should be telling you this, but it keeps me awake at nights. My ex-husband, Bernie, is not a forgiving man. He was extremely angry when he found out about my affair with John. I don't mind admitting I was unfaithful for two years before he found out, so I was in the wrong. Bernie was away from home a lot on business. He's a property developer, a very successful one, and also very hard-working. He'd be away on projects for days on end. I met John at a literary lunch. Do you want to hear this?"

"If you think it makes a difference, of course," Diamond said.

"It isn't easy, but I've said it all to lawyers and the mediator, so I suppose I can say it to you. Well, we happened to be seated next to each other on the top table and I expressed interest in John's field of study. I read English myself at Oxford and it was wonderful talking to him. It brought back golden memories of my student days. Bernie had been away on some development project for over a week and I was feeling sorry for myself. On the face of things, I was well looked after—a rich bitch, my sister called me once before this happened. The best of clothes, my own sports car and of course a show house to live in. But none of that can compensate for being ignored. John made me feel alive again. We went to the cinema a couple of times and then he took me for a meal and ended up in my bed. The old, old story. You'll have heard it all before."

"It's your life," Diamond said. "I'm not here to judge you."

She turned to face him. "That's kind. We got away with it for a surprisingly long time. I dreaded Bernie finding out, as he was bound to. In the end one of his business rivals saw us together and tipped him off, probably just to bug him. The showdown wasn't pretty and I got what was coming to me."

"Violence?"

"Bernie came from that sort of background. I expected nothing less. What I hadn't expected was that he'd get drinks in and turn me over to his friends. As I'd behaved like a whore, he said, I deserved to be treated as one. He sat in a chair and watched."

"That's horrible. Did you report it?"

"I didn't dare." She added slowly, spacing her words, "And I don't want you to follow it up."

"We could put him away for years, and the accomplices."

"I'd deny everything." She was cool, measured and determined. "So you see, it wasn't the sort of fight between man and wife that ends in reconciliation. The only thing we agreed on was divorce. I don't know if you've gone through the process."

"Fortunately, no."

"You have to spend time with a mediator, in case you can be reconciled. Some chance! It was only then that I learned Bernie had been having a series of one-night stands with women he employed as personal assistants. Life isn't fair, is it? I got gang-raped for admitting I was unfaithful. There was nothing I could do about his cheating."

"Sickening."

"If nothing else, his infidelities ensured I got a fair share of the settlement. I can still live in some style. John was a single man, so we were able to marry soon after my divorce came through. We bought a nice house near the Thames in Caversham. And now this." Her lip trembled. "I had to identify him."

"I don't understand why you decided to tell me so much," Diamond said to get her back on track.

"Because of Bernie and something he said. He's a powerful, ruthless man. You don't come up through the building trade from nowhere without getting in fights. And as he got bigger in the business, he had his own heavies, who crushed the opposition for him. People he once worked for got taken over and old scores were settled before he trampled on them. No one got the better of him. I dreaded the day when he would find John with me in the house."

"Is that what happened?"

"Thank God, no. John and Bernie only came face to face once, at the divorce hearing, outside the court. Too many other people were about for Bernie to start a fight. He walked right up to John and looked him in the eye and said, 'You'll pay for this.' I don't know what John thought of it. My blood ran cold."

8

The law can only function fully if people are willing to speak out. Many crimes go unpunished because victims are too frightened, or too traumatised, to describe their experiences and be cross-examined. Diamond knew he'd get nowhere trying to persuade Monica Gildersleeve to testify to the violence her former husband had unleashed. He understood why and sympathised, but he was appalled by the knowledge that such a vicious man was still at liberty and capable of repeating his crimes.

Stay focused, he chided himself. You're dealing with the professor and how he met his death. Weigh the information you've been given.

The story Mrs. Gildersleeve had told without an atom of self-pity had rung true. There was no apparent reason for her to have lied or exaggerated. Thanks to her candour, there was a new perspective on the case. The auction may not have triggered the killing, as he and his team had supposed, but simply served as the backdrop to a planned execution. The professor's affair with a married woman had brought him a dangerous enemy. A threat from Wefers meant more than mere words. Here was a vengeful man with the means to employ others to act for him.

Slightly less compelling, but not to be ignored, a second suspect had emerged. Dr. Poke knew he would not be offered the chair of Old and Medieval English while Gildersleeve remained in the job. Thwarted ambition can nurture jealousy, hatred, even murder. The motive is the insidious kind that eats away day by day at morality and respect for the law.

■ ■ ■

The team listened keenly when Diamond reported on his meeting with Monica Gildersleeve. The only surprise to him was the way Ingeborg reacted. He would have put money on her empathising strongly with the poor woman's ordeal. Instead she remained as calm as if he'd been reading out the latest crime figures. He didn't mind too much. Excesses of emotion never went down well with the team. Perhaps it was the way he'd told it, he reflected. Hearing the victim herself would have shocked them more.

John Leaman was the first to comment.

"I don't get it."

"Don't get what?" Diamond asked him.

"If this was a deliberate, planned murder, what's the point of doing it in such a public place?"

"It's smart. Everyone assumes the victim was killed in the course of a robbery that went wrong. That's what we've been thinking up to now. Maybe it's what we were meant to think."

Leaman shook his head. "That's too Byzantine for me."

Looks were exchanged, but no one asked.

"Plenty of people knew the sale was coming," Diamond went on. "It was well publicised, in the paper and online. Gildersleeve wasn't exactly silent about going there and bidding up for the carving. Anyone who knew about him and his interest in Chaucer could predict how he'd behave if he was thwarted. The auction was a very good cover for a killing."

"Except the killing wasn't all that efficient," Leaman said. "He died from a stomach wound rather than several bullets to the head, like you'd expect from an assassination squad."

Diamond shook his head and glanced round the room. "Did anyone hear me say the gunmen were hot shots? Plainly they weren't."

Paul Gilbert took some heat out of the exchange. "They don't get much practice here in sleepy old Zummerzet."

Smiles all round.

Diamond wasn't letting Leaman undermine him. "The

thinking behind it may have been intelligent even though the execution was poor. That's all I'm saying."

Then Keith Halliwell tried to move the discussion on. "It's progress. We're talking about suspects now. Real people. I never had much confidence in the British Museum as the killer."

"They have a high body count," Paul Gilbert said, on a roll with his homely wit.

"What do you mean?"

"All those mummies."

Halliwell rolled his eyes. "Get the names on the board, John. Let's get some background on these villains."

But Leaman refused to back off. "I don't think we should get carried away by what this woman said. Any rational assessment points to an armed robbery that went wrong."

Diamond relented a bit. "You're right about that, John, and it's still the main line of enquiry. These other suspects are side issues for the present, but we won't discount them."

Ingeborg said, "It sounds as if Monica Gildersleeve impressed you, guv."

He hesitated, sensing disapproval behind the remark. "I believe she was speaking the truth."

"It's just that she's got us all thinking about Wefers and Poke. Is that why she asked to see you—to finger them as suspects?"

"It's one interpretation. What's your point here?"

"Shouldn't we ask ourselves why?"

"Her husband was shot. She's entitled to an opinion."

"And the two people she named are her ex and the guy who wanted her husband's job."

"Go on. I'm listening."

"What's her agenda? That's my point. Can't she accept that her husband of six months got killed making a fool of himself over a lump of limestone? He'd been telling all and sundry how much he wanted the thing. It must have really got to her, him going on like that."

"She didn't say so."

"What's more, he was willing to pay twenty-four grand."

"I doubt whether money came into it. She's a rich woman."

"He died trying to hold onto the *Wife of Bath*, not the wife he'd recently married."

The words Monica Gildersleeve had used came back to him: *I was starting to wonder if he preferred her to me.* He nodded. "I follow what you're saying, Inge. It must be really tough for her to take."

"Well, it may explain why she favours another explanation."

"Okay. In matters like this it's helpful to get the woman's angle."

Her eyes narrowed and she said in a low voice, "Don't patronise me."

From nowhere, he'd got a putdown from the brightest of his team, the one he still hoped would volunteer to go undercover. He didn't fully understand how it had happened. He'd tried to give her credit for speaking out.

He had another try. "I was about to say we mustn't get deflected. It would be useful to find out more about the stone before it got into the auction, and I'm thinking of making a trip to Bridgwater tomorrow. We could take in North Petherton as well. Feel like a break from this lot?"

"Are you speaking to me?" she said in the same disenchanted voice.

"I thought I was."

She hesitated. "I'd rather not, if you don't mind. I'd like to be closer to home tomorrow. Personal reasons."

There wasn't much arguing with that. "Fair enough."

Leaman spoke up. "I'll go with you, guv. I'm getting interested in the history of North Petherton since I started researching online."

"Thanks," Diamond said without any gratitude. "I'll enjoy your company." His mind wasn't really on Bridgwater or North Petherton. He turned back to Ingeborg. "Can we have a chat in my office?"

She was more relaxed when alone with him. She smiled when he warned her not to trip over the *Wife of Bath*.

"It's easily done," he added. "I ought to push her into a corner out of the way."

"She might not appreciate that. You may not have noticed, but women like to know precisely what's going on."

He smiled. "You and I seemed to be on different wavelengths out there. I didn't set out to upset you."

"No problem. I'm a little edgy, that's all."

"Something I said?"

She exhaled like a smoker, using the pause to choose the right words. "All this stuff about suspects and deliberate murder got to me, guv. I spent a lot of the past twenty-four hours thinking over what you said about going undercover and my mind was made up. I was going to speak to you as soon as you were alone. So it came as a shock to hear you talking about these new theories fed to you by Monica Gildersleeve."

"That wasn't my intention."

"I know, but it seemed to show you don't have total confidence in the scenario we've been pursuing up to now."

"You've known me a long time, Inge," he said. "Keeping an open mind is the only way forward. In this job, it's essential. We don't know everything, so we have to stay receptive."

"I understand that."

"But . . . ?"

"But if I'm going to put my career and maybe my life on the line by associating with known criminals, I want to know it's for solid reasons. I want to be certain I'm not on a wild goose chase."

His mouth had gone dry. Now that she was on the point of volunteering, he was becoming unsettled instead of relieved. "Nothing is certain, Inge. I'd be dishonest if I promised you it was. The only solid fact we have is that three armed robbers held up the auction and shot the professor. None of our theories, however over the top, can alter that. I don't know how we're going to make progress without tracing the gunmen. This isn't the kind of stuff you get from talking to snouts in a pub."

She nodded, more reconciled, it seemed. "So nothing fundamental has changed since we spoke?"

"Nothing has, and nothing will if you're taking risks for us."

She fixed her flame-blue eyes on him, and they burned into his conscience. "If I do it, I want the freedom to act as I choose."

"Within the law?"

There was a long pause. "If not, I'll cover my tracks."

He didn't care for that answer, but he understood why she used it. "Fair enough. I trust your judgement."

"I won't report in until I get a breakthrough. It may take some time."

"I'm prepared for that."

"You'll cover for me at this end?"

"Goes without saying."

"What about the ACC? Will you be telling her?"

"It's better Georgina doesn't find out. She'll only think of what can go wrong. I'll keep her from interfering." He plucked at his ear lobe. "Is there anyone in your private life who might get suspicious?"

Her eyes flared again. "Why should there be?"

"You said you didn't want to come with me to Bridgwater tomorrow."

"Because I'm keen to get started."

"Where, exactly?"

She gave a short, nervous laugh. "There you go, wanting to keep tabs on me. I just said I need to be a free agent. I'm not going in blindly, guv. I've done my research. Okay, it's Bristol, but I'm not saying which part."

Anxieties he'd been suppressing bubbled over. "Shall I alert our colleagues at Trinity Road?"

"God, no. I don't want minders."

"There are places in Bristol where a white blonde woman is going to stand out."

"You're starting to talk like my dad. I'm a detective sergeant. I've got a game plan, and it doesn't include telling you or anyone else what I'm up to. You can leave messages on my voicemail at home if you want."

"Will you be armed?"

"It's all taken care of. I just hope you and the rest of CID survive without me for as long as it takes."

She'd avoided the direct answer. He continued to fret. "The gang culture isn't as clear cut as it's reported by the media. You'd think it was all youth crime, muggings and car thefts, but there's another, more sinister, layer. These are the people you'll be rubbing shoulders with, hardened professionals, men in their thirties and forties who keep a lower profile and authorise bigger crimes using guns rather than knives. They were there when I joined the force and the faces may have changed, but the level of violence hasn't. If anything, it's worse."

"Guv, I know this. When I was freelancing as a journalist I wrote a series of articles for the *Western Daily Press* on organised crime. I've kept up. I know who the head honchos are. I'm not cosying up to a bunch of fifteen-year-olds doing drugs on street corners."

He stopped himself asking for a second time where she would start. She was right. He had to act like her boss rather than her father. "Inge, I can't put into words how much I appreciate what you're doing. If you need back-up, call me any time, day or night."

In the CID room, John Leaman had been busy on the computer. The prospect of the Bridgwater trip had got him going. He gave an uncharacteristic cry of triumph when Diamond came in.

"Guv, I've found something."

"Yes?"

"Stradling's book."

"Stradling?" Diamond said without taking it in, still troubled by the risks he was asking Ingeborg to take.

"William Stradling of Chilton Polden, the antiquarian who owned the *Wife of Bath* before she was acquired by the museum. He wrote this book, *A Description of the Priory of Chilton-super-Polden*, about his weird collection of objects and how he built Chilton Priory to house them, and it's here online."

"Does it tell us anything?"

"The collection included the head of a Maori chieftain,

an ancient canoe-paddle, a bishop's mitre, a German execu-
tioner's sword, an oak chest from Glastonbury Abbey, a stone
cannonball from the Civil War, stained glass, a Roman hand-
basin, a tomahawk, a scarab from the breast of an Egyptian
mummy, a brass drum from the Battle of Copenhagen and
numerous chunks of masonry rescued when local houses
and churches were being knocked down in the name of
restoration."

"How do you remember that lot?"

"It's a knack I've always had. I'm unbeatable at that party
game with objects on a tray."

Diamond believed him. "But you left out the *Wife of Bath*."

Leaman cleared his throat. "She doesn't actually get a
mention."

"Because he didn't know what the carving was?"

"Nothing in the book sounds much like it, to tell you the
truth. There are plenty of carvings—busts, gargoyles, bits
of buildings scavenged from stonemasons' yards—and he
describes them. I've checked the whole thing more than
once."

"It isn't listed? So why are you telling me this?"

"Hang on a minute, guv. This isn't the whole story. I found
another website with the history of the Stradling family.
They go back a long way. They were Welsh, originally, from
Glamorgan. William traced them back."

"Cut to the chase, John. I haven't got all day."

"It's this. Edward Stradling, a direct ancestor, born about
1398, married Jane Beaufort, who was the granddaughter
of John of Gaunt, who was married to Catherine de Roet,
and—this is the interesting bit—Catherine's sister Philippa
was Chaucer's wife. The families were linked by marriage."

"My head is spinning."

"You said you wanted it fast. Listen, I'll say it again more
slowly."

"No, you won't. I get the point—a family link we didn't
know about."

"But old William Stradling, being an antiquarian, would

certainly have known about it, and been proud of being related to the father of English poetry. So it's not surprising he took a special interest in Chaucer."

"If he did." Diamond needed more persuading. "You just told me the *Wife of Bath* doesn't get a mention in his bloody book."

A superior look surfaced on Leaman's face, as if his overweight boss had just dropped into a tiger trap. "The book appeared in 1839. He lived another twenty years. Obviously he found the carving after publication."

It was a fair point. "That's possible, I suppose."

"We know for certain that Stradling once owned the thing. It's part of the provenance set out in the auction catalogue. That sort of claim has to be accurate, with money involved. And because of his family's link with Chaucer, I'm suggesting he recognised it for what it was, but never published the fact."

"Where's Chilton Priory?"

"We'll pass it on the road tomorrow. It's on the A Thrty-Nine, about five miles this side of Bridgwater."

"As close as that?"

"But there's nothing to see any more. It's privately owned."

"So it can't be far from the place where the Chaucer house once stood?"

"Eight or nine miles. The altar rails from North Petherton church were part of Stradling's collection, so he certainly scoured the area for relics."

Diamond was finally persuaded. He said with more enthusiasm, "I'd still like to know exactly how he came across the carving. I'm getting hooked on this myself. Do you think the professor found out the Chaucer connection when the thing came up for sale?"

Leaman shrugged. "It didn't take me long on the internet."

"We're not all computer geeks."

"He will surely have heard that a carving of the Wife of Bath was going to be auctioned. He must have done his research, or he wouldn't have bid so much."

"You're right. He was a Chaucer expert and he worked it

out. And so did the British Museum and the bidders from New York and Tokyo. You've done well, John. I can't wait to get started." He turned towards his office, his brain still reeling from the overdose of information. A long car journey with the anorak of the team would be quite an ordeal.

But Leaman hadn't finished. "I hope it's all right with you. I thought we might need some expert help tomorrow."

"You're an expert yourself. Is that necessary?"

"I don't know the place at all. I called the Bridgwater museum and they're providing a local history person to show us round."

"What did you tell them—that we're the Bath murder squad?"

"No, I thought that would put them off. I said we're writers researching Chaucer."

"Couldn't you think of anything better than that?"

"We do have to write stuff."

Writers. Marvellous as he was at absorbing information, John Leaman hadn't a creative thought in his head.

9

"Known to the police" is a badge of honour to certain people. They are the Teflon-coated tyrants behind most organised crime in the major cities. They preside over lawbreaking on an industrial scale without ever getting blood on their hands.

So Ingeborg had little difficulty targeting Nathan Hazael as the most likely supplier of the gun that had killed John Gildersleeve. This sinister individual was notorious in Bristol, ruthless, feared by the entire criminal fraternity—and just about untouchable. He occupied a unique position in the city, overseeing multiple scams, hold-ups and thefts enacted under threat of death, but impossible to trace to him personally. He was protected by layers of insulation: at the lowest level, thugs; at the highest, lawyers. And between, an army of hitmen, con artists, pimps and protection racketeers held in thrall by blackmail, old scores and threats.

Most professional criminals in Britain do not own firearms. For a "hard job" they approach people like Hazael and rent by the day and the going rate is high. The trick is not to fire the things. There is a good rebate on a gun that was used merely as a threat. The science of ballistics and the difficulty in recovering used ammunition means that after a weapon has been discharged it becomes identifiable and loses almost all of its value. Most "hot" guns are broken up or buried.

Getting under Hazael's radar was the challenge. Ingeborg believed she'd worked out a way to do it. She'd done her research, read everything on file, checked the man and his associates, familiarised herself with his methods. The precious snippet of information she had seized on wasn't in the police records at all. It was something she had found in a local arts magazine.

She knew she had to act on the discovery and she had thought of a way to do it. But of course there was a risk.

She needed to make a judgement about one of her oldest friends. Get this wrong and she could walk into a death trap. You can spend years being completely open with someone, sharing the ups and downs of life, but in the last analysis can you depend on them? She wasn't going into this blindly. She knew Sylvie May was loyal and wouldn't willingly betray her. This was a mate who stood by you, who wouldn't allow anyone to get away with a mean-spirited remark. Given the opportunity, she would defend you to the death. But that same fighting spirit that made Sylvie who she was also made her a loose cannon. She never gave a moment's forethought to what she was about to say. She was out with the response before she'd thought it through. Emotion ruled her, and that was the danger.

Yet she was uniquely placed to help.

She was the editor-in-chief of a popular weekly that covered the arts and entertainment in the southwest. There had been a time ten or so years ago when Ingeborg was freelancing as a journalist and Sylvie was the showbiz editor of a national daily and the two had helped each other to unearth the real stories behind the guff put out by the PR agencies. If you wanted the truth about some celeb's secret dealings or latest conquest, Sylvie or Inge would have discovered it. They knew where the action was and time and again they came up with scoops any other journalist would have pawned her iPad to get.

Heart-stopping as it was, the risk of confiding in Sylvie couldn't outweigh the opportunity. Ingeborg got in touch and fixed a meeting.

Any hope she might have had of a discreet *tête-à-tête* was quickly dashed. Sylvie's *tête* was emerald green in corkscrew curls. Against the backdrop of the scrubbed-brick walls in Flinty Red, the small restaurant on Bristol's Cotham Hill, the look was startling. Before they went to their table Sylvie loudly demanded a hug that had everyone else in the restaurant turning to see the two noisy women who had arrived. This wasn't going to plan.

Sylvie was a regular here and wanted everyone to know. She hugged the manager and the waiter. "They do the most amazing wine-tastings," she told Ingeborg. "I can never remember the name of anything I try, so I have to keep coming back. All the reds are superb. For starters let's plump for something Spanish and then we can think about France or Italy for the white."

Was this the worst mistake of Ingeborg's career? Today of all days she needed a clear head.

Sylvie had moved on to the lunch menu. "You haven't gone veggie or anything? You were never predictable. I want you to try the braised octopus with harissa, coriander and potato."

"Don't I get a choice?"

"Trust me."

After they'd ordered, Sylvie pitched her voice at a more normal level, which was a blessing, because she was straight into her journalistic Q&A mode. "You got made up to sergeant, I hear. How's the detective business going?"

Questions like this were to be expected. Ingeborg would normally be relaxed about them. She was clear in her mind how much she could safely say. The danger was that girl-talk loosens the tongue and that was without the assistance of alcohol. "Good and bad days. You get them in any job, don't you? I wouldn't go back to being a hack."

"And how do Bath CID take to a sassy blonde telling them Colonel Mustard did it with the candlestick in the library?"

"They're fine. Some are more serious-minded than others, but you need people like that. Policing isn't one big laugh."

"And the boss?"

"He's good."

"Yes, but what's he like? What makes him tick?"

"Now you're asking." She could picture Diamond's horrified

reaction if he ever discovered his personal qualities were the small talk in a public restaurant. "He brings out the best in the team. A good brain, which is essential. You think you can predict how he'll handle any situation because he's a seasoned cop, and then suddenly he'll surprise you. I've never known anyone quite like him. He plays up to his image of being all fingers and thumbs and at war with technology, but I suspect he could build his own spacecraft and fly it to the moon if needed."

"Sounds like you're a secret admirer."

Ingeborg smiled. "Give me a break, Syl. He's at least twenty years older than me. But if I wanted to bank on someone to save my life, I'd pick Peter Diamond every time."

"I bet he fancies you, whatever age he is."

"There you go. Don't you ever stop working? He's in a relationship with a smart lady who understands him better than I ever will." Ingeborg paused while the wine was poured, and told herself she really must go on with this. "And now that I've given you the rundown on my professional life, how's yours? Thriving, by the look of you."

Sylvie flicked the curls into motion again. "It's cut-throat, as always. Changes of owner, bosses who can barely speak a word of English. We're like one of those premiership football clubs, easy prey to foreign oligarchs. They hire and fire at will, and you can never be sure who'll be sitting in the chair when you walk into the boardroom."

"But you keep *your* job."

She gave a broad wink. "Made myself indispensable, haven't I? If they sacked me, they'd lose my contact list, which I guard like the Crown Jewels. It *is* the Crown Jewels."

"Can't someone hack into it?"

"No chance. The numbers aren't on any computer. They're in a battered old Filofax that stays zipped in my bag. It's there now. And if anyone nicked it they wouldn't be able to read my shorthand. You're under the letter S with all the other Smiths, in case you're wondering. I'm rather chuffed to have a private line into Bath CID."

"Not much use to you," Ingeborg said.

"No?"

"Absolutely no."

"Go on. I wouldn't mind betting you know secrets about the glitterati of Bath I could share with my readers. A hint about some celeb in the frame for pimping in the pumproom?"

"Sylvie, if it happened, you'd be the first to know."

"Says who?"

"You'd be on the case before I was."

"Oh, come on. Now I understand where the word 'cop-out' comes from. You must have any number of juicy stories crossing your desk."

"You wish."

The good-natured fencing continued right through the main course. It was becoming obvious to Ingeborg that she'd have to give a little to get the favour she wanted.

"That was truly out of this world," she said when she put knife and fork together on her empty plate. "You should write the food column for your magazine."

"Between you, me and the manager, I sometimes do."

"I still read your feature articles regularly. Even when you don't give yourself a byline the style is unmistakable."

Sylvie took a long sip of the Chablis and stared over the glass with a look that refused to be schmoozed. "And the reason we're here must be because some piece of deathless prose I wrote lately has caught your beady blue eye? Go on, nice cop. I'm listening."

No backing off now. Out of sight under the table Ingeborg's fingers laced together and squeezed. She hoped to God she'd judged this right. "The issue before last, you had a piece on a singer from the Far East who is moving up the charts."

"Lee Li. You saw it?"

"I did."

"Okay," Sylvie said. "She's definitely one to watch. She blends classical Chinese melodies with modern music of all sorts from reggae to soul. A bright kid who will make it big if I'm any judge."

"Was she pleased with what you wrote?"

"Over the moon. I'm quoting her actual words, as texted on the day of publication. She talks in clichés, by the way, and I found it rather endearing. English is her second language. What's your interest? Professional, no doubt."

"I downloaded her Cherry Blossoms album. The voice is special, thrilling on the lower registers."

"But that's not what we're here about," Sylvie said with her trademark directness.

"True. Towards the end of the article you throw in the names of some people who helped Lee in her career so far, producers mostly."

"Lifted straight out of the promo literature. They all like their credit if they can get it."

"One name stood out because I didn't know he has form in the popular music world."

"Who's that?"

"Nathan Hazael."

"Can't hear you."

Of course she'd heard. She just wanted a moment to think. Ingeborg leaned forward and repeated the name without raising her voice.

Sylvie laughed. "He's not a muso. He's a crook." She stabbed a finger in Ingeborg's direction. "Now I know what this reunion is really about."

"You could be getting warm."

"Well, I hope Bath police will be picking up the bill. I only mentioned the son of a bitch because the girl kept on about him and his many acts of kindness."

"So he wasn't in the promo material?"

She laughed. "He's the sugar daddy. She may be talented, she may have a voice in a million and a sweet personality, but it's who you know, isn't it? She needs Nathan's help to rocket her to the top of the music business."

"Is she living with him in his mansion on the Leigh Woods estate?"

"That's the price of success."

"And does she know he supplies the firearms for three-quarters of the serious crime in the southwest? Allegedly."

"Remarkable as it may seem to you, my precious, my interview with Lee didn't get round to the subject of guns. She spoke of him with unbridled admiration every time his name came up. That's what I'm telling you and that's what I'll tell Nathan's lawyers if they come visiting. Have you got something new on the scumbag, because it had better be foolproof."

"Don't I know it," Ingeborg said with feeling. "The last time a major investigation targeted him he walked out of court a free man and the DCI on the case and two others were suspended. No, I don't have an arrest warrant in my back pocket. I simply find it bizarre that this godfather figure suddenly has a stake in a pop singer from Taiwan."

"A peach of a singer. And a rising star. You said so yourself. It's the old, old story. He likes young flesh and Lee Li needs funding. It may be distasteful, but she's a grown-up. It's not against the law."

Trying to sound casual and not feeling it in the least, Ingeborg put the question she'd rehearsed in her mind a hundred times. "If I wanted to meet her what's the best way to go about it?"

"Meet her—or him?" Sylvie said. "You're too transparent for a super sleuth, darling."

"I can't knock on his door with my list of questions," Ingeborg said.

"I wouldn't recommend it. He's nobody's fool. And he's very, very dangerous. Even I know that, and I haven't met the guy."

"So the best approach is through Lee."

"And you want me to set it up? How, exactly?"

"It can't be too obvious. I'm thinking of telling her I'm a freelance."

"As you were."

"And wanting to do a photo feature."

"As you—" Sylvie rocked back in her chair. "Hold on, you're no photographer."

"Let me explain. I'd tell her I'm pitching an idea for a

regular two-page spot in one of the weekend colour magazines in the national Sundays, a new take on one of those 'day in the life' things. It would be called iPhone Diary and consist of up to a dozen shots taken with my phone to give a record of her wild and wacky day from wake-up to lights out."

"Wicked—but no picture editor I know would agree to use your fuzzy iPhone pictures."

"The fuzziness doesn't matter," Ingeborg said. "It's meant to have a slightly amateurish look, as if these are sneaky pics of something private. With an intro from you, I can convince Lee that I'm genuine. I'll flatter her by telling her she's been picked because she's so famous and attractive, my number one choice for the pilot feature."

"This is your passport into Nathan's fortress?"

"I reckon."

"Isn't there a tiny flaw? He's not going to let you and your iPhone anywhere near his stately home, sweetie."

"Oh, come on. You know as well as I do that the male ego knows no bounds. He'll be chuffed to bits to let the world see him sitting up bare-chested in bed with a stunning little creature like Lee. But if I have to settle for Lee in her bathrobe eating muesli, so be it. The object of all this is to get me under Nathan's radar."

"And then what?"

"I'd rather not go into that."

"I mean what happens when your photo feature doesn't make it into print?"

"I'll say the stupid newspapers turned me down. By then I'll be out of it, anyway."

"You hope. You're playing with fire."

"Not playing. It's my job."

"And all you want from me is the intro? What's wrong with approaching her yourself if she's going to be as eager to please as you say?"

"You bring credibility. She knows you. She likes you. If Nathan asks who the hell I am, she'll say I was recommended by the writer of that brilliant interview in *South West*."

"Greaser." Sylvie smiled and sighed. "All right, chuck, I'll call her this afternoon. How much am I allowed to say?"

The hours that followed weren't easy. Ingeborg could imagine any number of ways her fast-talking, well-lubricated friend could torpedo the plan. So it came as a welcome surprise when Sylvie called early in the evening.

"She swallowed the bait, darling. She wants to meet you first and she's suggesting—wait for this—tonight at midnight on the promenade deck of the *Great Britain*."

"Are you serious?"

"Am I ever not? She'll be there to film her next video, *Seabird*. A night shoot. All very hush-hush in case the fans get to hear of it, so keep it to yourself. The crew have to set up after dark and be out before sunrise. She'll talk to you between takes. Indulge her. This is her chance to be seen doing something glamorous. Get a few pics with your mobile and you're under way, aren't you?"

"I hope so."

"Come on, be positive. You're the big-time journo certain to boost her reputation."

"Is that what you told her?"

"In a nutshell. I'm not going to repeat all the stuff I said in case you get big-headed."

"Nothing was said about you-know-who?"

"Not a syllable. You're primed and ready to go and my job is done, right?"

The location and the timing may have been unusual, but the arrangement suited Ingeborg rather nicely. She would establish herself as the hotshot hack and give the appearance of being under way with the project before she had to meet Nathan Hazael.

10

Approaching on the A39, you could easily have mistaken it for a church. Chilton Priory, known locally as Stradling's Folly, was visible from some distance as a grey tower with battlements and gargoyles, but until you got close you didn't see the full extent of the building, mostly obscured below the steep banking at the side of the road.

They got out of the car. To Diamond's eye, this was a perfect setting for a horror film. Extending from the tower were a gothic nave and an oratory that must have been part of the original, housing the antiques collection. More parts had been added at intervals since. Perversely the late nineteenth century two-storey wings were in the Tudor style, but still constructed from the grim, grey lias found locally. So this much-enlarged building now boasted at least four different styles of window—lancet, oriel, stone-mullioned and casement. Turrets and chimneys sprouted from the otherwise flat roofs. On the east side of the building was a twentieth century feature, an integral garage that still managed to look sinister, as though it led directly through the Tudor section into Stradling's crypt below the tower. And the whole building was topped with battlements in an attempt to salvage some sort of unity from chaos.

"Is it me, or is it a mess?" Diamond said.

"Stradling called it his repository," Leaman said.

"Sums it up."

"You may be thinking of something else."

"Terrific view. I'll give it that."

The so-called priory—which had never housed a monk or a nun—stood on Cox's hill, a high point of the Polden ridge.

The peat moor stretched for miles below them, across the Vale of Avalon to the north where the Mendips made a dramatic blue backdrop. But in reality (difficult to grasp here) they weren't particularly high up. The flatness of the terrain below made the impression.

"He claimed that when he used a telescope from his tower on a clear day he could see across the Bristol Channel to his other house in South Wales," Leaman said.

"My second home is the nick," Diamond said, "and I thank the Lord I can't see it from my place. When did you say this was built?"

"1838–9 the same year the book came out." Leaman as always couldn't be faulted on his facts.

"So he wrote the book to promote his collection."

"I suppose."

"And as he didn't mention the *Wife of Bath*, we can assume he acquired her some time after?"

Leaman's eyebrows popped up in tribute. The boss seemed to have grasped the fundamentals now.

"But from where?" Diamond said.

"Some stonemason's yard, I expect. He found a lot of his pieces lying about when buildings were being renovated. He was on a mission. Victorian restoration, so-called, stripped bits from a lot of churches and great houses and he salvaged whatever he could."

Diamond was silent, thinking.

Leaman continued to prattle on like an audio guide. "The three pinnacles up there are very old and were originally part of the tower at Langport, which you can see from the other side of the road. He says in his book—he has a good way with words—that they now look down on their tawdry usurpers."

"What time are we meeting our local contact?" Diamond said, weary of words and gingerbread architecture. "We'd better move on."

As it turned out, they had time for a coffee in Bridgwater. Diamond ordered a Cornish pasty and a double helping of chips with his. "One useful tip I learned early on in my police career: never go past a food outlet or a toilet. It might be the last you see all day."

"I had a good breakfast," Leaman said.

"So did I. That was two hours ago." He leaned back in the chair. "I'm thinking when we meet this guy we'll straight away drop the charade of being writers or researchers, or whatever poppycock you told them. I believe in being honest with people."

"As you wish," Leaman said, piqued. "Sometimes they clam up when you tell them you're police."

"If you witter on about pinnacles like you do, they will. They can't get a word in. Let him do the talking, right?"

Leaman tilted his head in annoyance. "I thought you were interested."

"I was. This guy won't be. He could be the pinnacle of pinnacle experts. Leave him to me."

Leaman stood up suddenly.

"What's up now?" Diamond said, thinking he'd taken offence.

"Nothing. I'm taking your advice, or part of it."

"Oh, yes?"

"This seems as good a time as any to find the toilet."

The local contact waiting for them at the entrance of Bridgwater's Blake Museum appeared to be a woman until they got close enough to tell he was a slightly built man in his thirties with shoulder-length black hair and a white bandana. At home, Diamond sometimes caught a few seconds of *Time Team* when he was flicking through the TV channels and he'd noticed how most of the experts sported an impressive growth of hair. Once, the mark of a serious archaeologist would have been a beard. Not these days.

A friendly smile greeted them. "Mr. Leaman?"

"Detective Inspector, actually," Diamond said, to get things on the proper footing he'd announced to Leaman, "and I'm Detective Superintendent Diamond."

"Policemen?" The smile turned to something worthy of a dentist's chair. "I was told you were writers."

"You were told wrong."

"We do a certain amount of writing," Leaman added to compensate for the abruptness.

Diamond glared at him, but this wasn't the time to say the only writing they did was filling in endless forms.

"Am I missing something?" their guide asked.

"I don't know," Diamond said. "But we're missing your name."

"Tim Carroll, of the Bridgwater Archaeology Society." He continued to look at them as if they were from another planet. "I was told you wanted to be shown some of our local sites."

"That's the truth. North Petherton, for one."

Tim Carroll recovered himself a little. He nodded. "That will be because of the Alfred Jewel."

This was spoken with such confidence that Diamond enjoyed shaking his head.

Leaman was moved to say, "We've heard of it, of course."

"That's the reason people come to North Petherton," Carroll said. "Nothing else of note has turned up for over three hundred years. It doesn't deter the metal detectorists, who come in big numbers. I doubt if there's a square foot of ground that hasn't been checked many times over."

"We're not treasure hunters," Diamond said. "We're interested in the Chaucer connection. Didn't the Chaucers have some sort of official role as foresters?"

"They did, but there's nothing to see. Sorry to disappoint you. We don't have any Chaucer relics in the Blake." He stopped and raised his hand as a thought came to him. "Now I know why this interests the police. It's to do with that shooting at the auction, isn't it?"

"Spot on."

"Yes, I'd put it out of my mind and I don't know why, because there's been a lot in the papers lately. There *is* a Chaucer relic, or was, and it's the very thing they fought over."

"The *Wife of Bath*." Leaman was going out of his way to be helpful.

"You know about this, obviously."

"We'd like to hear your take on it," Leaman said.

"It was put up for auction by this museum. It had been in storage and unrecognised for God knows how long. When it came to light and the trustees grasped how valuable it might be, they decided to sell it and spend the proceeds on some refurbishing."

All this was familiar to Diamond. After more than two hours in Leaman's company, he wasn't sure if he could endure another anorak. To add to the discomfort, his stomach was hurting. The pasty had been undercooked. "Where was it stored?" he asked. "In a back room somewhere?"

"Not in this building at all. There just isn't the space. In a basement below the Arts Centre in Castle Street with a whole lot of other bulky items that weren't on display because they were thought to be of little interest."

"Take us there, would you?"

"The carving has gone now."

"I know that. I'm sharing an office with it, *pro tem.* I want to see where her ladyship was living before she moved in with me."

"Right now?" Surprise, if not annoyance, dawned on Tim Carroll's face. He'd not expected the awkward squad.

"Tomorrow's no use to us," Diamond said.

"We'll need a torch. I don't think the lighting works."

"They'll have one at the place. Lead the way."

Castle Street wasn't far off, so they walked.

"I don't see any castle," Leaman said, still doing his best to ease the tension.

"There isn't one."

After that, there wasn't much else to say except, "How come?"

Carroll seemed to be deciding whether he really needed to humour these pushy policemen. He walked some distance before saying, "There was a fine one built in the thirteenth century, everyone's idea of a castle with walls fifteen feet thick and a thirty-foot moat, but it was pulled down after the Civil

War. Castle Street was built over the site. Bridgwater people are rather proud of what we got in its place."

A handsome residential street it proved to be, of eighteenth century brick buildings glowing warm orange in the late morning sun. Distinctly different in material from Bath's honey-coloured blocks, the row of houses still had the pleasing Georgian proportions.

"What a location for an arts centre," Leaman felt moved to say. "They're usually on the outskirts, in buildings nobody wants to live in."

"Like Manvers Street nick," Diamond muttered. He knew for sure that the pasty had been a mistake. His belly-aching was real.

Carroll said, "It's Bridgwater's pride and joy, in use for the arts since just after the war. A theatre, art gallery, meeting rooms and bar. The council purchased it in the sixties, in more affluent times, and it's now leased at a peppercorn rent, but the upkeep has to be paid for. I used to work here until we were all laid off when the recession bit, and now the place is run by volunteers."

"You lost your job?" Diamond said.

"That's tough," Leaman said.

"It was, but you can't let the buggers grind you down, if you'll pardon my French." Carroll was sounding more confident now he was in guide mode.

"What do you do now, apart from showing visitors round?" Diamond asked.

"I get my hands dirty working for my brothers, doing house clearances. A change from arranging concerts and exhibitions, but it tides me over until I find something more to my liking."

Leaman said, "We appreciate you giving up time to see us."

"Local history is my hobby. Shall we go in?"

They'd stopped outside a three-storey building that Carroll entered as if he owned it. Inside, he greeted a volunteer by his first name and said they needed to go down into the basement.

"I wouldn't if I were you," the man said. "It's become a glory hole since you left. Everything gets shoved down there."

"These gentlemen came especially from Bath to see it," Carroll said.

"Watch your step, then. I don't think we're insured for anyone breaking a leg down there."

They borrowed a flashlight and picked their way down a set of steep steps. The door at the bottom creaked when Carroll pushed it open. He passed the light beam over the interior, whistled, and said, "See what he meant? Do you really want to go on with this? The museum stuff is on the far side, not easy to reach."

Immediately ahead of them was a drum kit and beyond that a stack of tall wood-and-canvas scenery flats. Other large hazards, less easy to identify, appeared to bar all progress.

"I'm blowed if I'm giving up now," Diamond said. He was going to see where the *Wife of Bath* had lived before coming to him, come what may.

"It doesn't smell too fragrant," Carroll said.

"You're telling me," Leaman said.

Diamond could have admitted he was having an attack of flatulence, but there were more elevating matters to pursue.

They persevered by pushing the drums to one side and forcing some of the scenery far enough to the left to make a space that even a man of Diamond's girth could pass through. Stacks of plastic chairs were easier to move aside. Beyond them were three massive papier mâché animal heads, a lion, a rhino and an elephant.

"The carnival is a very big deal here," Carroll said.

Now the flashlight picked up some bulky forms covered in drapes. "That's what we're looking for," Carroll said. "But if you're hoping to find another of the Chaucer pilgrims, you're in for a disappointment. It's only junk that's left."

"There's the source of the smell," Leaman said.

On the stone floor behind the animal heads were a sleeping bag and some blankets that clearly hadn't seen the inside of a washing machine for many a year. There were also empty cider bottles and pizza boxes.

"Someone's little secret," Diamond said, encouraged that his own little secret hadn't been detected.

"It wasn't here when I was on the payroll," Carroll said.

"That's the problem, I expect. The volunteers don't come down here." He sidestepped the bedding, and lifted one of the drapes. "What are these?"

"Chimney pots. Early Victorian. You wouldn't put them on display, but you wouldn't want to dispose of them either," Carroll said.

Leaman dragged the covering from a longer object the shape of a coffin. "Someone found a use for this."

The inside of the horse trough was filled with yet more empties.

Diamond turned his attention to another draped item, interesting because it was approximately the shape and size of the stone carving. "What's this, I wonder?"

He unveiled a small stack of weather-beaten gravestones. "I've heard of identity theft, but this is a step too far."

"Seen enough, gentlemen?" Carroll said.

"Where was the *Wife of Bath* among this lot?"

"Against the wall there." Carroll picked out a space with the torch. "It was facing inwards, so you couldn't tell what it was."

"I couldn't tell when it was in my office and pointed out to me," Diamond said. "You saw it here yourself, then?"

"Actually, I'm the guy who first dusted it off and took the trouble to find out what the inscription said."

"Really?" Diamond said in surprise. "And they still sacked you?"

Carroll shrugged. "There was nothing personal about it. First the Arts Council withdrew the funding and the county council followed and we all lost our jobs."

"They could still make good money out of your discovery."

He laughed. "Not enough to pay my salary even if they gave it all to me." If this young man was entitled to be bitter about his treatment, it didn't show. "Shall we get some fresh air?"

# # #

They used Leaman's car to drive the couple of miles through farming country to North Petherton. Diamond could feel more gas collecting in his stomach. He hoped he could hold on until they got out of the car. This pilgrimage had a subtext that Chaucer himself would have found amusing.

"It's hard to visualise," Tim Carroll said from the rear seat, "but in Chaucer's time all this was forest—royal forest. The king would come here to hunt. Well, it's known for certain King John did in the century before. He would stay at Bridgwater Castle, so it's quite possible Edward III and Richard II came as well."

"And Chaucer was deputy forester?"

"Towards the end of his life, yes. A reward for good services rendered."

"If he was the deputy, who was his boss?"

"I couldn't tell you without checking the records."

"Doesn't matter. Hardly a tree in sight these days. It's all farming round here, is it?"

"Used to be. When they built the motorway the village of North Petherton was turned into a commuter settlement."

The M5 ran in parallel, east of the A38 they were travelling along. "Bit of a shake-up for the locals."

"And how. It went straight through Petherton Park, where we're going."

"Did they make any interesting finds when they put the road through?"

"None that I've heard about."

"You must hate it."

"The motorway? Not really. We can't stand in the way of progress. The canals and the railways opened up the rural areas in their day. This is the modern equivalent. Take the next left and I'll show you Parker's Field, where the Chaucer family lived."

"Is that a known fact, about Chaucer actually living here?"

"A known fact? Maybe not. It's believed in these parts, I can tell you. We're proud of our connection with him."

"You don't think the forester thing was just a sinecure and he stayed in London?"

"Absolutely not," Carroll said as if he was speaking of his own career. "Being forester was a proper job. The forest brought in revenue for the royal purse. It was all enclosed and the locals had to pay to graze their cattle and pigs and there were tolls for using the forest tracks. Acorns and beech mast were particularly prized for pig feed. Managing all this was a big responsibility. You couldn't possibly do it from London."

"And you even know the house?"

"We know where it was sited. Tradition has it that the Chaucers lived in the Park House, or Parker's Field House, and there's usually some truth in tradition. The house was recorded as early as 1336. The family would have moved in later, of course, towards the end of the century."

The rows of modern housing they were driving past made it impossible to visualise how the view must have appeared to Chaucer. Tim Carroll gave directions from the back and they worked their way through a dull estate towards a more open area. "You can stop here."

"We'll need to," Leaman said. "The road ends."

"That's a mercy," Diamond muttered.

"What was that?"

"Touch of cramp. I'll be glad of a stretch."

"The developers never give up," Carroll said. "I don't give this much of a future as open country."

They got out and stood at the edge of a recently ploughed field. Diamond eased his stomach more audibly than he intended. "Noisy," he said at once. "If I was deputy forester I wouldn't buy a house here."

"That's the motorway you can hear."

"Thought so."

"Do we need to go any further?" Leaman asked. "We'll be up to our knees in mud."

"It's living history," Diamond said. "We didn't come all this way to sit in the car."

"I can show you the general area of the house, but there's nothing to mark the spot," Carroll said.

"We'll be right behind you," Diamond said. What he wanted most was a few more minutes in the open air.

After trudging some distance through the freshly tilled soil, Carroll stopped and looked right and left, trying to get his bearings. "To the best of my knowledge, this is where Park House was. There was a dig here a dozen years ago. Reading University."

"Led by John Gildersleeve," Diamond said. "They traced the foundations, but found damn all else."

"That isn't surprising," Carroll said. "Park House didn't last beyond the Tudor era. In those days the builders reused materials. It would have been cannibalised. It's likely most of the fabric was used for Broad Lodge, a house in Petherton Park erected in the seventeenth century."

"Still standing?"

Carroll shook his head. "And there's another reason why the Reading dig was unsuccessful. A local archivist has recently discovered a *Bridgwater Mercury* report of an earlier excavation in 1843. A vicar from Taunton brought a team here and they were digging for about six months."

Diamond chuckled at that. "And Gildersleeve hadn't heard? That's rich. I bet the Victorians dug up everything that was worth having."

"There's no record of what they found. My society made an intensive search of all the local press and documents held at the records office and came up with nothing more than that five-line report tucked away in the newspaper."

The laughter was working like a dose of Rennics. The discomfort eased.

"How about this for a theory?" Diamond said with more enthusiasm than he'd shown all day. "The Taunton vicar unearthed the *Wife of Bath*. She'd been sculpted especially to decorate Chaucer's house and lay buried right here where we're standing for all those centuries. Along comes the local magpie, William Stradling, and makes the vicar an offer he can't refuse. It would explain how it got into Stradling's collection."

"I rather like it," Carroll said after a moment's thought. "One thing we do know about Stradling is that he was alert to anything of interest turning up. And the date is about right. By that time he'd built his museum at Chilton Priory just a few miles north of here and by 1843 he'd be looking to add to his collection."

"We were there this morning," Leaman said. "It's all coming together rather neatly."

And so it was that out here in a Somerset ploughed field, with nothing to look at except mud, Diamond was moved to feel elated. The mystery of the *Wife of Bath*'s past was reasonably explained to everyone's satisfaction. They would never know the precise details, but this was a pretty good guess. The local expert approved. Even the hypercritical John Leaman had given his nod.

And the indigestion had all but gone.

A curious moment followed. They were returning to the car when Diamond had something like a vision from the remote past. The back view of Tim Carroll in his padded tunic, flannel shirt and black trousers, with his long hair swaying gently on his shoulders, made him appear remarkably like a flashback to the fourteenth century when it was fashionable to look like that. It was as if Geoffrey Chaucer himself had materialised to add his blessing.

11

"What I don't understand," Paloma said, "is why you had to go there."

After his stressful day in Somerset with John Leaman, Peter Diamond was restoring his sanity, having an evening in with Paloma at her house on Lyncombe Hill, enjoying a supper of baked salmon and asparagus helped down with Prosecco. He didn't mind discussing his work with Paloma. She was discreet, and she sometimes threw fresh light on the cases.

"The object of the visit was to get in the head that's behind this mystery."

"Do you know whose head?"

He smiled. "I wish. No, I'm coming at it obliquely, trying to understand why someone was so eager to own the *Wife of Bath* that they hired a team of gunmen to hold up the auction."

"How does a trip to North Petherton achieve that?"

"By improving my understanding. I needed to find out the history of the stone. I'm certain the person I'm pursuing will have done the research. I'm thinking they learned something I'm still not aware of."

"Even after visiting Somerset?"

He managed a wry smile. "I've barely scratched the surface."

"Why do you say that?"

"I can't understand why anyone is so eager to own the *Wife of Bath*. I wouldn't want her if she was pure gold."

"But you've got her."

"Yes and she sits in my office and reminds me how little I know."

"That lump of stone has really got under your skin."

"Fair comment. I won't be happy until I can shift it. I'm dealing with people who put a very high value on the thing. I can understand the victim, because he was a Chaucer expert. But the killer? What does he know that I don't? The key to all this is the back story and I'm doing my damnedest to root it out. North Petherton was high on my 'to do' list."

"Did Chaucer ever go there? Some of the experts say he didn't."

"The locals think he did. And there was a house—long gone—where Thomas the son definitely lived. It was in existence in the 1330s, so it's well possible that Chaucer senior lived there towards the end of his life."

"When did he get the job of deputy forester?"

"1391. He'd been incredibly busy up to then on all kinds of official duties that kept him in London, but with frequent trips to Europe. It's amazing, the travelling people managed all those years ago: Spain, France, Italy. But in middle age, he seems to have looked for a place in the country—first in Kent, where he was a justice of the peace and MP—but that didn't last and he came back to London as clerk of the king's works. Two years on, he retires—so some experts believe—to Somerset. His wife Philippa seems to have died in 1387. It's a fruitful period of his life when most of *The Canterbury Tales* are written."

"So he was a widower, like you."

"Mm." He looked away, never comfortable when the spotlight shifted to him.

"And it turned out to have been the most creative time of his life. Did you find out anything you didn't already know?"

"We were taken to the site of the house but there's bugger all to see now. It's been ploughed over many times."

"Shame."

"But what I did learn is that there was an excavation in early Victorian times led by a local vicar. This was 1843. There's no record of what was found in the dig, but about the same time, the *Wife of Bath* stone is acquired by William Stradling, the antiquarian."

Paloma smiled. "Someone did a smart deal."

"Stradling was the sort of man who missed nothing, a proper scavenger. He lived only seven or eight miles away."

"Didn't he admit where it came from?"

"I expect it was known locally, but there's nothing in writing. And after his death, people seem to have lost interest. It eventually got into the museum and was put in storage."

"So the theory is that the tablet was originally part of the structure of Chaucer's house?"

"It is now, but no one in recent times linked it to the 1843 dig for the simple reason that all news of the dig was unknown until quite recently when an archivist came across a small report in the local paper. When Gildersleeve came along in two thousand with his team from Reading, he thought they had an untouched site to explore and even a possibility of proving Chaucer himself was once the owner. They found nothing of real interest the whole summer they were there."

"Quite a blight on the professor's career, poor man," Paloma said.

He nodded. "Some cruel things were said by his so-called colleagues."

"I can understand how excited he was when the tablet came up for sale. A chance to have the last laugh."

"Yep. But who would want to frustrate him?"

"Some other Chaucer expert?"

"Another academic?"

"Depends," Paloma said. "You may not appreciate the competition that exists between universities and even within departments. I've seen it close up. Suppose some equally fanatical Chaucer expert knows he doesn't have the funds to make a decent bid. I've no idea what it would cost to fund a hold-up, but it may be less than Gildersleeve was able to pay for the stone."

"True. He'd married into money. But then the rival gets the thing by criminal means and what can he do with it? He can't write a learned paper or put it on exhibition. He's stuck with it and has to stay silent. What's more, if the Old Bill come knocking on his door, it's a big item to hide."

"That holds true whoever planned to steal it."

He smiled. "Dead right."

"You obviously have another theory," she said. "Let's hear it."

"I wouldn't dignify it by calling it a theory. I simply think if the tablet was going to be taken by force—and wouldn't be any use to the perpetrator—there must be an element of spite, a personal issue with Gildersleeve, closer to home."

"You've been delving into his private life," she said, unable to mask a note of disapproval.

"We have to. It's the job. There were people close to him who may have borne a grudge."

"Such as?"

"His wife's former husband, a property developer with a tough reputation. He's called Bernie Wefers and he was particularly brutal to Monica—savagely so—when he found she was having an affair with Gildersleeve. The fact that Wefers himself was unfaithful, sleeping with his PA, didn't seem to register. At the divorce hearing, he issued a personal threat to Gildersleeve—'You'll pay for this'—and he wasn't talking about money."

"Sounds like your number one suspect, then. Is he under investigation?"

"Of course. But one thing I've learned in this game is never to focus everything on one suspect."

"Are there others?"

"We talked about rival academics. There's one I met at Reading, a Dr. Poke, who shared an office with the victim. Extremely ambitious. I didn't care for him at all. He wants to become a professor, but there was no chance while Gildersleeve remained alive. There's just the one chair in the department and Gildersleeve looked like hanging onto that for the foreseeable future."

"Did Dr. Poke tell you this?"

"No, I got it from Monica Gildersleeve."

Paloma sat back in her chair and laced her hands behind

her head. "So she provided you with two suspects? Shouldn't you enquire into *her* motive? She could be diverting suspicion."

"They'd only recently been married. She's devastated by the murder."

"Are you certain? I notice you called her Monica and not Mrs. Gildersleeve when you started talking about her. Could it be that she appealed to your sympathetic nature?"

"Me—sympathetic?"

"You suffered a violent bereavement yourself when Stephanie was murdered."

"That's got nothing to do with it," he said, tight-lipped.

"Sorry," she said. "Shouldn't have spoken."

Suppressing the ache of the old scar, he said, "But I see what you're getting at. And she's a strange lady in some ways. She's staying with her sister in Camden Crescent, but doesn't want the sister knowing she spoke to the police. She said something about walls having ears, so we met in Hedgemead Park, on a park bench."

Paloma raised an eyebrow. "Good thing I didn't come by and see the two of you."

"It was all very proper. I can understand that she doesn't want her sister listening to her private business. Anyway, she didn't appear to hold anything back. And when we talked about the auction, she turned bright pink at the mention of the 'wretched carving' and said Gildersleeve went on so much about it that she was starting to wonder if he preferred the *Wife of Bath* to her."

"I can understand. If he hadn't been so keen to buy it, he wouldn't have got killed."

"True," he said. "But I don't seriously believe she was so jealous that she decided to have him shot. If she had murder in mind, her previous husband is the one who should have got it."

"So Monica is not a serious suspect?"

"Not until you can find me a motive."

"I'll work on it. Don't you worry." Paloma gave a faint smile. "Who else is there?"

"As suspects? We have to go back to the auction for that. Anyone who was going to be outbid by Gildersleeve had a possible motive for hijacking the auction. There were bidders on the phone from New York and Tokyo, and they dropped out quite early in the process. The main rival was a man called Sturgess, who told me—after I threatened him with a night in the cells—that he was bidding on behalf of the British Museum. Talked down to me in the way these upper-class types often do. I didn't like him at all, but that doesn't make him a suspect."

"Unless he was lying," Paloma said, "and wasn't anything to do with the BM."

Diamond shook his head. "He was telling the truth. The museum was sure to be interested. They get the auction catalogues and go through them and this was a major discovery."

"But why the secrecy?"

"Because everyone knows they can bid high, but they don't want to be pushed into paying more than necessary. It's not unknown for the seller to arrange for an accomplice to bid high and gee up the price when a big institution is involved."

"And would the British Museum have outbid Gildersleeve?"

"I'm sure of it."

"Well," Paloma said. "Here's a long shot. What if some friend of Gildersleeve got to know who he was going to be up against and arranged the hold-up?"

He thought about this. Then his eyes widened. "To thwart the museum?"

"Yes."

"That is . . . Byzantine."

And now Paloma blinked and looked impressed.

He didn't explain he'd heard John Leaman use the word the previous day. "What a monumental cock-up if the gunmen were doing him a good turn and he didn't realise and got shot."

She brought her hands together and laughed. "There. I've found a motive for Monica. She knew how much her darling husband wanted to win the auction—and found out he would be outbid—so *she* hired the gunmen. But it all went wrong. Gildersleeve knew nothing of this and panicked and was shot. And now Monica in desperation is doing all she can to point you to other suspects."

He chuckled too. "Clever. It's wacky, but it's a new theory, I'll give you that. And it's more than any of my team have come up with."

12

The steamship *Great Britain* stands proud in dry dock in Bristol harbour. Built originally in the city by the engineering genius Brunel and launched by Prince Albert in 1843, she was one of the first great ocean-going liners, making voyages to America and Australia packed with emigrants and fortune-hunters in the days of the gold rush. But the world's largest vessel had difficulty navigating the Avon and only ever made one start from Bristol. Her home port became Liverpool. Bristol had to wait a century and a quarter to reclaim the ship as its own. In 1970 the rusting hulk was towed eight thousand miles from where it had languished in the Falklands as an oversized coal bunker for over eighty years. Vast numbers of Bristolians lined every viewpoint along the Gorge one Sunday morning to welcome the old lady home. She was sited in dry dock exactly where she had been built. The renovation may not have left much of the original superstructure, but the refitting was faithfully done and created a visitor attraction that won the Gulbenkian Prize for museum of the year.

This symbol of Bristol's maritime history was where Ingeborg came with a flask of coffee and her press card at a few minutes before midnight. Nobody was there to challenge her, so she got aboard with some of the film crew as they were unloading lighting equipment from a large van on the dockside.

Nervous minutes. Not a good idea to introduce herself to anyone, she decided. She found a back-rest on deck against a raised skylight and settled to watch the show unfold. Enough lighting was in place to reveal what was going on while she remained in shadow.

The crew switched on more lamps and soon the full length of the deck, about a hundred metres with as many as six masts and a funnel, was visible, much of it covered in cables. On the starboard side a mobile camera was being given a trial run along a stretch of dolly track. Voices could be heard from the darkness above the floodlights and Ingeborg assumed there were TV crewmen perched on the yardarms. They had to be as surefooted as the sailors of old. It was all very workmanlike and professional.

A woman with earphones who had to be the floor manager patrolled the deck checking progress. Ingeborg squeezed further into the shadow. She was close enough to hear a bad-tempered answer to a query from one of the cameramen.

"Of course she isn't here yet. What do you expect? She's a fucking diva. She'll be at least an hour late. But that doesn't mean the rest of us go slow. It's got to work without a hitch when we get under way."

The floor manager was right. For Lee Li it would be playing to her image to keep everyone waiting. The legendary lateness of pop stars hadn't clicked with Ingeborg until now. She'd been too focused on her own part in the arrangement. Only a raw beginner would turn up at the appointed time. Then it would be all systems go to get the filming done before morning.

She resigned herself to a long, uncomfortable wait. The words "it's got to work without a hitch" were troubling. This tightly controlled exercise might run into a problem when she stepped out of the darkness and spoke to the star performer. Still, the invitation to do it this way had come from Lee Li herself and she was in a position to dictate terms.

A more disquieting thought had already crossed Ingeborg's mind: what if Nathan Hazael decided to attend the shoot and show support? She'd need to be ready to front it out with the man. She'd much prefer to meet him later, after she'd got to know Lee. Please God he's in bed and asleep, she told herself. He'd have to be keen to put in an appearance at this hour.

Twenty more minutes passed and there were signs that the preparations were almost complete and the real business of the night could begin—when the star finally deigned to turn up. Several of the floodlights were dimmed. At the aft end of the deck a group had gathered around someone who certainly wasn't the star. Ingeborg guessed he must be the director. They were in a huddle under the only lamp on full power and there was a definite air of anticipation.

Closer to Ingeborg one of the grips spoke up in a distinctively camp voice. "Has anyone phoned to see if madam is on her way, do you think?"

"She'll say she is, even if she's in some nightclub. And when she gets here, don't hold your breath. She'll be in make-up for ages."

"Where are they doing that?"

"Down below. The first class ladies' boudoir."

"Nice if you can get it."

"Eat your heart out."

Ingeborg was increasingly uncomfortable squatting where she was. She decided to take a walk along the port side, which was mainly in shadow and not being used, except for lengths of cable. If anyone challenged her, she'd tough it out.

She'd reached as far as the ship's enormous black funnel when a car horn sounded below. She looked over the rail at the various vehicles parked on the dockside.

A white limousine had just arrived. Someone stepped forward and opened the door and a slight, dark-haired figure stepped out and looked around as if she had all the time in the world.

Attendants moved towards her. A camera flashed repeatedly. This was definitely Lee Li. She posed for shots before strolling towards the steps up to the gangway. The minders followed at a respectful distance.

It was a relief to Ingeborg that they didn't include anyone with the body language of a gangster lover.

She checked her watch. 12:55 A.M. That earlier estimate of her late arrival had not been far out.

Would it be a good move to approach Lee Li while she was being dressed and made up? Probably not. Between takes,

Sylvie had said. Cool as she appeared, the singer was no doubt nervous about the video shoot.

So it was a matter of more waiting, more self-discipline.

More promenading.

Perhaps forty minutes went by before there was another stirring of interest on the main deck. Ingeborg glanced towards the stern and spotted a cluster of people under a floodlight switched to full power. She couldn't see the queen bee for all the drones. They spent more time fussing over her.

Even the crewmen nearest to Ingeborg were mystified. "What's the hold-up now?" one of them said.

"It's not easy," a woman's voice said. "They've got to fit the harness."

"And then what? Is she going for a technical run-through first?"

"Not much point. They might as well go for a take."

And shortly after, this was confirmed. The floor manager said, "Stand by, everybody. This is take one."

Recorded music came over the loudspeakers, a strong, clear voice soaring above a drum beat, Lee belting out the number they were creating in visual form. At the far end, the floodlit support group stepped away like the mechanics at a pit stop, leaving one slight figure alone under the light. She had dark hair to below her shoulders and was wrapped in a glittery white cloak.

Suddenly she was in motion, sprinting along the deck, her hair fanning behind her. The cloak opened and rippled into a twenty-foot train of flimsy material designed to float on the air. She was in a sequinned jumpsuit. The camera dolly moved in parallel, powered by two of the grips at full stretch to keep up.

She'd need to be fit to run the length of the deck at this rate, Ingeborg was thinking.

But then came the eye-opener. Lee Li spread her arms like wings and was airborne, lifted by unseen wires. A spotlight caught her swift movement upward between the ship's masts, a stunt made possible with wires worked by lift operators hidden high up in the darkness. Their skill, the costume designer's brilliance and Lee's grace of movement made the flying effect stunningly realistic. She swooped upwards in a great arc, poised for a split second at the limit of the movement, bunched her legs, stretched and somehow got her feet on one of the mainmast yardarms and came to perch there like a gull. The music stopped.

The crew applauded. Someone even gave a yelp of appreciation.

"Nice one," the floor manager said. "Let her down gently and tell her we need at least one more take."

The descent was less graceful. The lengths of muslin had wrapped themselves around the performer and she was more like an insect trapped on a web than a bird. But to her credit it was definitely Lee Li herself who had performed and not a double. On the deck, people were waiting to disentangle her and unstrap the harness from her chest and thighs. She shook off the last pieces of loose fabric and began walking back to where she had started.

Setting it up again would take twenty minutes or more. Ingeborg's moment had arrived. She stepped out of the shadows.

"Miss Li."

The star glanced over her shoulder.

"I won't hold you up," Ingeborg said, hurrying to draw level. "Ingeborg Smith. Sylvie May told me to introduce myself between takes."

"The writer?"

Ingeborg nodded. "You were sensational."

"Do you mean the track?" Lee had her priorities right. Commercially, the quality of the music mattered more than the aerial acrobatics.

"Loved it. I can't wait to hear more."

"It's a change of direction for me. I'm trying out new things. Variety is the spice of life."

"Obviously. But I mustn't interrupt."

"You can stay and talk while they fix my hair. I have to do the flying at least once more."

"You're so cool about it."

"We've been here all week. They rehearsed me Sunday

night, six times, I think. You feel ridiculous when you get it wrong and start spinning. With all the practice we should be able to get it right each time."

Ingeborg remembered reading about the aerial accidents that once plagued the Broadway production of *Spider-Man*—a thought she would keep to herself.

They'd returned to the start point. A chair was produced for Lee so that the people from make-up and wardrobe could get busy. The director, a tall, bearded man with an air of importance, said, "That was spot on, Lee. We may get away with two more takes to get the extra angles we need." He turned to Ingeborg. "And who are you, if I may ask?"

Lee said, "It's okay, Marcus. I invited her. Ingeborg is doing a photo feature about me for a colour magazine."

"Does she have permission to be on set? If so, I wasn't told," Marcus said.

"She has my permission."

"I don't see any camera."

"With my phone," Ingeborg said, tapping her pocket and wishing she sounded more believable.

Lee came to her aid. "It's the latest thing, a record of a day in my life, meant to look up-close and personal. A picture is worth a thousand words. Isn't that right, Ingeborg?"

"Well, yes. The photography won't be anything special, but it's the look that matters. It's supposed to bring more integrity, like hand-held camerawork."

"Which has been done to death," Marcus said, turning away with a sniff. "Listen to me, people. You may be thinking we have all night, but I felt a spot of rain just now. Can we go again on the hour?"

"Why don't you get some shots with your phone right now?" Lee said to Ingeborg when Marcus was far enough away. "Opportunity seldom knocks twice." Sylvie May had got it right. At some stage in her education, Lee had swallowed the Oxford Dictionary of Proverbs.

"You don't mind?" Ingeborg said. "I was thinking of leaving now we've met. I didn't want to start without your agreement."

"You mean a contract? There's no need for that, is there? I assume it's the usual understanding. I get to see what you plan to publish and right of refusal. My manager would insist on that."

"No problem. Who is your manager?"

"He's also my partner, Nathan Hazael. United we stand, divided we fall. He'll be along shortly. You've got to meet him."

13

"Nathan calls me Lily," Lee told Ingeborg. The conversation was easy with this buoyant young woman. "I don't mind. What's in a name? It was my nickname at school, so I answer to it automatically."

"It's cool."

"Sure, but in the music business I'm Lee Li. It's all about image, isn't it? Where does your name come from?"

"Sweden, but I'm not from there. My parents are English. They picked it out of a book."

"But your hair . . . ?"

". . . is natural, yes. I'm from several generations of blondes. My mother says I have her to thank for that. But my father, who is dark-haired, says it's down to him because the males in the family have a genetic preference for blondes. Somehow I doubt if that's good science." Ingeborg had been explaining all her life that her hair colour was unrelated to her name, so she didn't think of it as giving much away. Every word was being overheard by the team of attendants fussing over Lee's hair, make-up and costume. At least two more takes had been ordered by Marcus. "And from the way you speak, I'm guessing you've spent most of your life here."

"Not all of it," Lee said. "I was born in Taiwan. My parents brought me over. They had an import-export business in London. They're both dead now. I thought you already knew my life story from Sylvie's article. You're doing a picture feature, right?"

"I am, only I like to hear about the lives of the people I

photograph. Have you trained as a dancer? You managed the flying as if you'd been doing it all your life."

Lee twitched her shoulders. "I enjoy anything physical. Athletics, gymnastics, karate."

"I won't pick a fight with you, then," Ingeborg said, actually thinking it would be fun. She was a black belt herself and Lee was a good mover and probably no slouch at karate. It was weird to be more relaxed with this stranger—even with all these people listening—than she had yesterday with Sylvie. Lee was calmer than Sylvie, which was remarkable considering the heart-stopping feat of agility she had just performed, and was due to repeat in a short while. "Will there be more flying in the video?"

"Quite a bit. Most of it's in the can already. What you saw is just one tiny sequence—the last of many. We wrap tonight."

"All of it featuring you?"

"And some genuine seabirds." She smiled. "They're smarter than me. They do theirs in one take. And they refuse to work nights."

"That'll be the seabirds' union," Ingeborg said.

Lee's laughter was a joy to hear, a true expression of delight. "It's such a pity you've come at the end of filming. I don't know what else I can show you about my day that will make a good picture feature for you."

"Not a problem," Ingeborg said. "What my readers really want to see isn't you in performance. Plenty of magazines cover that. This is about the everyday things you take for granted, your mealtimes, hobbies, pets, sports, the house you live in, your bedroom, all that stuff."

A guarded tone entered Lee's voice. "Some of that might not be possible. I'll need to talk to Nathan first. He can be a little touchy about visitors. He's a rather private man."

"But I expect you have parts of the house you can call your own."

"Sure. I have a purpose-built studio to practise my singing and there's a gym that Nathan never uses, so I have that all to myself."

"Would he mind if I took shots of you there?"

She hesitated. "We can ask him. If he isn't happy about it, we'll need to think of somewhere else."

"I really want to photograph you at home," Ingeborg pressed her. "That's the premise for the series and as you're my first interviewee this will set the standard for everything that follows."

"I understand," Lee said with an effort to be helpful. "I'll have to persuade him, won't I? After all, it's not as if he has anything to hide."

Ho-hum was Ingeborg's silent comment on that.

The director called from across the deck, "Two minutes. Let's have you at your mark, Lee, and make it snappy."

"Listen to old bossyboots," Lee said. "You'd think it was World War Three, the way he carries on. Take your time, ladies. Slow but sure wins the race."

"Wouldn't it be easier for you if I'm not around when Nathan gets here?" Ingeborg asked.

"Not at all. I want him to meet you and see what a sweet person you are. He wouldn't say so to me, but he's partial to blondes. I've watched him give them the eye."

Marcus called to her a second time. "For Christ's sake, Lee. Everyone is waiting for you—again."

"How can he be so mean?" Lee said without moving a muscle. "Am I looking good?"

"You're done," said the make-up woman.

The dresser nodded as well.

Lee yawned and stretched. "Help me into that horrible harness, then. The sooner begun, the sooner done."

The two minutes had long gone by when she ambled to her mark.

Nathan's face was well known to Ingeborg from mugshots. He'd been photographed after his arrest by Bristol CID three years ago—the abortive court case that sent a shockwave through every police authority in the country. The look said it all, the gaze of a man in custody who knew he was still streets ahead of his captors. Dark, cavernous, intimidating eyes. A suspect under arrest will often stare back at the camera as an act of defiance. This was something else, total disdain. He knew he would come out the winner.

And now she saw him in real life, standing in the shadow of the ship's funnel watching the third take. His eyes caught the glare of the floodlights and glinted with all the arrogance of the police photos. Nothing was going to faze Nathan Hazael, not the technical wizardry of the production, nor the sight of his protégée being swung upwards by unseen wires. Smart, in a black overcoat with a velvet collar, he kept his arms folded, feet slightly apart. His hair was cropped so close that it was difficult to tell what colour it was.

Behind him waited two large men wearing shades who certainly weren't anything to do with the film unit.

Ingeborg, standing among the make-up team and hoping to appear as if she was one of them, had a momentary loss of nerve. If police officers of far more experience had taken on this ogre and lost, what hope did she have? Then she reminded herself that she wasn't in combat with Nathan. She was after intelligence about the shooting in the auction room and the source of the weapon. Nathan might be an accessory, but someone else would have fired the fatal shot.

Even so, it had become obvious already that she'd need to deal with him in person. Any hope that Lee Li knew about the supply of the murder weapon had vanished with that last remark: *it's not as if he has anything to hide.* The singer was so absorbed with her own career that she hadn't worked out—or wasn't willing to admit to herself or anyone else—that she was living with a crime baron.

For tonight, at least, Ingeborg would keep her distance from Nathan. She'd settle for the introduction she'd been talked into and keep it as brief as possible. She would rely on Lee Li to get her inside the house in the next day or so. The rising star's eagerness for publicity would play to her advantage.

Applause broke out for the third successful take.

Marcus announced, "All right, boys and girls, we'll wrap on that. Thanks for being so patient and professional." Which sounded like a strong dig at Lee Li.

All the lights came on and the clear-up started. The make-up team were the first to return below deck, leaving Ingeborg isolated if she remained where she was. She stepped out of Nathan's field of view behind the nearest mast.

From above, Lee was lowered slowly to the deck. Two of the wardrobe people stepped forward and released her from the muslin drapes. Unhitched from the wire, she ran across to Nathan. Ingeborg couldn't resist peering around the mast to see the embrace. It didn't happen. Nathan kept his arms folded.

"How was I tonight, then?" Lee said, eyes shining.

"You finished?" he asked, ignoring the invitation to compliment her. "It's late."

"I know. Before we go, I want you to meet Ingeborg. She's still here—or she was a moment ago."

This couldn't be ducked. Ingeborg broke cover and crossed the deck. Considering that Nathan was supposed to be partial to blondes, the introduction was a letdown. They didn't shake hands. He condescended to give her a nod and a glance with the nail heads that were his eyes.

Chilling.

Ingeborg settled for, "Hi."

Lee said, "She's a journalist doing a piece about me."

Nathan behaved as if he hadn't heard.

"Covering a typical day in my life," Lee went on as if unaware how offensive the man was being. "It means taking lots of pictures. Ingeborg was recommended to me by that nice woman who wrote the beautiful piece in *South West* magazine. You won't object if she comes to the house tomorrow and shadows me? You and I might think my day is boring, but I've just been told the ordinary stuff is what the magazine readers want to see. East, west, home's best."

Nathan spoke again. "She's not coming to the house."

"Late in the day," Lee said, continuing to pour out words.

"It had better not be before noon. We always sleep in after a night shoot, don't we, my love?"

"I don't have press in my house," Nathan said. "Tell her to piss off."

"She's not from a newspaper. She's a freelance showbiz writer."

"You heard me."

There was a pause of several uncomfortable seconds. "But I need the publicity," Lee said. "It's essential in my work. My fans want to read about me or they won't buy my music. Why do you think I've been busting my ass every night this week? Give me a break, Nathan."

"Are you going to change out of those stupid clothes, or what?" Nathan plainly wasn't impressed by his lover's moving appeal.

"You're my manager," Lee tried to remind him. "You should be celebrating when I get the chance of a photo feature. Listen, my love, why don't we talk about this in the morning?"

"You know where the car is." Nathan turned his wrist and checked the shiny chunk of metal attached to it, a thing more like a weapon than a timepiece. "You got five minutes. If not, find your own fucking transport."

His eyes hadn't returned to Ingeborg in the whole of the exchange. He'd dismissed her.

This couldn't have got off to a worse start. Trying to contain her anger, she said to Lee, "We'll work something out. I've got your number. I'll call you."

She expected Lee to be close to tears. Strangely, she wasn't. If anything, her eyes had a faint gleam of triumph. Extraordinary, Ingeborg thought. Maybe she got off on treatment like this. Was she one of those women who was switched on by bullying? A willing victim? It might explain why she'd been drawn to such a scumbag in the first place.

"No problem," the singer said with a smile, and ran down the steps to the saloon where she'd left her clothes.

Nathan turned in the direction of the gangway, closely followed by his two heavies.

Ingeborg wasn't troubled by being treated as if she didn't

exist. She knew the criminal class don't like journalists. If the evening had panned out the way she intended she wouldn't have met Nathan at all. She'd have gained entrance to his house before he was aware who she was and why she was there.

She had the chance to leave now, but she didn't. She was interested to see whether Lee would throw on her clothes and dash upstairs in obedience to her less than charming lover, or whether she'd play the pop star again and keep him waiting. If she chose to defy him, would he be true to his word and leave without her? Or was he a softie when it came to the crunch?

Here was an opportunity to get a sense of the real relationship between these two. For her own safety, Ingeborg needed to know she could rely on Lee. That look in the young woman's eyes after Nathan had played the heavy was deeply unsettling.

She decided to go below and check the First Class Ladies Saloon for herself and presently found herself in a lavishly reconstructed, well-lit and carpeted corridor, with passenger berths at either side. Victorian grandeur was everywhere around her. She could hear voices from the end where the saloon evidently was. She entered the saloon through a gilded arch and took in more luxuriance, the white and gold columns, the arabesque pilasters, the ornate mirrors and the tiered sofas. But she couldn't see Lee Li. One of the women she'd met on the promenade deck was packing make-up jars and brushes into a case.

Ingeborg asked where Lee was.

"She's come and gone."

"I don't think so. I was on deck a moment ago and she didn't pass me on the stairs."

"She left two or three minutes ago—definitely. She was in a hurry."

"But I would have seen her."

"That isn't the only way to the top deck. She could easily have used one of the others."

"Why would she do that?"

"Don't ask me, love. She's in a world of her own. I expect it's the blood rushing to her head when she's up there on the wire."

Ingeborg turned and ran out of the saloon and along the corridor until she found another companionway. At the top of the stairs she found she was on the other side of the funnel on a deserted stretch of the deck. She went to the rail and looked over. Nathan's two bodyguards were standing beside an expensive-looking black limousine a little apart from the vans that had brought the heavy equipment. Presumably their boss was inside, waiting.

In that case Lee hadn't been hurrying to order. She was still somewhere aboard the *Great Britain.*

The sensible option was to remain above deck and keep watching the gangway—the only way off the ship. Ingeborg started in that direction and found a few of the TV crew packing up equipment in near darkness. The floodlights had all been turned off and were cooling and the cables were being reeled in. She asked if anyone had seen Lee. They shook their heads. None of them showed any concern. The unpunctual singer wasn't anybody's favourite.

Her own first impression of Lee had been positive, probably because she hadn't had to put up with several days of lateness. She'd thought her charming and easy to get along with, but she couldn't understand her present behaviour. Baiting her dangerous lover to this extent was asking for trouble.

The car still parked on the dockside told its own slightly different story. Lee appeared to have succeeded in calling Nathan's bluff.

Ingeborg looked over the rail again and checked that they were still down there fully fifteen minutes after Nathan had threatened to leave without her. One of the minders was rubbing his hands to keep warm.

Her own little Ford Ka was parked at the other end. The sight of it was tempting. She could be home and in bed in under the hour. This had been a long stretch without sleep. But her curiosity wouldn't allow her to leave.

More lights and cables were humped across the gangway and down to the vans. The dolly track had been lifted and stacked away and so had the cameras. The crew had been swift to dismantle everything. The lateness of the hour made for a slick operation.

A woman's voice carried to her and for a second she thought the wait was over. Then the last of the make-up and wardrobe people came by. The woman Ingeborg had spoken to in the saloon said, "Are you still waiting for Lee?"

"She doesn't seem to have left the ship yet."

"Playing games with her boyfriend, I wouldn't wonder. Rather her than me. He's a nasty piece of work, but she has him on a string."

"I wouldn't know about that."

"We all think so, anyway. Goodnight, love."

Presumably someone would be along soon to close the gangway and secure the ship. Ingeborg was in a dilemma now. Almost everyone had gone ashore—except for Lee. Without the TV lighting, the deck had become a stark, eerie place. Streaks of moonlight were the only illumina-tion. She was tempted to leave, yet strongly suspected one more dramatic scene would be played here, and she would be a fool to miss it.

The sound of an engine being started prompted her to look down at the dockside again. The last of the TV vans was moving off. She watched it head for the gate at the end and disappear from view.

Now only two vehicles remained: her own at the far end and Nathan's, much closer. She faced a practical difficulty she hadn't foreseen. When she came off the ship she'd have to pass the black limousine to reach her Ka. But the longer she stayed here, the more suspicious her behaviour was going to appear—as if she was implicated in Lee's non-appearance.

A car door slammed.

Then someone from down there shone a flashlight beam straight at her. She backed away from the rail.

"She's up there," a man's voice said.

This was getting worse by the minute. They'd mistaken her for Lee.

"Don't fucking stand there, then, you moron," she heard Nathan say. "Get after her."

She didn't fancy waiting where she was to explain the confusion. The top deck offered nowhere to hide except behind the funnel and the masts, so she made for the nearest companionway and down the stairs and then down another flight to the deck below. It was in darkness.

This would be where the steerage passengers had once been housed. She pressed her hands to the wall and edged sideways until she felt a door handle. One of the cabins? She would never know because it was locked.

Heart pounding, mouth dry, she groped her way further from the stairs, furious with herself for getting into this situation. Here she was, acting the fugitive, trapped in a dark corridor in the bowels of the ship. Stupid and demeaning. She should have stuck to her original plan and left immediately after meeting Nathan.

She still couldn't decide what the real agenda was. There was clearly more to the relationship between this oddly matched couple than she had been led to believe. What was Lee's game—to be discovered cowering somewhere and then dragged off the ship and bundled into the car, driven home and punished? Was she sexually aroused by Nathan's anger? That strange gratified look when he'd blown his top and threatened to leave had had more than a hint of masochism about it. Or was she more assertive than she appeared and deliberately defying him?

A long interval passed and Ingeborg heard nothing. Looking at the situation coolly and sensibly, it's unlikely they'll come down here, she told herself. The vast ship was more than three men could search. They would be bound to give up before long. They might even have left already.

She allowed more minutes to go by. Then she retraced her way to the stairs and crept up them, alert at each step for the sound of anyone nearby.

It remained quiet.

At the top of the second flight she paused. Out on deck she would be conspicuous. There wasn't much light, but the moon's silver glow would make any movement obvious. If Nathan and his heavies were still about they'd surely expect her to head for the gangway. They could be waiting some-where near. The smart way to avoid them was surely to come out on the starboard side. She might then outflank them, move a safe distance away and cross to the port side and discover if the car was still down there.

She held her breath and took the first heart-stopping steps out onto the stretch of deck where the filming had taken place. So far, so good. For a short distance she would have the great black funnel between herself and the gangway. After that only a series of skylights projected above deck level. Her movement was more like gliding than striding, a steady progress towards the aft end of the ship. Good thing she wasn't wearing heels. The smallest sound would have been like drumming on the deck. She was prepared any second to be caught by the flashlight beam. You can't escape the speed of light.

But her eyes were getting used to the conditions and her confidence was growing with each step. She kept as close as possible to the side at this stage and must have gone thirty yards when she spotted something lashed to one of the posts supporting the rail.

A rope ladder hanging over the side of the ship.

She leaned over the rail, but it was impossible to see how far down the ladder went.

Now she could make an informed guess as to what Lee Li had done. She'd made an escape bid. She wasn't staying to face Nathan's wrath. The stupid thug had been lulled into thinking the gangway was the only possible means of quitting the ship. Stupid—or merely guilty of failing to think outside the box? Ingeborg herself had fallen for it.

Maybe, after all, it was understandable.

She peered over the side again. The sturdy ladder of thick,

coarse rope with wooden rungs looked reasonably new. Even so, using it for a descent must have called for strong nerve and agility. The curve of the enormous iron hull meant that she would have been dangling free of the side, further away with each step down. And she couldn't possibly have seen what was below.

From the other end, near the gangway, came voices. Ingeborg froze. Then, as her heart beat faster, she felt a rush of blood from her head to the pit of her belly. Turning, she saw the flashlight beam being played over the funnel. Nathan and his heavies hadn't given up. Worse, they were coming in her direction. It only needed a speculative sweep of the flashlight and she'd be caught in its glare.

If she wanted to avoid being caught, she had no option.

She grasped the rail, got her legs over and her feet on a rung of the rope ladder and started descending. Briefly she toyed with the idea of clinging on shortly below the rail where she would be screened from the light. But she guessed they'd soon spot the ladder and point the beam over the side. The only practical option was to keep going, rung by rung, right down.

It wasn't easy. The ladder was swaying dangerously, and the movement increased the further she went. She didn't know what she was lowering herself into. They called this a dry dock, so presumably she'd be going right down to where the hull was stabilised in a system of buttressing.

But then she glanced down and saw to her horror that there was water below her. It couldn't be. She stopped, clung on and looked again in case she was hallucinating.

No. Against all reason she was swaying over a sheet of water. She could see the ripples. The hull's black immensity was darkly reflected in the moonlight.

This was crazy. The *Great Britain* was in dry dock, laid up for over forty years. The ship hadn't moved and the sea hadn't flooded the dock.

She moved down a few more rungs and looked again. She was about six feet from getting her feet wet. Then she realised that the surface had a strange stillness. The ripples were an effect of the moonlight filtered by clouds.

"Bloody idiot," she said aloud.

A memory had stirred in her brain of a news report about the ship. A survey in the late 1990s had revealed that the hull was corroding badly in the humid atmosphere of the dock. The owners had come up with a remedy. At the original waterline, sheets of toughened glass were fitted, allowing dehumidifiers to keep the space below at a steady and safe level. The glass was shaped and coloured to look like sea water.

Deeply relieved, she let herself down the remaining rungs and felt her feet come in contact with the firm glass. But it was like stepping on ice. She had some difficulty getting a footing before she allowed her smarting hands to let go of the sides.

She looked up to where she had come from. Nobody was there yet. She was well placed to climb out of the dry dock and make a dash for her car.

Which was when she experienced a sensation of warmth on the back of her neck. She turned to look and felt hot breath on her cheek. Nathan Hazael had been standing right behind her. He must have been waiting there, watching her climb down. He grabbed her right wrist and twisted her arm violently up her back.

14

On the rear seat of Nathan's limo, wedged between the crime baron and one of his bodyguards, her wrists tied behind her back, Ingeborg cursed herself for making such a disastrous start to her so-called undercover assignment. If Diamond or any of the others in CID could see her now she'd be mortified. She'd made the wrong call over and over. Her cover story of the photo-journalism was looking like a non-starter. Lee Li clearly wasn't the single-minded wannabe she'd taken her for. There was a strong possibility she had been using Ingeborg as a distraction device rather than the other way round. Lee's getaway down the rope ladder had fooled everyone. Yet it was Nathan who had been quickest to work out what was happening and ambush Ingeborg when she'd wrongly supposed he was still aboard ship with his two henchmen.

Humiliating.

However . . .

There was one thing on the plus side, even though she couldn't take much credit for it: her objective had been to gain entry to Nathan's house and it looked likely to happen. They were definitely driving in the direction of Leigh Woods. They had crossed the Avon on Brunel Way and looped northwards on the west side of the gorge, cruising at speed along deserted roads into millionaire country.

"Technically, this is abduction," she said in as calm a voice as she could raise.

The minder on her right said, "Shut it."

Nathan told her without a glance in her direction, "You don't seriously expect to throw shit at me and walk away?"

"I've done nothing. I only met you an hour ago."

"Don't give me that. You and Lily pulled this off together."

"If you're talking about Lee Li, I only met *her* for the first time tonight."

Nathan didn't answer. But the reason Ingeborg was his prisoner was made clear. He now believed she and Lee had conspired against him. Lee had chosen this night to cut loose and because Ingeborg had used the same escape route, it was taken to be a joint arrangement.

She, too, lapsed into silence.

The hanging woods towering over the river on the Somerset side of the gorge rank high among the glories of the British landscape, making even Brunel's suspension bridge look a modest structure. By night the blue-grey gap between plunging masses of black is decorated by the necklace-like lights of the bridge. From Rownham Hill the glow of the city on the opposite side confirmed to Ingeborg that she had correctly predicted the route. She was urging herself to be positive. Her earlier mistakes shouldn't matter now she was being driven in style to Nathan's mansion—even though her wrists were bound.

Near the top they took a right. The road map in her brain told her they were now heading towards North Road, a haven of affluence in an area known as Nightingale Valley, where many of the major properties were sited.

Sure enough, they reached a T-junction, turned left and travelled a short distance before braking in front of a substantial entrance between high stone walls. The driver pressed a remote. In silence the steel gate rolled aside.

A dog was barking nearby. Escaping from here wouldn't be a breeze, Ingeborg noted as they started up a long drive. It wasn't surprising Lee had chosen to decamp from the ship, rather than this penned-up place. Exactly what had prompted the escape bid was less certain. Things must have gone badly wrong for her to cut loose at this point. Nathan's support of her career in pop had seemed to underwrite the relationship.

Well, he wasn't Prince Charming, for sure.

Security lights blazed as they approached a tall, coal-black building with gothic features any director of horror movies would have sold his birthright to acquire.

Someone was awake at this hour of the morning and stepped forward to open the car door. He looked a clone for the other bodyguards.

Nathan stepped out without a word and made a gesture for Ingeborg to follow. She felt a cautionary hand on her shoulder from the heavy who had shared the back seat.

They passed through an arched doorway into a tiled entrance hall the size of a barn, with suits of armour displayed on the walls, along with shields, swords and lances. What message was that supposed to give out? An owner with delusions of grandeur? An interest in medieval history? Or a need to divert suspicion?

The collection of modern weapons would be stored somewhere less obvious, Ingeborg decided.

The doorman helped Nathan out of his coat. The pinstripe three-piece underneath definitely hadn't been bought off the peg.

"Will the lady be in the guest room, sir?" the doorman enquired. Perhaps, on consideration, he was a butler.

"The tower room," Nathan said.

"I need a bathroom first," Ingeborg said.

"It's en suite, madame," Nathan said with mock servility. "Tonight you're my guest."

"Your prisoner, you mean."

"Have it your way." He turned to the bodyguard. "Search her. She's got a phone in her pocket. I need that."

It wasn't pleasant being frisked, but the handling was workmanlike. The man didn't make it an excuse for a grope.

Nathan was handed her iPhone. He pocketed it. "I'm going to get some sleep. We'll talk later. You will, anyway."

The hand on her shoulder tightened. She was steered across the hall and through a door. A stone staircase spiralled upwards. They were in the tower already.

"Move it," the minder said.

"It would be easier if you untied my hands. I'm not going to take you on."

The suggestion was ignored. She climbed two floors and waited while a door was unlocked and a dim light switched on.

"The penthouse suite?" she said, stepping inside. Her wit was lost on the bodyguard.

In this house they must have been used to unwelcome guests. The light was mounted on the wall in thick glass behind a steel grille. The furniture consisted of a wooden camp bed that looked a relic from the 1950s, with two thin brown blankets lying across the canvas slats. The en suite was a bucket with a lid and no other comforts. A cat might have squeezed through the narrow lancet windows, but no human would.

"Now do I get my hands untied?"

This small mercy was conceded without comment. The door slammed behind her and she heard it locked. At four thirty in the morning you don't spend long fretting over accommodation, especially when there's nobody to listen. In under ten minutes Ingeborg was out to the world.

When she woke, she didn't need long to recall where she was. Judging the time of day was more difficult. Although it still seemed early she looked out of one of those niggardly windows and saw that the sun was high. It could have been noon already. Lack of illumination was why she was disorientated.

The camp bed had not been comfortable, but she'd had enough sleep to get her thoughts straight and ponder what might happen next. Nathan had said they would talk later, as if he expected to find out things. She hoped his questioning would be confined to Lee's disappearance. She could handle a grilling about that. The danger was that he might suspect she wasn't after all a journalist. From there it was a short step to discovering she was more interested in him than in Lee—in which case she would be exposed as either from the police or a rival gang.

The next hours would be a minefield.

She heard steps on the stairs not long after, and the door was unlocked and opened inch by inch. Greatly to Ingeborg's surprise, a woman was standing there in a pink sweater and jeans. She looked about fifty, short and a bit overweight. She said in the Bristol accent, "I'm not alone, so please do exactly as I say. My name is Stella and I'm Mr. Hazael's housekeeper. Follow me and you'll get a chance to shower and freshen up. Then you'll get coffee and whatever you want for lunch."

Good call. Things could only get better now.

The same bodyguard from last night was standing to the right of the door, looking as meek as a muscleman can. Starting a fight didn't feature at all in Ingeborg's thoughts. A shower would be bliss.

At the bottom of the stairs they emerged from the tower, crossed the hall and entered a more furnished section of the house, a corridor carpeted in red, with wood panelling hung with ancient jousting shields. Nathan clearly had pretensions of grandeur, with his interest in weaponry extended to this archaic décor.

The bodyguard remained in tow as Stella the housekeeper led them into a lift at the end.

The doors parted a level higher in what was clearly a woman's dressing room, with a wardrobe, dressing table and shower cabinet. A disquieting probability was put to rest when Stella instructed the bodyguard to go through to the bedroom and wait behind a screen. "I'll tell you when to come out."

To Ingeborg, she said, "Take your time. He'll behave himself. You can wash your hair if you want. Everything you need is in there."

The glass sides of the shower were part-frosted, but Ingeborg had no inhibitions about stripping. She was confident from Stella's superior manner that she outranked the bodyguard in this household and God help him if he stepped out of line.

After such a wretched night, the soft spray on her skin couldn't be bettered as a restorative. Expensive gels and hair treatments were ranged along a glass shelf. She showered and shampooed and used the thick white towels from the heated rail outside.

"Help yourself to a change of underwear," Stella told her. "It's brand-new and top quality. I know, because I do the shopping for him. There's a range of casual clothes in the wardrobe if you want. He likes his lady guests to feel pampered."

Pampered? It was tempting to comment that a night in the tower room wasn't pampering, but why complain to Stella, who was being helpful? White jeans and a black cashmere sweater were a comfortable fit. Feeling infinitely better outside and in, Ingeborg used the range of make-up at the dressing table and then declared herself ready to eat.

"Good. We'll go down to the dining room." Stella put her head round the door and told the henchman they were ready. He followed them tamely to the lift.

The dining room had a panoramic view across sunlit lawns to Leigh Valley woods. "Take a seat and don't hesitate to tell them what you want and how it should be cooked," Stella told her. "I must get to my other duties now. Enjoy your meal. If you want a tip from me, the savoury crêpes are to die for."

"You've been kind."

"It's my job. I expect he'll join you shortly." The first unwelcome thing she'd heard this morning.

Places for two had been set at one end of a long polished wood table, so she did as she was asked and a waitress arrived at once to take her order. Nathan might be a barbarian, but he knew how to live.

Coffee and freshly made crêpes were served. A variety of fillings made the meal a delicious guessing game. She recognised spinach and ricotta and red pepper and tomato, and there were other combinations with shrimps and mushrooms that were harder to identify.

Then a less welcome side-dish appeared. "Are they looking after you?" Nathan's voice came from somewhere behind her. A whiff of aftershave had crept in with him.

"I can't fault the cooking," she said evenly as he took the seat opposite. He was in a black silk robe decorated with dragons.

This guy didn't underrate himself. "Is this the softening up process after the tower room treatment?"

"That was a security measure," he said, eyeing her with that penetrating stare that recalled the mugshot. "The alternative was to put you in a guest room with a minder for company and you might not have appreciated that."

"I don't know why you want to put a guard on me. I'm not likely to run away."

"Lily did, so why not you?" He raised a hand to stop her from answering. The waitress had appeared from the kitchen. "My usual," he told her without making eye contact, "with a slice of liver."

When they were alone again, he made a performance of offering Ingeborg more coffee. "So what do you think of my house?"

"I haven't seen much of it," she said.

"I'll show you some more soon. I think you'll be impressed. I've made a lot of changes since I bought the place. I'm modernising."

"The bits I've seen don't look modern."

"It was owned by a baronet. Been in his family for centuries. He was the last of the line, saw out his days here and died a few weeks before his hundredth birthday. They put it up for sale full of all the crap he'd collected. It's a good location and there's plenty of ground with it, so I made an offer and bought it, house and effects. This was three years back. We had a massive auction on the lawn outside to get shot of the bloody effects. Two days it took. Marquee, dealers from all over. A lot of the stuff was antique and I came out of it pretty well."

"Who did you use as auctioneers?"

"I don't know. A Bristol firm, out of the yellow pages. Why do you ask?"

"I met an auctioneer recently called Doggart, but he was doing his stuff in Bath. They get about, don't they?"

"I wouldn't know about that. Anyway, I decided to hold on to the armour on the walls until I redecorated, so that didn't go into the sale. You know how it is. You plan to make changes and the years go by and you don't. I'm getting round to it now, having it valued, and it turns out that some of the armour is very old. The trouble is, who wants to buy bloody suits of armour these days?"

"Can't help you there," Ingeborg said.

"The buyers take some finding, I can tell you, and it's slow progress. I want a fair price. I'm not giving the stuff away. So that's why the place hasn't been given a makeover."

Nathan's eyes slid to the right, waiting for the waitress to leave the room. Then he stopped talking like a TV presenter on one of those house transformation shows and got round to more personal matters. "We can sort this out in a civilised way. I won't deny Lily and I have the occasional spat, but I've never roughed her up. We always kiss and make up. Always. That's what couples do, isn't it?"

Unsure how to deal with this soul-baring, she watched him top up his cup. An insight into Nathan's private life might be of use, but it wouldn't be smart to put herself into a position where he felt he'd said too much and was getting nothing in return. She said, "I haven't the faintest idea what's on Lee's mind."

"Don't give me that crap," he said, dropping the civility straight away. "You're close, you two. You must be."

"I only met her yesterday."

He brushed that aside. "Who supplied the rope ladder?"

"I've no idea."

"She didn't bring it with her. I drove her to the ship for the shoot. I know a woman can stuff a lot in her bag, but I'm bloody sure there wasn't a ladder in there."

"I can't help you with this," Ingeborg said, doing her best to sound cool.

"What's your name?"

"Ingeborg Smith."

His lip curled.

She had a response she'd used a hundred times before. "I can't help being called Smith, if that's what bothers you.

There are seven hundred thousand Smiths in Britain and I happen to be one of them."

"You're a writer. Get a pen-name."

She took this as humour and smiled. "It's what I'm known as. Why change it now?" On an inspiration, she added, "Wilbur Smith is one of the most famous writers in the world and he doesn't find it a handicap."

Nathan was unimpressed. He didn't look like a book-lover. "If you didn't know about the rope-ladder," he doggedly returned to his main line of enquiry, "how come you used it to get off the ship?"

"It was hanging over the side when I ran along the deck. I was being chased. Your men were shining flashlights at me. What would you have done?"

Nathan wasn't interested in replying.

"They could have been armed," she added, becoming more confident. "Someone comes after me in the dark, I don't hang about."

Another temporary halt was called for the arrival of Nathan's lunch, a plate piled high that made her think fleetingly of Peter Diamond. In this situation Diamond, like Nathan, wouldn't have ordered the crêpes. But he might have approved of the way she was coping with the interrogation.

"What was that about my men being armed?" Nathan asked when the waitress was gone.

"You're a major player," she said. "I expect you need to defend yourself."

He didn't deny it. "Tell me what you know. Is Lily playing silly games or has she really jumped ship?"

"I can't answer that. I keep telling you we aren't friends. My dealings with her are professional. She's someone I arranged to interview, that's all."

He used his knife on the fried liver, served so rare that blood oozed from it. "I don't like being pissed about. I invested a fortune in that girl. I treated her well." He looked up from his plate. "Did she say something was bugging her?"

"Not to me. We hardly talked at all."

"After the shoot finished, did you speak?"

Ingeborg shook her head. "I went to the dressing room and they told me she'd already left."

"How soon was that?"

"Not long after the wrap."

"Was she with anyone?"

"They didn't say so."

Nathan used his blood-stained knife to stress what he said next. "She wasn't acting alone. Some toe-rag supplied the ladder and fixed it to the side of the ship. She knew where to go, and she had wheels to get away. It was all arranged."

Ingeborg had worked this out for herself. It didn't require great deductive powers. She sipped her coffee and said nothing.

"Am I reading it right?" Nathan asked.

Difficult. Neutrality was her preferred stance. "I'm not in a position to say."

"Come on, I've checked your phone. You took pictures of her. You were with her."

"On and off."

"Was she nervous? Excitable? Angry?"

"How would I know? We'd only just met."

He pointed the knife at her. "You're not helping."

"I'm being honest." And she added something which was not honest at all. "If you want to know who's angry, I am. I'm angry with Lee. She played me for a sucker, letting me think I could get a magazine piece out of this."

The mean eyes widened a fraction. Maybe she'd made a telling point. "Where was this going to appear?"

"In one of the Sundays, probably."

"A national?"

She nodded.

Nathan was clearly interested. He pressed his fingers to his lips and tapped them thoughtfully. "It's not like Lily to turn down the chance of publicity."

She was content to let him think the matter through in his own time. If he came to the right conclusion this could be helpful.

"The silly little bitch is bound to come to her senses soon," Nathan spoke his thoughts aloud. "She'll find she can't hack it as a pop star without me backing her every inch of the way. She'd never have got this far without me. She's not answering my calls. All I get is some recorded message." He put down the knife and fork and leaned back in the chair. "But I know what to do."

Ingeborg waited.

"You can talk some sense into her."

She shook her head, acting dim. "I don't know how."

"Like I just said, she needs to be in the papers all the time, or she'll find herself at the bottom of the heap. Tell her you still want to write about her, even though she let you down."

"But we don't know where she is."

"She'll have her phone with her. Call her on your mobile."

"You took it off me."

"Play along and you can have it back. I don't know why you're bothered about the phone. There's fuck all on it."

"It's brand new," she said, which was true. "I got it especially for this project. It's supposed to take better pictures than my old one." In reality she would have been idiotic to have brought her own phone with all its data. "Can I have it back now?"

"All in good time. You and I are going to strike a deal. She's not answering my calls, but you can bet your little cotton socks she'll talk to you. What did Mrs. Thatcher call it? The oxygen of publicity?"

"Something like that." In her wildest dreams she hadn't expected to hear Margaret Thatcher being quoted by Nathan Hazael.

"It's neat," he said, leaning back and rubbing his hands. "I'll tell you what to say. We'll soon find out who she's shacking up with."

"And what do I get out of the deal?"

"Your ticket of leave. You'll be free to go after I get her back."

"I can't guarantee she'll come back."

"Don't you worry about that," Nathan said. "When I know where she is, I'll fetch her." A simple statement of intent with a grim subtext. He dipped his hand into a pocket of the robe and produced Ingeborg's phone and held it out. "Call her now."

She took the phone and let it rest in her palm as if she'd never seen it before.

Put on the spot like this, she felt her veins ice up. She hated the idea that Lee would be tricked into revealing where she was and brought back by force. But if Nathan didn't get his way, the ferocity would swing in another direction. He was in charge here.

Crunch time.

The bigger picture was that she couldn't allow herself to fall out with Nathan. Her reason for being here was to get the truth about the hold-up at the auction and the fatal shooting. She needed to stay on speaking terms with the man. She felt a strong empathy with Lee, but it wasn't a case of Lee being totally ignorant about Nathan's intentions. The singer would be expecting him to come after her. She'd lived with him and she knew he wouldn't be dumped without a fight.

Lee had the intelligence to work out what was going on.

The bigger picture had to win.

"If I get through, do you want to speak to her?"

He shook his head. "She'd cut me off. Besides, we don't want her knowing you're with me. You're calling for yourself, got it?"

Lee's number was one of the few she had stored. She called it.

There was still a chance of getting a recorded message.

But Lee's voice came through. "Hi. Is this Ingeborg?" As chipper and friendly as if nothing had gone wrong.

"How are you? We seem to have lost contact."

Across the table, Nathan made a fist and held it up in triumph.

Into the minefield.

"I'm good," Lee said. "Hey, I don't know what to say about last night, leaving so suddenly. But at least we met."

"Where are you?" Ingeborg asked, and saw Nathan's nod of satisfaction at the question.

"Right now? With a friend."

"In Bristol?"

"I'd rather not say, if you don't mind. Change in my personal arrangements. I'm not at Nathan's place any more."

"The thing is . . . are you still up for the photo shoot?"

After a pause, Lee said, "Sure. We can do it, only it won't be exactly as we planned, and we may have to wait a few days."

"Sorry, but I can't wait that long," Ingeborg said and improvised: "I pitched the idea to the *Sunday Times* and the magazine editor is keen to use it. I promised to deliver by the end of the week."

"The *Sunday Times*? Diggety dog, that's cool." The excitement was so clear in Lee's voice that Ingeborg felt a stab of conscience. It was one thing telling lies to Nathan, but this young woman wasn't remotely evil.

"I can't mess them about," Ingeborg felt compelled to say. "I was counting on doing most of it today."

"Aw, shoot. That's so difficult. I can't tell anyone where I am, not even you. Ask no questions and hear no lies. Well, I'd better say this much: I've split with Nathan. My life was getting impossible for all sorts of reasons I won't go into. So, you see, we can't do the photo shoot at his house like we said we would."

"That *is* a problem," Ingeborg said, her brain in overdrive, conscious that Nathan was hanging on every word she spoke. "It's supposed to be a typical day in your life."

"Can't you change the format?"

"Not at this late stage. Really it doesn't matter where we do it, as long as it's about you from morning till night. I took those shots on the ship last night. They'll go in nicely and show you at work. Great publicity for the video, too."

"You're right. Oh, God, this is difficult. I'm really up for it, only I don't see how it's possible."

The conflict in Lee's voice was painful to hear and Inge-borg felt desperately mean, but she couldn't allow this call to end yet. "There must be a way round this. Can we meet somewhere and talk it through?"

Nathan raised both thumbs.

The pull of publicity was too much for Lee to resist. "Righty. I'll meet you. Only it has to be somewhere I can feel safe. What the eye doesn't see, the heart doesn't grieve. Let me think."

Ingeborg was tempted to tell her she'd think better if she stopped trotting out these stupid proverbs.

"Do you know Queen Square?" Lee asked.

"I do, but where in Queen Square? It's huge."

"The middle, where I can see in every direction."

"Where the statue is? Okay, what time?"

"What is it now? Half-twelve? I can be there by two, just to meet, right, and work out what we do?"

"Two it is."

Nathan had a smile like sunrise over the Bristol Channel when the call ended. He didn't ask for the phone back. "I heard your side of it. Queen Square. Did she say where she is now?"

"No. She was being careful."

"She can't be far off if she's meeting you at two."

"True."

"Not long until I get her back."

"That isn't what she's expecting."

He chuckled. "Women like surprises."

"Do you need me there, or can I go now?" Ingeborg asked, already guessing what he would say.

"You've got to be there."

"I feel like Judas."

"Relax. She'll come to her senses when she knows how much I care about her." And his eager voice suggested he really did care. "Have you seen the sound studio I built for her? Come on, I'll show you."

Recording studios held no particular interest for Ingeborg, but the chance to see more of the house was unmissable. She followed Nathan from the room and through a spacious sitting room equipped with a plasma TV, on the lookout all the time for anything resembling an armoury. But this was a place to relax, more modern in style than the other living rooms she'd seen, with deep armchairs, sofas and subdued lighting.

"We're entering her private quarters now," Nathan said, pushing open another door. "I don't often come in here. Had it built for her only three months ago. You can still smell the paint. There's also a small gym. She's quite an athlete, as you saw on the ship."

"Do you have your own gym?" Ingeborg asked.

He laughed. "Christ, no. What do you think I am?"

"What's in your section, then—a cocktail bar?"

"You don't want to know what I get up to."

"But I do. Let me try. Men's stuff. Snooker and darts?"

"I'll own up to that." He was leading her along a white-walled corridor into the extension.

"A gun-room?"

He turned to stare at her. "What makes you say that?"

"You're a powerful guy," she answered as smoothly as she could. "I can see you target shooting and hitting the bull, no problem. Wouldn't surprise me if you have some kind of shooting gallery as well."

"You'd be wrong," Nathan said.

"About the gallery? Then I reckon you have a range somewhere outside. Or do you just shoot squirrels and pigeons?" She was pressing him harder than she intended because she could see he was practically purring over the macho image she was suggesting for him. "As for foxes, I bet they know better than to come visiting your estate."

"Did Lily speak to you about me and guns?" he asked after an uncomfortable pause.

"No."

"What put this in your head, then?"

Stay cool, she thought. He's not suspicious. He's trying to be friendly, making conversation.

"If you remember, I was squeezed between you and one of

your employees in the car last night—close enough to feel what was clipped to his belt. And if your men are armed, I'd expect you to know how to handle a weapon."

Satisfied, apparently, he gave a shrug and moved on. He hadn't denied a strong connection with guns. He hadn't denied anything except owning a shooting gallery.

They reached the door at the end of the corridor. "The studio."

She entered a large oval room with chairs and cushions behind a semi-circular console and plenty of light from high windows. "You expected it to look like a bunker?" Nathan said. "So did I before we designed this. It's a myth that a studio has to be totally enclosed. Your musician needs to feel relaxed. Look around you. Everything she needs. She's had a band in here and made recordings. I don't clip her wings, whatever she may have said to you."

"It's got a nice feel to it. I would have been happier here last night than in that tower room."

"Not so secure," he said with a smirk. He stepped behind the console and pressed a couple of switches and a track from *Cherry Blossoms* came through the speakers, surrounding them.

"What do you think?" Nathan shouted, to be heard.

"Great. I bought the album myself."

"The studio acoustics."

"Ah—outstanding." But the purity of Lee's voice surrounding them was disturbingly at odds with the duplicity to come.

"Want to see the gym?" Leaving the track still playing, Nathan strode towards a door at the end and led her into another well-lit space furnished with enough state-of-the-art exercise machines to train an Olympic team. "If she gets stressed in the studio she can step in here and work out any time she wants. Would you walk away from all this?"

"Not for long. But I'm not a singer or a sports girl. All I need is my laptop and I can work anywhere."

"You would have been a cheaper deal."

She smiled. "Is that a compliment?"

"No offence," he said. "You can't budget for love is what I'm saying. You just have to go with it."

It was bizarre to hear this kind of talk from a hard-nosed criminal. Nathan had convinced himself he was in love with his pop singer and he was starting to convince Ingeborg, too.

"Seen enough?" he said. "I'm taking you back to the TV room now and one of my staff will sit with you until we leave. I have arrangements to make."

"This is all very neat for you," she said, "but I can't see my story getting filed. She won't trust me any more."

"You're wrong," he said. "Lily will play along, whatever she thinks of you. When it comes to PR, she doesn't miss a trick."

"But you heard what I said on the phone. I have to meet a deadline."

"Sure. We'll bring you back here and you can take as many pictures as you like. You can spend another night here, no problem."

"Not in the tower room."

He slid his brown eyes sideways and fixed them on her. "Listen up, Miss Smith. Prove you're on side when we get to Queen Square and you can have the five-star guest room."

15

The first thing Keith Halliwell told Diamond when he arrived at work was that Ingeborg wasn't in.

"I'm not expecting her. Gave her the day off, didn't I?" he said. If Halliwell hadn't cottoned on, he didn't deserve to be called a detective.

"I don't think I heard about that."

Diamond understood now. There was a subtext to this conversation and it was about confidences being shared between senior colleagues. Reasonable enough. But another principle was in play here, the need to know. The fewer people who were privy to Ingeborg's undercover mission, the safer she would be. If her personal safety was weighed against Halliwell's dignity, there was only one winner.

Diamond relented enough to give a wink. "We'll manage without her. What's the real news, then? What have you got to show for a day without me in the office?"

"Mainly we were getting the background on Monica's 'ex.'"

"Tell me all."

"He's a huge name in the construction world, as we know, but it's not your conventional CV. Mr. Bernie Wefers has form."

"Violence?"

"Plenty of it. He spent most of his youth in young offenders' institutions. Gang stuff, mostly. Shoplifting, leading to robbery with violence—and then absconding from one borstal after another."

"Where was he raised?"

"A council estate in Swindon. A single mum with multiple

relationships and four kids. He was the youngest and she'd just about given up by then. He was always in trouble."

"Firearms?"

"Flick knives. The usual pattern, threatening shop-owners and nicking the cigarettes and the contents of the till."

"Gangs, you said."

"He had his own mob of tearaways from an early age. He was a kid with leadership qualities, without a doubt. Even when he was locked away, he was the main man, organising the scams. There was a riot and a fire at one place and he was definitely the ringleader. The probation officers seemed to give him up as beyond redemption. But then at seventeen, he comes to his senses. He's learned a trade inside as a bricklayer and he gets employment in Birmingham in the early nineties when there is plenty of construction going on. He disappears from criminal records and just about every other record for ten to twelve years and then he turns up in the south of England as a vehicle owner in Surbiton and the vehicle is a new BMW."

"Did all right as a brickie, then."

"Suspiciously all right. Nice address, paying his council tax. Nothing worse than a couple of speeding fines. He was changing cars all the time, buying the new models as they came on the market."

"Not laying bricks any more, I'll warrant."

"He'd become a contractor. The Wefers name starts getting on vans and lorries. But he isn't content with that. He starts a private construction company and it takes off in a big way and is floated on the stock market."

"And the rest is history. How we all wish we'd bought a slice of it. What's he doing these days?"

"Still very active in management. He excels at land deals, identifying prime sites, dealing with the owners and seeing off any objectors."

"What with—power drills?"

Halliwell shrugged. "Better than that, he has a team of planning experts who run rings round the local authorities.

They're paid almost entirely on commission, and are known in the trade as the piranhas. Even in the leaner years of this century he's managed to forge ahead of the opposition. His developments always include an element of affordable housing along with the profit-making four- and five-bedroom houses, so he gets the blessing of the government."

"In short, he's got it made."

Halliwell nodded. "Got it made. That wouldn't be a bad motto for Wefers Construction, unless it's 'concrete the country.'"

"Do I detect a note of bitterness?"

"Only about developers in general. Another lot built a car park over the churchyard where my grandparents were buried. The church was closed and became a pub restaurant and the gravestones have been moved to the boundary and set into a new stone wall as someone's weird idea of respect for the past. They're passing it off as the wall of remembrance—as if wc ought to be grateful."

"That's sick, Keith. I sympathise. I'd feel the same." Diamond let a suitable interval go by before saying, "Okay, that's the business side of Bernie. Instead of nicking cigarettes at knife-point, he grabs land with his piranhas and builds on it. That's known as channelling your talent. Smart guy. No doubt he'll end up with a knighthood. Did you get anything on his private life?"

"Twice divorced, with any number of broken relationships as well. He has no problems attracting the women, but he doesn't keep them long. If you Google images of him you'll see him with his arm round any number of women, all different."

"Kids?"

"None that he admits to."

"So how does he spend his money?"

"Cars, holidays abroad, night clubs, racing."

"Not a student of fourteenth century poetry, then?"

"No, but he has a sideline in old carvings."

Diamond laughed in disbelief. "Get away."

"I mean it. One of his companies deals in statues and garden ornaments."

"A salvage yard?"

"They have a massive warehouse called Stone Rescue in the London dockland area. The stuff is harvested from all over the country as he buys old property for redevelopment. And then they're sold at a tidy profit. But I don't think he'd be in the market for the *Wife of Bath* unless it was dirt cheap."

"As far as I'm concerned, he could have it for nothing if he'd cart it away."

"Who does it belong to now?" Halliwell asked.

"Bridgwater museum."

"Not the auctioneers?"

"No, they're the middle men. It didn't go under the hammer, so technically it still belongs to the seller. The museum people are only too pleased to have it under police protection now they know it's worth a small fortune." He hesitated as a thought distracted him. "It is still with us? I haven't looked yet."

"It's unlikely to walk."

Just to be certain, Diamond got up and opened his office door. The slab remained defiantly in front of his desk. There was still a faint whiff from the decontamination. "My cactus has had it."

"Shame."

He closed the office door. If there was ever an incentive to work in there, it had gone. "I'd better interview Bernie myself. Send someone else and they could end up as part of the foundations of a luxury home. Where is he based?"

"All over. He hops around the country in his private helicopter."

"But where does he live?"

"Several houses. The closest is Maidenhead."

"Long drive. Get on to his office and find out his schedule for this week. With a bit of luck that chopper could be landing closer to home."

While Halliwell was on the phone, Diamond started a slow patrol of the CID room, checking progress on the investigation. Just as he reached John Leaman's desk, he felt a tap on his shoulder. He swung round in annoyance. No one in the team dared touch him.

He was faced with Georgina Dallymore, the Assistant Chief Constable. She was in the full dress uniform with the silver buttons strained to the point of separation. "A word, if you don't mind," she told him.

"What's that, ma'am?" he said, privately thinking a word of four letters. A visit from Georgina never brought welcome news.

"In your office, if you don't mind."

Seven words already, and not to his liking.

"As you wish." He led her across the room and opened the door. "Mind you don't trip."

She peered at the *Wife of Bath*.

"Don't ask," he said as he stepped over and moved behind his desk to open a window and let the fumes out. "Have a chair."

She sat down and said, "DS Smith."

"Ingeborg? Not in today," he said with an effort to subdue the alarm going off in his head.

"Unwell?"

He did his best to appear casual. "Unlikely. She's very fit."

"Hasn't she called in?"

"Not yet. No doubt she will."

"She isn't pursuing enquiries, then?"

He hesitated. How much did Georgina know? "She could be. I allow my team some scope, as you appreciate."

"She drives a Ford Ka—is that correct?"

"To the best of my knowledge, she does."

"The reason I ask is that a query came in from Bristol. A foot patrol making a routine check of the harbourside area early this morning came across a vehicle apparently left overnight close to the *Great Britain*."

"The old Brunel ship?" Now he was puzzled himself.

"They did a vehicle check with the PNC and found it was registered to DS Smith. She doesn't live in Bristol."

"No. She has a flat here."

"Then why would she leave her car overnight in Bristol?"

"I'll ask her when she comes in."

"You don't have any enquiries currently going on in Bristol. Anything over there would be handled by their CID."

"Goes without saying." He knew those silver buttons couldn't possibly take the strain if Georgina learned that one of Bath's officers had been authorised to go undercover in Bristol. Better she learned the truth at the conclusion of a successful investigation than now when it was barely under way. "I'll certainly look into it."

"And report to me."

"Directly, ma'am."

She stood up and took a long, unadmiring look at the *Wife of Bath*. "I take it this is the item that provoked the fatal shooting at the auction last week?"

"So we understand," he said.

"You're not certain?"

"It's not impossible that the shooting was premeditated and made to look like an argument over the carving."

Georgina frowned. "That's rather skewed thinking, if I may say so."

"Say whatever you like, ma'am. We prefer to use the term Byzantine."

16

Keith Halliwell was through to the head office of Wefers Construction. No music, no voice asking him to hold and then telling him he was moving up the queue. He'd picked a good time and was through to Bernie Wefers' personal assistant, Colleen. He raised a thumb to Diamond across the room. The big man shimmied between the desks and joined him.

Halliwell stressed the urgency of the request. "If you give me the locations, we'll arrange to meet him at the most convenient one . . . Very important, yes . . . His helicopter, yes. We know that . . . No, it's a personal matter . . . Thank you. I have a pen ready."

Diamond stood at Halliwell's side vetting the place names as they appeared on the notepad. Hastings was a no-no. Brighton out of the question. The Isle of Wight still too far to travel. The route seemed to be moving in their direction along the south coast. Then it veered north. Marlborough.

Marlborough was possible.

"Is that it, then?" Halliwell asked Colleen. ". . . He's back to London after that?" He looked at Diamond, who nodded. "We'll meet him in Marlborough. What time will he land there? . . . And where exactly is the site?"

Before getting on the road, Diamond spoke to the youngest of the team, DC Paul Gilbert. "You were looking for some action."

Gilbert looked up from his computer screen, eyes shining. "Ready to go, guv."

"This won't be quite what you had in mind. I'm not asking you to go undercover, but it will get you out of the office and it's a solo mission."

"Cool."

"The ACC is fussing over Ingeborg. A query came in from Bristol police this morning about a vehicle left overnight on the harbour-side where the *Great Britain* is. Do you know where I mean?"

"That'll be the car park for the Maritime Heritage Centre."

"Sounds like you know it better than I do. If Bristol haven't got more urgent things to do than check on parked cars, they need downsizing, in my opinion, but I suppose this red Ford Ka stood out. Maybe it's illegally parked. Turns out it's registered to Ingeborg."

"That's what she drives."

"And I expect there's a very boring explanation."

"She isn't in today."

"I know. She took a few days off with my blessing. What I want you to do is keep everyone happy by going over there and checking it out—if it's still there. See if there's any sign of a breakdown, a flat tyre, or whatever. The wardens could have served a parking notice by now. Make sure they don't tow it away."

"Is Ingeborg interested in old ships?" Gilbert asked.

"Not to my knowledge."

"There isn't much else there. She could have left the car and taken the harbour railway from there, I suppose. Shall I ask the *Great Britain* people if they saw her yesterday?"

"If you like. We're not too fussed. This is mainly to keep Georgina sweet. Do you understand me?"

Gilbert returned Diamond's grin. "Sure thing, guv."

There was ample time. Marlborough was not much over thirty miles east along the old Bath Road.

"If Bernie is building in Marlborough, nowhere is safe," Diamond said while they were on the stretch between Chippenham and Calne. "It's the ultimate NIMBY town. If you're seen in the High Street without an old school tie you're up before the magistrates."

Halliwell looked surprised. "I've often stopped there for a cup of tea. Nobody ever bothered me."

"I was exaggerating. But you know what I mean. It's a picture postcard. All those old buildings and quaint little lanes down to the river. It's not ripe for development."

"Bernie seems to think it is."

"He must know something we don't."

Halliwell drove through Calne—not a picture postcard—and out into open country again.

Neither man spoke about Georgina's rare appearance in the CID room and the conversation behind the closed door of Diamond's office. Halliwell must have guessed Ingeborg had been under discussion and decided not to ask. And Diamond preferred to wrestle silently with his thoughts and fears. He couldn't understand why Inge had parked her car at the dockside overnight. Such a dumb thing to do. If you're going undercover, you don't leave an obvious trail. He racked his brain for an explanation. She may have gone there on surveillance, acting on a tip, and then got distracted in some way. He hoped this was the case, but feared she might be in trouble. He'd been checking his phone repeatedly for a text and nothing had come through. He kept reminding himself that she'd urged him to trust her and he was trying. But he wished he understood what was going on.

"Makes you feel desolate, doesn't it?" Halliwell said suddenly.

"Not at all. I'm going to be positive."

"Nothing personal, I was speaking about the landscape. Miles and miles with scarcely a sign of life."

"I can't agree with that. It's teeming with life. Grass, sheep, butterflies. That's Wiltshire. I like it. I'm a green fields man myself. Don't need to see housing estates."

"Have you ever lived in the country, guv?"

"No, but I appreciate it when I see it. You could take this more slowly. You don't have to drive as if you want to leave it."

"We're only doing fifty-five."

They drove through Avebury and soon the distinctive Bronze Age mound called Silbury Hill appeared on their left.

"There's your sign of life," Diamond said.

"It's a burial mound, guv."

"Man-made, I meant." He glossed over that one. "Almost there. Do you know where to make for?"

"She gave me some directions. Shouldn't be difficult to find. Marlborough is built around the High Street, basically. We drive right through and look for a field that comes off on the left."

"Should have brought my wellies. What's happening in this field?"

"Nothing much. It's a project under discussion. Bernie is meeting the landowner there."

But plenty was happening when they had driven through the town and turned up a side road that Halliwell believed would bring them to the proposed building site. Cars—expensive cars mostly—were backed up as far ahead as they could see. They were parking on the left, leaving only a narrow through-way.

"We'd better join them," Diamond said. "Something must be on."

Halliwell parked behind a Range Rover and they got out and joined the stream of pedestrians all heading one way. "Do you think it's a meeting?" he asked Diamond.

"Could be a march. Some of them are carrying banners."

"They won't march far in wellies."

Wellingtons, Barbours, cords and flat caps were clearly the dress code of the day. Diamond, in his trilby, suit and walking shoes, stood out, and Halliwell had no headgear at all. It didn't seem to matter while they were on the move. The mood was hearty, with plenty of raised voices in well-bred accents hailing friends by name. Some distance up the road was a gate and everyone was filing through it. By the time Diamond and Halliwell reached there at least a hundred people were standing about in a large field.

Some of the banners were visible now. One said: ENOUGH IS ENOUGH and another: STUFF YOUR PLAN.

"We're not the only ones with something to say to Bernie," Diamond said.

"Be lucky if we get a word in."

Just to be certain, Diamond turned to a man in a tweed jacket with leather shoulders and said, "Is this about the Wefers development?"

"We're all in the wrong place if it isn't," the man said. "And who are you?"

"We're not locals."

"I can see that."

"Down from Bath."

"Nothing to do with the Wefers lot, I trust?"

"Far from it," Halliwell said.

Diamond nudged his colleague and said, "We can watch it from over there." He didn't fancy being put through more questions.

A section of the field had been staked and roped and a huge whitewashed letter *H* marked inside. A man with a loud-hailer was telling people with the utmost courtesy, "Kindly keep well back from the landing area, ladies and gentlemen. We don't want any accidents."

Two of the local police were watching from a distance, appearing content to leave the stewarding to the great and the good of the town.

"The British at their best," Diamond said to Halliwell as they took up a new position. "No other nation on Earth could stage such an orderly demo." He took out his mobile to check once more whether Ingeborg had sent a text. Normally she was a regular texter. She'd even taught him the basics.

Nothing.

No use trying to reach her and risking blowing her cover. He pocketed the phone just as the leather-shouldered man approached them again.

"I say, you people, what exactly is your business here?"

Diamond looked up in surprise. He'd quite forgotten that the well-educated aren't all polite. They can be downright rude.

Halliwell said, "Just observing at this stage."

"I think I have a right to ask."

"I'm not sure that you do, but I'll tell you anyway," Diamond said to silence him. "We're police officers."

"You're not in uniform."

"That's obvious, isn't it?"

"And a moment ago you were taking pictures with your phone." This busybody was cranking himself up into quite a state. "Is that what you're up to, covert surveillance, getting a record of decent, law-abiding people on a peaceful demonstration?"

"Not at all. I was checking for a text."

Halliwell added, "If we were doing surveillance, we'd use better equipment than a mobile phone."

Diamond told the man, "I suggest you aim your protest at the cause of all the fuss. That speck in the sky seems to be heading in this direction."

The interrogator moved off.

Others had seen it and the anticipation mounted as the helicopter announced itself with the engine drone and the flash of sunlight on its fuselage. On the ground, jeering began and banners were raised.

"Please stand well clear of the landing area," the man with the loud-hailer appealed once more.

But there was a bigger hazard.

From behind them at the edge of the field, a black four-by-four with lights on full beam powered through the gate and made swift, bumping progress across the turf, horn blaring to force a passage through the crowd. Fitted with a bull bar, it could do that if necessary. Word quickly passed round that this was the owner of the field making a last-minute appearance. If so, he must have been parked just outside, ready for this. He wouldn't have wanted to announce his presence any sooner. A chorus of booing from the demonstrators left no doubt what they thought of the maneuver. The British at their best were getting fractious. Some young men ran at the vehicle and thumped the bodywork. A banner was smashed over the bonnet. This made not a jot of difference. The black Jeep came to a skidding halt at the edge of the landing space and brought down one of the iron stakes and a length of the rope. Wisely, the driver remained in the vehicle with the engine running.

Meanwhile the small silver helicopter had swooped in and was hovering about fifty feet overhead, the pilot evidently taking stock of the scene below. The long grass in the marked, enclosed area was flattened by the action of the rotor blades. A few hats were dislodged.

Two men were seated at the front of the aircraft: the pilot and a passenger in a blue windbreaker and black knitted cap. If this was Bernie, he didn't look bothered by the scene. In fact he was grinning. His face was close to the side window, getting a sight of what was going on.

"Look at him, the smug bastard," the man with the leather shoulders said to no one in particular. "You can tell it's a done deal."

The helicopter descended the last few feet and touched down.

"You know what's going to happen?" Halliwell yelled to Diamond. "Bernie will transfer to the Jeep and be driven off. They'll have their discussion well away from all this."

"If they escape," Diamond said.

The door of the four-by-four opened and a short, slight figure in black jumped out and was practically knocked over by the downdraught from the rotor blades.

"Bloody hell—it looks like a woman," Halliwell said.

No question about it. The headscarf she was wearing was wrenched off by the draught and a mass of blonde hair fanned out behind her. She looked far too young to be a landowner.

Her youth and gender didn't stop a chorus of jeers from the crowd.

The door of the helicopter opened and Bernie jumped out, an agile, middle-aged man with cropped hair going grey. Years in a hard trade had left their mark. It was a weatherbeaten face, coarse-skinned and deeply creased. Several gold chains nestled in the chest hair revealed by his open Hawaiian shirt. His swagger suggested he would yield to nobody and certainly not a crowd of nimbys in a field he was shortly to claim as one more piece of his empire.

Without so much as a handshake, Bernie and the blonde climbed inside the Jeep and slammed the doors—the signal for the crowd to close in and try to stop them. But the blonde was having none of it—as she made clear by jamming her foot down and punching the horn. Her acceleration wouldn't have disgraced a rally driver. The best the protesters could manage was to flail with their banners, and even then several slipped over. It was more by chance than design that nobody fell under the wheels.

With the engine revved to screaming level, the clear winner in this contest surged across the field to shouts of "madman" and "swine." A few brave souls tried blocking the exit gate until it was obvious they were inviting serious injury, if not death, and they leapt aside. The targets of all the mayhem were through and away.

"What did you make of that?" Halliwell said. "Who the hell was she?"

"How would I know? The crowd seemed to think it was the landowner, but she looked too young to me. Could be one of the staff. In any case, she's a tough lady. She wasn't taking prisoners."

"So what now, guv? We can't give chase."

"While the chopper is here, we're okay. He's got to come back some time to return to London."

Among the crowd the outrage at how dangerous the escape had been was giving way to disappointment. Some insisted they had made their point by being there. Others said they had been cheated out of a chance to put their arguments to Bernie Wefers—as if there was a code of behaviour for demonstrations and it had not been observed. Muttering groups discussed what to do next and a number gave up and left. Some looked over their shoulders at the helicopter, now standing silent, with the pilot still in the cabin.

As if they sensed the threat of damage or even injury, the two uniformed police officers moved towards the landing space and raised the fallen stake and forced it into the turf again. Then they stationed themselves inside the rope and started making calls on their hand radios.

A large section of the crowd remained, debating what to do next. The mood wasn't friendly.

"They're looking for someone to blame," Halliwell said. "Might be wise to put your phone out of sight, guv."

Diamond was checking once again for a text. He looked up and saw what his colleague meant. "A good moment to make ourselves known to the local fuzz, I think."

They moved fast, brandished their IDs, and stepped over the rope. The men on duty greeted them as brother officers volunteering to help out. One said, "There's a fair amount of anger out there. I asked for some back-up."

His mate said with a grin, "Didn't think they'd call up Avon and Somerset."

"Sorry, my friend," Diamond said. "We're not the US cavalry. We're on an enquiry. We're going aboard the chopper to interview the pilot. But it's nice to know we have you guys protecting us."

The pilot appeared to be asleep. Diamond reached up and tapped the glass and pressed his ID against it when the pilot showed signs of life. The door opened, the steps were let down and they climbed up to the cabin.

"Nothing to worry about. You're in the clear," Diamond said, sensing this as a promising unplanned opportunity. "What's your name?"

"Sinclair. Percy Sinclair."

"Good to meet you, Percy. Any idea when Mr. Wefers is expected back?"

The pilot hesitated, torn between loyalty to his paymaster and submission to the law. "Couldn't say, except he wants to be back in London before tonight, so he shouldn't be all that long."

"We'll sit down then." Diamond parked himself in

Bernie's seat and Halliwell squeezed through to one of the passenger seats behind. "Who was the blonde with the Jeep? Do you know?"

Percy Sinclair had decided to cooperate. "She's the one selling the land. Miss Thompson. Her father died suddenly and left everything to her. She's an air stewardess, I believe, with no interest in farming, so she wants a quick deal."

"She's got guts, in addition to her other assets. I'd think twice about driving into a demo like that."

"They have to be confident in her job, don't they?"

"You have to be confident in yours," Diamond said. "You landed the chopper to perfection and there was a lot to put you off. How long have you been flying for Bernie Wefers?"

"Couple of years, no more."

A couple of years would be sufficient to get the pattern of Bernie's trips.

"You've got to know his sites like the back of your hand, I'll bet."

"Most of them, anyway."

"All over Britain?"

"Just about."

"We're from Bath. Where's the best landing spot there?"

"Down there we always go to Castle Combe," Sinclair said. "He picks his hotels. If they're comfortable and have a helipad he keeps going back. Do you know the Manor House Hotel?"

"By reputation. Nine or ten miles from where we work."

"Yes, if he visits Bath, he'll be driven in from there."

"Do you get to stay in the Manor House as well?"

"I do."

"Lucky you. Have you done the trip recently?"

"Two or three weeks ago, maybe. Bristol first, then Bath."

"Where do you stay in Bristol?"

"Some way outside. Thornbury Castle. They have the helipad there."

"Not slumming, exactly. You say you were there recently. I expect you keep a log of your trips?"

"I do." A cautious note had entered the pilot's voice.

"Do you have it with you?"

He was right back in his shell now. "I can't show it to you without Mr. Wefers' permission. He doesn't allow me to discuss his business."

"We wouldn't be doing that," Diamond said as if he, too, thought it was an appalling liberty. "It's just a matter of knowing who was where on a particular date last month. Where do you keep it—somewhere within reach?"

Sinclair flexed his legs and tucked his heels in.

"Under your seat?" Diamond said.

"I can't show you."

"I know exactly how you feel, but we have a duty here, and there's an offence known as obstruction."

Sinclair was tight-lipped for a few seconds as the words sank in. Then he exhaled sharply, leaned forward and felt under his seat. "You won't tell him?"

"Percy, it's entirely between ourselves."

With definite misgivings, a battered notebook was handed over.

Diamond opened it at random and quickly got a sense of what the columns represented. He turned several pages in rising anticipation. "All the flights are logged here?"

"Every one."

His finger went down the left column and up again. But there was crushing disappointment here. "That trip you mentioned to Bristol and Bath was all of four weeks ago."

"Sorry. It seemed like less."

"Nothing more recent? I'm interested in the week beginning the twelfth."

"Whatever is written there is correct," Sinclair said.

"According to this, you didn't fly anywhere on the fifteenth."

"There are days when I'm not needed. He tells me in advance, so I can take time off if it's due to me. We're often away at weekends and I make up my rest days when I can."

Diamond exchanged a look with Halliwell. The fifteenth had been the day of the auction.

"Does he ever travel by other means?"

"Short trips, around London."

"But if he wanted to visit Bath, he'd ask you to fly him there?"

Sinclair nodded. "He isn't one for spending hours in a train or car."

"On the sixteenth, you flew to Norwich."

"Yes, he's got a big building project there. Do you want to know where we stayed?"

"Doesn't matter," Diamond said in a mood of resignation. A promising line of enquiry had led nowhere. "Did you ever fly his ex-wife Monica anywhere?"

"Monica?" He blinked several times. "There were trips when she joined us. She'd visit friends or go shopping. That was way back last year. There was a serious falling out." He stared back at Diamond. He'd finally made the connection. "Is this about her new husband getting shot?"

Diamond nodded.

"Tragic."

"Indeed. Did you ever meet him?"

"The professor? No." Sinclair made it obvious he wanted to end this conversation, shifting in his seat and glancing left and right as if deciding whether to open the door and leap out.

"I expect you heard about him from Bernie. He talks to you on these flights, doesn't he?"

"Not much. There's nothing more I can tell you."

"That's okay," Diamond said smoothly. "You've been really helpful. I'll mention it to Bernie when I speak to him."

"Christ, no, don't do that. He won't be pleased at all. I could lose my job."

"Has he got something to hide, then?"

"No, no—don't get that idea."

"Have *you* got something to hide?" More than just a hunch, the possibility had surfaced in Diamond's mind when Sinclair had reacted so sharply to the mention of Monica. "Did you know about the affair before Bernie found out? A little secret between you and Monica? I've met her, by the way, and she talked very freely. I feel sorry for her."

"Me, too." He was less guarded now. "There was one time while Bernie was away in America, and a rail strike was on. I flew her to Reading, to the university there, and it didn't go into the log. She asked me to keep it to myself. We were there overnight. I stayed with friends in Caversham. I guessed what she was up to, but I thought it was fair game. Bernie has girlfriends all over."

"That emerged in the divorce court," Diamond said.

"I'm not criticising. He treats me fairly. If that's how he wants to lead his life, so be it. But I have a lot of sympathy for Monica."

"Has he ever spoken to you about the professor being shot?"

"Not a word. None of my business."

"Of course not." Diamond looked out at the demonstration. Most of the protesters had given up. A police van had arrived and the reinforcements were chatting amicably among themselves. He turned to Halliwell. "Don't get too comfortable. You and I had better move, or Percy will have some explaining to do when Bernie comes back from his business meeting."

17

"So how shall we play this?" Ingeborg asked.

She was seated with Nathan in the rear of his black limousine, trusted enough to travel without one of the minders beside her. Another car was following with at least four heavies inside.

"Leave it to me," Nathan said.

"That isn't good enough. I need to know what to expect."

Pressured, he took a deep, impatient breath and said without looking her way, "Me and my back-up will be out of sight when you meet Lily. Be natural with her and keep talking. We'll take over when the time is right."

"No shooting?"

"Christ no, I don't want her getting hurt."

"Or me, I hope."

"You're one of us. You have as much interest in reeling her in as I do—almost."

Ingeborg doubted whether Lee would appreciate being "reeled in." The runaway pop star might ultimately forgive Nathan, whose actions really did seem to be driven by his heart, but she was certain to feel betrayed by Ingeborg. This assignment had already been stripped of any glamour it had at the beginning. Going undercover, even in a worthy cause, is a dirty, demeaning trade.

And there was no way to pull out now.

Precisely what had prompted Lee's bid for freedom was uncertain. She had said on the phone that her life had been getting impossible for reasons she wouldn't go into. She was with a friend. The first thought had to be that the friend was male, younger than Nathan, more attractive and less demanding. The regime in the Leigh Woods mansion must have been pretty repressive for any young woman, least of all one getting empowered by fame in the music business. She may have needed Nathan's backing at the start of her career and now decided she was successful enough to go it alone.

Whatever the outcome of this afternoon's adventure, it was a game changer. Posing as a journalist would get more difficult, if not impossible, when Lee turned angry and refused to cooperate.

Time for a rethink.

The obvious way forward was to work on Nathan. "Prove you're on side," he'd said earlier, and now he'd called Ingeborg "one of us." By building on his confidence, she need no longer rely on Lee as her ticket into the Hazael household.

Using people like this was alien to her nature, but it had to be done.

"Will you help me with Lee?" she asked Nathan. "She's going to feel I haven't been honest with her."

"Sure. I'll talk her round. She'll be pleased we went to all this trouble to bring her back. I'm not a total beginner with women. You all enjoy the chase."

Dream on, she thought.

"We'll put you down in the Grove, south of the square," Nathan continued, with a switch to a managerial tone. "You walk up Grove Avenue and there you are. Do what she said, go to the middle, where the statue is, and talk to her. She'll want to come to some arrangement about this thing you're doing for the Sunday paper. Fall in with whatever she says. Put her mind at ease, okay? Don't say a single word about me. And don't ask who she's with or what her plans are. When she's ready to leave, you say goodbye, walk back to the Grove where we dropped you and wait for the car. Is that clear?"

"Where will you be?" she asked.

"Watching," he said. "She's right about Queen Square. It's bloody big and she can see all around. Advantage Lily. But when the talking is done, she has to leave and we'll see exactly which way she goes. Advantage Nathan. We'll be there to pick her up. Game, set and match."

The logic was persuasive. Nathan was no beginner in the art of reeling people in.

The limo cruised sedately south of the river by the road that runs alongside it, Coronation Road. They had more than twenty minutes in hand, but getting to Queen Square early and waiting would be no hardship. A short break from present company would come as a relief. Nathan's efforts at friendship made Ingeborg's flesh creep.

At the major roundabout that linked with the A38, they turned left and crossed the Avon at the first opportunity, the bridge at the western limit of Redcliffe Way, and so arrived in the Grove.

Nathan turned to her before the car stopped. "Keep it simple, right?"

"I hear you."

She got out, crossed the street and started up Grove Avenue.

Bristol has never treated its architecture with the same respect Bath has. Queen Square, one of the glories of the city, the largest Georgian square in the world, has suffered terribly over the years. In 1831, much of it was burnt down during three days of rioting over the rejection of the Reform Bill; and, in 1937, another act of violation occurred when the Inner Circuit road was thrust diagonally across it. Only in 2000 was the abuse corrected and the space restored.

The few surviving eighteenth century houses bordering the square—including the first American embassy—are along the south side where Ingeborg emerged, but her eyes were fixed ahead, on the rendezvous, the intersection of the broad walks where the equestrian statue sits on a tall plinth of Portland stone. A few people were about, and several were using the park seats facing the centre. She couldn't tell from this distance whether Lee was among them. She was still some ten minutes early.

The sense of space here was a joy after being confined

for hours in the Leigh Woods mansion. She had no difficulty empathising with Lee. Any woman who took on Nathan
was depriving herself of independence. His involvement in
the criminal culture meant that he demanded control and
unquestioning loyalty.

But there was a real danger of what military strategists
called mission creep.

Don't side with Lee, she rebuked herself. This is about you
and the job you have to do.

She moved straight across the lawn towards the centre,
mindful that space shouldn't be confused with freedom. She
knew her every step was being watched by Nathan and his
henchmen, no doubt dispersed at each side of the vast square
with a sightline avoiding the few mature trees.

Be vigilant. These are dangerous people.

About a minute of steady walking brought her to the centre.
Nowhere could she see Lee. She circled the perimeter of the
gravel area checking the people on seats: three old couples,
two women with dogs and one young mother with a tod-
dler in a stroller. There's time, she told herself. I have a few
minutes in hand.

Even so, no one resembling Lee was moving in this direction across the square.

She looked up at the statue, an idealised rendering in
brass of King William III as a heroic Roman figure on a
high-striding stallion—which was ironic considering William
had died after a riding accident when his horse tripped on a
molehill. The statue had also suffered the indignity of being
shifted off-centre when the dual carriageway was put through
and only returned to its original position in 2000. Blokes and
their delusions of grandeur, she thought. Better watch out,
King William. There could be worse to come. Brass is fetch-
ing record prices as scrap metal.

For something to do, she took out her iPhone and snapped
a picture of the king.

Out of nowhere a male voice said, "Want me to take one
of you?"

Get lost, buster, she thought. The last thing I want is to be picked up by some man on the make.

"That's okay." She made her wishes clear by returning the phone to her pocket.

"You know who I am."

More of a statement than a question. She'd been avoiding eye contact. Now she gave him a glance, still thinking it was a try-on.

Tall, fortyish, black leather jacket and jeans. And bearded.

She knew him.

"You're Marcus, from the TV crew."

"And you're the writer doing the piece on Lee Li. She's not coming. She asked me to meet you."

Her spirits plunged. Nothing is certain but the unforeseen, as Lee would surely have said.

"Why?"

"She has to be ultra-careful. She dumped Nathan—her boyfriend—and he's bound to be looking for her."

"And how do you come into it?"

"I gave her some help. She stayed with me last night. But she's still dead keen to see you. I'm here to take you to her."

Better.

Last night's events made more sense. Lee had spent several nights with the crew shooting the video, ample time for a friendship to develop. She must have poured out her troubles to Marcus and he'd aided her escape, using the rope ladder and transported her away from the *Great Britain*.

All very sweet—except that it created a problem. This changed scenario would surprise the watchers at the borders of the square. What would Nathan make of it if she wandered off with Marcus? Would he even recognise Marcus? He should do. Would he have the sense to guess Marcus was leading her to Lee?

It was a chance she had to take.

"Lead on, then."

They crossed the lawn and approached the row of houses on the west side, walking as briskly as if they were doing it

for their health. She couldn't see Nathan's car, but she was
in no doubt he was watching, revising the plan, plotting his
next move. She hoped he didn't suspect she had prearranged
this. When push came to shove—another thing Lee would
say—she was still in Nathan's camp.

"Where are we heading?" she asked Marcus.

"Not far."

Actually she could see they were making a beeline for
Middle Avenue, one of the main exits from the square. Queen
Square is built on former marshland surrounded on three
sides by water. Ahead of them was an area she knew well,
Bordeaux Quay, a trendy haunt for the young where old
warehousing had been inventively converted into centres for
the arts. The Arnolfini Gallery was to the left and the Watershed media centre across the bridge and to the right. It was
well possible Lee had chosen one place or the other for the
meeting.

"Good call," she said to Marcus. "This is less obvious than
the square."

"Her idea, not mine."

At the end of Middle Avenue they turned left towards the
giant arches of the Arnolfini. Ingeborg was thinking Nathan's
stalking ability would be tested in this more confined area.
His presence still wasn't obvious.

But the Arnolfini wasn't the meeting place. Halfway along,
Marcus turned right, towards the quayside. Ahead of them was
the footbridge known to most locals as the horned bridge, but
officially called Pero's Bridge, after an Afro-Caribbean slave
who had worked in Bristol in the eighteenth century when
it was said that "there is not a brick in the city but what is
cemented with the blood of a slave."

The horns were huge sculptures at either side of the section
that sometimes lifted to allow river traffic to pass. They acted
as counterweights and looked like the monstrous loudspeakers of antique gramophones. Suiting the slave theme, they
were said to be symbolic of the Caribbean flair for music.

At this moment Ingeborg wasn't interested in symbolism.

Every sinew of her body tensed at the sight of one of Nathan's musclemen standing with arms folded at the far side of the bridge.

"Keep going," Marcus said, and she felt his hand against the small of her back. She started forward. There was just a chance she could let the man know with a look that he should allow them to pass. No one else was on the footbridge at this time.

She hadn't taken more than three steps when a voice from behind called out, "Got you, Marcus. Let the woman go."

She swung around. Nathan had blocked off their retreat.

Marcus reacted fast—and mistakenly. He said, "You crafty bitch"—and grabbed a fistful of Ingeborg's long hair close to her scalp. "Come any closer," he shouted at Nathan, "and she goes over."

She was trained in martial combat, but when your head is forced back to the point where your spine feels ready to snap there is little you can do except kick aimlessly. She tried and didn't connect. She was his hostage now.

She heard Nathan shout, "Where's Lily?"

To hell with Lily, Ingeborg was thinking. I'm the victim here.

"Let me pass," Marcus said. He was desperate and outnumbered.

"Sod off. What have you done with her?"

She was trying to go limp as her training taught, ready for a surprise counter-attack, but as long as her head was held back at this agonizing angle, she could do nothing.

Marcus dragged her to the side of the bridge. It felt as if he'd pulled a hank of hair out by the roots. She caught him in the ribs with her elbow and he gave a grunt of discomfort, no more. He still had the advantage.

Now it appeared he meant to force her off the bridge into the river. He slammed her against the side rail. A little below shoulder height, the ironwork had an angled top to dissuade people from climbing over.

"I'm on your side," Ingeborg tried to tell him.

"You suckered me into this," he said.

"How could I? I didn't even know where we were going."

The logic seemed to penetrate his brain. Ingeborg felt his

grip relax a little. At the same time she got some purchase from the railing. With her shoulder hard against it she kicked with her left leg and felt the toe of her shoe sink into the soft flesh behind his knee. His leg jackknifed and he lost balance. Still gripping her hair, he toppled backwards, taking her with him. But he must have landed on his arm, because his fingers opened and her head was freed.

On the floor of the bridge, she wrestled him, sliding her right thigh across his hip and bringing her weight to bear on him. She grabbed his arm and forced it upwards in a half-nelson.

She was in charge now.

She heard the thud of footsteps.

"Okay," Nathan rasped in her ear. "We'll deal with him."

"What was that about?" she said as she disentangled herself from Marcus. He made no attempt to rise.

"You did good," Nathan said.

"You ruined everything. He was taking me to Lee."

She got to her feet and brushed off her clothes. Her neck ached and her cheek was sore from the contact with Marcus's coarse beard.

Four of Nathan's henchmen were standing there.

"Thanks for coming to the rescue, guys," she said with sarcasm.

"Stand back." Nathan forced his foot under Marcus's shoulder and tipped him face upwards. "Where's Lily?"

"How would I know?" Marcus said, eyes stretched wide in alarm. "She'll have run a mile by now."

Nathan stooped and slapped his face and hit the other cheek with the back of his hand. "Have you been shagging her, you dickhead?"

"No," Marcus said in a yelp of denial. "Absolutely not." His lip was starting to bleed.

"Because if you have, you're never shagging anything again."

"I offered her a place to stay last night, that's all. She appealed to me for help. She sounded desperate."

"So desperate she still wants to do her bloody interview."

"It was important to her, a career opportunity."

"She was at your place? Where's that?"

"Clifton. She isn't there."

"Where were you heading just now, then? What was the meeting place?"

"I honestly don't know. She didn't trust anyone. She said we were to cross the bridge to the other side and she'd meet us."

"Right here?"

"Yes."

Nathan straightened up and took a long look at the small, interested crowd that had started to gather on the Watershed side of Bordeaux Quay. Some of them took this as the cue to move on.

"I'll tell you what we'll do," he said to his team of heavies. "If she's here, we'll give her something to look at. We'll tip this piece of shit over the side."

Marcus yelped in protest, but they moved in fast, keen for some action after standing by for so long.

"Don't," Ingeborg said. "He could drown."

But they already had him by the arms and legs and hoisted him off the floor ready to swing him high over the railing.

"On a count of three," Nathan said.

"You're mad," Ingeborg said. "This won't help us find Lee." She knew the gravity of what was happening in full view of witnesses and she was implicated. She'd fought Marcus to the ground and disabled him. The cardinal rule of going undercover is that you don't get involved in violence. Serving officers had got sent down for long terms for conniving at the commission of a crime.

Marcus was whimpering like a puppy. They swung him back at the count of one.

"Two."

There was a scream of, "Don't do it," from the crowd and somebody sprinted to the bridge and towards them.

A woman. Dark hair, slim, East Asian.

Lee Li.

She must have been among the bystanders, uncertain

what to do until the brutality to Marcus got to this intolerable point.

Nathan dropped the leg he was holding and said, "Get her."

Marcus hit the floor with a thud and the team dashed after their new quarry.

Lee turned to escape, but she only got a few yards. The quickest of the henchmen grabbed her by the shoulder and swung her about. With ease, he grasped her round the waist and carried her, struggling, back to his employer.

"Put her down."

For a moment, Ingeborg thought Lee Li was going to get a face-slapping, but she did not.

Nathan opened his arms and embraced her. The man really was besotted.

Lee looked dazed and not at all happy.

This touching reunion came to a stop when a police siren sounded. One of the watchers must have used a phone.

"We're leaving," Nathan said.

In the black limousine, Ingeborg was allowed to sit beside the driver. Nathan was in the back seat with his arm around Lee, who was grim-faced and silent.

"Some hard things were said back there," he said to Ingeborg. "Heat of the moment."

She turned her head. "Is that an apology? I could have been badly hurt."

"You looked after yourself pretty good. Where did you learn to fight?"

"I did a course," she said. "Every woman needs to know the basics, journalists even more so."

"You hear that, Lily?" he said. "If you'd learned self-defence, none of this would have happened." Apparently he'd persuaded himself that she had been abducted by Marcus, who right now was probably giving his account of the affray to the police response team. And if Marcus had any care for his future well-being, he'd deny all knowledge of his attackers.

"Where are we going now?" Lee asked, staring ahead.

"Back to the house," Nathan said. "You still want to do that piece for the *Sunday Times*, don't you?"

"Not right away. I'm a mess. I need a shower and a change of clothes."

"No pressure," Ingeborg said, thinking ahead. "We could do this tomorrow and I'll still make my deadline."

Nathan said, "Stay another night and keep Lily company. I have some business back at the house."

"What is your business?" Ingeborg was bold enough to ask. Nathan's mood was distinctly friendlier now that he'd rescued his lover. If ever there was a time to get him to open up, it was now.

"I supply the hardware for various projects," he said, embracing the chance to give an arch response. "I'm a middleman, really, specialising in goods not obtainable from the manufacturer."

"Who are your clients?"

"That's confidential. Household names, some of them."

"Not the government?"

"No, my customers tend to operate independently." He was basking in the interest and clearly enjoying giving these cryptic answers.

"You obviously made a terrific success of it," Ingeborg said.

"I always thought the way to get ahead is to corner the market in something and I've proved it over and over. They all know me and my reputation—here in the southwest, for sure, and some of them come out from London to get the best service and no questions asked."

"Are they a bit dodgy, then, some of your customers?"

He chuckled. "I wouldn't say that, if I was you, not to their faces, anyway. Lily's met one or two ripe specimens passing through in recent months, haven't you, my precious?"

"Too true," she said.

"They wouldn't get into a garden party at Buck House, if you know what I mean," Nathan added. "In my line of business, you can't be too choosy."

"It sounds intriguing."

"A job of work, that's all."

"Maybe you'd consider letting me do one of my photo features on you. A day in the life of a millionaire middleman."

"No chance," he said. "Publicity is the last thing I need."

"Don't you advertise?" She was starting to enjoy this game as much as he.

"It's all done by word of mouth."

Lee piped up, "And some of the words are unprintable."

The car arrived at the security gate of Nathan's house and a volley of angry barking reminded Ingeborg of the dangers of overplaying her hand. They passed inside and up the long drive.

"I may see you before you go, depending on my business arrangements," Nathan told her. "I appreciate what you did today—more than you bargained for when you took on this project. You can have the guest room tonight, fresh towels and all that. Make yourself at home."

"I'll look after her," Lee said. "It's a treat for me to have a guest in my part of the house—a female one, that is."

The last remark drew a sharp glance from Nathan. He got out and walked into the house.

Lee gave a girl-to-girl smirk at Ingeborg. "Let's freshen up and then we can chill out together. I'm really sorry for all you had to put up with."

"Not your fault."

"I know. Nathan doesn't have a clue about women. Later I'll tell you how he really earns his money."

18

Light rain was falling in Marlborough, persuading more of the demonstrators to lower their banners and quit. The diehards amounted to thirty or so and they kept themselves going by taunting the police on the inner side of the rope. Their numbers were now up to ten—excluding Diamond and Halliwell. As often happens in protests, the local bobbies were sympathetic to the cause and uncomfortable facing their own townspeople across a dividing line. Officially, they were protecting the helicopter from potential damage, but their presence gave the appearance of siding with the property developer from London.

The two in plain clothes known to nobody came in for extra derision. Word had been passed round that they were police spies, seen photographing individuals in the crowd.

They needed some allies here. They'd identified themselves to the police, but hadn't said anything about the investigation they were on. "We wouldn't be standing with you if we were spies," Diamond said to the local sergeant. "We'd be mingling with that lot, passing ourselves off as part of the demo."

"I wouldn't argue with them, even so," the sergeant said. "They're getting in a strop, some of them. It's been a long afternoon with not much to show for all the shouting."

"Will Wefers get permission to build here?"

"Likely he will," the sergeant said. "It's government policy to stick more houses everywhere, get their figures up, whatever the local needs may be."

"Houses will sell here?"

"That's for sure. It's a nice place to live. But adding a big estate makes it a little less nice for those already here."

"The march of progress."

"Which anyone can slow up if they're well organised. This lot will fight all the way to the courts, if necessary."

"Expensive, once they employ lawyers," Diamond said. "Personally, I'd think about a cheaper option."

"Such as?"

"A dormouse."

The sergeant's long look at Diamond suggested he was being sent up. "Dormouse?"

"Protected species. You're not allowed to build over the habitat of a dormouse."

"I get you now. I doubt if there's one to be found in this field."

"That's not what I'm saying."

The sergeant smiled at last. He seemed to have latched on. "No chance. It wouldn't wash with the planning people. They're up to all the tricks. Anyway, a dormouse favours woodland and hedgerows."

"I'm not a countryman," Diamond said, "but I reckon other protected species make their homes in fields like this."

Unexpectedly, the helicopter door opened and the pilot climbed out and approached them. "Just letting you know I'm taking off now. You'd better stand well clear. Thanks for the protection."

Caught unprepared, Diamond couldn't let this happen. "Taking off without your passenger?"

"Mr. Wefers just phoned me. Change of plans. He's stopping overnight at the farmhouse."

"Is he, indeed?" Diamond said with a knowing look at Halliwell. Bernie was living up to his reputation as a stud.

"He told me to move the chopper to a field nearer to where he is. It's only a short hop and it'll be safer there."

This called for a rapid rethink. Bernie could be playing a clever game of avoidance, making his getaway from another location. "Did you tell him about us waiting to see him?"

"No, it was just a short call."

"And where exactly is this farmhouse?" A new plan was forming.

"A short way north across the fields, he tells me. There are twin silos I should be able to spot from the air."

"We'll join you and help you find them," Diamond said, a statement of intent, not a mere request.

Percy Sinclair plucked nervously at his hair. "I'm not sure about that. He's expecting me on my own."

"That's all right. Tell him we're police officers and we insisted."

"He'll go bananas."

"You reckon?" Diamond turned back to the sergeant. "Tell the mob the party's over for today." He strode towards the helicopter, Halliwell at his side.

Percy Sinclair followed, shaking his head.

Inside, the pilot made one more appeal. "He won't want to see you."

"It's a funny thing," Diamond said, "but people never do."

The twin engines spoke, the rotor blades stuttered into action and soon the whirring aircraft was fifty feet above, allowing a fine view of the last action of the demo, much shaking of banners and fists. A pull on the control stick, and they veered sharply away. The excitement of swift movement through the air took over. Speed above ground didn't trouble Diamond in the way a car moving at more than fifty-five did.

The joyride was short.

Diamond nudged the pilot's arm and shouted, "Twin silos!" The farmstead was in view, with that squeaky-clean look buildings have from above ground. The house and kitchen garden stood at the end of a lane. A yard beyond contained the silver silos, a large barn, machinery shed and cowshed.

Sinclair was a careful pilot. He circled the area, seeking the best place to touch down. Nobody was on the ground to help. Several speculative rotations took as much time as the rest of the flight. Finally the choice was made and they landed at the edge of a green field that looked like some kind of pasture.

The engines were switched off. The rotor blades flicked round a few more times before anyone could speak with ease.

"Not much of a reception," Diamond said to Sinclair. "They must have better things to do. Remind me of the lady's name."

"Tess Thompson."

"Okay. Keith and I will see if we can rouse the inmates. You can keep your distance. I expect you have to put this thing to bed in some way."

Close-up, the farm was more real than it had appeared from the air. The mud, smells and cowpats were all too obvious. Sidestepping where necessary, the two CID men crossed the yard to the square, two-storied house and knocked at the red-painted door.

A long interval passed before it was opened by Tess Thompson, barefoot and holding a glass of red wine. She was a little older than the earlier glimpses had suggested, closer to forty than a blonde in a black satin top with generous cleavage wishes to appear.

"Oh," she said. "I wasn't expecting more than one."

"There are three of us. The pilot will be along shortly." Diamond showed his ID. "We're from Bath police, needing a few words with Mr. Bernie Wefers."

"Someone mention my name?" a disembodied voice said, and the Hawaiian shirt and gold chains materialised in the dim interior.

"They're policemen," Tess Thompson said in a tone suggesting they might have been whirling Dervishes.

"What's wrong?" Bernie asked, stepping forward. He was shoeless and carrying a wine glass. He put his free hand against the doorpost, making it obvious they weren't welcome. His shoulders filled most of the space.

"Nothing is wrong," Diamond said. "It's a routine enquiry."

"What about?"

"The shooting of your former wife's husband."

He didn't move. He seemed to be absorbing the information slowly.

"Professor Gildersleeve," Diamond added. "You must have heard."

Bernie found his voice. "I wasn't there. Can't tell you a thing. How the hell did you find me?"

"May we come in?"

"It's not my house." Bernie turned and raised his eyebrows at Tess. "It may not be convenient."

She froze, uncertain what to say.

"We can do it at Marlborough nick, if you prefer," Diamond said. He'd played this game many times before.

Bernie swore, turned his back and beckoned at the same time. They followed him into a spacious living room that must have been in Tess Thompson's family for generations. It looked out of the 1930s, a three-piece suite in chintz, dining table and chairs, standard lamp and Welsh dresser laden with crockery. Framed family photos adorned the walls.

Having thrust himself into the main armchair beside the stone fireplace, Bernie said, "This had better not take long."

The owner of the farm hesitated in the doorway. "Do you want me here?"

"It's your gaff, gorgeous," he said. "No reason for you to leave."

She crossed to the other armchair, leaving the sofa for Diamond and Halliwell.

Diamond came straight to the point. "Do you recall where you were on the day Professor Gildersleeve was shot?"

"Not in Bath, if that's what you want to know," Bernie said. "I was home in Maidenhead or London. Can't remember which." A problem only ever faced by a man with about five different places of residence.

"So how do you know you weren't in Bath?"

"I read about it in the paper next day and thought bloody good thing I wasn't about when that happened, or some of your lot would come knocking on my door."

"Why? Why would you expect a visit from us?"

"Obvious, isn't it? He was having it off with my slag of a

wife for the best part of two years before I got to know about it. I had good reason to plug him. But I didn't, because I was a hundred miles away."

"He was shot by one of three masked gunmen."

"So?"

"Somebody may have hired them to carry out a contract killing."

"Oh yeah?" Bernie folded his arms. "And you're thinking I'd pay good money to rub out a waste of space like Gilder-sleeve? I'm a businessman. I spend my profits on good causes."

Diamond's eyebrows shot up. "Such as?"

"My yacht and my house in Spain. Anyway, I'm not a violent man."

"That isn't true, is it?" Diamond said.

Bernie didn't answer.

"You have a criminal record."

A moment of tension was broken when he laughed. "Pathetic. That's ancient history. Kids growing up do daft things. They all do. Me, I was unlucky, got caught, paid my dues and reformed. I'm a success story, in case you haven't noticed."

Diamond chose not to mention the violence to Monica. There was no advantage in stoking up aggression before he'd explored another avenue. "Four weeks ago, you travelled to Bath and Bristol. What were you doing there?"

"You're well-informed," Bernie said, looking less confident. "Who told you that?"

"We have our sources. It wasn't a secret trip, was it?"

"You must be joking." He reached for the wine bottle and topped up his glass, trying to recover his poise. "I was checking previous work we undertook. We always follow up, however small the project, just to make sure our clients are well satisfied."

"Dealing with complaints?"

He shook his head and glared. "Come off it, mate. We finish to a high standard."

"What was the project in Bath?"

"Outside the town. You probably know it, if you come

from there. Two hundred houses off the A46, forty percent of them affordable."

"What are the other sixty percent—millionaires' row?"

"Don't get sarcastic with me. You bloody know it's government speak, affordable homes for first-time buyers."

"And then you went on to Bristol."

"What's wrong with that?"

"More business?"

"A satisfied client took me for a meal. We built a major extension for him six months ago—fitness suite and sound studio. All the latest gear. He was well satisfied, but I've handled jobs for him before and he knows it's always top quality." He looked at the clock on the mantelpiece. "This is getting us nowhere. Any more questions? Because I want to get on with my evening."

"Here's one," Diamond said. "Did you ever meet Professor Gildersleeve?"

"Only once, at the divorce court. I wasn't impressed."

"You threatened him. You said you'd make him pay."

Bernie leaned forward and stabbed the air with his finger. "Listen, I was the mug who did the paying. My ex came out of it ten million quid better off."

"The words said to Gildersleeve weren't about money. It came across as a physical threat."

His voice became a growl. "How would you know what I said? Has Monica stitched me up?"

"The law works on hard evidence, not hearsay, Bernie. If it wasn't said, it can't harm you."

"Loads of things are said in the heat of the moment. Doesn't mean shit."

"So you used the words—about making him pay—and did no more about it?"

He seemed to regard the question as too trivial to answer. "If that bitch decided I had Gildersleeve killed, she'll do everything in her power to frame me. She hates my guts. I'm no angel, but this won't stick. I wasn't there and I didn't put a contract on the guy."

"Who do you think was responsible, then?"

He held out his hands like a salesman with nothing left in stock. "That's your job, isn't it, not mine. All I'm saying is don't take what Monica says as gospel. She's second to none at stringing blokes along. Happened to me, the day we first met in the London casino. She saw I had money and made a play for me. Terrific while it lasted. Heavy sex, nothing barred and a quick wedding. I see it now for what it was, but at the time I was blind to what was going on. She was everything I'd ever wanted in a woman. I'll say it—I loved her."

From Bernie, this was a startling admission, yet, oddly enough, it came across as sincere. "What went wrong?"

"Nothing for the first year or two. She treated me well and I pulled out all the stops to make sure she was happy. Holidays abroad, meals at the best restaurants, smart clothes, jewellery. I paid her credit cards every month without even looking at the stuff she'd bought. But then the rot set in. I was flat out running my business and left her alone too much. Sometimes I'd come home from a trip just needing to crash out when she wanted a tumble. I always said she had enough energy to build a pyramid all on her own. But the thing she wanted needed two of us. A man as busy as me was never going to keep her happy for long. And she was always on about culture and stuff. That's how she came to join the Diphthongs."

"The what?"

"Some sort of club for weirdos studying old-time writing. They gave themselves this stupid name as a kind of clever-dick joke. Do you know what a diphthong is?"

"I've some idea."

"More than I have. Any road, this was more about thongs than diphthongs. They were all at it, as far as I can make out." As if remembering a lady was present, he winked at his client Tess. "The things some people get up to."

Bernie's narrative had changed the mood. The stonewalling when they had first arrived and announced their business had given way to this free flow of reminiscence. He seemed eager to tell the story of his marriage, perhaps to justify his later brutality.

"Where was this going on?" Diamond asked. "In Maidenhead?"

"Reading. It's only a twenty minute drive from my place. Started out as some kind of course at the university on Wednesday evenings. She was forever complaining her brain needed stimulating. I stimulated everything else, no problem, but not the top storey. She'd been to college, got the degree and wasn't doing nothing with it. I could see it was a problem for her. I didn't mind her signing up for this course. In fact I encouraged her. It was supposed to be a couple of hours, but from early on she was coming home after midnight. A bunch of real keenos, the younger ones on the course, some of them full-time students, got used to going on to the pub with the lecturer and that's how the classes grew into something else. I thought nothing of it. I enjoy a drink and a bit of company myself."

"Who was the lecturer?"

"You think I'm going to say Gildersleeve, but you're wrong. It was a guy called Archie Poke."

Diamond did his best to hide his surprise. He'd heard nothing from Monica about a friendship with Poke. She'd spoken of him only with contempt. "He's known to me. In fact, I've met him."

"I can save my breath, then," Bernie said. "He's told you all this."

Diamond shook his head. "It's new to me."

"There isn't much more to tell. After a bit, they started meeting Friday nights as well as Wednesdays."

"In the pub?"

"And sometimes people's houses. Like I said, they called it a club and gave it that crappy name. One Friday night I had a call from Monica saying she thought she was over the limit and unfit to drive, so she was staying over. I was a mug. I still thought nothing of it. It sounded like the right thing to do. These were college people. I thought they spent their time talking about stuff I'd never get my head round."

"Is that what she told you?"

"They studied bits of ancient writing. She called it texts. I thought a text is what you send on a mobile. It was brain-fagging work, but they all liked it because they knew Anglo-Saxon and stuff. After a couple of hours of this they had to unwind, so they'd have a drink and a laugh and sometimes another drink. She had the sense not to get into her car."

"That sounds believable," Diamond said. "In your shoes, I wouldn't have been suspicious."

"Yep, she said when she got home in the morning it had been like her student days, bedding down on someone's floor. I swallowed it. I don't have time to question everything. Maybe if I didn't have a business to run I'd have seen a warning light. Anyhow, this happened a few times. Not every week. But one evening the call didn't come from Monica. It was one of the others. I didn't know her, but I could tell from her voice she'd had a skinful. She wouldn't give her name. She said she was one of the Diphthongs and Monica—she called her Mon, which I never did—Mon had asked her to say she wouldn't be home that night. There was giggling in the background as if a bunch of them were listening to this. I asked her to put Monica on the phone and she said she'd already left with Arch. I asked who Arch was and she just laughed and put the phone down."

"What did you do?"

"Nothing that night. I didn't sleep much, I can tell you. I'm not used to being treated like some schoolkid. I'm a major player, a managing director. I get respect wherever I go. When she came home next day we had a real set-to. She gave me some bilge about feeling ill with stomach pains in the pub the night before and Archie—that was the lecturer, Dr. Poke—had driven her to hospital to A&E and she'd spent most of the night there. I didn't believe a word of it. The others wouldn't have been pissing themselves laughing if she was on her way to hospital. I went over to the university and found Poke and got the truth of it. They didn't go near a bloody hospital. He'd taken her back to his flat and shagged her and it wasn't the first time."

"He used those words?" Diamond said in disbelief.

"That's what he meant. He said when an attractive grown-up woman like that came on to him he wasn't going to say no."

"Did you hit him?"

Bernie scratched his head. "It's strange. I don't know how to explain it. Educated people like him have a way of talking to you that stops you in your tracks. I didn't like what I was hearing, but it came across as the truth. If he'd bullshitted me, I would have landed one on him for sure. He didn't."

"So did you take it out on Monica?"

"Not that time, no. Well . . ." He grinned at a secret memory. "Not really. We had a run-in for sure. I'd caught her out big time. She cried buckets and said she'd been scared to tell me the truth. She'd got in with this crowd and there was heavy drinking and most of them were pairing off. She was chuffed when this Archie started chatting her up rather than any of the other women, telling her she was the star of his class and he might be able to get her a higher degree or some such. She said it made her feel young, like she was a student all over again. I was broken up, but I knew where she was coming from. It was a part of her life I'd never be able to share. But I didn't want to lose her. So we patched it up."

"How?"

"Do you really want to know?" Bernie said, his face reddening. He glanced in Tess's direction. "Cover your ears, sweetheart. I pulled her pants down and smacked her bare arse, followed by the best fuck we ever had. She was amazing. Squealed like six pigs, but didn't shed another tear. After it, she said I should spank her more often and I was the only man she'd ever loved. She promised to leave the course and never go drinking with them again. She meant it. She could have killed Poke for telling me everything."

"She stopped seeing him?"

"Totally. I'm sure of that."

"So how did she meet the professor?"

He sighed and shook his head. "This was the real kick in the teeth. I only found out the truth of it when the divorce was going on. It happened like this. After she left the Diphthongs, she had this gap in her life to fill, so she joined a fund-raising group for the local hospital. They were all women and some of them had been through college like her, so she enjoyed the company. I encouraged her. She liked talking about it. They put on a charity swim and a painting exhibition and all kinds of money-making stunts. One of these was what they called a literary lunch, with some jerk from the television talking about his latest book. All sorts of guests were invited and she was supposed to take care of Gildersleeve, sitting next to him, but, being Monica, she was all gooey-eyed at chatting up a real live professor." He sighed and shrugged. "Same old story."

"Except this time it ended in divorce," Diamond said.

"Two years it went on, under my nose. Other people knew—I still don't know how many—and I only found out when I was laying into one of my business rivals, a dickhead who gazumped my offer for a brownfield site, a power station in London. We were having this up-and-downer and he says you're so thick you don't know what's going on—your own wife having an affair with some poncey professor. I thought he was dragging up the thing with Poke until he told me he was on about heavy sex going on right then. Broke me up, it did."

"You faced her with it?"

He nodded. "Turned out she started seeing Gildersleeve the same year I forgave her for the other affair. We was finished. Anyway, she'd had enough of me. She wanted the divorce and she got it. I'm not a saint. I've had one-night stands, but nothing you could call a relationship. And she knew I was like that."

"She says you treated her savagely when you found out."

His expression didn't alter. "If you want to pull me in for that, it's a fair cop. In the world I come from, she got what was coming to her. I lost all respect for her the day I learned the truth."

There was a silence, broken only when Tess said, "What happened?"

Bernie said, "You don't want to know, darling." He turned back to Diamond. "There's nothing else I can tell you."

The two detectives were driven the short distance into Marlborough by the pilot, who borrowed Tess's four-by-four. He would be staying the night in one of the best hotels in the high street.

Halliwell's car stood alone in the approach to the field. You wouldn't have guessed that the street had been lined with vehicles from end to end only an hour before.

As they left the town and headed for Bath, Diamond said, "What did you make of all that?"

"It's like any witness statement—one side of the story," Halliwell said. "You heard Monica's side of it. I didn't."

"She tells it differently, but they don't disagree on the basics. What you heard from Bernie doesn't conflict with what I got from her, except he added some detail. They both behaved badly—really badly—and they admit it. The bit that was new was Monica sleeping with Poke. It brings another dimension to the case."

"In what way?"

"Come on, Keith. The rivalry between those two shoved together in adjoining offices in Reading University. We knew Gildersleeve had the professor's job—the only one going—and was a block on Poke's career. Now we have another issue altogether."

"But she'd finished with Poke before she met Gildersleeve."

"Yes, and she despises him. He shopped her. He told Bernie she invited him to sleep with her. But we haven't heard Poke's take on it. He may still carry a torch for Monica. Imagine how he felt when he learned his arch-rival was seeing her."

"Even more of a motive."

"Conceivably." Diamond waited while they overtook a rider on horseback and then said, "It's funny."

"What is?"

"Bernie's marriage could be straight out of Chaucer."

19

While Halliwell was negotiating the series of roundabouts at Chippenham, Diamond checked his phone yet again for a text from Ingeborg.

"Did it beep?" Halliwell asked.

"I'm wondering if the damn thing is broken," Diamond said. "It's turned on, but nothing has come through all day."

"There won't be a problem. She'll be in touch when she's ready."

"She's a compulsive texter. It's been a couple of days."

Halliwell smiled.

"What's amusing you?" Diamond asked.

"Just a thought. When it finally comes through, will you understand it? Texting is like another language."

"She knows my limitations. She'll keep it simple. I just wish she'd send something, so we know she's okay."

"Infiltrating the enemy takes time. Shouldn't be rushed. What's she going to text, anyway? 'I'm all right, guv. Don't fret.'"

"Sarcastic bugger."

But he understood the point. Ingeborg herself had told him he sometimes sounded like her father. The responsibility for sending her undercover was hard to live with. He'd pressured her into doing this because she seemed the right choice at the time, and now her initial reluctance kept coming back to torment him. But he had to keep reminding himself that she'd said she might not be in contact for some time. He'd taken that to mean twenty-four hours maximum. She must have meant longer.

She was no babe in arms. She'd worked as an investigative journalist, taking on tough assignments. Treating her as a raw recruit did her no favours, but deep down he had an old-fashioned instinct that women needed protecting.

He said to Halliwell when they were on the long stretch to Corsham, "Am I out of touch?"

"How do you mean, guv?"

"In that field, if you remember, we were talking about endangered species."

"The dormouse."

"Right."

"No way are you a dormouse," Halliwell said.

He seemed to have missed the point and Diamond wasn't going to labour it, so he went back to staring out of the window.

They had almost reached Batheaston when Halliwell picked up the conversation as if it was continuous. "There's the great-crested newt, but I wouldn't compare you to that."

"Thanks."

"And then there are butterflies. When I was growing up I was into butterflies in a big way. Some of them are protected. Do you know what the rarest butterfly in Great Britain is called?"

"No idea."

"It's so rare, it may be extinct."

"Tell me. I can't stand the suspense."

"The large copper."

His phone finally beeped when they reached Bath and were parking in the reserved area in Manvers Street police station. He snatched it from his pocket.

"It's a text."

"There you go," Halliwell said.

"But not from her. It's Paul Gilbert." He'd almost forgotten sending his eager DC to check on Ingeborg's parked car.

The message raised more questions than it answered:

CAR STILL HERE. NO DAMAGE. I WAS ON GB FOR NIGHT VIDEO SHOOT. PRODUCER MARCUS TONE AND BLONDE MAYBE I SEEN FIGHTING BRIDGE NEAR ARNOLFINI. G2G SEE TONE CLIFTON.

He handed the phone to Halliwell. "Impress me. Make sense of that."

"Tricky. 'GB' must mean the *Great Britain*."

"But he says he was on it for a night video shoot. He couldn't have been. He only went this morning."

Halliwell frowned. "Then the 'I' must stand for Ingeborg."

"*She* was at a video shoot?"

"Look, the second 'I' makes it clear. 'Blonde, maybe I.' If so, it seems she got into a fight. Doesn't sound like under-cover work."

"What's 'G2G?'"

"Got to go," Halliwell said. "Our Paul is on his way to Clifton right now to meet this Marcus Tone."

"Idiot. I only gave him instructions to check the car."

"He's always wanted a piece of the action."

"Tell me about it! I had him volunteering to go under-cover." Diamond swung the car door open. "Tone sounds bloody dangerous, whoever he is. Let's see if we've got any-thing on him."

In the CID room, they asked John Leaman to check crimi-nal records for Marcus Tone. Nothing. He had more success when he Googled the name. The man was well known in the pop music industry as a producer of videos. He had his own website and an office in Clifton.

"What time is it?" Diamond said. "Will his office be open as late as this?"

They obtained Tone's home address—also in Clifton—from the electoral register. Diamond was on the point of sending a response car when another text came through.

Paul Gilbert again:

TONE SAYS I AND SINGER LEE LI DRIVEN OFF AFTER FRACAS BY NATHAN HAZAEL WITH MINDERS. NH LIVES WITH LL LEIGH WOODS. FOLLOWING UP. G2R.

"Following up? Is he out of his mind?" Diamond said, hand-ing the phone to Halliwell.

"You can text him, guv."

"Do it for me, and fast. Tell him he's to get back here

now. On no account is he to go to Leigh Woods and mess with Hazael."

Halliwell's thumb pressed out Diamond's instructions. "This may be too late. He'll be well on his way, if not there already. 'G2R' is 'Got to run.' From Clifton he only has to drive over the suspension bridge. Under ten minutes, easy."

Diamond clasped both hands to his head. "He's going to foul up this whole operation and put Ingeborg in more danger than she is already."

Halliwell sent the message and looked up. "Does he know Hazael is a crime baron?"

"He must know, but he won't know Inge is undercover." Diamond hesitated, weighing the new information. Plenty had been conveyed in Gilbert's two messages. On reflection the emergency wasn't quite as desperate as first appeared. He said in a more controlled tone, "On the face of it, she could be doing precisely what she planned, infiltrating the main arms supplier in Bristol. It's starting to make sense: a video shoot on the *Great Britain* of some pop singer who lives with Hazael. If Inge has linked up with her and tricked a way into his house, she's succeeding."

"What about the fracas?"

"Could be the Trojan horse."

Halliwell looked as if the logic had passed him by.

"A way of conning Hazael into taking her in," Diamond explained. "Ingeborg stages a street incident involving this singer. What's her name?"

"Lee Li."

"And comes to her rescue and is invited back to the Hazael mansion. Mission successful. If that's where she is, I'm not in the least surprised she hasn't been texting me."

"Let's hope Paul opens our message, then. Do you want to drive over there?"

Diamond shook his head. "Mustn't put Ingeborg at more risk."

"Surely he'll have the sense to know he can't do anything alone. If 'following up' means putting the house under obser- vation, he can't cause too much of a problem."

"We just have to mark time and stay calm, Keith," said the man who a few minutes before had practically torn out his hair—what there was of it.

They drank coffee and updated Leaman on the Marlborough trip. He kept his usual poker face and said, "Do I gather from all this that Bernie Wefers is no longer the prime suspect?"

"Put it this way," Diamond said. "He had a powerful motive for killing the man who stole his wife, and he didn't deny threatening him outside the divorce court, but it became obvious his anger was directed mainly at Monica."

Keith Halliwell added his own observation. "And the pilot's log in the helicopter suggests Bernie wasn't in Bath on the day of the auction. He'll have needed to arrange a contract killing."

Leaman nodded. "But that's what happened. Someone hired a set of gunmen."

"Which raises the question whether Bernie would murder by proxy," Diamond said. "I could be wrong, but my impression is that he'd want to be there to witness the killing. He's not the sort to take revenge at arm's length."

Leaman got up and crossed the room to the whiteboard where the faces of the principal witnesses and suspects were displayed. As the architect and manager of the incident room, he never missed an opportunity to demonstrate its usefulness. "So Bernie moves down in the pecking order and Dr. Poke moves up."

"Certainly. Until today we had Poke down as a suspect because of professional rivalry, but we didn't know he'd slept with Monica," Diamond said. "Neither of the pair said a word to us about the Diphthongs."

"They wouldn't volunteer it," Halliwell said. "Doesn't do either of them much credit."

"I haven't met Poke," Leaman said, "but isn't he just the sort of creepy guy who would think up an underhand way of removing the professor from the scene?"

"No question," Diamond said, "and there would be extra satisfaction from having him killed just at the moment he was bidding for the big prize—the Wife of Bath. We need another session with Poke."

"And Monica?" Halliwell said.

"Monica, too." Diamond's thoughts returned to the conversation he'd had with Paloma, the wacky theory that Monica had hired the gunmen herself to prevent her husband from acquiring the *Wife of Bath* and the plot had literally misfired and resulted in Gildersleeve's death. Too way out to mention to colleagues? He still thought so. "She has some explaining to do as well."

Allowing that it had been a long, stressful afternoon, Halliwell was sharp this evening. "How about this? Secretly, Monica was still attracted to Dr. Poke. She discovered she'd made a terrible mistake marrying Gildersleeve. He was boring and locked into fourteenth century poetry. The sex was a disappointment—if it happened at all. We know she has an appetite for sex."

"I can see where this is going," Diamond said.

"Doesn't the auction present an opportunity to get rid of him and also reward Poke with the professorship? She could have hatched the plot on her own or in collaboration with him."

"Not bad," Diamond said. "They were cool about each other under interview and that's what you'd expect from two killers working together."

Leaman nodded. "I like it. But they'd still need to find the gunmen to stage the hold-up."

"She'll have met all sorts in her time with Bernie," Halliwell said. "She'd know who to contact."

Leaman picked up a marker pen and drew a line on the whiteboard linking Monica's name to Poke's and adding a question mark. Then he pointed to another name. "Shouldn't we also look at Sturgess, the British Museum man? He was the rival bidder."

"When you say 'British Museum man,' he was only acting as an agent for the museum," Diamond said. "His firm is independent. They must get some kind of commission or fee."

"They'd be under pressure to acquire the carving for as little as possible," Leaman said. "When the bidding went way past the valuation, Sturgess must have been worried. It could have gone higher. The gunmen put a stop to that."

"You're not suggesting Sturgess is behind the hold-up?"

"We haven't looked into his background. There could be other stuff we don't know about."

"Do it, then," Diamond said.

Leaman continued to study his board. "Is there anyone else from the auction we might be overlooking?"

"The glass lady," Diamond said.

"Who's she?" Halliwell asked.

"Miss Topham, from Brighton. The only witness able to give us anything useful on the gunmen, a scar like a moon crater on the back of the neck of the one who stopped the auction. She's known as the glass lady because she specialises in glass objects."

"We don't have a picture of her, unfortunately," Leaman said, ever the perfectionist.

"I'm not losing any sleep over that," Diamond said. "I can't see Miss Topham having anything to do with the shooting."

"The auctioneer?" Halliwell suggested.

"I got his picture from the internet," Leaman said, pointing to the beaming apple-cheeked face above a pink cravat. "Denis Doggart. He's well known."

"And in the clear," Diamond said. "I can't think of any reason why he would sabotage his own auction, can you?"

"Who's left?" Halliwell asked.

Apart from the victim, the only other individual displayed on the board was the Wife of Bath.

Two hours on, they remained in the CID room. Diamond had sent out for beer and sandwiches. He didn't want to leave without hearing from Ingeborg. But he was in a better frame of mind now, satisfied that she must have got inside the Hazael mansion. Her silence was understandable.

Finally, about nine thirty, his phone went.

It wasn't a text this time. He was grateful for a real, old-fashioned call. But not so thrilled to see on the display that it was from Paul Gilbert.

"Yes?"

The voice was little more than a rustle.

"Is that you, Paul? Speak up. Where are you?"

"Leigh Woods." He was still barely audible.

"At Hazael's place?"

"I told you I was going there." The voice trailed away.

Diamond turned to Halliwell. "It's no use. I can barely hear him."

Halliwell took the phone and worked the keys.

The volume improved by a few microdecibels. Gilbert was saying, ". . . up a tree."

"I missed some of that," Diamond said. "You did what?"

"Climbed over the wall."

"You said something about a tree."

"I'm up the tree now. There's a guard dog."

"And now a dog has got you trapped?"

"For the time being. It's getting dark here. I'm hoping it will lose interest and I can make a run for it."

"I wouldn't count on it. Didn't you get my text?"

"Yes, but too late. I was already inside. I thought I was doing the right thing, guv. Ingeborg is with this singer, Lee Li, who was being filmed on the ship. They all think Inge is a journalist."

"You didn't let on that she isn't?"

"To Marcus the director? No. But there was an ugly scene on the horned bridge at the quayside. The thing is, Lee Li wants out. She's been trying to escape from Hazael. Marcus was roughed up and both women were driven away by Hazael and his minders. It's likely they're being held here. I came to check, but the place is a fortress."

"No one told you to go there."

"I used my initiative, guv. Sorry."

"You'd better use it to get out, you pillock. And without anyone knowing. I can't send a rescue party and risk a major alert. Keep us informed."

With a sigh and shake of his head, Diamond pocketed the phone. He liked young Gilbert, but this was a near disaster. He told the others to leave. He'd stay on for a while and see this through. They knew better than to argue.

He would use the time catching up on emails and paperwork in his office. There was sure to be masses of stuff to be got through. He stepped inside and sank into his comfortable leather chair and eyed the in tray without disturbing it. He reached out to touch the spacebar on the keyboard and watched his screensaver light up, an old film poster of the Margaret Lockwood and James Mason classic from 1945, *The Wicked Lady*. After today, the title had extra resonance. He continued to gaze at it and thought about Monica and her talent for picking up unsuitable men, a brute of a builder, a one-track professor and a diphthong. With better judgement, she might have had a long, fulfilling marriage. Too lusty for her own good, she'd made terrible choices. But was she a wicked lady? He couldn't see it—yet.

A sense of unease with his surroundings was keeping him from opening the emails. Something wasn't right. Subconsciously he'd noticed an abnormality, but subconscious it remained. He scratched his head, rotated his chair and looked at the ceiling for inspiration. His eyes returned to the screen and the film title.

Then he knew.

The *Wife of Bath* was missing from the room.

20

The shower was bliss.

Ingeborg lingered longer than she normally would, trying all the adjustments, especially the massage, easing her back against the powerful jet and enjoying the relief on her aching neck and shoulders. She didn't think Marcus had caused any serious damage yanking her head back, but some of the muscles had stiffened. It wasn't much consolation that her attacker would be nursing a sore leg.

Taking a shower always stimulated her brain. Better be honest with myself, she decided, and admit that the under-cover work hasn't yet delivered anything, in spite of all the action in the last twenty-four hours. The good news is that I'm in Nathan's house and on speaking terms with him, but I still have no proof that he supplied the Webley that killed Professor Gildersleeve, a necessary step before—hopefully—winkling out the identity of the killer.

So she wouldn't be calling Peter Diamond to report on progress.

Not yet.

Even so, she was tantalisingly close to finding out. She wanted keenly to be the one who nailed the killer. It could be as simple as getting the name from Nathan. How cool it would be to pull the rabbit from the hat and let the CID team conclude that all the painstaking work at the crime scene and by forensics, all the interviews and statements, the trips to Reading, Bridgwater and North Petherton, were superfluous. In reality they wouldn't be, because evidence is needed for the trial, but it would feel like a triumph. She could picture the long faces, hear the comments, taste the bitterness. Mean—but understandable. John Leaman's face would be a picture.

Getting the information was another thing. Extracting the name of the secret client was a tough call. She doubted whether Nathan kept records on paper or computer of his dealings. He'd shown in the car that he was canny, well capable of discussing how he operated without giving anything away that could incriminate him or anyone else. He hadn't amassed his fortune by shopping his clients.

How could it be done, then?

She ran through the possibilities. Talking to the staff was an obvious one, except that they acted as if they'd rather cut their own throats than give anything away even if they knew it. She was pretty certain Lee wasn't privy to all of Nathan's secrets even though she'd said something about telling all. Loosening his tongue with drink was another option she rejected. He wasn't going to be around for drinks. He'd said he had business to deal with.

Then an idea came.

If Nathan had a weak point, it was his enchantment with Lee. The pretty little singer had obviously got to work on him to further her music career. More recently she'd put her efforts into plotting her escape. He'd already forgiven her. She wouldn't welcome it, but he was in thrall to her.

Lee had to be persuaded to get him off guard so he would spill the beans.

That settled, Ingeborg stepped out of the shower and reached for one of those fluffy white towels.

At Lee's suggestion, they took a chilled bottle of Chablis and two glasses into the jacuzzi in her gym. "We can talk there in private. I'm still tense from this afternoon and I'm sure you must be aching all over. You can use one of my costumes."

Ingeborg was at least a size larger, but the bikini had ties so it was easy to get into. She followed Lee into the churning water and sat beside her.

"Your arm is bruised," Lee said after they'd clinked glasses.

"It's nothing."

"Did Marcus hurt you?"

"Only at the time. He was forcing my head back. I thought my hair would come out at the roots. His ribs came off worse."

"What was the fight about?"

"He thought I'd led him into a trap. I didn't. When Nathan and his men blocked off the bridge I was as surprised as Marcus was."

"I saw it from a little way off. I was waiting on the other side, in front of the Watershed," Lee said.

"What you don't know is that Nathan kidnapped me on the ship—tied me up and brought me here. When I phoned you this morning, he was sitting right beside me. He was using me to get you back."

"That's awful. I'm sorry."

"Me, too. It wasn't nice, deceiving you. But I know why he went to all that trouble. He adores you."

Lee squeezed her eyes shut as if the words hurt and then opened them. "I know, and I feel guilty. I encouraged him. In spite of everything, he's . . . Well, look around you. He altered his house for me, built this huge extension. I went along with it, slept with him, let him think I was in love with him, but I wasn't. I was faking. He's been so helpful in my music career that I *am* fond of him, but not enough to share his life forever."

"You tried to escape."

"I'm getting really well known in the pop world now and I need professional help to guide me. Nathan calls himself my manager and tries his best, but in all truth he doesn't know much about the business or the people in it. It's not what you know, but who you know. If I want to make it big, mega big, I need to be in there with the movers and shakers."

"Makes sense."

"I was saying this to Marcus when we first discussed the video and he said he was thinking himself that I needed a better manager. He thought I could simply walk away. He didn't understand that I'm a prisoner here. Nice prison, yes, but not easy to escape from. I told him my relationship made breaking away from Nathan incredibly difficult. So Marcus offered to help. He said I could stay with him in Clifton until I got my career sorted out. No hidden agenda. Actually I think he's gay. He was acting from the goodness of his heart."

"And probably didn't know much about Nathan. He does now."

"You're so right—which is why I feel so bad that he got roughed up. He had no idea what he was taking on. I should have warned him Nathan wouldn't give me up without a fight, but I was thinking only of myself. Do you think he's okay?"

"Marcus? He'll be fine. It could have been a lot worse. They could have used guns."

Lee put her hand to her mouth. "That would have been awful." Significantly, she didn't show disbelief that Nathan might have access to a gun.

Ingeborg said, "I tried to make sure they weren't armed. Nathan told me he wouldn't put you at risk and he meant it." She took a long sip of the wine. "But you were going to tell me more about him. I'm interested."

"You won't put this into print?"

"God, no. I may be a hack, but I have my standards."

"Okay." Lee rested her glass on the side and brought her arms around her raised knees. "Nathan won't ever say how he got to be so rich, even when I ask. He gives the sort of smart answers he was giving you in the car today. I'm naturally curious to know the truth about the man I go to bed with."

"Who wouldn't be?"

"He does heaps of business on the phone and then people—nearly always men—come to see him here. They never stay long. And he doesn't employ a PA or a secretary like you would expect for somebody running a business. The guys who work for him are all part of the housekeeping side of things."

"Or protection," Ingeborg said.

"He calls that housekeeping as well. I guess it is, in a way.

But you'd think he'd need someone to keep records of his dealings. There don't seem to be any records. It's all word of mouth. I asked him once if he employed an accountant and he laughed and said something about mental arithmetic."

"So what's the explanation?"

"I can't say for certain, but I'm afraid it must be illegal."

"I can't disagree with that," Ingeborg said.

Lee looked right and left and then leaned forward. "I was thinking drugs."

"Really?"

"When he talks about dealing in hardware I think he must mean hard drugs, like cocaine and heroin. It's a play on words, and it obviously amuses him."

"That passed me by, I have to say," Ingeborg said in all sincerity. "Is there any proof?"

"Nothing for certain. He doesn't do drugs himself, I'm sure of that. But then dealers are in it to make money, not to use the stuff themselves."

"If he's dealing on a big scale he must have a stash in the house somewhere. Where does he store it, do you think?"

"I haven't seen all over the house. There's a locked room on the same floor as his bedroom. One afternoon when he was out, I did some exploring upstairs, hoping to find out more. I've often heard him go up there with his customers, as he calls them."

"Why would he do that?" Ingeborg asked, trying to sound calm while her heart was pumping harder than the jacuzzi. "The customers don't need to see what he stores up there."

A look of uncertainty crossed Lee's face. "I hadn't thought about that."

"It would be a huge risk, showing them his stash of drugs. A dealer doesn't want people knowing how much he has."

"That's true." She was crestfallen.

"Did you get into the room?"

"No. Like I say, it's kept locked." Lee hesitated. "If he doesn't deal in drugs, what else could he have in there? A machine for printing banknotes? No, he wouldn't invite people in there to see. How about fake paintings? He'd need to let the customers have a sight of them if he was selling."

"He isn't the artistic type," Ingeborg said. "Believe me, I've met a few artists and Nathan doesn't cut it as a Leonardo. Even a Picasso."

They both laughed.

"I don't think I've seen a single picture in this house."

"You're right." Lee sighed. "I'm running out of ideas. Do you have a theory yourself?"

Ingeborg did, but she wasn't ready to reveal it. First, she needed to coax more information from Lee. "Maybe there's something to be learned from the people he calls his customers. Are there any regulars?"

"I don't think so. The ones I've seen have been different each time. And they're all sorts, going by their cars, beat-up old bangers to Rolls-Royces."

"Local people, would you say?"

"I can't tell. I haven't spoken to many of them."

"Do they come alone?"

"Nearly always, and almost all of them are men."

"Thinking back over the last two or three weeks, can you remember any in particular?"

"Now you're asking." Lee sank up to her neck in the churning water, and for a moment Ingeborg thought she was about to duck the question as well. "I did open the door last week to a man who came in a Range Rover and said he was sorry he was early, but he'd miscalculated the journey, so I guess he came from a long way off. He said his name was Rollo, and he was expected at three. This was about two thirty and Nathan was having a siesta, as he calls it. Anyway, I sat Rollo down in one of the living rooms and gave him a magazine to look at. I'm sure it was his first time here. He was so twitchy, as if he was nervous of meeting Nathan."

"Do they often seem nervous, his visitors?"

"Now you mention it, they do. A man who came one day last month asked if he could use the toilet as soon as he came through the door. He almost pushed me over, he was in such a hurry. I never discovered what his name was. As a rule, they're not keen to give their names."

"And none of them say what they're here for?

"Not to me. They'll say they have an appointment with Nathan, or Mr. Hazael, if they're really being polite. And of course, most times Nathan or one of the staff lets them in. The exceptions are the valuers, who come to look at the armour and stuff we're trying to sell off. They nearly always have a visiting card and show it as soon as they arrive. And they treat the place as if they own it."

"Nathan was telling me about this. He wants to give the house a more modern look."

"Yes, but he discovered that some of the armour is really old and valuable, and he doesn't want it undersold. That's why he had a series of valuations done. Most of the swords are worth four or five grand and some of the armour even more."

"Wow! Nathan could ditch his main business and live off the proceeds of what's hanging on the walls."

"I don't think he'd enjoy that," Lee said, treating the remark seriously. "He gets a lot of pleasure from his business. It seems to give him a sense of power, and guys can't get enough of that. I'm different. I want fame and attention and loads of awards. He's happy to keep a low profile, as he calls it. And he seems to make plenty of money."

Ingeborg decided this was the time for straight talking. She dipped lower in the water, on a level with Lee. "Have you ever thought he might be supplying criminals with guns?"

Lee bit her lip. "I don't want to believe that. I hate guns." Something in her eyes suggested she'd known all along and refused to admit the truth. She glanced away. "Where would he get them from and where would he keep them?"

"I can answer the second part. He'd have them in that locked room."

The singer's look returned to Ingeborg, fixing on her as if she'd only just noticed her. She didn't speak.

"It could be the reason why he invites his customers up there, to choose which weapon they want."

Lee had lost all the colour the warm water had given her. "Oh God, you could be right. I'm living with an illegal arms dealer."

"Have you ever seen him with a gun?"

"A shotgun, but he says he has a licence for it. He shoots rabbits and pigeons sometimes. I don't go anywhere near."

"Small arms? Revolvers and automatics?"

She swallowed hard and nodded. "At one time he set up a target behind the house and was firing at it with one of his customers. They were using handguns. When I asked him about it later, if it was legal, he said pistol shooting is an Olympic sport."

"Sounds more like a demonstration than a competition. There are strict rules about firearms. He'll need to have a firearms certificate as well as one for the shotgun. The guns have to be stored securely to prevent unauthorised persons from using them. The law doesn't state exactly how, but you get inspected by the police and they insist on a steel gun cabinet that locks."

Lee shook her head. "I've never seen anything like that in this house."

"It needs to be flush to the wall and secured with coach bolts so it can't be prised away."

"How do you know all this?"

Went overboard there, Ingeborg chided herself. "I'm a journalist. We're picking up information all the time."

"I'm scared now."

"It's only a theory," Ingeborg said, backtracking a little.

"But he must keep the shotgun somewhere. And the handguns. It all adds up," Lee said, crossing her arms over her chest.

"You'll be okay. He'd never point a gun at you."

"If I threaten to leave him, he might."

"He loves you."

"But I need to break up with him. What am I going to do?"

Lee's distress was getting to Ingeborg and it was impossible to give honest advice—another consequence of going undercover. She dug deep for the right words. "I think you need to empower yourself more."

"How exactly?"

"By learning the truth about him and what goes on here. If we can find out for certain that he's providing criminals with firearms, you've got every reason for leaving him. And if he objects, you threaten to report him."

Lee clasped her hand to her head. "That seems so ungrateful."

"Don't look at it like that. He's kept things from you that could get you into trouble as an accessory. If he's investigated and you're living with him it will be difficult to prove you didn't know what was going on."

She nodded. "I know what you're going to say. I must work out a way of getting inside that room. God knows what I'll find there."

Enough evidence to put away Nathan for the foreseeable future, not to mention some of the top criminals in the south-west, Ingeborg thought. Ballistics would have weeks of fun finding which weapons had been used to commit crimes in and around Bristol. But the main prize would be a list of Nathan's clients. Surely he must need to keep a record of who hired or bought which weapons. And surely it was inside that locked room.

"Listen, if you can get the key," she said, "I'll look inside while you keep Nathan distracted. Does he carry a set of keys with him?"

Lee nodded.

"You can bet the key to the gun room is one of them. Will he want to sleep with you tonight? He was all over you in the car."

"I guess he will."

"He's mentally shaken. He's looking for reassurance. When he undresses, where does he put his clothes?"

"Over a chair mostly. If he's had a few drinks or he's eager to get into bed with me, they'll be scattered over the floor."

"Does he remove the keys from his pocket?"

"No."

"Do you think you could get them and pass them to me if I wait outside the bedroom?"

Lee looked alarmed.

"When he's in the bathroom or something?"

Lee was looking as if she wished she'd never started this conversation.

Ingeborg said, "Is he a heavy sleeper?"

"Not especially."

"After sex he is—I bet."

"I suppose."

"Could you do it then? Is he likely to make love to you soon after going to bed?"

She nodded.

"Let me guess. He doesn't take long."

A fleeting smile. "That's how I put up with it."

"You could wait twenty minutes and, when he's breathing deeply, slip out of bed, get the keys and put them outside the door. I'll be ready outside. Could you do that? It's really important that you know the truth about what's going on."

"I suppose. But how will you get them back to me?"

"Same way. I'll open the door—or you can leave it ajar—and I'll put them inside. You can choose the right moment—go to the bathroom or whatever—replace them in his pocket. Job done."

"You make it sound so simple."

"I'll need to do a recce first, so I know which door to unlock. Is the gun room anywhere near the guest room I'm in?"

"Very close. We can go up there now if you like. We both need to change into some fresh clothes." She hesitated. "I just remembered a saying: good clothes open all doors."

"Nice," Ingeborg said, "but I think we'll need the key, even so."

21

The risk was high, but the prize was the big one.

Ingeborg sat on the bed in the guest suite, ready for the night's adventure. She'd changed into black sweatpants and a loose-fitting top Lee had found for her and she was wearing her own trainers.

These nervous minutes before anything happened were a chance to focus on the whole point of the undercover operation. Getting into the locked room wasn't just about confirming Nathan was the major supplier of weapons to armed gangs. She needed evidence that linked him to the saleroom killing. Logic suggested that some record of transactions was kept secure, inside the room, with the arsenal itself. *Surely* Nathan kept an inventory or something. He would need it in there each time he made a visual check of the guns. The best guess was a notebook with everything listed by date. Another possibility was a card index. She doubted whether he trusted a computer with such sensitive information.

She had her phone in her pocket. Some photos of the interior of the gun room would be useful. Even better, if it existed, the notebook. If she could find and photograph the names of recent clients, the weapons themselves would be of secondary interest.

She checked the time. Eleven twenty. Lee had said Nathan would be ready for bed before midnight. Right now the couple were in the main sitting room downstairs watching a film that was due to end soon. At Ingeborg's suggestion Lee had arranged for one of the staff to serve champagne in celebration of her homecoming.

"Make sure Nathan drinks most of it," Ingeborg had stressed, bearing in mind that Lee had already sunk a couple of glasses of Chablis. She didn't want her accomplice falling asleep or falling over.

The couple would come past the guest room on their way up to bed, so she was listening up.

Another ten minutes went by.

Huge relief when she heard footsteps in the corridor. Soft giggling, too. The champagne seemed to be working.

The steps grew fainter and she heard the click of their bedroom door being closed.

Now it was a question of how long to wait before making a move. She didn't want to risk stationing herself outside before they were settled. There was always a risk Nathan would think of some reason to go downstairs again. Allowing time for him to undress and use the bathroom (he didn't shower at night, Lee had said), he ought to be in bed and proving his manhood inside the next twenty minutes. Lee, never short of an apt idiom, had confided that the lovemaking was like two shakes of a lamb's tail. After that, it was a question of how soon lover boy would drift into a deep sleep.

Say half an hour from now.

Just after midnight.

Ingeborg didn't want Lee in more trouble over this. There were limits to Nathan's tolerance, however much he doted on his pet pop star. Lee's openness was both brave and troubling. Subterfuge was foreign to Lee's nature. She was deeply uncomfortable about breaking up with Nathan after he had spent so freely to launch her in the music business. But she was driven by this overwhelming ambition to succeed as a singer and she knew the time had come to move on. The complicating factor was Nathan's emotional state. From all that had been said, the relationship had started out in a businesslike way with Lee trading sex for Nathan's backing. He'd invested money, not love, and neither of them had expected much to change. But Lee's winning personality had softened and mellowed the tough professional criminal and his desire had grown into love. In this state he was capable of being badly hurt.

If tonight's plan went wrong, and he knew he had been betrayed, all bets were off.

Once again, Ingeborg was forced to remind herself that her mission came before everything else. Come what may, she must get inside that room.

The minutes dragged by. She fastened and unfastened her hair a couple of times. Putting it up made her feel more positive. She wasn't sure why.

Midnight arrived.

Taking care not to make any sound, she eased the door open and tiptoed along the corridor, sidestepping the boards that might creak. The whole house was as silent as falling snow.

On her right, she passed the locked door. The location of everything was all so convenient—and so fraught with danger.

At the end of the corridor she flattened herself against the wall to the left of the door. Really there was no way she could hide if Nathan got out of bed and looked out, but the semblance of stealth helped her nerves.

No sound from within.

She imagined Lee, tense and apprehensive after the lamb's tail had stopped shaking, waiting for the regular breathing that would mean Nathan had drifted into post-coital slumber. Slipping out of bed wouldn't be a problem. If the movement woke him, she could say she was going to the bathroom. The dangerous part would be picking up his trousers and rifling the pocket for his keys. Difficult to explain that away. And next there was the added challenge of creeping to the door, turning the handle, opening it and handing over the keys, all without making a sound.

What could she say if he woke up? I must have been sleepwalking?

Ingeborg snapped out of this destructive train of thought. How many times did she have to tell herself that empathising with Lee was unhelpful? What mattered was her own plan of action.

More time went by and there was no sound from inside the bedroom. She checked. Almost 12:15.

Doubts crept into her mind. Had Lee fallen asleep? Or become so petrified that she couldn't go through with the plan?

And now her right leg started cramping below the knee, a familiar but excruciatingly painful spasm that usually made her cry out. All this tension was getting to her. Gritting her teeth, she tried stretching the muscle, working her foot up and down, hoping the stiffness would go, but now it was in her thoughts, it was difficult to shift.

About 12:25, the door opened and a small hand emerged with a set of keys resting on the palm.

Lee had delivered.

Heart going like the climax of a drum solo, Ingeborg closed her fingers over the bunch and backed away.

The door closed.

Now it was up to Ingeborg. She crept the few steps to the door of the locked room and stood outside in the dim light examining the keys on the ring. Two at least were of the Yale type. This was more of a mortise lock, needing a longer key. She found one and tried it, her hand shaking.

It wouldn't turn.

A second key made a metallic rasp as she pushed it in.

She froze, fearful she must have been heard.

After waiting a few seconds, she turned her wrist and felt the key engage and shift the lock. She grasped the handle and eased open the door.

The interior was even darker than the corridor. She had to keep the door ajar for a source of light. For a couple of seconds she stood in the doorway, allowing her eyes to adjust.

But she wasn't standing in an armoury. She was in a bathroom. There wasn't a gun in sight.

Her expectation dashed, she closed the door behind her and felt for the cord that switched on the light. It was no illusion. This was a fully tiled bathroom in duck-egg blue and white, with an oval bathtub set into the corner, a shower cabinet, toilet, bidet, vanity cabinet, wash basin, towel rail and mirrors. There were matching blue towels, a white candle-wick bathmat, facecloths, soap and toilet paper. Toothpaste, electric toothbrush, shampoo and a shaver. Even a toilet bag.

She couldn't have been more devastated if she'd gone through the gates of heaven and found it was Terminal 3 at Heathrow. All the speculation, the planning, the risk-taking—for this, a sodding bathroom. She could have wept.

But why would anyone keep a bathroom locked from the outside? It appeared to be set up for regular use, but who would use it? Only Nathan or Lee, and they had an *en suite* bathroom. Did Nathan have this as a back-up, for when Lee was using the other one? It had the look of a man's bathroom.

She felt the towels and the facecloths. They had the fluffy texture that you only find straight from the shop. The tooth-paste tube was new. The shampoo and the shower cream hadn't been used. Did he insist on everything being fresh each time he came in here?

Her suspicion grew that this bathroom wasn't all it appeared.

What if the guns were stored out of sight? They could be in the vanity cupboard or behind the cladding around the bathtub or even in the toilet cistern.

There were drawers and a cupboard in the vanity unit below the hand basin. The cupboard contained spare toilet rolls. Too bloody obvious, she told herself. If this was built to frustrate a search, you wouldn't use the cupboard. That was the first place anyone would look.

She opened each of the drawers and found more towels. As silently as possible, she removed all three drawers completely from the unit and stacked them on the floor. The space inside was dark. Kneeling on the mat, she reached inside and felt with her hand. Her palm flattened against the solid wall. She probed up and down. Nothing was hidden there. Nor was there any kind of opening in the floor.

The wood cladding was more promising. The bath had been plumbed into a corner and had substantial space around it. Moreover, it was set into a platform at the end of the room with two low steps up from the floor level, all built with the same veneered board. Behind and out of sight there was enough room for several rifles and assault weapons as well as handguns.

Was there a simple way of getting inside? Presumably Nathan needed easy access to show his wares to his customers.

On hands and knees Ingeborg made a search for a panel that could be lifted, or a hidden hinge. She spent the next fifteen minutes examining the joins. Everything appeared to be tightly screwed in and each piece was flush with the next. Whoever had made this had done a professional job, which encouraged her to think there must be a clever way in, a sliding panel or a loose board that lifted up.

She broke two fingernails trying.

Finally she accepted that if there was a trick, she hadn't detected it. The only way she would get a look behind the cladding was by forcing a piece out. Any damage would then be obvious.

It didn't take long to come to a decision. Tonight's opportunity wasn't likely to be repeated. But what could she use as a tool?

In the toilet bag was a manicure set, with scissors and a nail file.

The nail file would make a serviceable screwdriver. She chose a large panel in front of the bath and got to work. Getting the screw to move at all wasn't easy, but with strength born of desperation she got it to turn. Out it came.

She started on the screws directly below. They would have been driven in using a power tool and she had only muscle power and a four-inch nail file. Each one was a brute to move. Only the extreme urgency and her persistence finally brought a result. The two extra screws came out and she was able to prise out one end of the panel. It made a horrible squeak and she gasped and froze.

No sound came from along the corridor.

She got her fingers behind the panel and tugged. The gap widened.

She put her arm right in and groped in the space. Nothing was there. Her fingertips made contact with the underside of the bathtub.

No guns. All this effort had achieved nothing.

In despair now, she pushed the panel back into position. It would have to be left without screws. She didn't have the strength to replace them.

One last possibility remained: the cistern. Every police officer who has ever done a drugs raid knows water tanks are favourite hiding places for items wrapped in waterproof bags and strapped to the sides.

Maybe a handgun or two could be secreted in this one.

She stepped close and lifted the heavy porcelain lid.

It was a normal, functioning cistern filled with water. Nothing was in there that shouldn't be.

At this of all moments, the cramp in her leg returned, rock-hard and agonising, sending a shockwave through her entire body. Her fingers flexed and lost their grip on the cistern lid. It slammed down with an impact loud enough to wake the entire population of Bristol.

In panic and in pain, Ingeborg's reaction was to get out fast. She limped to the door and started along the corridor towards her own room.

Before she'd hobbled more than three steps, she heard the door at the end thrust open, followed by Nathan's voice yelling, "Stop right there," followed immediately by a shout from Lee: "Don't run, Ingeborg. He's got a gun."

She wasn't stupid. Hand-held guns are never wholly accurate, but there was a strong chance of being shot or hit by a ricochet. She raised her arms and waited. Ahead of her, someone else appeared, one of Nathan's minders wearing nothing but boxer shorts. He, also, was pointing a gun.

"Grab her," Nathan ordered.

She backed against the wall, hands spread in a calming gesture. "It's okay. I'm not in for a fight."

The minder made sure by stepping up to her side and pressing the muzzle of the gun into her neck.

The bathroom door was still open and the light was left on. Nathan—in silk floral pyjamas—padded towards it and looked inside. Lee, in a baby-doll nightdress, was framed in the doorway of their bedroom looking terrified.

"I should have known better than to let a fucking journalist sleep in my house," Nathan said. "How the fuck did you get hold of my keys?"

Before Lee could say a word, Ingeborg said, "You were both asleep so I crept in and took them. I need drugs. I thought you must have some hard stuff hidden in the locked room." In the situation, this was the best story she could think up. If nothing else, it shifted any blame from Lee.

"You're a bloody junkie?" Nathan said. "You came to my house looking for drugs? I don't believe this. Roll up your sleeves and show us your arms."

"Cocaine," she said at once. "I snort coke."

"Cobblers. You wouldn't come here if you wanted coke."

"It's got to be somewhere," she said, at full stretch to sound convincing. "You live in style. Everyone says you're importing. How else could you make it so big?"

"Someone's been stringing you along," he said, giving just a suggestion that he believed her. "Drugs are a filthy trade. I wouldn't lower myself to deal with the scum who take them. Tell her, Lily. She's got it all wrong."

In a strained, small voice, Lee said, "Nathan doesn't sell drugs."

Nathan advanced on Ingeborg and she thought he was going to strike her. Instead he put his face so close that she could feel and smell his bad breath. "You made one hell of a mistake coming here, Miss so-called Smith, telling a load of shit to Lily about getting in the papers, when all you wanted was to invade our privacy, abuse my hospitality, nick the keys from my trouser pocket and look for flake in my bathroom. You don't have a clue who you're dealing with.

I ought to feed you to the dogs, but I'll think of something better." To the minder holding the gun, he said, "She can go in the tower room for the rest of the night. Get her out of my fucking sight."

22

Locked in the tower room, Ingeborg refused to give way to despair. There had to be positives. She was still in the place where she needed to be, Nathan's mansion, even if she no longer had the guest room. She remained undercover. No one knew she was a police officer. If her hastily concocted story was believed, she was a cokehead journalist on the hunt for drugs. And she still had an ally in the house. By telling Nathan she'd actually entered the bedroom to steal his keys, she'd removed any blame from Lee—provided Lee had the inner strength and wit to deny any part in the incident. But she wasn't pinning her hopes on Lee. She had to find her own way of dealing with the setback.

That was how it was in her thinking: a setback, not a disaster.

Nathan's appalled reaction to her suggestion that he had drugs in the house had come over as genuine. And he had revealed more than he intended with his comment that she didn't have a clue who she was dealing with. He may as well have said that while he was not into drugs, he was still a supplier, but not a supplier of what had been suggested. It was as if dealing in firearms was a clean trade.

His outrage at having his secret bathroom invaded was more than just anger that his privacy was violated. His near panic suggested Ingeborg had come close to exposing him.

But she'd found only soap and towels.

The bathroom remained a mystery and a challenge. Lee had said Nathan often took his visitors in there. *Took visitors into a bathroom?*

Before tonight, she'd been confident the room was used

for storing the guns he supplied to his gangster clients. Lee had appeared to agree.

In her head she reconstructed that bathroom unit by unit: cupboards, drawers, bath, shower, hand basin, toilet. The tiling was sound, the walls and ceiling solid. The floor had been covered in square ceramic tiles that felt firm underfoot, suggesting they were on a base of cement. None were loose. There were no tell-tale gaps between them. So far as she could tell, it was a fully equipped, fully functioning bathroom, except that it didn't function. It was not in regular use.

Again she asked herself why. Nathan and Lee had the *en suite* shower and toilet. If they didn't choose to share, Nathan could easily have stepped along the corridor. Evidently he didn't, because all the toilet items were shop new.

She was convinced the room was used for something more sinister. The washing facility was just a bluff. Had to be.

She tried putting herself into Nathan's situation. Suppose she were storing weapons on a big scale. Suppose it was common knowledge that she was an illegal supplier, known to the police as well as the criminal world. Wouldn't she need a secret armoury tucked away in some part of the house no one would suspect? Suppose it appeared to be a bathroom. Suppose the bathroom was just a front.

An idea dawned.

A big, bold concept.

She was going to need a second inspection of the secret bathroom. And it had to be tonight, before dawn. After being woken in the night, people invariably sink into a deeper sleep. This basic physical reaction would apply to the minders, as well as Nathan and Lee. By defying her body clock and stay-ing awake, Ingeborg could gain an advantage. The remaining hours of the night offered her the best opportunity of not disturbing the others—or being disturbed.

First challenge: how to escape from the tower room. The floor and walls were solid, the window too narrow to squeeze through.

What about the ceiling? Presumably she was in part of the original house, so the ceiling would be constructed of traditional lath and plaster. Logically, this was the escape route. The room was at the top of a virtually free-standing tower with a conical tiled roof over it. She was certain she was the only inhabitant, so it was unlikely she'd be heard. She could scrape, scratch, hammer at the plaster to her heart's content. But what with?

The ceiling was out of reach, about nine feet above floor level. She upended the latrine bucket and stepped on and off to test the extra height it would give her. Not enough. She tugged the blankets from the primitive camp bed and examined the wooden frame. Hinged at the centre and mounted on six folding legs, it would make a cumbersome battering ram, but it might do. It was not too heavy to lift. She grasped one end and hoisted it to the vertical. Balancing the frame on its end, she stepped on the bucket. Then she braced herself and thrust the bed upwards so that one corner struck the ceiling with a satisfying crunch at a point quite close to the wall.

Some powder came down.

She tried a second time. The noise was louder than she expected, a boom like a bass drum. To hell with that. You can't make an omelette without cracking eggs, as Lee would say.

She began a regular pounding of the ceiling, hitting it with all the strength she could muster. She was glad of her state of fitness. The weight of the bed worked to her advantage as a destruction implement, but was hell for her back and biceps. And the hinged legs swung loose more than once and rapped her knuckles.

Thankfully, the plaster started coming down in chunks. She used one of the blankets to protect her head.

After fifteen minutes, the progress slowed. Not much more was shifting.

She paused and stared up. So near and yet so far. A sizeable dent had appeared, revealing some of the laths. A few small lumps of plaster hung down, attached to the animal hair once used as a binding agent. She'd removed about half an inch, and she was tiring with the effort to penetrate those close-packed strips of wood. She couldn't hoist the cumbersome thing to that level and she was tiring with the effort. She needed to get up there herself and force a way through, but how?

Before being locked in, she'd been subjected to another body search. This time the minder had enjoyed himself and it had been a revolting experience. He'd taken her phone, of course, and made sure she wasn't armed. But in the process of running his hands over every curve and fold of her figure, he'd failed to check inside her shoes—where she had slipped the metal nail file she'd been using as a screwdriver in the bathroom.

Nail files aren't designed to be cutting tools. This small round-ended strip of metal was impractical for working on the laths, but she had another use for it. The bed frame was held together by L-shaped angle plate brackets screwed into the lengths of wood. They were a handy size. If she could free one of them, she'd have a useful tool.

She lowered the bed to the floor and got to work with the nail file. Difficult. The four screws weren't round-headed, like those in the bathroom. They were flat to the wood and difficult to shift. The curved end of the nail file got in the slot, but kept slipping out.

Resolved not to be beaten, she jammed the file into the door frame and snapped off the end with a kick of her heel. She was left with a flat tip that made a better tool. Now she had some purchase on the screw and got a little movement that with more effort became a forty-five degree turn and then more. Fortunately she had always had strength in her wrists. The other screws followed and the bracket was freed. As a tool it felt good in her hand. It was at least three inches along each side, thin galvanised steel.

The next task was to get up to a level where she could work on the ceiling, and the only way was by propping the bed against the wall and using it as a ladder, hoping the canvas slats would bear her weight. Removing the bracket had made it a distinctly unsafe structure.

For the present, the frame held together and she climbed

within reach of the damaged ceiling and got to work with her new tool. The laths were nailed to the undersides of the joists. They had to be forced downwards if possible. Get one out and the others should follow.

Whoever had made this ceiling had built it to last, using a strong bond. But by probing steadily with the bracket she eventually found a weak point and forced the end right through. By much jiggling and gouging she enlarged the slit and felt a small movement of the lath. She worked at it with such energy that the camp bed bounced against the wall. And at last the lath gave way and split at one end.

Elated, Ingeborg forced the strip of wood downwards, levered out the other nail, and threw it on the floor. With the space to reach through, the others were easy to remove.

In under ten minutes she had made a hole wide enough to scramble through. The bed slid down the wall a fraction when she raised herself to the next slat and it fell all the way and clattered on the floor when she made a grab for the exposed joist and hauled herself into the loft.

She paused briefly to enjoy the moment. She was crouching in the dark, cone-shaped loft.

The next task would be easier: removing tiles from the roof. In fact, she was thinking ahead to how she would cope so high up in the open air. She had a faint memory of the tower's position at the corner of the house, but she couldn't be certain of its structure. She needed to break out on the side closest to the rest of the building. Difficult to judge in a round tower.

She could only make the attempt and hope.

The bracket was the perfect tool for ripping through the felt underlay. She rapidly exposed a section between two rafters. Tiles that had resisted more than a century of gales and snow lifted easily from the battens supporting them. A square of grey light was revealed and cool air fanned her face. One row of tiles was nailed and needed some leverage. Two slid into the guttering, but she was able to scoop them up and stack them inside with the others. The opening got larger.

She had got lucky with her choice of where to break out.

An almost full moon gave her a view of the house, mostly in silhouette, with long shadows cast across the drive and lawns below, and streaks of silver light along the extremities picking out the angles of the roof and battlements. She was higher than she expected, but there wasn't time to dwell on a potential attack of vertigo. Getting started was paramount.

She needed to reach the battlements that linked the tower to the main house and they were at least a body length below. Could she trust the guttering to take her weight?

A scary moment.

She wriggled through the opening and pressed her torso against the tiles still in place, keeping one hand curled under a rafter. Little by little, she allowed herself to slip down the angled roof and over the edge until gravity took over and she slithered into space, made a grab for the curved gutter and hung on. It creaked under the strain and shifted slightly. Please, she thought.

The next stage was crucial and the most dangerous yet. Her feet were some inches short of the nearest battlement, but hanging in mid-air from an ancient gutter she didn't have the option of waiting.

She let go, dropped, slipped, made a grab and hugged the stonework. With a huge effort, she raised her knee and got astride the battlement as if it was a horse. Not an experience she would ever want to repeat.

Now it was a matter of working her way along the battlement to where it connected with the east-facing side of the main house, a relatively simple manuever. Somewhere below in the grounds a dog was barking. She couldn't think how she had disturbed it from this far away, and anyway she had to keep going. Concentrating on her footing, she eased round each toothlike projection of the battlement until she reached a rampart and was able to get the support of a wall. The moonlight showed her a drainpipe just within reach. Once again she would need to put her trust in rusty Victorian fittings. There was no other way down.

This side of the house was bathed in moonlight and—wonder of wonders—she spotted a lattice window partly ajar. It was some nine feet below her and she thought she could reach it by transferring from the drainpipe to the ledge below the stone window frame. A chance to get into the house without triggering the alarm system would be a massive bonus.

Hand over hand, she lowered herself until she was level with the ledge. The distance between was not huge, but from her position hanging on to the drainpipe, it was no simple move. She couldn't leap across. She had to stretch out her right leg as far as she dared and feel blindly for a toehold. At the third attempt her foot lodged against something solid. Without pause for thought, she pushed herself away from the pipe and got a grip on the top of the stone frame.

The sense of relief was profound. Her heart was racing.

The open window was the farthest of three. Still moving mainly by feel, she sidled across the ledge, got a hand inside the open window, leaned down, lifted the stay from its notch, and pulled the whole thing open.

She was so excited to have completed the move without mishap that it wasn't until she was lowering herself into the house that she had an alarming thought: a window left open at night could well be in a bedroom.

It was.

The muffled sound of someone turning rapidly in bed was followed by a panicky, "Who's that?"

Ingeborg froze. Just as she'd thought the gods were on her side, this had to happen.

The voice sounded female. One of the staff? She hoped so.

The woman in bed fumbled for a light switch.

Ingeborg still hadn't moved. But when the light came on, she recognised the raised face of Stella, the housekeeper, the woman who had taken her to breakfast. Critical memories flashed through her brain. Stella had been reasonably friendly. She had no cause to make trouble now. She hadn't appeared in the corridor when half the house found out that the secret bathroom had been invaded. She must have slept through. In which case, she wouldn't know Ingeborg was enemy number one and was supposed to be locked in the tower room.

"It's me, Ingeborg Smith. We met yesterday."

No response.

This called for some improvisation. "I'm really sorry about this," Ingeborg said, thinking fast. "I was trapped outside and couldn't find my way in. There's a guard dog out there."

Stella said in an expressionless voice, "Now I know who you are."

Ingeborg developed her cover story. "I saw the open window and climbed up a drainpipe. I didn't know it would be your bedroom."

"What were you doing outside?"

"I couldn't sleep. I needed fresh air. Stupidly I let the door shut behind me and I was stuck. I'm really sorry. I'll find my way back to the guest room. Where exactly are we?"

"You turn left outside the door and go up the stairs at the end." Stella yawned heavily, sank back on the pillow and reached for the light.

Ingeborg pulled the window back to its original position and secured it, crossed the room, closed the door behind her and turned left. Maybe the gods were with her after all.

But the biggest test lay ahead. She still needed to find her way back into Nathan's secret bathroom. And this time she must do it without the assistance of Lee Li passing her the keys.

At the top of the stairs in the dim light she confirmed she was back in the corridor where the locked room was—with the door to Nathan's bedroom facing her at the end.

Could it be, she wondered, that after the ruckus in the small hours Nathan hadn't relocked his secret bathroom?

It was worth finding out. She crept forward, remembering to sidestep the part of the floor that creaked, and tried the handle.

No short cuts in this mission.

Needing to rethink her strategy, she retreated along the passage, opened the guest room door and slipped inside.

The stress of the last half hour was getting to her. A stretch on the big, soft bed was a huge temptation she knew she must resist. She stepped through to the hand basin in the shower room and splashed water on her face.

The keys would be back in Nathan's bedroom, either out on a table or some other surface or, more likely, secure in his trouser pocket again. Being realistic, she knew it was unlikely she could get in and out without waking anyone.

The bathroom had a solid, sturdy door with a modern cylinder lock, not the sort you can open with a plastic card—if she had one. But there was no other way in, short of using an enforcer. No window. Breaking in through the ceiling wasn't practical and would wake everyone in the house.

She looked at her watch: 3:25. Time was slipping by. At daylight, the minders would discover the damage to the tower and her chance would be gone. She needed to be away from here before then. How galling if she came away with no evidence after all this effort.

Some lateral thinking was wanted. Understandably, her brain wasn't functioning at its best. Go back to the practicalities, she told herself. Nathan has the key. Rather than repeating the earlier trick and taking it without his knowledge, there must be some way of getting him out of bed again to unlock that door himself. A sudden noise in the corridor would surely bring him out to make a check. Rattling the door? If he then came out and no one was in sight, he'd be suspicious and want to make sure all was well. He'd unlock the door and go inside.

Was she capable of taking him on? She wasn't entirely confident. Karate-trained, she reckoned she could defend herself against anyone, but this would place her in the attacking role. She would need to follow him into the room, slam the door behind her before his minders arrived, disable him, locate the hidden firearms and the logbook she was confident he kept, and then, armed with one of his weapons, make her escape.

Not easy.

Even if she got that far, past the minders and out of the

house, she'd need transport—which meant hijacking one of his cars.

While these thoughts were still running through her head, the unexpected happened. A piercing two-note electronic alarm sounded in the corridor outside, the sort of signal that means a building has to be evacuated.

She moved fast to the door and looked out. No smell of smoke. The sound was ear-shattering. Maybe somebody had found she'd escaped and raised the alarm. She closed the door again.

An emergency or an opportunity? If all the attention was on the tower room, and Nathan got up and rushed there to check, this could work out better than any plan she had devised.

In the brain-numbing din, it was difficult to hear anything else, but she thought a door opened and someone was shouting in the corridor. She released her door a fraction and caught a glimpse of a figure dashing past, away from the bedroom at the end. She couldn't tell for certain, but who else could it be but Nathan?

She swung the door fully open and met Lee Li scuttling towards her, tugging on a bathrobe, eyes like searchlights when she saw who it was.

Lee was lost for words.

"Go with Nathan," Ingeborg told her, shouting to be heard. "Keep him busy as long as you can."

Swerving past the bewildered singer, she hared into the bedroom, eager to find those keys. His suit was on a hanger on the front of the wardrobe. She pulled the jacket aside and ran her hands over the trouser pockets. Flat, as if they'd been freshly pressed.

Where then?

The king-size bed stood against a wall unit with lighting and shelving across the centre and matching bedside cabinets. Nathan slept on the side closest to the wardrobe. Some coins were stacked on his cabinet top, probably the loose change he had emptied from his pocket. A leather wallet, card-case and gold Omega wristwatch were with them. There was a digital alarm clock. But no keys. Had he grabbed them before rushing from the room?

She tugged open the cabinet drawer. Only paper tissues, packs of condoms, sleeping pills and baby oil. She ran around the bed and checked Lee's drawer, just in case. Without result.

More in frustration than necessity, she swept a bunch of paperback thrillers off the shelf above. Nothing was behind them.

Increasingly frantic, she cast around, taking in every surface in the room. If the keys were still here, they certainly weren't in sight.

She scooted through to the shower room and checked the shelf where the toothbrushes were. And the vanity unit. The only items were those you would expect to find.

Hand tugging distractedly at her hair, she returned to the bedroom. The big bed was in disarray, the duvet doubled over where the sleepers had roused themselves when the alarm started. She flung it back, with no result. Tossed the pillows aside. He wouldn't leave the bloody keys on the bed, she chided herself. This is desperation.

What does a man do with a set of keys he knows have been removed once from his room? He makes sure no intruder can sneak in and steal them a second time. He can't rule out the possibility that his sleeping partner assisted in the first theft. He places them within reach, his side of the bed.

Under the mattress?

Ingeborg lifted the mattress, slid her hand in the space above the box spring and found nothing. She dropped to her knees, put her head to the carpet and checked under the bed.

I made a big mistake, she thought. I should have asked Lee.

Then her eye was caught by the glint of something metal. Large mattresses are fitted with handles. This one, tight to the side, was made of padded fabric at least an inch in width. Wedged behind it, so close to where Nathan slept that he could have reached down and checked them at intervals through the night, were the goddamn keys.

Come on!

She tugged them free and ran out of the room, back to the locked door. She found the right one, inserted it and turned the lock. After pocketing the ring of keys, she entered Nathan's secret bathroom and slammed the door behind her.

Everything was still in place. She knew already what she needed to check. She'd been over and over it in her mind.

The shower unit.

Guns wouldn't be hidden under the shower floor. If she was right, this was much more ambitious. She stepped up to the curved glass doors and tried them. They glided smoothly aside. The fittings appeared genuine enough: power selector, temperature control, riser rail, flexible hose, soap dish and drain. The two walls forming the corner were tiled in the same duck-egg blue as the rest of the room.

"All right, you bugger," Ingeborg said aloud, "let's see if I'm right."

She stepped back, closed the doors and put her weight against the metal framework. It didn't shift a centimetre. With a sharp, impatient sigh, she moved to her right to try from the other angle. The shower was robust and entirely unyielding.

But so was Ingeborg.

She tried pulling instead of pushing, still without success.

"There's got to be a way," she said. "Got to be."

Outside, the house alarm stopped its nee-na. She didn't have long now.

She checked along the floor and up the sides for a release switch. Thwarted, she took a step back, arms folded, and tried to bring some intelligence to the problem. There *had* to be an answer.

And it came.

She forced the sliding doors apart and stepped inside. She pressed her foot on the drain and there was movement. The criss-cross grille with its circular flange disconnected from the floor and sank an inch. It had a spring mechanism. The drain had been acting as the brake.

She stepped out, gave the sides a push and the entire shower unit including the two tiled walls slid forward on rollers. She had found the way in.

23

Neat.

On small wheels set into twin tracks, the shower unit had glided forward from the bathroom into another room: Nathan's gunroom. To enter, you stepped in and made your exit on the right. Ingeborg found herself in a space not much larger than a holding cell, narrow in depth, but appreciably longer in width, that must have been created by partitioning when the bathroom was installed.

Efficient use had been made of the space, amounting to about twenty square metres. Rifles and submachine guns were racked vertically at head height along the walls, and handguns and ammunition displayed in glass-fronted cabinets. Two wooden crates at the far end contained more handguns. She picked one up and it was lighter in weight than she expected, clearly a replica. Firearms manufacturers turn an extra profit by franchising out their designs to dealers in imitation weapons. These "air-soft," pellet-firing guns are marketed as collectors' pieces, but in practice are often used in armed robbery. They can be modified to fire live rounds. When a villain takes aim, the shopkeeper doesn't ask if it fires real bullets. He opens the till and hands over the cash.

The range of weapons in the cabinets was impressive. Ingeborg was no expert, but she had done the firearms course and recognised the Glock 9mm self-loading pistol as a type she had fired. Five of them were together on the top shelf, along with Smith & Wesson revolvers, Berettas, Walthers and, yes, some older handguns, including two tarnished silver Webleys. She opened the cabinet and—taking care not to handle it—used one of Nathan's keys to lift a Webley by the trigger guard and feel the weight. This was no replica. The metal was chipped in places and it had the look of a much-used weapon. She replaced it.

The police ballistics experts would have a field day with this collection. No wonder Nathan's storage facility was so cunningly disguised.

For now, Ingeborg focused on the mission she'd taken on, linking Nathan to the shooting of Professor Gildersleeve. Having got this far, she wasn't leaving without the evidence and—if possible—the name of the killer. Where was the paperwork? She'd persuaded herself Nathan kept records of his dealings. Surely it was sensible to store the log in this secure place.

Out of the corner of her eye she spotted something hanging from a hook high on the wall behind her. She reached up to a clipboard loaded with several sheets of what looked like accounting paper. Found! Elated, she allowed herself a yelp of self-congratulation.

The handwritten entries were made in columns. They weren't headed, but to Ingeborg's eye they were easy to decipher. The date of each transaction appeared in the left column, then abbreviations for the make and type of the weapons (the giveaway was *H&K MP5* for the Heckler & Koch carbine), more initials for the hirer, followed by the date of return and space for a tick when the transaction was complete. Nothing about the money that had changed hands. No doubt Nathan kept that information in his head.

She didn't study all the sheets. After unclipping them, she folded them roughly and stuffed them in her pocket. High time she thought about getting out of this place alive.

She took a Glock 17 from the display and loaded it. The seventeen-round magazine capacity and the lightweight polycarbonate body would help anyone's confidence in a shootout. She helped herself to a shoulder holster and strapped it on, leaving both hands free if she was scaling walls.

From now on, she would have to wing it. There were too

many unknowns. Any plan was likely to run into trouble straight away.

Pity she no longer had her iPhone. Some pictures of this place would have been strong evidence. She took a last look round and then re-entered the shower cabinet and crossed the bathroom to the door and opened it a fraction.

The corridor was eerily silent. Nathan's bedroom door remained ajar, as Lee had left it. Lights were on along the corridor, but outside it would still be dark. She needed to make her escape now.

She stepped out, down the stairs and past Stella's room. No one could have slept through that alarm. Was the entire household gathered obediently at some assembly point? She couldn't picture it.

From this point, she would rely on instinct to orient herself. Another staircase would bring her to ground level and she'd need to be extra cautious there. She drew the gun before taking the last steps down. Ahead she saw the armour displayed on the walls that meant she'd reached the entrance hall. Not the preferred route. She'd be crazy to make her exit from the main door. Instead she started along an unlit corridor she hoped would bring her to a less obvious way out of the building.

Then she froze. She could hear someone coming towards her.

This wasn't one of those helpful corridors with doors on either side. It was probably the route to what had once been the servants' quarters, a narrow passage not much wider than the telescopic corridor used for boarding an aircraft. Faced with the choice of turning and running or taking a stance, she drew the gun and took up the classic position she'd been trained for, legs astride, knees slightly bent, both hands steadying her aim.

"Hold it!" she called out, heart stuttering.

The footsteps ahead stopped.

"Stay right there. I've got a gun and I'm coming towards you."

The brief, tense silence was broken by Lee Li's shrill voice. "Ingeborg, is that you?"

"Are you alone?"

"Yes."

Ingeborg lowered the Glock and stepped forward.

Lee, still in her white bathrobe and flip-flops, stared like a choked thrush at the pistol. "Where did you get that?"

"Never mind." She shoved the thing back in the holster. "What's going on outside?"

"Some trespasser broke into the grounds. The dog found him and woke people up with all the barking. They were saying he fell from a tree. I think he's dead. Nathan told me not to look and sent me back to bed."

If some unfortunate had come to grief, he wasn't Ingeborg's concern. "Do they know about me? Does Nathan know I got out?"

"He didn't say anything. I don't think he knows."

She made a rapid assessment. Lee's knowledge of the house could be useful, even though she would add to the risk of being spotted. "Do you still want to get away?"

"I'm not dressed," Lee said.

"If you want out, it's now or never. I'm leaving now."

Lee bit her lip and pulled the bathrobe tighter across her chest. "All right."

"I've got his keys. One looks like a car key to me."

"That'll be for his Aston Martin. It's in the garage."

"Take me there."

Lee didn't need convincing of the urgency. She turned and led Ingeborg briskly through two doors and down some stone steps. "In here."

They entered a basement garage spacious enough to park a fleet of cars in addition to the two limos and the open-top sports car already in place. What the hell if the Aston Martin Roadster was an eye-catching sunburst yellow? It would go some. Ingeborg stepped over to it, opened the door and made sure the key fitted. "How do we open the garage door?"

Lee was already seated beside her. "You've got a remote on the dash."

She found it and pressed the top button. A rollerglide

door started moving in the far corner. "Which way when we get out?"

"Up the ramp and right. It takes you to the front of the house and you'll see the drive ahead."

"Let's go, then." The 4.3 litre engine started with a satisfying *vroom* and they cruised out and upwards with the lights on full beam. "Where exactly is Nathan?" Ingeborg asked as they swung right.

"You'll see them in a second. They've got flashlights."

She hoped to God they had nothing more lethal. Nathan and three of his bodyguards were under some trees partly illuminated by the security lights at the front of the building, not more than thirty yards from the drive. They had a dog with them and there was a figure prone on the ground. They spun about at the sound of the car. Nathan thrust his hands up in alarm and two of the minders reached for their guns.

"Head down," Ingeborg told Lee. "This could be ugly."

She gave the car an injection of speed and spun the wheel to control a skidding turn in front of the house. A shot screamed over her head and another hit the bodywork somewhere, fortunately without hindering the forward movement. Ingeborg ripped through the gears on squealing tyres to get out of range of the guns. More shots were fired, but handguns are notoriously inefficient at distance, even when the target is stationary, and in seconds they had belted up the gravel drive to relative safety.

"You all right?" Ingeborg asked.

"Thanks, yes."

"We need to get through the gate. Can he control it from the house? I'd rather not smash it down."

"I don't know. The remote should open it."

"We can only try." She squeezed the brakes as she began to run out of drive.

Those gates looked huge and impenetrable. The car would never burst through them and still be usable. She pressed the remote control and waited, her stomach clenching. Agonizing seconds passed before anything happened. The two of them didn't need to speak their thoughts. By now, Nathan would have collected something from the garage and started in pursuit.

The gates shuddered and started inching open.

Impatient to be in motion again, Ingeborg stared into the rear-view mirror and saw headlights make the turn in front of the house. She drew a sharp breath and exhaled at once, switching her attention back to the slowly widening space between the gates. Judging the gap to a centimetre, she engaged the gear, jammed her foot down and swung on to the road.

24

Diamond's speech was slurred when Ingeborg phoned him from her Bath flat. He must have been asleep. She hadn't appreciated how early it still was. But he soon grasped what had happened and was touchingly anxious to know if she was unhurt. He told her not even to think about coming into work before she'd got some rest. Was this really Peter Diamond talking? At this end of her mission she didn't object to the paternal treatment. She rather enjoyed it.

She cooked an early breakfast. Lee, still in the white bathrobe, was on the sofa with her arms folded around her knees. The chase through Leigh Woods was a pleasing memory now. The Aston Martin had easily outpaced Nathan's limo and lost it on the empty roads before crossing the suspension bridge, courtesy of Nathan's crossing card. Ingeborg had felt a pang of regret at having to abandon the magnificent beast at the dockside near the *Great Britain*, where her little Ford Ka still stood in isolation. She was sorrier still to have to smash the window of her own vehicle and start it with the spare key she kept taped under the dashboard, but the minder had taken hers when he searched her the first time.

"We'll get some sleep after this," she called from the kitchen. "I need to go into work after a couple of hours, but you're welcome to stay on as long as you want."

"You're so kind," Lee said.

"Nonsense. I wouldn't have got away without your help."

"You're not really a journalist, are you? I saw the mail waiting on your doormat . . . Detective Sergeant Smith."

"Sorry," Ingeborg said. "Really sorry. Let me explain."

"You don't need to. I could tell you were more interested in Nathan than my singing, and when I saw how you handled the gun, I guessed."

"You're quite a detective yourself."And she might have added, *But thank God you seem to trust me.*

"What will happen now?" Lee asked.

"To Nathan?" Ingeborg scooped the fried egg from the pan and transferred it to the plate with the strips of crisp bacon and the mushrooms and tomatoes. "I expect we'll raid his house before he moves the firearms to some other place. He's not stupid. He's probably started shifting them already."

"You knew he was dealing in arms?"

"It's well known. Proving it is altogether different. If we can nail him this time, he'll get a long sentence. You could be called as a witness."

Lee thought about that and frowned. "I don't know if I'd want to testify. He's bad, I know, but he was kind to me. And he definitely helped my career. Even the devil isn't as black as he's painted."

Ingeborg smiled at yet another axiom, a debatable one. "In my scale of things, Nathan is among the worst. I don't know how many serious crimes could be traced back to him and his guns. Probably dozens." She brought the laden tray over to Lee. "With that new album to launch, you'll find another sponsor, no problem."

"Will he come after me, do you think?"

"Right now, he has too much other stuff to deal with. The dead man in the grounds, for a start. Even if the death was accidental—and I have my doubts—he'll want to dispose of the body somewhere else. He won't want an investigation on his home patch."

"Who do you think it was?"

"No idea. Not one of ours, for sure. I was on a solo mission. Just some chancer who needed a gun for a job and heard the rumours about Nathan, I guess." She took her own breakfast from the oven and brought it to a chair opposite

Lee. "Do you have friends you can stay with until you sort yourself out?"

"I'll have to think."

"I could call my friend Sylvie, the one who interviewed you. She has plenty of contacts."

"Thanks. She was nice."

This was as good a moment as any to ask the key question. "Did Nathan ever speak about the shooting at the Bath auction house a week or so ago?"

Lee frowned and shook her head. "What was that?" She truly didn't appear to know.

"A man called Gildersleeve, a university professor, was gunned down. We're trying to find out if Nathan supplied the murder weapon."

"He wouldn't have told me, anyway. I wasn't supposed to know that side of his business."

"Is there another side?"

"Import-export, he calls it."

Ingeborg laughed. "Helping the country's balance of payments? Let me ask you about his customers. Was one of them by any chance a university lecturer by the name of Dr. Poke?"

She hesitated. "I didn't find out who they were. Only a few I happened to meet, and he wasn't one of them. I'd remember a name like that."

"A woman called Monica?"

"I'd certainly remember a woman. No."

"A property developer, Bernie Wefers?"

Lee sat forward in surprise. "He came to the house, yes."

"Are you sure?"

"But not to buy guns. Bernie built my studio and fitness centre. Didn't personally build it, I mean, but did all the planning with Nathan and me and brought the contractors in to do the job. He's a large man, a bit rough at the edges, as they say, but I don't think he's a crook."

Ingeborg smiled. "You can't tell a book by its cover."

"Very true, but I rather liked him."

"He was married to Monica, the woman I mentioned."

Lee shook her head. "I wouldn't know about that."

A new thought formed. "Did you get the impression Bernie had done work for Nathan before?"

"They seemed to know each other, certainly."

"I was thinking he may have built the secret bathroom and the gunroom. It must have been one large bedroom originally."

"If he did, it was before I arrived."

The need for sleep was becoming irresistible. Ingeborg returned the trays to the kitchen and found some bedding for Lee, who was happy to stretch out on the sofa. Two and a half hours would have to do. Ingeborg set the alarm for nine and sank exhausted into her own bed.

Diamond was at work early that morning feeling as if he'd hardly been away. Actually he'd been home a few hours and not slept well for fretting over Paul Gilbert. Nothing more had been heard from the young DC since the phone call of the evening before. Diamond's irritation with Gilbert had long gone. The lad had gathered valuable information about what was happening at the Hazael mansion. Thanks to his good work, it was clear that Ingeborg had successfully infiltrated the place after befriending the pop singer who was Nathan Hazael's girlfriend. Relief all round.

But now there was deep concern over Gilbert. Diamond was unburdening himself to Halliwell. "You heard what I said to him on the phone and I'm not proud of it now. The whole situation was a farce, him up the tree with the guard dog waiting underneath. I was sure he'd be humiliated if we sent a rescue party. He wasn't supposed to be there, anyway. That's why I told him to fend for himself. You heard me, Keith. Were those my words?"

"You told him to use his initiative."

"Exactly."

"And you called him a pillock."

Almost the last word he'd spoken. He winced. "Okay. I was rattled. He put Ingeborg's undercover mission at risk."

"He didn't know about that."

"He wasn't supposed to know." Diamond ran a hand over

his head and scraped back hair that was no longer there. "What do you think happened, Keith? Is he still up the bloody tree? Is he a prisoner inside the place now?"

"Looking on the bright side, he could have done what you said and escaped. He may have thought it was too late to call in and let us know."

"He hasn't been in and he hasn't called us. I'm getting jack shit from his mobile."

"Try calling him at home. There's a landline."

"I already did. All I got was the recorded message."

"Give him more time, guv."

Muttering to himself, Diamond crossed the room and opened his office door. "And another thing: the *Wife of Bath* is missing."

"That's all right," Halliwell said. "John Wigfull wanted her for a photocall."

"For crying out loud."

"He came up with a trolley and six burly constables some time yesterday."

"Where is it now?"

"Still outside the main entrance where they took the pictures. It was when I came in, at any rate. I think Mr. Wigfull had trouble getting anyone to hump it back here."

"So it sat in front of the building all night? It's worth a fortune. What if someone nicked it? Doesn't Wigfull realise a man was shot in a hijack attempt to snatch the thing?"

"I'll get onto him."

"I've been here long enough to remember a member of the public coming in and informing us that we had cannabis growing in the concrete planters outside the front. It took years to live that down."

When Ingeborg walked into the CID room in the middle of the morning and went straight to her desk and checked the computer, there was no sense of surprise, no applause. Almost nobody noticed—which, perhaps, is what an undercover officer should aim for.

Some minutes after, she knocked on Diamond's door and got a more satisfying reaction.

"You're back. Thank God for that."

"And I've got some juicy things to report. Is this a good time?"

"As good as any. Let me call in some of the others first. They didn't all know you were undercover, but they should now."

Halliwell and Leaman joined them and gave Ingeborg more of the welcome home that was her due. She launched into a snappy account of her adventure, from the night on the *Great Britain* to the escape with Lee Li. "I brought the sheets from the gunroom for you to study," she said in conclusion. "I haven't been through them myself." She took the sheaf of papers from her pocket, unfolded them and handed them across.

Diamond said, "This is terrific. You didn't get any photos of his collection, I suppose?"

She shook her head. "They took away my phone."

"Not to worry." Diamond brandished the gunroom log. "This is the star prize. With any luck we'll recognise some names when we go through it."

"I also brought away a gun, a Glock 17, for self-defence. It's got my prints all over it, but it's evidence that he deals in firearms."

Leaman in his usual downbeat way said, "I doubt if we'll find the rest of the guns. He'll have shipped them out already. Even if we raided the place right now, we'd be unlikely to recover much."

"We could find the room where they were stored," Halliwell said.

Leaman shook his head. "I wouldn't even count on that."

Ingeborg said, "He may not have done anything about the guns. He's got plenty else to keep him busy."

"Repairing all the damage you caused?" Diamond said with a grin.

"I meant disposing of the body."

"Which body?"

"Didn't I mention the dead man in the grounds?"

25

Two busloads of armed police and the dog unit accompanied the response car that drove Diamond, Halliwell and Ingeborg to Leigh Woods—and for once there was no complaint from the big man about the speed they were going. Uncomfortable in their body armour, the three detectives were suffering far more aggravation from the mix of grief and anger in their minds. The only way to get through was to concentrate on practicalities. During the journey, Ingeborg described the layout of Nathan Hazael's mansion in as much detail as she knew. "And there are at least four resident bodyguards armed with handguns," she said.

"From what you were saying, they have an arsenal of weapons to choose from," Halliwell said. "We could be facing carbines."

"And there's the dog, a Dobermann."

Diamond emerged from a brooding silence to say, "Let's be clear about this operation. The top priority is to discover what happened to Paul. To achieve that, we must arrest Hazael and question him. And we need the evidence to back up the charge. Inge, your first duty is to identify the spot in the grounds where you saw them standing over the body and tape it as a crime scene. I've already asked for a CSI team. There should be evidence of firearms use or other violence. I'm assuming they'll have moved the body elsewhere."

"And then shall I join you in the house?" Ingeborg asked.

"Soon as you can, yes."

"Do we have a search warrant?"

"Leaman is arranging it as we speak. We'll go through the

place with a fine toothcomb. But the focus of all our resources right now is Paul. The gun-running is secondary."

"This may sound dumb, but did you try calling his mobile?" Ingeborg said.

"Switched off, or destroyed."

"They've had several hours," Halliwell said. "They'll have worked out that Ingeborg was undercover and they'll be expecting a raid from us."

"So?"

"They could have chucked him in the river by now. It's only a short drive."

Diamond inhaled sharply while his imagination dwelt on the remark. "You can go straight down to the garage in the basement and check the vehicles, Keith, unless they're out front. Two limos, you said, Inge, apart from the Aston Martin, which we assume is still abandoned on the quayside?"

Ingeborg nodded.

Persevering with the task in hand, trying to keep his darkest fear from taking hold, Diamond said, "We know one of the limos was used in the chase, but we can find out if they were driven after. See if either engine is still warm and check the boot, of course."

"Are we nicking the bodyguards, as well as Nathan?" Halliwell asked.

"You bet we are."

Already they were speeding along North Road with Nightingale Valley to their right, through the lush vegetation and millionaire estates of Leigh Woods. The resentment against Hazel and his crime-sourced fortune was almost tangible, but went unspoken.

Ingeborg alerted the driver when the turn came. They pulled up in front of the tall iron gate she had last seen from the other side.

Diamond stepped out and buzzed the intercom on the gatepost. There was some delay before a woman's voice responded over the static.

"Yes, who is it?"

"Police. Open up, please."

"Mr. Hazael isn't here."

Ingeborg told Diamond, "Sounds like Stella, the housekeeper."

"Open the gate or we'll take it down."

After more hesitation, the ironwork was activated with a shudder and began its slow inward movement.

They drove through the woods towards the house, already visible ahead, overblown and pretentious with its turret and battlements. Ingeborg said to the driver, "Slow up a bit, would you?" She was concentrating on the swiftly changing view across the turf, trying to visualise the scene she'd passed in a very different light. This time there were no flashlights and no people under the trees to mark the spot. A massive oak came up on the right. "We're coming to it, I think. Stop. I'll get out here."

"Are you certain?" Diamond asked.

"As near as I can be."

"They'll have police tape and cones in the bus. See you presently."

The car and the second bus drove right up to the house. The armed police in their Kevlar jackets poured out and spread wide across the frontage. Diamond marched up to the already partly open front door and flashed his ID to the middle-aged woman barring the way. She looked aghast at such a large police presence.

"You must be Stella, the housekeeper."

"Yes, sir."

"We're coming in to search the building. A warrant has been issued. Where's Nathan Hazael?"

"He went out earlier with some of his staff. He didn't say where."

"Some of his staff, or all of them?"

"The catering people are still here."

"So has he taken all the cars?"

"I expect so. I didn't see them leave."

"Step aside, please. We're coming in now."

"I don't know if Mr. Hazael would like that."

"We don't give a toss what he would like. Do you want to be charged with obstruction?"

She stepped back to avoid the inflow of armed officers. Halliwell asked her which way the garage was and she pointed to a passage on the right. He led a group straight through.

Diamond remained with Stella, reminding himself she was only one of the staff, low in the pecking order. He'd let rip at the door and now he needed to keep his emotion in check. In a measured tone, he said, "I'm going to warn you that withholding information is an offence. We have reason to believe there was a violent incident here overnight. A man was attacked and possibly murdered in the grounds. You must have heard the alarm go off."

She nodded, wide-eyed. "I didn't know anyone was murdered."

"Come on. Everyone must have been talking about it. What did you see?"

"Someone came through my bedroom in the night, a woman, a journalist who was staying here. I don't know what it was about."

"That was before the alarm, right? What did you do when you heard the alarm?"

"I got out of bed and ran downstairs. I thought there must be a fire, but there wasn't. One of Mr. Hazael's personal staff was in the front hall and told me to go back to bed. He said a guard dog had found a trespasser in the grounds and they were dealing with it. I took him at his word and went back to my room. Soon after that I heard shooting."

"Where from?"

"Outside."

"More than one shot?"

"I wasn't counting. Several."

"And when you got up in the morning? What time were you about?"

"My duties start at eight, so I was up soon after seven."

"What was going on at that time? Did you speak to anyone? See anything?"

"Plenty was going on, but I'm not sure what. People up and down stairs, in and out of the house. I was told by the kitchen staff that no one was eating breakfast. They were all too busy with other stuff. Lily—that's Mr. Hazael's partner—had left the house in the night with the journalist and taken the sports car from the garage. They drove off while the men were out in the grounds dealing with the intruder."

"Does anyone know what exactly happened with this intruder? Did they attack him?"

"He was hiding up a tree, I was told, and fell out."

"Fell out? He wasn't shot?"

"I don't know about that. I wasn't there."

"Who told you this?"

"The cook."

"But you say you heard gunfire in the night. Didn't you get up to look?"

"In this house it's not wise to be too curious. I covered my ears and stayed in bed."

"Was an ambulance called for the man?"

She shook her head. "I couldn't tell you. I didn't hear one."

"The man was a police officer keeping the house under surveillance," Diamond told her. "It's possible he was murdered. You won't need telling how serious that is. I've warned you already about withholding information. The man isn't out there now. Do you know what they did with him?"

"I was told they took him away." She was clearly frightened and the answer sounded genuine.

"The cook told you this?"

She nodded.

Diamond's phone buzzed. It was Halliwell. "The garage is empty, guv."

"Get onto the PNC and find out which vehicles are registered to Hazael. Do we know what make the limos are? Ask Ingeborg. And then get an all-units out. Two black limos, possibly together." He turned back to the white-faced Stella. "Did you see them lift the body into one of the cars?"

Her voice shook. "I didn't myself . . ."

"Someone else did?"

"Cook mentioned seeing something."

"Take me to him now."

"Cook is a lady."

The lady—the fount of all knowledge about the morning's events—was in a white linen jacket outside the kitchen door, mid-fifties, reed-thin, twitchy and lighting a cigarette. Diamond went through the necessary cautions and added some veiled threats of his own. These women knew their employer was a monster and must have realised instant dismissal would be the least of their problems if they grassed to the police. But they were up against another ogre and today he was fired up by emotions of his own. Last night he'd left young Gilbert to fend for himself, unarmed in this hostile place. Conscience strikes deep into the soul.

"Did you hear the shooting in the night?"

She was a cooler character than Stella. She took her time stubbing out the cigarette on the stone wall, then gave a nod.

"And was that before the alarm went off or after?"

"After."

"How many shots?"

The answer was a shrug.

He moved on to the more crucial incident. "I heard what you witnessed this morning. I want to hear it in your own words. What time was it?"

"Six, or soon after."

"And where were you?"

"In the dining room, trying to find out if anyone wanted a cooked breakfast before I started. No one was in, so I looked out the window." She was probably lying about her reason for snooping, but it didn't matter if she spoke the truth about what she had witnessed.

"What exactly did you see?"

"One of the cars on the drive with the back open. Mr. Hazael under the trees with two of his staff. There was shouting, but I couldn't hear the words. He seemed to be angry. I saw the men bend down and pick something up and carry it across the grass towards the car and when they got nearer I could tell it was a person."

"Dead?"

"You should have seen the way it was being carried. They dumped it in the boot and shut the lid down."

The "it" was chilling. "Then what?"

"Nothing."

"What do you mean—*nothing*?" For all his good intentions, he was getting irritated with this cold-eyed woman.

"Nothing happened for a long time." After some hesitation she seemed to sense his anger and decided more had to be revealed. "No one came in for breakfast except Stella, the housekeeper. I told her what I'd seen and we talked about the disturbed night we'd had. After she went, when I was clearing plates, I saw them drive off."

"Who?"

"Mr. Hazael and his men."

"So how long had the limousine been waiting on the drive?"

"An hour, easy."

"With the man shut in the boot?"

"Must have been, mustn't he? The second car came round the side of the house and they all drove off."

"Which car was Hazael in?"

"The first."

"The one with the body?"

"Yes."

Diamond checked his watch. "That was about two hours ago and they haven't returned. How many were in each car?"

"Three in the first. I'm not certain, but there must have been two in the second."

"And you didn't overhear anything about their plans?"

"I told you already. They were too far away."

He left her and rounded the house to the front. Ingeborg

and her team had taped off the area under the oak. The dog-handlers were making a wider search of the grounds. He went over.

"Plenty of shoeprints," Ingeborg told him, "and four shell cases we spotted and left where we found them. There could be more."

"They were firing at you when you drove past."

"Right. So I expected to find something."

"I'm trying to find out precisely what happened, and when. The housekeeper heard some shooting, several shots, and I assume that was the bodyguards firing at you in the Aston Martin. Whatever happened to Paul must have been done before then, right?"

"The body was under the tree when I drove past. They were there with the dog."

"So Paul could have been attacked at any time in the night?"

Ingeborg tapped a finger against her lip, remembering. "When I was escaping from the tower, out on the battlements, I heard a lot of barking down below. I reckon he was still alive then."

"What time was that?"

"Not long before the alarm sounded. Say about four or four thirty."

"But you didn't hear shooting?"

"No."

"Up the tree he'd be an easy target, so I doubt if it was a volley of shots."

"Even a single shot so close to the house would surely wake people," Ingeborg said.

"Both the women I just questioned talked of shooting after the alarm, but not before. It's possible we're hearing the truth—that he wasn't shot, but fell from the tree."

"Or was pushed."

"The bodyguards went up the tree, you think? I can't see it happening. Has Keith asked you about the make of the limos?"

She nodded. "They were both Daimlers."

"Where would they be making for?"

She spread her hands. There were limits even to Ingeborg's knowledge.

The image Halliwell had mentioned, of Paul's corpse being slung into the river, was haunting Diamond's thoughts. Hellish as it was to face the unthinkable, he had to be professional and outguess the perpetrators. "They'll dispose of the body first and then go into hiding. They may well make for the airport. He probably has houses abroad. We'd better alert all the ports and airports. Would you get onto that?"

"Keith has already done it, guv. Every patrol in Avon and Somerset is looking for them."

The next phase would be tough to endure. The real action—if any—was out of his immediate control. He would remain here in Leigh Woods until there was some sort of breakthrough. Unlikely as it seemed, Nathan could yet return.

Back in the house, he used his abundant manpower to begin a search of the building and outhouses. He called everyone to the hall and announced his wish list of items, starting with Nathan's passport, credit cards, wallet, iPhone, address book and keys, any of which might have been left in the house in the hurry to get away, and going on to documentation for the cars. He added that there might also be stray firearms about the building, even though it was known where the main cache was stored.

"Do you want to take a look at the gunroom now?" Ingeborg asked him. In all the concern over Paul's fate, her big discovery had been pushed down the agenda.

"It's as good a time as any." Action of any sort was welcome.

She led the way up the main staircase to the corridor she knew floorboard by floorboard and pointed out Nathan's room at the end, the door still open. "While I'm here, I must remember to collect some of Lee's clothes," she said. "She's only got her night things with her."

"Is she still in your flat?"

"I left her asleep. I doubt if she'll leave. She should be safe from Nathan there."

"I hope so, for both your sakes." To Diamond's eye, the décor in the bedroom was nauseatingly kitsch, the huge double bed under a coronet drape in pink chiffon and the oversized soft toys on the lace-edged pillows. Lee's choice, he imagined. He didn't say anything to Ingeborg in case she, too, had the home life of a fairytale princess, but he doubted it. He opened every one of the cupboards and drawers and found nothing of help to the inquiry. "So where's the gun collection?"

The panic in this place a couple of hours earlier must have been extreme, because the door to the secret bathroom had been left ajar. Ingeborg showed him inside. "You've got to give them credit for deception," she said. "It's amazing. Doesn't it look genuine? The plumbing is in place and it works. The only thing that doesn't work is the shower and you're unlikely to turn that on and risk getting a soaking if you're making a search. It took me two goes to suss it." She gripped the sides of the shower cabinet and rattled it to demonstrate how robust it was. Then she pressed her foot on the drain and demonstrated how it clicked to its lower position, allowing the cabinet to move.

"Full marks," Diamond said. "I'm damn sure I would never have worked it out."

With the confident air of one who had been here before, Ingeborg pushed the whole structure forward and slid the door open and a dog leapt at her throat, teeth bared, snarling hideously.

The Dobermann had been shut inside the gunroom, making no sound. Ingeborg swayed back, karate-trained to react against sudden attacks, if not from dogs. But her shoes slipped on the metal floor of the shower and she keeled into Diamond's arms with the dog's front paws clawing at her chest. All three, a shrieking, growling melee, crashed heavily on the bathroom floor. Forced away from Ingeborg's neck, the dog closed its jaws on Diamond's shoulder. He was wearing his suit, but he felt the points of the teeth penetrate the cloth. With a yell, he rolled away, taking Ingeborg with him. His right hand came in contact with soft fabric that he supposed was Ingeborg's cotton shirt until he felt how chunky it was. He'd grasped the bathroom mat, a large oval of white candlewick. Taking a stronger grip, he tugged. He rolled some more, got to a kneeling position, jerked the mat from under Ingeborg and swung it free.

Extreme situations call for extreme reactions. In a continuous movement, Diamond flung the mat over the Dobermann, wrapped, lifted and slung the snarling and snapping beast through the shower cabinet into the gunroom and shut the sliding door.

Ingeborg sat up. "Christ almighty."

"Are you okay?"

"I think so. How mean was that, leaving the dog in there?"

"There are no rules in this game." He held out his hand and helped her upright. She was shaking, and so was he. "At the back of my mind, I knew something didn't add up about this place. I clean forgot to ask where the dog was. Are you sure you're not hurt?"

She shook her head. "I'm fine. More than I can say for your jacket."

He checked it. The sleeve was ripped from the shoulder.

Ingeborg said, "Thanks, guv. It would have had me. The gunroom will have to wait for another day."

"Not necessarily. I'll get one of the dog-handlers to subdue the brute."

As if in defiance, there was growling from the other side.

They returned to the entrance hall and told Halliwell about their experience.

Inside ten minutes, the Dobermann was caged and brought downstairs.

"Are you game to resume the tour?" Diamond asked.

Ingeborg stepped through the shower and said, "Shit."

The gunroom had been cleared of every weapon, every

piece of ammunition. The cupboards and racks remained, but there was nothing left to incriminate Nathan.

"Now we know what kept them busy for an hour this morning," Diamond said when he'd followed her in.

"The place was stacked to the ceiling," she said. "What did they do with everything?"

"Lugged it all downstairs and loaded up the limo in the garage," he said. "That's why they didn't drive off immediately with Paul in the boot of the other car. They knew you were certain to be back shortly."

"I'm an idiot. I should have collected the two Webleys when I had the chance. I didn't want my prints all over them."

"Don't beat yourself up over it. You were trying to escape. And the law wouldn't look kindly on evidence seized undercover."

She was incensed and it showed in her voice. "Where would he take all those guns? He can't fly out of the country with them."

"He'll have a safe address somewhere near, a lockup maybe. The guns are his source of wealth and also his biggest risk. He would always have had an emergency plan for them." He rapped the inner wall with his knuckles. "This isn't a plywood partition. It's brick. Whoever built it did a good job."

"Oh my God." Ingeborg clapped her hand to her forehead. "There's something I didn't tell you when I reported on what happened last night. I heard it from Lee when we got back to my flat this morning. The sound studio and gym, which you haven't yet seen, were built by Wefers Construction."

"Bernie?" He gave a low whistle.

"He came here in person. He knows Nathan. And it wouldn't surprise me if he installed this gunroom as well. They go back some way, apparently."

Diamond took this in, frowned and made the considerable mental effort to shift his attention from the current emergency to the case that had started all this. "Bernie and Nathan? Who would have thought it?"

"I meant to tell you sooner. It got overtaken by all this."

"It's okay," he said, still making the connection and trying to see how it played.

Ingeborg filled him in more fully. "I asked Lee about each of the main suspects. I think she's in a little bubble of her own. She didn't know about Gildersleeve being killed and she hadn't heard of Dr. Poke or Monica, but when I mentioned Bernie, she knew him straight away as someone who came here and discussed the specifications for the studio and the gym."

"Monica hasn't been here?"

"Not to Lee's knowledge, anyway."

"But Bernie has definitely done business with Nathan?" He was still absorbing, still calculating.

"I got the impression they were thick as thieves."

He leaned back against Bernie's solidly constructed wall and gave his verdict. "This takes us into uncharted waters. If Bernie is a regular here and very likely built the gunroom, he wouldn't think twice about borrowing a handgun. We know he threatened Gildersleeve at the time of the divorce. It's not looking good for Bernie. Your undercover mission has really paid off."

"I still wish I'd picked up those bloody Webleys. One of them is almost certainly the murder weapon."

"Let's not assume anything," he said.

"Did you look at the list I brought back?" she asked, hardly listening. "That could clinch it."

"Personally, no. I haven't had time. Someone in the office is going through it looking for initials we can recognise, but they may be in code."

"Is Nathan as careful as that?"

"I don't know. You've met the man. I haven't yet. Going by his actions, I'd say he's a smart operator."

They returned downstairs and inspected Lee Li's purpose-built annexe, the sound studio and the gym. "I'm sure he genuinely loves her, to provide all this," Ingeborg said.

Romantic deeds didn't feature in Diamond's take on

Nathan. "He didn't stop his bodyguards shooting at her when you were escaping in the Aston Martin."

"They wouldn't have seen her. I told her to keep her head down."

The search of the building continued. The entrance hall was being used as the headquarters and Halliwell was presiding. Little of interest had been found so far. Of Diamond's wish-list, only the logbooks of the Daimlers and the Aston Martin had been found. The registration numbers had already been obtained from the Police National Computer.

"No news of sightings, I suppose?" Diamond asked.

"I'd tell you, wouldn't I?" Halliwell said. "But the crime scene team have started work under the tree."

"I won't hold my breath."

Diamond took off the ripped jacket and slung it over a chair.

"That's blood on your shirt," Ingeborg said.

"Nothing serious."

"You should get some antiseptic on it."

"Don't fuss."

"You saved my life. I have a right to fuss. I'll get the first aid kit from the car and don't try and stop me."

In five minutes he was shirtless and being fussed.

"Do you mind if I ask something?" Ingeborg said.

"Ask away."

"Why did you send Paul Gilbert here?"

"I didn't. I couldn't understand why your car was left on the dockside. Georgina got wind of it and wanted action, so I gave Paul an outing. In no time he was hot on your trail."

"But we agreed that I wouldn't report in."

"Absolutely."

She changed abruptly from caring nurse to counsel for the prosecution. "You couldn't let me get on with it, so you sent Paul to check?"

"Are you listening Inge? It wasn't like that at all. He took it on himself to put the house under surveillance. The first

I knew of it was when he started texting me. I finally get a phone call late last evening and he's up the tree with the dog in attendance."

"What a mess. What did you do?"

"I was angry. I told him to use his initiative and get the hell out of there." He made a movement of his shoulders that could have been taken for a shudder. "If I could turn the clock back, I would."

Ingeborg nodded, more accepting now. "You know he lives with his mother. Should we let her know?"

"As yet, we don't know for certain ourselves."

"If he's not been home since yesterday morning, she'll be worried."

"Don't you think he would have phoned her?"

"To say he was on a job? I suppose."

"If there's bad news to pass on, I'd rather be certain about it," he said. "And I won't do it over the phone."

Late in the afternoon, with no more news and nothing to show for the search, he released the armed response team and they got in the buses and returned to Bath. But in the grounds, the CSI team continued the painstaking examination of the area under the oak. Nothing new of any significance had been found.

Even the Dobermann had given up barking and was asleep in the caged area behind the house where it was kept.

As time passed, Diamond was thinking increasingly about Paul Gilbert's mother. Maybe Ingeborg was right and they should contact her soon.

Then Halliwell took a phone message from Bristol Central. A corpse had been sighted in the River Avon.

26

Bristol police informed Diamond that the location was difficult. The body was beached three hundred metres downstream from the Clifton suspension bridge, on the Leigh Woods side. The sheer sides of the gorge made access a problem.

"So how do I get there?" Diamond asked, his thoughts more on the grim task of identification than the practicalities.

"Where are you now?"

"Still at Nathan Hazael's place."

"You could leg it through the woods but it would take at least an hour."

"Too long. Oh Christ, I'll work something out."

"A bike?" Ingeborg said, when he came off the phone.

"Are you serious?"

"That's the quickest way I can think of. The cycle path runs the whole way along the gorge. I did it once."

He hadn't sat on a bike in twenty-five years, but this was an emergency. "Where do I get one?"

"I'll come with you," she said. "We can phone ahead and have two bikes waiting for us at the car park in the woods. Won't take us long to drive there and then we can cycle down to the river."

"You don't have to come," he said, wanting to spare her the ordeal at the end.

"You'll never find your way alone."

In the car they exchanged hardly a word. Each of them was grappling with anguished thoughts. Diamond kept telling himself this tragedy could have been averted—as it certainly could if he'd responded to Paul's distress call the night before. But going to the young man's aid with a police team would have put Ingeborg's mission at risk and placed her in danger. A balance of risks with a bad outcome whatever he'd done.

For Ingeborg, the mental pain was more about grief than guilt. She was reflecting on a young life lost, on memories of duties she'd shared with Paul, like last year's search of the Walcot Street pubs and clubs on the trail of the Somerset sniper. Wide-eyed and innocent, the young DC had tried hard to play the alpha male and amused her at the time. Now she remembered that evening with affection, but much more with a sense of loss. Paul's death would leave a huge gap in the CID room.

The bikes were ready in the car park.

"Small wheels," Diamond said.

"They make them like that now," Ingeborg said. "Haven't you noticed?"

"Let's go, then. You'd better lead."

If she sensed him wobbling behind her, she had the tact not to turn and look. After a few minutes he steadied a bit and felt more in control of the thing, but the character of the terrain soon undid any confidence. The agreeable flat stretch didn't last long. They swung right towards the gorge and started to descend. Of course the shortest route to the river was straight down the side of the gorge and would have ended in disaster. Whoever had designed the cycle trail had worked out a way of going diagonally across the steepest angle. Even so, once they started freewheeling and gathering speed, Diamond felt like closing his eyes.

"Still with me, guv?" Ingeborg shouted.

"Do I have any choice?"

They sped down the ramp and in no time the gleam of the river showed below. Ingeborg had been right. This was certainly quicker than walking. Quicker than most forms of transport on this incline. Finally the angle of descent eased and they took a gentle right turn and linked with the river-side route.

"If we kept going, we'd end up in Bath," Ingeborg said.

He didn't comment. His legs were stiff as tree trunks, not from pedalling, but the tension of being on a runaway bike for the past three minutes.

On level ground they progressed along the base of the gorge in the shadow of the enormous cliff. The trick was not to study the scenery, or your steering suffered. But one feature stood out. Round an outcrop of limestone, a pale blue forensic tent came into view on a small strip of shoreline, a uniformed figure beside it.

They dismounted and leaned the bikes against the rock face.

Walking like a swan with sciatica, he needed a moment to get himself together.

"Are you okay?" Ingeborg asked.

"I'm trying to work out the mechanics of bringing a body all the way down here without a car."

"I don't suppose they used a bike."

"Well, they wouldn't have used ropes and pulleys either. They must have been some way upstream from here. The tide would make a difference. Places to stand on the bank. The water will have been many feet lower than it is now."

"Near the bridge you can get a car closer to the river."

"Now you tell me."

Both of them knew this was facile conversation, a way of filling a nervous interval with words, like people outside a crematorium talking about their journey. He hobbled across the cycle path and down a bank of rubble towards the tent.

"Damaged your sleeve on the way down, sir?" the sergeant on duty said.

"That was earlier," Diamond said. "Let's get on with this."

The sergeant raised his hand as if on traffic duty. "I wouldn't go in yet. The pathologist doesn't want to be interrupted."

"How did *he* get here before us?"

"I wouldn't know."

The big man folded his arms in frustration. "So how was it found?"

"A sighting upriver. The current tends to bring them to this side, so we were waiting. This isn't the first jumper to have ended up on this little stretch of mud."

"Jumper?" Diamond said. "You're not thinking this was suicide?"

"I'm not thinking anything else," the sergeant said. "I know they made it more difficult by raising the height of the barrier, but we still get four or five a year hell-bent on killing themselves. It's the loveliest bridge in Britain, spectacular, but more saddos have topped themselves here than any other spot except Beachy Head."

"We suspect he was dead before he entered the water," Diamond said.

"Get away."

"There was a fatal incident at a house off North Road last night that we're investigating."

"That's news to me," the sergeant said as if he didn't believe a word.

"It shouldn't be," Diamond said. "We put out an all-units call. Two black Daimlers."

"That? Yes, I heard about that. Didn't connect it with this."

"Four or five bodies a year, you said. How many do you reckon to find in a day?" Diamond said, getting irritated—and it wasn't the fault of the sergeant. The pathologist was making a meal out of this, considering he would have the postmortem to decide on the cause of death. It wasn't as if the ground they were standing on was a crime scene. This was only the place where the corpse was beached.

Ingeborg must have seen her boss was on a short fuse because she chipped in with a question of her own. She asked the sergeant if he'd helped to recover the body from the river and he confirmed that he had.

"Any signs of violence you wouldn't expect? We wouldn't be surprised if he was shot."

"Shot? I didn't see any bullet wound."

"They're not always obvious, especially if you were already thinking he'd drowned."

"They don't drown," the sergeant said. "They hit the water at seventy-odd miles an hour. That's what does for them."

"The impact, you mean?"

"Water is like a brick wall at that speed."

"He wasn't tied up, or anything?"

A disbelieving frown. "Christ, no."

At last the pathologist emerged—Bertram Sealy, who had crossed swords, or scalpels, with Diamond many times before.

"Hey ho," he said, "are you so short of work in Bath that you come looking for it here?"

Diamond wasn't interested in sparring with Sealy. "How exactly did he die?"

"If I may say so, that's a pretty dumb question to put to me before I've done the autopsy."

"We want to know if he was dead before he entered the water."

"Can't tell you, old sport. I may discover more after I've opened him up, but don't count on it."

"But you'll know if he was dead?"

"Not necessarily. There will be extensive impact injuries, probably multiple fracturing of the thoracic cage and maybe the skull, but that would happen regardless. If you have information that someone was seen pushing a lifeless body off the bridge, you'd better tell me now."

"Nothing like that. We're thinking he could have been murdered and placed in the water further upstream."

"Unlikely. He hit something pretty damn hard, I can tell you. But then it's seventy-five metres down. Quite some drop."

Diamond exchanged a shocked look with Ingeborg. It was starting to sound as if they had pushed Paul off the suspension bridge.

Sealy unzipped his white paper overall and started pulling it off. "I've done all I can here. I'll perform the necessary tomorrow morning. Move him as soon as you like," he told the sergeant.

"We'll wait for low tide, sir."

"Sensible, yes. Did you hear that, superintendent? Tomorrow morning."

"I heard." Diamond wasn't thinking about tomorrow. He was steeling himself for what he would see inside the tent. Turning to Ingeborg, he said, "You don't have to come in unless you want to."

"I'll be okay, guv."

They stooped, stepped inside and looked at the body flat on its back, the clothes coated with mud, the face smeared with filth and blood, but wiped clean around the eyes, nose and mouth.

Ingeborg said, "Oh my God!"

Diamond said, "That's not Paul."

Ingeborg said, "It's Nathan."

27

Diamond's first action after returning to Bath in the afternoon was to send Ingeborg home. She needed some proper sleep. But before that, she would have the thankless job of breaking the news to Lee Li about Nathan. The cause of death wouldn't be confirmed until the autopsy was performed, but Sealy, the pathologist, had been confident the firearms supplier had fallen from the suspension bridge.

Suicide?

It seemed the only explanation. Difficult to credit, a millionaire criminal choosing to top himself. Even allowing that his secret gunroom had been found by an undercover police officer and he faced a long prison term if convicted, he'd got the weapons off the premises before they could be used as evidence. He'd quit the house in time. He had other places to go, a reasonable chance of staying at liberty. From his point of view, the raid on his house should have been more of a setback than a disaster.

But as Ingeborg had reminded Diamond on the drive back from Bristol, Nathan had suffered a devastating emotional wound. Lee Li had dumped him. If he had been under any illusion that she still loved him after seeking sanctuary with Marcus Tone, he couldn't ignore the fact that the next day she had run off a second time. "He doted on her, guv. He built that studio and the gym and he bankrolled her singing career. Whatever she thought of the arrangement, he was crazy about her."

Supplying guns to murderers and bank robbers didn't sit well with unrequited love, but Diamond had seen the recording studio and the gym. He'd seen the bedroom the couple had shared, the king-size bed draped in pink chiffon, the matching soft toys and the wardrobe stuffed with designer clothes. It all testified to a man hopelessly besotted.

Nathan must have driven across the suspension bridge thousands of times. He would have known it was Britain's leading suicide bridge and from time to time he would surely have given thought to what it would be like to jump. No great surprise if he preferred that way to blowing his brains out with one of his own revolvers.

For Diamond and everyone in the team, the overriding question was what had happened to Paul Gilbert. No reports had come in of a second body. The Daimler limousines had not been sighted.

And it wasn't only Bath CID who needed to know. Somebody else would be going out of her mind with worry. Diamond found a safety pin and reattached the torn sleeve to his jacket.

"Can't leave it any longer," he told Halliwell. "I'm off to visit his mother. She'll expect him home tonight."

"I could do that," his deputy offered, thinking, perhaps, of the poor woman finding Diamond, grim-faced, on her doorstep. The boss in his dark suit looked uncannily like a harbinger of death.

A shake of the head. "You can do me another favour."

"Nathan's autopsy tomorrow?"

A faint grin. "How did you guess?"

He was back within the hour, looking relieved.

"How did she take it?" Halliwell asked.

"She didn't. She isn't there. The neighbour told me she's on a bus tour in the Lake District and not expected back until the weekend."

"We may have found him by then."

He gave a melancholy nod. "I suppose it will spare her the extra pain of not knowing for certain."

This state of limbo was, of course, weighing on everyone

in Manvers Street police station. Nothing active they could do. It was a matter of waiting for the confirmation they all dreaded. The right way forward was to keep occupied on the investigation, do the painstaking work they were trained for.

Diamond went over to his most reliable civilian assistant, a woman in her fifties called Penny. She had been given the task of analysing Nathan's paperwork recovered from the gunroom. "What did you discover?"

"He was selling or renting firearms at the rate of three or four a week," she said. "A variety of weapons, too, from Kalashnikovs to nine-millimetre pistols."

"I'm interested in the two Webleys Ingeborg saw."

"It's not an inventory," Penny said. "It's a record of the guns that went out. Nobody rented a Webley, not even one."

"Pity. That was the type of gun that killed Professor Gildersleeve. How about the customers? Can we identify anyone?"

"You might," she said. "I haven't—but then I only have initials to go by."

"Was he using a code, or are they the real initials?"

"They look real to me. Four months ago, there was an armed robbery at a jeweller's in Keynsham. A Bristol man by the name of Leslie Beech was charged and is now awaiting trial. He was found in possession of a Browning self-loading pistol. If you look at November seventeenth, you'll see a Browning nine millimetre out to someone listed as LB."

"No argument about that," Diamond said, studying the sheet, now enclosed in a transparent filing pocket. "Is there any link to our suspects Bernie Wefers, Archie Poke or Monica Gildersleeve?"

"Sorry, Mr. Diamond, but their initials don't feature at all."

"Too bad. We know Bernie oversaw the building of the sound studio and the gym and probably the gunroom as well, so he had opportunities to help himself and not be listed here, but the others, no." He dropped the sheet on her desk. "I was hoping we'd learn more from this. I was thinking it might be in code, but you say it makes sense the way it is."

Penny looked up at him. "You like a puzzle, do you, Mr. Diamond?"

"Not sure about that. I like a challenge."

"Crosswords?"

"I don't do crosswords." His face softened as the memory of an earlier time stirred in his brain. "When Steph was alive—she was my wife—we did the occasional jigsaw, but I was more of a hindrance than a help. We'd use up all the pieces we'd got and find one missing and it would be stuck to the bottom of my shoe."

"But you found it in the end."

"Most times, yes. I don't give up easily." He returned to his office and found the *Wife of Bath* back in occupation, returned from her photocall. "And neither do you."

He'd come to another decision. He picked up the phone and spoke to Bristol police about organising a search of Leigh Woods at first light next morning, using dogs.

"It's a big area," the inspector said. "Forest terrain."

"I know. I cycled through it this morning. You'll need everyone you can spare, and more."

"Are we looking for a corpse?"

"Unhappily, yes."

"Will you be there to supervise?"

"Sorry. I'm needed here, but someone from Bath will definitely join you."

He sank into his chair and reflected on twenty-four hours he wished to God he could re-run. This time yesterday he had been receiving texts from Paul Gilbert. He'd forever blame himself for consigning the young DC to his fate.

Don't dwell on it, he told himself. If nothing else, you have a duty to put the investigation to bed. That won't be redemption, but it's the least you can do if the boy's death isn't to be completely wasted.

What have you learned from the whole debacle?

He'd pinned too much hope on the log sheets from the gunroom. The best they could provide would be information for other investigations. Another disappointment was the removal of the gun hoard to some new hiding place. Difficult to track down now that Nathan was dead. No doubt the criminal world would find a way of bringing the weapons back into use.

The bodyguards, too, would disappear into the underworld. He had no great hopes of detaining them. Lowlifes like that were adept in merging with the background and leaving no trace.

The one breakthrough was learning of Bernie's involvement with Nathan. The boorish property developer had become the prime suspect in the shooting of Gildersleeve. The case against him had strengthened markedly in spite of the fact that under questioning he'd claimed to have an alibi—on the day of the auction he'd been at one of his homes in Maidenhead or London. He wasn't even sure which one, and it was just his word.

Diamond called Wefers Construction and got a recorded message saying that the office was closed. Easy to forget that the rest of the world worked to civilised hours like nine to five.

Plenty was still going on in the incident room. He shouted for Keith.

Halliwell put his head round the door. "Guv?"

"Do we have Bernie's mobile number?"

"I'll get it."

Bernie's recorded voice said, "I'm out of the country right now. Leave a message and I'll get back to you."

"Out of the country?" Diamond said. "Has he done a runner?"

"I doubt if he'd record a message if he had," Halliwell said. He scratched his head. "What was the name of his PA?"

"Colleen."

"She must keep a diary of his appointments. I'll phone her in the morning, find out where she thinks he was on the day of the shooting. And I'll have another go at Monica. I need more background on her ex."

"She's got her second husband's funeral tomorrow."

"Where? Reading?"

"The crematorium at eleven thirty."

"We must be there. We can make it, can't we?"

"You mean you and me?" Halliwell said. "If you remember, I'll be at Bristol mortuary."

"How come you get all the luck? It will have to be John Leaman, then. Not my first choice of companion at a funeral."

Halliwell gave him a look that was not overburdened with sympathy and left for home soon after, and the CID room entered ticking-over mode, with just two DCs and a sergeant on duty.

Diamond remained in his office until ten thirty waiting for the news that refused to come. When fatigue finally hit him and he signed off, it was with instructions that he should be phoned at home as soon as a report came in of an unidentified body.

Somewhere between Membury services and junction 14 on the M4 next morning, John Leaman made his first intelligent remark of the day: "There's a toll on the Clifton suspension bridge. Does it have cameras?"

"It must do, for security," Diamond said and then sat forward so abruptly that the safety belt tightened across his chest. "Good point. It's the obvious route out of Leigh Woods. Nathan ended up on the bridge for sure."

"He ended up in the river," Leaman said with his dogged logic.

"Okay." Diamond took out his mobile. "But there should be footage of the limos at the bridge. I'm calling Manvers Street now to get those cameras checked."

After the call was made and the instructions issued, Leaman said, "So what was the sequence of events after the two Daimlers drove away from the house yesterday morning?"

"Another good question," Diamond said, and meant it. With so much else on his mind, he hadn't looked at Nathan's actions in a systematic way. "Whatever opinion we have about the man, he was well organised. He'll have moved his precious guns to a safe place first. A lock-up is the most likely.

Leigh Woods isn't noted for them, but across the bridge near the docks there are storage facilities in plenty. The place is stiff with old warehouses and lock-ups. He'll always have had some place in mind. That would be his first stop, definitely."

"You don't think he'd trust his men to unload the stuff later?"

"He was too controlling."

"Then would he also want to supervise the disposing of Paul's body?"

Diamond composed himself, resolved to accept the gruesome reality as impassively as Leaman spoke of it. "I believe so."

"Difficult. It would have been almost daylight by then and people were about."

"They could have shoved him into a lock-up with the guns. They back the limo up to the entrance and no one sees."

Leaman nodded. "There is another possibility."

"What's that?"

"They dropped him off the bridge."

"Before Nathan jumped? Difficult. There are cars crossing the bridge all the time and sometimes pedestrians. I've seen how high the barrier is. You'd have a job heaving a body over it without being seen."

"Agreed."

"Besides," Diamond added, now thinking as coolly as his ultra-cool companion, "I'm pretty certain Nathan was alone when he climbed up and jumped. You don't commit suicide in front of your staff. He told his men to drive away and get the cars off the road before the hunt started. Then he made his own way to the bridge and put an end to himself."

"You must be right, guv," Leaman said after weighing what had been suggested. "It makes more sense."

A mile or two more along the motorway, Diamond got through to Colleen. "At last! Am I really speaking to a human being and not a cassette?"

"Who is this?" Colleen said.

He introduced himself and asked where her boss was. It turned out that Bernie had a meeting in Paris to discuss a building project and would return on Eurostar in the evening and stay overnight at his London address.

"So I can see him tomorrow."

"He's extremely busy," Colleen said.

"And now he's going to be busier still."

After running through Bernie's appointments they agreed that the best location would be Melksham, where a new shopping precinct was to be officially opened by the mayor at eleven.

"Excellent," Diamond said. "If the mayor is attending, there'll be champagne with salmon and cucumber sandwiches."

When they left the motorway at Reading, Leaman seemed to have a good grasp of the direction, so Diamond didn't offer help with the navigation. Once before he'd asked this cerebral DI why he didn't use a sat-nav and had been told he preferred to memorise the route. Around Reading's maze of roads, this was a formidable challenge. Unerringly they cruised through to Caversham, north of the town, and All Hallows Road where, appropriately, the crematorium sits.

With time to spare, they sat in the car park watching the other arrivals while Diamond called Bristol Central to ask how the search of Leigh Woods was progressing. And there had been a development. They had found Paul Gilbert's car parked on the verge in North Road some two hundred yards from Nathan's front gate. He must have left it there when he went to the house.

He spoke his thoughts to Leaman. "It's a step forward, I suppose. It confirms he didn't get back there."

"Not good news," Leaman said.

Trying to be positive, Diamond turned his attention back to the mourners.

"The high and mighty of the university will turn out for this," he told Leaman. "One of their professors cruelly gunned down. They have to be here, don't they? The vice chancellor and the dean and most of the senior common room. What interests me is whether Dr. Poke puts in an appearance."

"Why shouldn't he?" Leaman asked.

"They were rivals, weren't they? Sworn enemies. He had scarcely a good word to say for Gildersleeve. It's a dilemma for him. He's sweating on Gildersleeve's job, so he'll want to rub shoulders with the people who have a say in the appointment. I reckon he'll want to be seen here. Some will call him a bloody hypocrite, but if he stays away it will look worse."

The turnout was impressive, in dress as well as numbers. This was a more formal funeral than some others Diamond had attended. So many immaculately tailored dark suits, white shirts and black ties emerged from the cars that he wished his second-best suit had been a black pinstripe like his first instead of chestnut brown. He used the rearview mirror to check his tie, which was mainly black with hints of brown. "Let's get in there."

"At the double," Leaman said. "The hearse is coming up the drive."

Everyone was waiting outside for the principal mourners to appear, but the undertaker—in top hat and tails—ushered them in first. Diamond felt more conspicuous than ever, a brown slick in the sea of black. Even Leaman was in a leather jacket and black jeans.

Monica came in last with a woman who was presumably her sister Erica and a bearded man who must have been the brother-in-law. The widow had gone to some trouble with her outfit. She had a cape not unlike the garment Diamond had worn on rainy nights as a young copper in the Met, a fascinator hat with jet beads on tendrils (which he hadn't), tight black trousers and startlingly high heels.

The humanist service took a lot of the formality out of the occasion. Instead of hymns they listened to taped music from Duke Ellington and the Modern Jazz Quartet and some of the congregation joined in with the Beatles' "Let It Be." When the eulogy particularly mentioned John Gildersleeve's admiration for Chaucer's joy in poking fun at religious and secular institutions, Diamond didn't feel so bad about being the standout in the brown suit.

Just before the curtains moved and put the coffin out of sight, he scribbled G2G on the order of service and showed it to Leaman, who of course knew all about texting, but wasn't amused.

A footnote invited everyone to a reception afterwards at the Griffin, a pub-restaurant close to Caversham bridge. There, sure enough, Dr. Poke's shock of red hair was much in evidence as he sashayed from the vice chancellor's group to the registrar's to the dean's.

"Keep him in your sights," Diamond told Leaman. "When he's finished sucking up, I want a word with him."

He also wanted a word with Monica, but it was she who found him—courtesy, no doubt, of the suit. He didn't get the kiss she was giving most people, but he was warmly received. "How kind of you to come, detective superintendent. I've been telling people you're close to making an arrest and I hope it's true. Living with this uncertainty is a trial."

"I wouldn't say I'm close, ma'am, but I'm working on it."

"Did you catch up with my former husband?"

"Bernie Wefers? Yes. In Marlborough the other day."

"I expect he denies everything."

"He did tell me something I didn't know and I'm wondering if it's true. Can we, em, speak somewhere more private? I notice there's a patio nobody seems to have populated yet."

She followed him outside, accepting sympathetic kisses on the way from various friends. They had the patio to themselves. "This is heated for meals in the evenings," she said. "I used to come here with John, bless him. Shall we sit down? These heels are murder."

The chance of being interrupted out here was less likely, especially if they were seated and in conversation.

Diamond cleared his throat. "I'd better come straight to the point."

"Bernie told you about my little fling with Archie Poke," Monica cut in. "That was a long time ago and has no bearing on your investigation."

"Why didn't I hear it from you, ma'am?"

"Heaven help us, when we met in Hedgemead Park, you were a total stranger. I wasn't going to titillate you with lurid details of my sex life."

"You spoke about Dr. Poke as a rival of your husband with no chance of becoming professor while he was alive."

"It's true. Didn't you see him in there just now, schmoozing the vice chancellor?"

"Your relationship with him ended when you left the group called the Diphthongs, is that right?"

"Emphatically. I wouldn't spend another minute with the man who ratted to my husband," she said with such force that the jet beads bounced with each syllable.

"But it's possible he still carried a torch for you."

"He had a funny way of showing it."

"What I'm getting at is that he may have taken it badly when you started seeing his rival, the professor."

She looked down thoughtfully and tapped her fingertips on the table. "Archie never said a word of reproach to me— and if he had, I would have had his guts for garters. I don't know what goes on inside that calculating head of his, so I won't say it's impossible, but I saw no sign of it. Speaking for myself, we were finished the day he betrayed me to Bernie."

"Can you think of anyone else your husband had reason to fear?"

"Apart from Bernie and Archie?" The beads were exercised again, laterally.

Recalling Paloma's tongue-in-cheek theory that Monica herself hired the gunmen to seize the carving when she heard the British Museum was bidding, he asked, "Did you know in advance that there was so much interest in the auction?"

"I heard about it constantly from John. He knew as soon as the catalogue went out that Chaucer scholars across the world would put two and two together. He was extremely nervous, losing sleep over it. I promised him I'd underwrite whatever bid he had to make."

"But did he know he was up against the British Museum?"

"I expect so. I imagine even they had an upper limit."

"Did you discuss what it was worth with him?"

"No. He simply *had* to possess it. You have to remember the background to this, the crushing disappointment of the dig at the Chaucer house in Somerset in two-thousand when nothing except a few worthless shards turned up. John was a broken man. He'd staked his career on finding some proof that Geoffrey Chaucer lived there. So when the *Wife of Bath* piece came up for sale and he realised its provenance, he felt it was fated to be his, a sort of vindication. He planned to publish papers and probably a book."

"It seems there was a dig in early Victorian times that cleaned out the site. The stone was probably excavated then."

"I've heard something of the sort. John didn't ever find out about that, certainly not in two-thousand."

"It was in a local newspaper archive. These days plenty of them are digitised. All you have to do is put the words 'Chaucer' and 'excavation' into the search engine and it takes you straight to the right paper."

"John knew about that sort of thing. He did a lot of research."

"But he didn't find the 1843 report in the *Bridgwater Mercury*."

"He'd lost heart."

"You told me he never returned to North Petherton."

She shook her head. "Too painful . . . But he will be going back."

He raised his eyebrows.

"I intend to scatter his ashes there, at the site of Chaucer's house," she said. "It seems symbolic, a recognition that he was right after all and a triumph over the disaster that dogged him for so long. I can't think of anywhere else he'd rather be. Have you been there?"

Diamond nodded. "It's only a field now, as you know, but there's a guy called Tim Carroll who knows exactly where the house once stood. You could contact him through the Bridgwater museum."

"Or I could ask you, as you've been there and it's down

your way." The request didn't come across as heartfelt, more like an afterthought.

Scattering ashes wasn't strictly in Diamond's job description, but it was difficult to say a straight no to the principal mourner. "If my other duties allow it and you really can't find anyone else, certainly."

"Thanks." She glanced behind her at the reception still going on. "If we've finished, I ought to be going back."

"Before you do, I haven't asked if you attended the auction. I didn't see your name in the list of witnesses."

"I kept away," she said. "It was John's domain."

"But your money."

"I'm sure Bernie will have told you I did rather nicely out of our divorce. I wasn't worried how high the bidding would go."

"So where were you?"

"On the day of the auction? At home here in Caversham. We hadn't long moved in. There was plenty to keep me occupied."

"Is that where you were when you heard the sad news?"

"By then I'd gone out for a walk by the river. They contacted me on the mobile."

"What time would that have been?"

"I don't know. I was far too shocked to take note of the time. In the afternoon. Why do you need to know?"

"It's routine, ma'am. We try to fix where everyone was."

"But you don't think I had anything to do with it? I'm the tragic widow. Get that very clear in your head, superintendent." With that, she rose from the chair and teetered away on her murderous heels.

Diamond emptied his glass and went to look for Dr. Poke.

28

"He's scarpered."

"Already?" Diamond said, his voice rising in annoyance. "But I particularly asked you to keep an eye on him."

"I did," Leaman said in the obstinate tone he used when he felt he was in the right. "If I'd followed him, you wouldn't have known where either of us was."

"I carry a phone these days."

"But is it switched on?"

The team were taking his old habits for granted. In fact, in the last twenty-four hours the damn thing had not only been switched on, it had been used so much that it would soon need recharging. He ignored the last question. "Are you sure he's left the pub?"

"As soon as the vice chancellor went, so did Poke."

"I can't have that. How long ago?"

"Three or four minutes."

"He's probably still in the car park saying goodbye to people. You don't rush away from funerals."

But when they looked outside it was clear that Dr. Poke wasn't the lingering sort. The vice chancellor and his party were still in conversation beside the chauffeur-driven Mercedes, but no one else was in sight.

"He's not giving me the slip." Diamond strode over to the vice chancellor and introduced himself. "I'm investigating the shooting of John Gildersleeve and it's of some importance that I speak to his close colleague, Dr. Poke, who seems to have left in the last few minutes. Would your office have his mobile number?"

It was swiftly arranged that Poke would receive a call from the vice chancellor's office asking him to be available for an interview with the police in his own office on the campus at three.

"That should guarantee it," Diamond said when he rejoined Leaman. "He's so desperate to become professor that if the vice chancellor asked him to strip to the buff and jump off Caversham bridge he'd do it without a second's hesitation."

"I expect he'd prefer that to meeting us," Leaman said.

"I got on well enough last time. But he bobs and weaves. I'll be glad of your help to get some straight answers."

They drove across town to the Whiteknights campus, one of the few partially green areas left in Reading's urban sprawl. Poke was waiting for them in the corridor outside the Old English suite, arms folded, ready for a confrontation. "Why did you have to involve the vice chancellor?" he asked before he opened his office door.

"He was the obvious person to ask. He's a human being, not a tin god," Diamond said.

"Did he recognise my name?"

"Straight away."

The start of a smile appeared as he allowed them inside.

Diamond added, "I don't suppose there are too many Pokes in the senior common room."

After they were waved towards chairs, Diamond introduced Leaman.

"I saw you both at the funeral," Poke said. "I can't imagine why you need to speak to me again."

"You were helpful last time," Diamond said. "But there are one or two matters we didn't touch on."

"Such as?"

"The Diphthongs."

The face looked suddenly as if it was coated in chilli powder. "You've been talking to Monica."

"Her ex-husband, in fact."

"Him?" he said with contempt. "I should have guessed. Only a philistine like Wefers would stoop to parading such a private matter before the police. This has no conceivable bearing on your investigation. Our short-lived liaison ended at least a year before Monica started up with Gildersleeve."

"But how did it begin?"

"When she joined my university extension course."

"Extending to the pub afterwards and your bed."

He caught his breath in annoyance and the fine red hair danced in sympathy. "That is *so* unnecessary. It's all in the past."

"You had a visit from Mr. Wefers after he found out."

He dismissed Bernie with a flap of the hand. "He came here with all guns blazing, and I treated him with the utmost civility and it spiked his guns, so to speak. Perhaps it was ungallant, but I left him in no doubt that Monica made the first approach—which is true. She felt neglected, and rightly so. He devotes far too much time to his business."

The emphasis was different, but the facts agreed with Bernie's own account.

"Were you in love with her?"

"Certainly not. I was a shoulder to cry on."

"You provided more than just a shoulder."

"Nothing that wasn't welcomed at the time. Do we have to dissect everything like this?"

Diamond ignored the last remark. "And did it stop after Wefers complained to you?"

"It did. She didn't appear at my classes again."

"When did you learn that John Gildersleeve was having an affair with her?"

"A long time after. I'm generally the last to hear of any gossip from the senior common room."

"Bit of a shock," Diamond said.

"Now I see what this is about. You think I was jealous."

"Weren't you?"

"Absolutely not. I knew from my own entanglement with Monica that he was playing with fire. He was welcome to her."

"This wasn't the reason why you and he had difficulty working together?"

Poke rebutted the suggestion with a sniff. "Not at all. That went back years. It may seem churlish of me to say so after that toe-curling eulogy we sat through this morning, but the truth is that Gildersleeve was a pathetic figure, unpopular with his students, delivering dull lectures and writing dull books. There, I've done it, speaking ill of the dead, but I want to make clear that sexual jealousy didn't motivate me. The man was a pain in every way."

"When you say it went back years, was there some incident that caused the falling out?"

"I wouldn't say we were ever friends. We tolerated each other rather better in the early years than recently. He had this personal crisis you and I discussed before."

"The dig that didn't deliver?"

"Yes. The experience soured him. He was never the same after that ridiculous misadventure. You wouldn't get me under canvas with a bunch of disaffected undergraduates for a single day, let alone a whole summer. Is it any surprise that when nothing was found after weeks of scraping, they took to sitting around smoking weed? He took it personally, stupid fellow."

"Monica told me one of them was sent down."

"For a later offence on the university premises, yes. The last straw, as far as Gildersleeve was concerned."

"The final spliff." Dr. Poke's high-handed manner was bringing out the jester in Diamond.

"Do you remember the name?" Leaman asked.

"Of the student? It's difficult enough to hold in one's head the names of all one's present intake."

Becoming more flippant by the minute, Diamond couldn't resist saying, "Jack Flash?"

Poke looked out of his depth, and was.

"Rhyming slang for hash."

"Oliver Reed," Leaman said, taking up the theme.

"Not now, John." Two jokers on the team was too much. "You said the professor was a pain in every way, as if there were other defects we haven't covered."

"How much time have you got? Personal habits, lack of professionalism, dangerous driving."

"Let's do the driving."

"The man was a menace on the roads. He drove as if he was drunk, frequently having minor collisions. I don't think he was capable of giving proper attention to the task."

"Did he injure anyone?"

"He wouldn't have told me if he had, and I'm certain he wouldn't have informed your lot. But I saw him once attempting to park in Redlands Road, shunting back and forth. He owned a thing like a tank, known as the Defender."

"Land Rover," Leaman murmured.

"He dented the cars either side of the space and then got out and walked away as if nothing had happened."

"Wouldn't it have been obvious to the other owners?"

"They would have noticed the damage to their own cars, but the Defender was already a mass of dents. He'd deny any memory of it."

"Did he drink?"

"Not to excess. He drove badly because his head was filled with more important matters."

"Such as Monica?"

A shake of the head. "Some trivial point from *The Canterbury Tales*, more likely."

"With the damage he did to other cars, he must have had a reputation around the university."

"And in the town. Whenever he was caught, he paid up. He preferred to cover the damage himself. No insurance company would have done business with him if he'd claimed every time."

All this was new information, to be followed up. "I wonder if he had a record," Diamond said to Leaman.

"For his driving? I doubt it," Poke said. "He didn't speed. He poodled along, but with his mind on other things."

Leaman had his phone out and was checking the police computer. "He poodled over a pedestrian crossing with people about to step on it, three penalty points, and a set of traffic lights, three more points."

"Didn't I tell you?" Poke said, hands outstretched.

Diamond prised himself out of the chair. "I need another look at his office."

"There's nothing in there," Poke said. "It was emptied, ready for the new professor—whenever he may be appointed."

"Emptied?" Riled, Diamond asked, "On whose authority?"

"Mine. Nobody said we should preserve the room as a morbid shrine. You took away the items you were interested in, the computer and some of the books. I had the rest boxed and put in storage for Monica, when she gets back from her sister's."

"We should have sealed the place," Diamond said to Leaman as if it was his fault.

"I wasn't here, guv. This is my first visit."

"I'd still like to look at it," Diamond said, advancing on the connecting door.

"As you wish," Poke said in a world-weary way, becoming used to Diamond's cussedness.

Emptied it was. Not a stick of furniture remained. Even the carpet tiles had been taken up. The void seemed to affirm Poke's triumph over his old adversary. Although the shape of the office was identical to his own, he planned to shift his things inside as soon as he got the go-ahead.

"It's in need of some redecoration," Diamond said.

"That's been arranged."

"I'm sure." He stepped closer to a cream-coloured oblong on the wall defined by the fading emulsion around it. "This was Chaucer on the stunted horse, the Ellesmere portrait."

"You have a good memory," Poke said.

"I need it. When we talked before, you told me about another portrait, a drawing thought at first to be of Chaucer, but identified by Professor Gildersleeve as Thomas, the son."

"What of it?"

"Quite a coup for Gildersleeve, I imagine, being consulted by the National Portrait Gallery."

"It's not unusual to be asked for our professional opinion."

"He saved them some embarrassment, not to mention a vast amount of money."

"And naturally he basked in the publicity."

"Yes, you said it made the national press. Do you remember when?"

A little gasp of impatience. "I have more important things on my mind than Gildersleeve's five minutes of fame."

"He's a lot more famous now he's dead. No matter. We can check the date."

"Why would you need to?"

"Because it wasn't only a triumph for Gildersleeve. It was clearly a disaster for the person who was selling the drawing."

Poke shrugged, not interested in someone else's misfortune.

"What would a new portrait of Chaucer have fetched?" Diamond went on. "A six-figure sum? More? I don't suppose Thomas Chaucer rates more than a few hundred—and I doubt if the National Portrait Gallery would want to buy it. All of which leaves us with a pissed-off seller and a possible motive for murder."

"That's stretching it."

"Not at all. People can hold grudges for a long time, particularly if they don't seem to be getting the breaks themselves."

You could have guillotined a man with the look Diamond got from Poke.

Untroubled, the big detective added, "I expect an art dealer was involved. Was the owner's name made public?"

Leaman said, "We can easily check the report now."

"On Dr. Poke's computer? What a good idea."

Back in Poke's office, with Diamond at his side and Poke with hands on hips looking like the kid whose toys are being played with, Leaman downloaded a newspaper report from April 2004 in a matter of seconds:

PORTRAIT IS NOT POET, EXPERT SAYS

An ink drawing believed to have been of the poet Geoffrey Chaucer, likely to have been purchased for the nation by the National Portrait Gallery, has now been identified by an expert as the poet's son, Thomas (c1367–1434). The drawing was discovered on parchment used as backing for a fifteenth century treatise on crop management. The name Chaucer clearly appears above a coat of arms at the side of the portrait and the drawing—a full-length study—was sent to be authenticated by Professor John Gildersleeve of Reading University, who has made a lifetime study of Chaucer.

'There is a distinct resemblance to other well-known portraits of the poet,' the professor reported. 'However, the coat of arms establishes it quite certainly as his son Thomas, who later in life preferred to use his mother Philippa de Roet's family arms. Philippa had noble connections in her own right. Her sister was the third wife of John of Gaunt. So it is understandable that in the hierarchical society of the time, Thomas preferred to be linked to his mother rather than the author of *The Canterbury Tales*. Thomas was a significant figure, Chief Butler of England and a long-serving Speaker of the House of Commons. His tomb in Ewelme Church bears the de Roet arms.'

The new identification makes a substantial difference to the value of the drawing. The National Portrait Gallery was thought to have been ready to buy the drawing for as much as a million pounds. It is now valued at about £3000. A representative of Matlock & Russell, the art dealers selling the drawing, said, 'Our client is understandably disappointed and prefers to remain anonymous.'

"'Understandably disappointed' was on the tip of my tongue when I said 'pissed off,' Diamond said. "Sorry about that. With my language I doubt if I'd get the job as Chief Butler of England. Can you print it?"

Leaman did so without even asking Poke. "I don't see it, guv."

"Don't see what?"

"How the client could blame Gildersleeve, who was just doing his job."

"You'd feel like kicking someone, wouldn't you? Gildersleeve's name is the only one here."

Leaman stayed unconvinced. "It's like blaming an expert witness in court."

"Suppose a few years later you discovered the same Professor Gildersleeve was dead set on buying another piece of Chaucer memorabilia. Wouldn't it be sweet to hijack it from under his nose?"

He nodded. "I can see the appeal of that."

"What do you say, Dr. Poke?" Diamond asked.

The lecturer was saying nothing.

Diamond pressed for an answer. "I was thinking you'd have an opinion, as someone forced to work with a colleague who was a pain in every way."

"That's unfair," Poke said. "You shouldn't stigmatise me for being honest. Most of the people at the funeral this morning would have agreed with me if they had any integrity. Have you finished with my computer now?"

"I'd like to know who the disappointed client was," Diamond said. "Won't the all-powerful computer tell us?"

Leaman said, "I doubt it, if he chose to be anonymous."

"The dealers would know. Can you get their phone number?"

He worked the keys again.

And again.

And again. "Looks like Matlock and Russell have gone out of business, guv. This is a directory of all the art dealers in the UK."

"I wonder if the National Portrait Gallery know the name."

"I can get a contact number for them."

The speed of the computer gives the impression that information is always instantly on tap. Twenty minutes on the phone with various individuals at the gallery was a salutary corrective. Finally everyone was forced to conclude that anonymous meant anonymous and even if some trusted high-up had known the name at the time, no record or memory of it had survived.

"I'll think of a way of winkling it out," Diamond said.

"He probably will," Leaman said to Poke. "That's one of his strengths, winkling things out."

Poke seemed unwilling to be impressed.

■ ■ ■

Before leaving the campus, Diamond wanted to winkle out
something else. He called at the registrar's office and asked
if they kept records of students who were sent down. They
referred him to the alumni office, who talked about data
protection until he said who he was and that he was investigating the shooting of one of their own professors. They
agreed to allow him access but said it would involve making
a special search of files that hadn't been computerised.
The archives were stored in another part of the university
known as the Old Red Building. He said he would make
the check himself if someone would show him where the
records were.

His persistence paid off. One of the staff was freed to
help him make a physical search. They drove down to the
Old Red Building, where he learned that no file existed of
excluded students. The only way of finding the names was to
compare the records of thousands of enrolled students with
the lists—almost as many—of thousands who had gone on to
complete their degrees. Anyone who didn't feature in both
lists could be assumed to have dropped out. However, the
dropouts would include students who had left the university
voluntarily, transferred to other universities, failed the first
year exams, or became too ill to continue, or died.

"This could take days," he said. "All I want is the name of
one bad egg sent down by the dean for dealing in drugs."

Leaman came to the rescue. "Can't we narrow it down?"

"Good thinking. They were studying English and History."

"In the session two-thousand to two-thousand and one,"
Leaman added.

The task was still daunting, but more manageable. The
helpful admin officer said she thought she could compile a
list of all the dropouts by next day.

Diamond told her she was a star.

Outside the Old Red Building, Leaman said, picking his
words with tact, "Are you thinking someone held a grievance

all these years and hired professional hitmen to kill Gilder-sleeve? To me, it doesn't seem likely."

"Me neither," Diamond said. "It's a loose end I wanted tidied up."

"Well. I hope that woman doesn't lose much sleep over it."

On the drive home through Reading at the rush hour, he kept making audible intakes of breath.

"You all right, guv?" Leaman asked.

"I wish you wouldn't drive so close to the car in front, that's all," he said. "This isn't the Defender, it's a little old Honda with bodywork that buckles on impact."

"It's my car."

"It's my body you have in the passenger seat."

"We're crawling."

"Try creeping."

As they approached the motorway on the A33 everything came to a complete stop.

"What's up now?" Diamond said.

"Someone up there heard your prayer."

"That's a first, then."

"Do you feel more comfortable now?"

"Don't get snarky with me." He took out his phone.

"Are you going to check what's happened?"

He nodded. But it wasn't the traffic hold-up he was checking. He got through once more to Bristol and asked if there was news from the search in Leigh Woods. Nothing had been reported. Neither had there been a sighting of Nathan's two limos.

"Are we checking the CCTV footage at the suspension bridge?" he said into the phone.

They were, and it was still going on.

"I want to be informed as soon as—"

The line went dead. He didn't like to think they might have cut him off deliberately.

Leaman found the local radio station and learned that the westbound section between junctions 11 and 12 had been closed because of an accident and was unlikely to be opened again for two hours.

Ahead, cars were making U-turns. Leaman checked his mirror and started to do the same.

"Where are we heading now?" Diamond asked.

"Back through the town to find the back way to the next junction."

To keep his mind off the driving, he tried to think of the positives from the funeral. Basically, he'd got what he came for, the interviews with Monica Gildersleeve and Archie Poke. And there was an intriguing new lead to pursue. Who was the anonymous seller of the Chaucer portrait who had missed out on a fortune when John Gildersleeve gave his expert opinion?

29

Ingeborg arrived early at Manvers Street next morning to find Diamond already there making waves, on the phone to Bristol, asking if the search of Leigh Woods had resumed, firing a series of questions at the hapless inspector on the line. How much of the woods had they covered? Were they still using the dog team? How many dogs? How many men? He went on to ask about the camera footage at Clifton suspension bridge. The check had been completed, a long, laborious process, and it emerged that one of Nathan's limousines had definitely crossed the bridge in the Bristol direction at 5:50 A.M. on the day Nathan's body was recovered from the river. The second limo had not been spotted.

"They split up, then," he said, talking to the Bristol inspector as if he was up to speed on every detail of the case. "It makes sense. The car caught on camera must have been carrying the gun collection to some secret lock-up in the docks area. The other was used to dump the body somewhere in the woods. Then that second car crossed the river by another route, most likely using Brunel Way and Avon Bridge. Nathan will have known every patrol car in the county was looking for those limos. He will have got them off the road and out of sight as soon as they'd shed their loads. Then he'll have told his men to disperse and lie low. He'll not have told them he was about to make his way on foot to the bridge to commit suicide."

There was a short pause in Diamond's flow when the inspector got a few words in.

Then: "I don't know if you've got the manpower, but somebody needs to search for the weapons and the cars. I'm strongly of the opinion that you'll find them in the docks area. But the search for DC Gilbert has priority over everything. Do you understand me? Top priority."

Then he put down the phone and sighted Ingeborg, calm and groomed again, with her blonde hair in the ponytail she usually wore and her lightly pencilled eyes giving no clue as to the tough time she'd been through.

"Rested now?"

"Rested and ready to go."

"How did Lee Li take the news of Nathan's death?"

"Like I expected. Shock. Some tears. She felt responsible, she said, and I soon knocked that on the head. She's now come round to the view that she was lucky to escape when she did. He could easily have turned angry and *she* might have ended up dead in the river. Now she can get on with her life and her singing career without looking over her shoulder every minute."

"Is she still at your flat?"

"Only until this afternoon. She'll be staying with a friend."

"You like her, don't you?"

A shrug and a smile. "She's sweet, but not empty-headed. She'll have more success, I'm sure."

"When she collects her Brit Award, you'll get a mention in her acceptance speech: 'And finally Ingeborg Smith who rescued me from the clutches of a major crime baron.'" He updated her on the Reading trip. "So you see, there's a lot happening," he concluded. "I'm off to Melksham presently to waylay Bernie Wefers."

"Want me to come?" she offered.

He needed her instead to get on the trail of the mystery seller of the Chaucer drawing. "I have a strong hunch it's worth finding out," he said. "We know the dealers were Matlock and Russell, who seem to have gone out of business. But it was only ten years ago. Someone must know the inside story."

"Were they London-based?"

"I'm not even sure of that. Would one of your contacts from the newspaper world be able to help?"

Before she could answer, another fresh morning face in the CID room set Diamond on a different tack. "Hello, here's the myrmidon of the mortuary."

"The *what?*" Keith Halliwell said.

"Never mind. What did you glean from yesterday's autopsy?"

"That you're unlikely to survive if you jump off the suspension bridge. You hit the water at thirty-three metres per second. Your thoracic cage is crushed and the ribs penetrate your vital organs. Lacerated lungs, ruptured liver and heart. Do you want me to go on?"

"Drowning didn't come into it, then?"

"Didn't need to."

"I thought I once read about a woman who survived."

"The famous case of the Victorian lady in a crinoline that acted as a parachute. Tragically, Nathan wasn't wearing his crinoline on this occasion."

As a reward for that mortuary duty, Halliwell found himself driving Diamond to Melksham, where Bernie Wefers was due to touch down in his helicopter. "What are we trying to achieve?" he asked Diamond.

"Some straight answers. When you and I met Bernie at Marlborough we didn't explore his links with Nathan."

"It didn't come up," Halliwell said. "Can't say I blame him. If you're being interviewed by the police you're not going to throw in a mention of Bristol's leading arms supplier."

"Actually, it did come up."

Halliwell frowned.

"But Nathan wasn't mentioned," Diamond went on. "If you cast your mind back, Bernie told us he went to Bristol to build an extension for a client, including a gym and a sound studio. We didn't pick up the significance because at the time we hadn't heard from Ingeborg about what she found at Nathan's."

"So he gave us the partial truth."

"We wrung it out of him. We knew he'd been to Bristol."

"Did we?"

Diamond shook his head. As a memory man, Halliwell wasn't in John Leaman's class. "The pilot told us about flying Nathan there and we checked the log and found it."

"Percy Sinclair."

"Come again."

"The pilot."

"You remember all the stuff it's safe to forget. I sometimes wonder about your reports on the autopsies, whether you give me every blessed detail about the stomach contents and then forget to say that the head was sawed off."

"If you doubt me, you could attend the autopsies yourself."

"One of these days, I might," Diamond said, a boast about as likely as his completing a triathlon. Then he moved on smoothly. "Bernie remains the prime suspect."

"But he has an alibi for the day of the killing."

"So does everyone else. He could still have hired some gunmen to hold up the auction. His motive is stronger than anyone's. He threatened Gildersleeve outside the divorce court."

" 'You'll pay for this.' "

"You're doing better now. And going by his brutal revenge on Monica when he caught her out with Gildersleeve, he takes a strong line on retribution."

"But he didn't attack Dr. Poke when he caught her out with him."

"I'm sure he meant to. Poke is a special case. There's something about the squeaky voice and the wispy hair that disarms people. I noticed it myself. Are you an apologist for Bernie, or what?"

"Devil's advocate," Halliwell said. "I agree he's got questions to answer."

Melksham was only twenty minutes from Bath, even at the modest speed Diamond insisted on. A small working town that was also a traffic hub, it had few friends. "Of all the small towns of Wiltshire," wrote Nikolaus Pevsner in *The Buildings of England,* "Melksham has least character and least enjoyable buildings." Whichever way you approached the place, you saw a sewage farm or a caravan park or the twenty-eight acres of tyre manufacturing. So it was possible that Bernie Wefers was doing Melksham a favour with his new shopping centre.

A centre maybe, but central it was not.

They followed the Wefers Construction notices by way of several small roundabouts to a site on the eastern edge of the town surrounded by the rutted mud of months of building work.

THE PALACE PRECINCT, declared the ironwork arch over the entrance to a concrete barrack block. "Who would have thought it?" Diamond said.

"Some jerk with a degree in public relations," Halliwell said.

"I don't know. If you planted a few trees, you might make it easier on the eye—in about thirty years."

"I expect they sawed down some fine trees here before they started."

"That's known as landscape architecture, Keith. Let's get to those sandwiches. I'm ready for them."

They were pleased to see Bernie's helicopter standing in a corner of the field. They'd timed this trip to perfection. The speeches were over and about twenty guests were being treated to drinks around a non-functioning fountain in the echo chamber that was the new precinct. Not one of the twenty-four shops was yet in use or even spoken for, so the excitement was limited to the potential of the concept. A few helium-filled balloons anchored to the fountain advertised Wefers Construction and a scratchy sound system was playing Elgar.

"You've got to hand it to the Brits," Diamond said to Leaman. "We know how to celebrate."

They each took a drink from a tray (sparkling wine, not champagne) and helped themselves to eats (mixed nuts, not salmon and cucumber sandwiches). Then they honed in on Bernie, who had broken away from the mayor's group and was looking at his watch.

"Not thinking of leaving already, were you?" Diamond asked him.

"You two again?" he said. "I'm starting to feel hounded."

"We work just up the road. Couldn't miss a chance to see your latest triumph and ask a couple of follow-up questions. When we last spoke, you didn't mention your business link to Nathan Hazael."

"Nobody asked me."

"We know you built the major extension to his house at Leigh Woods. Did you also design the first-floor bathroom with the sliding shower cabinet?"

He frowned. "What's it to you?"

"The hidden gunroom behind the shower."

"That's news to me. Goes in for field sports, does he? I never asked what he planned to do with it," Bernie said in a virtuous tone, wide eyes mocking them.

"Come on, everyone knows how Nathan made his money. A collection of illegal weapons that featured in God knows how many recent crimes."

"Fancy that."

"You must have become a personal friend, doing so much work for him."

"We got on," Bernie said. "Didn't talk guns at any point. Is that what you wanted to know?"

"Didn't you inspect the collection, even to judge how it would fit into the room?"

He raised a warning finger. "Lay off, will you? I told you I didn't know it was a bloody gunroom. He wanted a hidden room. That was the deal. For all I knew, it was for storing inflatable sex toys. You don't ask questions of somebody like Nathan."

"You must have spent plenty of time with him setting up all these projects."

He shrugged. "Not 'specially. I have staff, you know, architects and surveyors."

"All sworn to secrecy? He wouldn't have wanted his gunroom known to all and sundry."

Bernie grinned. "After they done the work, he took them out and shot them."

Now it was Diamond who wagged a finger. "Let's have some

honesty here, Bernie. Did you personally design and build the sliding shower?"

A shake of the head. "His design. My execution." And another grin. "Except I lived to tell the tale."

"It's an expert job, I'll give you that. When did you build it? Before the gym and the recording studio?"

"They were done at the end of last year for some pop star he was shacking up with. The bathroom was an earlier job. I'd say four or five years ago."

"While you were still married to Monica?"

"Must have been."

"Did she ever meet Nathan?"

"Monica?" He thought about it and shook his head. "Not to my knowledge. 'Work is work and wife is well out of it is my philosophy.' Hers, too. Long as the money kept coming in, she was happy."

Not the impression Diamond had got from Monica. She'd been far from happy when Bernie was off on his business trips. "Didn't she know you were doing work for a notorious arms dealer?"

He reconsidered, as if wary of a trap. "You'll have to ask her. Too far back for me to remember."

"She didn't take much interest in your work?"

"I just said."

"Were you interested in hers?"

"You're starting to sound like that bloody counsellor we had to see when we was getting divorced."

"Fourteenth century English texts."

"Give me strength. What would I know about that?"

"The poet Chaucer?"

"Are you enjoying this? Because I'm not."

"But you know about building materials. Did Monica ever speak of a block of limestone that was said to come from Chaucer's house in Somerset?"

"Now I see where you're going," Bernie said. "No, mate, leave me out of it. The first I heard about that thing was what I read in the paper after Gildersleeve was shot."

■ ■ ■

Angry—she couldn't disguise it—to be grounded, stuck in the CID room for the morning when a suspect was being interviewed not far away, Ingeborg was at her desk waiting for phone calls. They'd brought in the whiteboard and lots of photos and called it the incident room as if it was all action here, but who were they kidding? This remained the same old place where she spent far too much time sitting on her butt. After her undercover work, research on the phone was safe and boring. To say she was unhappy with Diamond was an understatement. For one thing she suspected he'd invented this task as a time-filler for her. He'd talked blithely about having a hunch. Jesus Christ, she thought, if she'd had the brass to mention a hunch, he'd have shot her down in flames. She'd heard him before going on about women's intuition. And for another thing, she *deserved* to be in the front line after all she'd done.

In the last hour she'd put out feelers about the drawing of Thomas Chaucer and the former art dealers Matlock and Russell and now she was waiting for various journalist contacts to get back to her. John Leaman was with her, as smug as the cat who had finished the cream. She didn't need reminding that he'd joined the boss on the outing to Reading.

"Any joy?" he asked. Not the best choice of words.

"On the phone, you mean? No. I'm waiting for someone to call back."

"Is this just a red herring?"

"We'll find out, won't we?" she said.

"He's losing confidence," Leaman said. "He's got three people firmly in the frame—Dr. Poke, Monica Gildersleeve and Bernie Wefers—and he hasn't nailed one of them yet. The more he questions them, the more confused he gets."

"Is that why he's having hunches, do you reckon?"

"Desperation, isn't it?"

She'd heard John Leaman in this vein before. There was

always a point in an investigation when he rubbished all the theories. Normally, she wouldn't have listened, but this morning his pessimism chimed in with her bolshie mood.

"What about forensics?" she said. "Won't they come up with something?"

"We won't get much more from them. We know the gun that fired the fatal shot was probably a Webley, but we haven't recovered it yet. The gunmen left no traces and they were all wearing balaclavas and rubber gloves. What does he think—that one of his prime suspects dressed up in a balaclava—or all three?"

"There were two Webleys in Nathan's collection. I saw them."

"Pity you didn't bring them back with you."

"I couldn't."

"Tough."

Leaman seemed to regard that as the last word. Ingeborg had no desire to explain the difficulties of her mission to old misery guts, so they each returned to their computer screen and silence—until her phone beeped.

"Inge? This is Klaus."

Klaus Harting, one-time arts correspondent on the *Daily Telegraph*.

"Good to speak again," Ingeborg said.

"*Sergeant* Smith, the switchboard said. So the change of job worked out for you."

"Most days, yes. How is it with you?"

"The same. I've done some rooting around, without much success. Whoever was selling the drawing you mentioned—of Thomas Chaucer—went to some trouble to stay anonymous. I can tell you it was withdrawn from sale when the value plummeted because it wasn't of Geoffrey Chaucer. The National Portrait Gallery were willing to buy it at a much reduced but not unreasonable price—Thomas being a significant man in the fifteenth century, if not quite a celebrity—but the seller refused to negotiate and the drawing hasn't been heard of since."

"Waiting for a more favourable time to sell?"

"Very likely. If it was billed as the main item in a new auction of historical portraits, it might do better. After the disappointment that it wasn't the poet, there was the feeling it was second-rate."

"But it hasn't come up for sale yet? Is it still with the original seller?"

"The mystery man—or woman. I presume so."

"Did you find out any more about Matlock and Russell?"

"The dealers. They ceased trading in two-thousand and five, I'm afraid. It was an old-established firm based in the West Country."

"Where I am," Ingeborg said.

"The kingpin was a guy called Austen Chalk. When he died, the firm died with him."

"Where in the West Country?"

"Bath. They had premises in Broad Street. It's probably selling fish and chips these days."

She was already on her feet. "I'll find out. Klaus, you're a star."

Fish and chips? Unlikely. Broad Street specialised in antiques, crafts, upmarket homeware, fashion and, of course, public houses. The best thing about it this morning was that Ingeborg could walk there in five minutes.

Out of the police station and with a mission in mind, she felt better already. The sun was out, turning the paleness of the stonework a richer cream and giving the colourful shop fronts more pizzazz. Broad Street has no desire to compete with the formal elegance of its neighbour, Milsom Street. Not particularly broad except in style, it caters for the independent-minded, some of whom might not object to being called broads.

The shop once owned by Matlock and Russell had changed hands at least twice to Ingeborg's knowledge and was now selling ethnic clothing, so she had no great hope that the present incumbents would know anyone who had worked there. But she knew of a gallery long

established in Broad Street called Mary Cruz and decided
to try there.

The assistant she spoke to had no memory of Matlock and
Russell, but in the street outside someone tapped her on the
shoulder and said, "Excuse me, I couldn't help overhearing
you in there. I take an interest in art and I remember the
gallery you were asking about, long since gone, I'm afraid."

"I know," Ingeborg said. "That's my problem."

"A Mr. Chalk managed it, but he died."

"So I heard."

"However, he had an assistant, who did all the paperwork,
a Miss Brie. We used to call them Chalk and Cheese, for
obvious reasons. That's how I remember her name. She's
still living here. I've seen her about."

"Do you know where?"

"Couldn't tell you, I'm afraid."

Rather than returning to Manvers Street to look up Miss
Brie's address, Ingeborg called in at the library. An assistant
at a gallery must surely have had an interest in reading.
If not, it was likely she would be on the electoral register,
which they kept there.

The librarian didn't need to consult the records. "We all
know Miss Brie," she said with a faint smile. "She's often
in, a very observant lady."

"How do you mean?"

"Whenever she returns a book, she supplies us with a
handwritten report on it. She lets us know of any gram-
matical errors or spelling mistakes or unsuitable language.
I don't know what we're supposed to do about it. Books
are full of mistakes. If it isn't the author's fault, it's the
publisher's or the printer's. We've tried explaining, but
she doesn't give up."

"You have her address, then?"

"Always at the top of her report. Mon Repos, Saville Row,
Bath. She's a bit old-fashioned, so she leaves off the postcode."

Mon Repos wasn't exactly modern either. "Saville Row is
the alleyway behind the Assembly rooms, isn't it?"

"Yes, but Miss Brie wouldn't put it like that. She's proud of the address, even though it's over a shop."

Ingeborg wasn't discouraged by what she'd learned so far. A punctilious woman was likely to remember the clients she'd met at Matlock and Russell. With Miss Brie's cooperation this phase of the investigation ought to be concluded shortly. Diamond's shocked face would brighten up the day.

She toiled to the top of Broad Street, across George Street, through Bartlett Street and on to Saville Row, uphill all the way. Anyone living here and regularly borrowing books from the library would need to be fit.

A black door squeezed between two shops had a card set into a metal frame with the legend: *Mon Repos, press bell and take stairs to first floor.*

She did as she was asked. The stairs were unlit and uncarpeted. At the top, a second card advised: *Mon Repos, privacy please, no free newspapers, no uninvited callers.*

Sorry, Ingeborg silently said, but this uninvited caller isn't going away. She rang the bell.

A delay of half a minute wasn't promising. She looked up and about her and was reassured that it was nothing personal. A lady who hadn't yet entered the age of postcodes was unlikely to be equipped with CCTV.

Then there were footsteps and the door opened a fraction. Ingeborg could just about make out a face not far above the level of the safety chain. Nothing was said. She had a suspicion that the door was about to be slammed shut, so she put her foot against it and said, "Miss Brie, I'm Ingeborg Smith, from Bath police. May I come in?"

"Is something the matter?" a voice suitable for a National Trust guide (but not so welcoming) asked.

"It's all right. I just need your help."

"Are you in trouble?"

"Not at all." She pressed her ID close to the gap. "It would be easier if you let me in."

The sound of the chain being released was encouraging. The gap widened and Ingeborg looked with awe at Miss

Brie, so close to being a stick insect that she might have squeezed through the door with the chain still in place. A hint of eau de cologne was left in her wake as she led the way through a small entrance hall into a sitting room that could have been an interior from a 1930s René Clair film, with lace edging everywhere, on the curtains, the lamp-shades, the tablecloth, the antimacassars and over the bird cage. Now that she was seated, ankles crossed, tiny hands resting in her lap, the top of a lace petticoat showed at the divide of her white blouse. She was at least seventy and probably half blind if the way she applied her lipstick was anything to go by.

"I do hope you're not here to sell me something," she said, having waved Ingeborg to the only other armchair.

"Not at all. I'm hoping you can tell me a little about Matlock and Russell. You worked there, I understand."

"For twenty-seven years, typing, filing and occasionally showing people round."

"Until when?"

"Until the manager, Mr. Chalk, decided to retire and died within a matter of days. That was two-thousand and five. It was a difficult time. People weren't buying so much. Has there been an art theft?"

"Not to my knowledge, but it's an item of art I would like to ask you about, a fourteenth century drawing that turned out to be of Thomas Chaucer."

"I remember. It was towards the end of my time there."

"Two-thousand and four, I believe."

"You really are well briefed. Would you join me in a pre-prandial glass of Courvoisier?"

Not while on duty, Ingeborg realised she ought to say. A lager top would go down a treat, she was tempted to say. "How kind—I'd love to," was what she actually said. Warming up the witness was a sensible move, even if she wasn't quite certain what she was letting herself in for.

Two balloon glasses were produced and she remembered what Courvoisier was. "I was born and brought up in France," Miss Brie volunteered as she poured generously from a cut glass decanter. She went on to open a tin of biscuits and arrange some on a Limoges plate that looked as if it, too, was made of lace. This was evidently a daily ritual. "I do insist that you have a Bath Oliver with it. I've survived on them for most of my adult life."

"They're hard to find now," Ingeborg said, taking one, a hard, bland version of a cream cracker.

"Not if you know where to shop. It's a well kept secret."

"Are you going to share it with me?"

"Certainly not. A secret shared is a secret lost."

This was not promising. "We were speaking about the Thomas Chaucer drawing," Ingeborg prompted her.

"I remember because it was so unusual. You don't see much pen and ink work from such an early period."

"I believe it was first thought to be of the poet, his father."

"The seller firmly believed so. We kept an open mind and insisted it was authenticated by an expert, a professor who made Chaucer a life study."

"John Gildersleeve."

"Correct."

"Unfortunately, he was shot a short while ago."

"I heard on the radio. A dreadful incident. Is this why you're here?"

"Indirectly, getting background information."

Miss Brie took a long sip of brandy and began to talk more freely. "When the professor recognised the subject as Thomas, he saved us all, and not least our client—who wasn't best pleased at the time—from a professional faux pas. Imagine the embarrassment if it had been sold to the nation for a fortune and later turned out to have been incorrectly identified."

"Who was the client?" Ingeborg asked, and immediately saw from Miss Brie's eyes that she'd asked one brandy too soon.

"I can't tell you that. We had an anonymity clause."

"But it's history now. You're not in business any longer."

"I have my standards, dear."

"It's become a police matter now. It's gone past personal ethics. We're investigating the professor's death."

Miss Brie smiled. "You don't scare me in the least. My parents stood up to the Gestapo. I'm unlikely to be bullied into submission by an English lady policeman."

"I'm not here to bully you."

"And I'm not betraying a confidence. Not now. Not ever."

"That is a disappointment. And Mr. Chalk is dead?"

"He wouldn't have told you, either."

"But the client is still with us?"

Miss Brie chose not to answer and emphasised it by tilting her little chin a fraction higher.

Ingeborg said, "If the client was also dead, there'd be no reason to keep this up."

Miss Brie said, "Are you secretly recording this?"

"Good heavens, no."

"Even if you leave a hidden microphone here, you won't catch me out. I'm not going to make a phone call the minute you leave."

"There's no question of hidden mikes."

"I'm sober, you know. Being French, I can take brandy like water."

"I wouldn't dream of doing anything underhanded," Ingeborg said, setting aside the fact that she'd only just returned from an undercover mission. "I believe in appealing to people's public spirit. I wonder if I can persuade you that there's a higher morality at stake here. For everyone's sake we need to catch the person who shot the professor before there's another shooting."

Miss Brie swirled the brandy and looked over the glass. "All I will say is this. Our client couldn't possibly have fired the shot."

"Why do you say that? How do you know?"

"You can go on all afternoon trying to trick me, Sergeant Smith. It won't succeed. I'm holding fast to my principles, even in a world that I hardly recognise any more."

Half an hour later, Ingeborg realised that the old lady was right. She would no more get the name of the client than she would learn where to buy Bath Olivers. And after several top-ups from the decanter, she was starting to fear that she, too, wouldn't recognise the world any more.

30

This lunchtime three homeless men known to each other as Shakes, One-Eye and Junior were sharing a single can of Red Bull under a horse chestnut tree near the mortuary chapel in Brunswick Cemetery in the St. Paul's district. Not one of Bristol's most salubrious public spaces, it was still intended for public use. The gravestones had been moved to the edges except for a few raised tombs and most of it was grassed over and mown. As an amenity it was not much used, for all the good intentions of the planners. Razor wire fencing along the edges to protect the neighbouring buildings didn't help and neither did the fact that the cemetery was limited in access. To get in, you had to come through a private car park in Wilder Street. Most locals regarded the place as unsafe.

The homeless men weren't troubled. They would remain in the cemetery for hours yet. A short walk away was the night shelter in Little Bishop Street, run by the Julian Trust. Getting one of the eighteen beds in the dormitory was a lottery considering that eighty to a hundred men turned up each night for the free dinner at 9:30 P.M., but obviously you needed to turn up at the door to make any sort of claim.

Shakes was the only one of the three who had so far enjoyed a night in the Julian and it gave him extra status. "I wouldn't say it's the Ritz," he was telling the others. "You wouldn't have to share with seventeen others at the Ritz, but they do your laundry while you're kipping and it's ready for you in the morning. There's a proper toilet and a shower and all."

"What about breakfast?" One-Eye asked. "Do you get that

in bed?" It was meant in fun and he may have winked. It was impossible to tell.

"No, mate. You have to get up for that, and if you want it, you have to be in the dining room by six thirty."

"That's early," Junior said. "I'd rather stop in bed."

"They kick you out at seven thirty anyway."

Junior shook his head. "Definitely not for me. I'll stick with the underpass."

"They ought to make you a special case," One-Eye said as he handed the can to Junior.

The young man took this as sympathy and looked pleased. "Why?"

"You could do with the laundry. You really stink."

"No more than you."

"Mine's honest sweat. Yours is piss and puke. Doesn't he stink of piss and puke, Shakes?"

"Could be where we're sitting," Shakes said. "You never know who's been here."

"Downwind of Junior is where I'm sitting," One-Eye said. "Look at you. You're a fucking disgrace. How old are you?"

"Dunno," Junior said.

"He knows sod all," Shakes said. "He's simple. I can tell you when I was born, 1952, the year the king died. He doesn't know shit. He can't even tell you his name."

"Me, I was born the year we landed on the moon," One-Eye said as if he'd personally completed the Apollo Eleven mission. "When was that?"

"Don't ask me," Shakes said. "And don't ask him. He wouldn't know. Work it out yourself."

"Where was you before you came to Bristol?" One-Eye asked Junior, shifting the attention away from himself.

There was no answer.

"I'd say you're from round here, going by the way you talk. Brissle, born and bred, you be."

"D'you think so?"

"Bloody obvious."

■ ■ ■

With her head feeling divorced from the rest of her, Inge-borg stood at the end of Saville Row near enough to the corner of Alfred Street to back out of sight when necessary. She expected Miss Brie to emerge from *Mon Repos* before long. The Courvoisier-lubricated meeting had not delivered much, but she was confident there was more to come. She had seen the way the old lady's mind was working, the paranoia about hidden mikes and tapped phones. In her statements about surveillance, Miss Brie had revealed more than she intended. By denying that she would make a phone call, she had confirmed that she had it in mind to get in touch with somebody. Out of loyalty to her previ-ous employer, she planned to warn the anonymous client as soon as possible about this attention from the police.

How would a paranoid old lady make contact if she was convinced her house was bugged?

She'd go out.

If the client was local she'd visit in person. If not, she'd use a public phone. She was unlikely to own a mobile.

Worth waiting to find out? Ingeborg believed so.

The day had reached that busy time between one and two when office workers were out on the streets along with tour-ists, students and shoppers. Busy only in the sense of large numbers—No one was especially active. There was much standing about in groups, laughing, gossiping and generally enjoying the spring sun. This suited Ingeborg nicely. If you are tailing someone, you take advantage of every opportunity of cover and the chance to linger unnoticed on street corners.

The alcohol may have had something to do with it, but she was feeling buoyant again. She'd wanted more action and this was it. Tailing an innocent old lady didn't have the cachet of tangling with an arms supplier, but it beat sitting at a desk in Manvers Street with John Leaman for company.

Fifteen minutes later, some of the elation had drained away. Miss Brie had not made the expected move. Be patient, Ingeborg told herself. Old ladies don't rush. She'll be choos-ing what to wear, dabbing on more of the lipstick and eau de cologne, checking herself in the mirror and making sure all the lights and appliances are switched off before she steps out.

She looked at her watch. Nearly two. The lunchtime crowds were already thinning out. Saville Row was getting into afternoon mode, with just a few window-gazing at the antiques.

Then she took a sharp breath. A petite figure in a grey coat and black straw hat had stepped into the alley and started walking towards her with a firm step. Miss Brie was on the move at last.

Ingeborg backed out of sight a short way along Alfred Street and waited. She expected her quarry to continue straight down the hill towards the centre of the city by way of Bartlett Street, a wider walkway lined with yet more restaurants and antique shops, and she was right. Without a glance right or left, Miss Brie moved on, definitely on a mission. Steady on her feet and with a clear eye, she showed no effect from the several shots of brandy.

So it became a sedate pursuit, suited to a civilised city like Bath, keeping the black straw hat in sight, but remaining alert, ready to step aside into a shop doorway if necessary. At the foot of Bartlett Street, Miss Brie turned into George Street and used the pedestrian crossing. She was still so purposeful that it was tempting to get closer and trust she wouldn't suddenly look round and realise she was being followed.

Don't risk it, Ingeborg urged herself.

At the corner of Gay Street, a voice unexpectedly said, "Hi, Ingeborg. How are you doing?"

Not what she needed. James, her karate instructor.

"Sorry. Can't stop," she told him. "I'm late for a meeting." And she knew how unconvincing she sounded, especially as she was moving at Miss Brie's plodding rate and couldn't allow herself to speed up.

"No problem," James said, frowning a little and turning to watch her ambling past.

The hazards of stalking so close to home. Meeting a friend rather undermined the drama of the mission. Back on track, she continued down Gay Street and past the Jane Austen

Centre hoping fervently that the man outside dressed as Mr. Darcy and built more like Mr. Pickwick didn't invite her in. Mercifully he didn't.

Meanwhile Miss Brie progressed down the hill as true to her line as if she was pushing a surveyor's wheel. She'd now reached the west side of the most elegant roundabout in Britain, John Wood's majestic Queen Square, where traffic circulated around lawns, boules pitches, tall trees and an obelisk, all enclosed by railings and bordered by palatial buildings—in the grandest of which Dr. Oliver, the inventor of Miss Brie's favourite biscuit, had once lived. How galling, the thought crossed Ingeborg's mind, if it turned out that Miss Brie had come out only to replenish her stock of Bath Olivers.

The dignified pursuit moved on towards the opposite side of the square. Here the route was more open, so Ingeborg allowed Miss Brie to get even further ahead, just in case she had a sudden loss of confidence and looked behind her.

And now, as Ingeborg was crossing Old King Street, behind the back of Jolly's, someone else she hadn't spotted spoke up. "What's this, Sergeant Smith? On patrol, are you?"

Of all the people in all of Avon and Somerset, Georgina, in civvies, carrying a large bag that looked like clothes shopping.

You couldn't cold-shoulder the Assistant Chief Constable—even in the course of duty.

The remark had been pitched in a friendly way. Best be civil and keep it short. "I'm on my way back to the station, ma'am. I had to speak to a witness in Saville Row."

"One of the people at that auction?"

"Not exactly, but someone with information."

"And how is the investigation progressing?"

Where do I start? Ingeborg thought. What a question to ask, and what a time and place to ask it. She noticed Georgina had manoeuvred the shopping bag behind her ample thighs, but not swiftly enough to hide the name on the side. Honey of Bath, in Lilliput Court, was a well-known boutique. This unnecessary conversation was a deflection, just to cover

Georgina's embarrassment. "We're doing as well as expected, ma'am."

"That's good. I haven't seen you around the station for a few days."

"I had some time off."

"Really? In the middle of a major investigation?"

"Not exactly time off. I was on surveillance." At all costs, she must avoid using the word undercover.

"And was it a success?"

"In some respects, ma'am."

"Well done, then." Georgina was sidling past Ingeborg, still keeping the Honey of Bath bag hidden behind her. "Keep up the good work." And then, glory hallelujah, she moved swiftly on.

Ingeborg breathed a massive sigh of relief—and then discovered that Miss Brie was nowhere in sight.

Damn you, Georgina.

She started sprinting along the side of the square. It didn't matter any more if heads turned. The one head that wouldn't turn was Miss Brie's, because she wasn't here any more. But which way had she gone? She hadn't continued around the square or she'd still be in sight. Barton Street was straight ahead, Wood Street to the left, each of them leading towards one of the busiest pedestrian thoroughfares in the city. In that sea of people it would be hopeless trying to pick out the little old lady in the straw hat.

Then she stopped running and stood still with her hand pressed to her mouth like the actress in a silent film suddenly confronted with the sheikh. Ahead on the northwest corner was the board for Morton's Auction Rooms, where all this had started. Could Miss Brie be visiting there?

Of course she could.

She crossed the road and went inside. A receptionist behind a desk looked up. A sign above her said VALUATIONS TODAY: ANTIQUE CLOCKS AND WATCHES.

"Did an elderly lady in a black straw hat just come in?"

"She did."

Ingeborg was through the door and into the main auction room, now cleared of all the sales items that were here on the day of the shooting. Alone in the room, a bored-looking clock and watch expert in a tweed jacket and black jumper with an eyeglass hanging from his neck sat waiting behind a table covered with a black cloth. But no Miss Brie.

She asked the man the same question.

"Yes, indeed," he said. "But she didn't want a valuation."

"Where is she?"

"In the office at the back. She came especially to see Denis Doggart, the auctioneer."

"You want to get that cleaned up," One-Eye said.

The three were still in the cemetery, but Shakes was horizontal and appeared to be asleep.

"Get what cleaned up?" Junior asked.

"Your head. If that goes septic, your brain's going to get pickled completely. You'll be more confused than you are already."

Junior put his hand to his head and ran his finger down the length of an ugly-looking scab reaching from his crown to above his right ear. "It's cleared up."

"Don't scratch it, then. You'll make it worse. How did you do it?"

"Can't remember."

"Looks like you were in a fight."

"Was I?"

"Or fell off your bike. D'you ride a bike?"

"Dunno."

"You don't know nothing. Take my advice and get it seen to. Go to a hospital and see a nurse. That's their job. When I lost my eye, I was well looked after. Years ago, that was. They was all for giving me a false one, but I didn't want it. I wore a patch for a while, but people started calling me Nelson and I got fed up and slung it out. Now they call me One-Eye and I don't mind at all."

"That's all right, then."

"Can't you remember nothing?"

"Walking through the woods, that's all. And round the streets. Sleeping in the underpass."

"You poor pathetic sod."

As if the remark was meant for him, Shakes woke up, yawned and propped himself on his elbows. "Was I asleep?"

"Dreaming of a night in the Ritz, I reckon," One-Eye said. "Have you ever slept in a real hotel?"

"Only in my dreams."

"What's the best place you've ever slept in?" He turned to Junior. "Shakes has been around, you know. He's a traveller. A real traveller, I mean. A gentleman of the road, they would have called him in the old days. Up and down the country. There isn't a dosshouse he hasn't been to."

"That's stretching it," Shakes said.

"You could write a book. *Shakes's Dosshouse Guide.* We'd be queuing up to buy it."

"Five stars for the best," Shakes said, entering into the spirit of this.

"And where would that be?"

He scratched his white curls, pondered the question for some time and finally decided. "There's a small town near the coast, down Portsmouth way, except it isn't Portsmouth. Christ, my memory is going like Junior's. Anyway, the nightstop was the best I've ever stayed in and it was called Stonepillow."

"Doesn't sound all that comfortable."

"Stonepillow, yes. You weren't sharing with seventeen others. You had privacy. They fed you dinner and breakfast, gave you a bed, bath, laundry. And if you played your cards right you could stop there for twenty-eight days guaranteed."

"Did you hear that, Junior?" One-Eye said, tapping his own head. "Salt it away if you can. You may be glad of it one of these days."

"Young fellow his age doesn't want to know about dosshouses," Shakes said. "He wants a woman."

Junior continued to look blank.

"Stone woman," One-Eye said, laughing. "Better to have a stone woman than a stone pillow."

Junior blinked several times. "I know a stone woman."

One-Eye may have winked again. "Tell us about her."

He looked eagerly to each of the others, as if they could unlock the memory for him. "Hold on. It's coming back to me. About this size." He stretched his arms like a fisherman describing his catch.

"That's wide," Shakes said. "Too wide for me."

"Was that her waist or her bust?" One-Eye asked.

"She's carved on a lump of stone and she's not just a woman, she's a wife."

"What's he on about?" One-Eye said.

"A stone wife," Junior went on, digging deep through the layers of his concussion, trying to connect with the image. "My boss brought her back to the office. Him and her together was kind of comical. I can see her now. I can see him. If only I could remember his name."

31

"Is he back from Melksham?" Ingeborg asked John Leaman, still on duty in the incident room he thought of as his own.

"He was."

"I've got something urgent to tell him. Has he gone out again?"

"He's down in the yard with the fleet manager."

"Transport? What's that about?"

"He didn't say. He's more restless than ever. You'll have to ask him."

Deep in the bowels of Manvers Street where the vehicles were kept and maintained, Diamond was examining a two-wheeled trailer. He gave one of the tyres a kick. "It'll need to be strong."

The fleet manager, a civilian, said, "It's meant to take loads. How much weight are we talking about?"

"It takes six strong men to shift her. She was too heavy to carry down to the evidence room, which is why she ended up in my office."

"And now you want your office back?"

"That's the plan."

"If six guys can lift her, this'll do the job, no problem. What have you got to do the towing? Not your old banger?"

"Probably not."

"Day after tomorrow?"

Diamond nodded, looked behind him and saw Ingeborg fidgeting with her ponytail. "I doubt if her Ka is suitable either. Let me think about this. I may need one of your Land Rovers."

"You will, by the sound of things. Also ropes and a tarp," the fleet manager said. "We can supply them. How about a motorcycle escort?"

"Are you being sarcastic?"

"Only jesting."

"I could take you up on this. If robbers can ambush an auction, they can hijack a trailer."

"Do they know you're making the trip?"

"Not yet, but they could find out. A couple of outriders aren't such a bad idea. Put me down for the Land Rover and trailer and I'll let you know what else I need." He walked across to Ingeborg. "In case you're curious, I've decided to take the wife back to where she belongs."

"Bridgwater?"

He nodded. "The museum is still the owner. They should take responsibility now. I'm there on Saturday for the scattering of the ashes. Monica doesn't know where the Chaucer house stood. I promised to show her. She wants company. I know how she feels."

"That's very noble, guv."

"Not entirely. It's a chance to kill two birds with one stone."

"Hasn't the stone done enough damage already?"

This earned a broad grin. The prospect of unloading the wife on to someone else made him feel as if he'd got out of jail. "Okay," he said. "There's a certain look in your eye. What staggering news have you got to tell me?"

Strange how one decision changed everything. It was as if the *Wife of Bath*, faced with the prospect of being sent back to the museum, decided the game was up and she would end her sport with Diamond. Little had gone right from the moment she had been dumped in his office, but the stubborn old cuss had refused to accept that he was jinxed. It was only a lump of stone, for God's sake. Bad luck was just that and nothing more.

In the course of the next hour, he made calls to the auction rooms, followed by Bridgwater, Bristol and Reading. When he finally put down the phone, the truth about the killing of John Gildersleeve had become as obvious to him as how he would deal with it. He was at peace with himself, quietly elated. At this stage he said nothing to the team. The right moment would come.

Instead, he got out of his chair, rounded the desk and stood facing her. Since her return from the photo session she had been left at an oblique angle, so that she seemed to be riding towards the door. Pure chance? Much against his lifelong insistence on commonsense behaviour, he started speaking to her in a low voice inaudible to everyone in the CID room. "I don't accept for a moment that you had any influence over me or anyone else. I'm not superstitious. Every case I've ever investigated had a rational explanation and I've proved it over and over. Just because you were the start of all this, it doesn't mean you ran the show. You were the start and I'm allowing you also to be the finish, but that means nothing. Nothing at all. I think we understand each other, don't we?"

Let's not give the *Wife of Bath* any credit for what occurred next. Diamond didn't, then or later. The former US Secretary of State Donald Rumsfeld could have been speaking for Diamond when, in another context, he uttered the immortal words, "Stuff happens." At least ten minutes passed before any stuff did happen. It was an incident in the incident room. There was a shout of surprise followed by a scream overtaken by an outbreak of shouting and shrieking the like of which Manvers Street had never experienced.

Diamond moved fast and flung open his door.

Everyone was in a huddle at the far side. The noise level wouldn't have disgraced Epsom on Derby Day and mercifully they were sounds of joy. At the centre of the crush, smiling, shaking his head, at a loss as to how to accept such an outpouring, was Paul Gilbert, alive and back with the team.

Diamond went forward, wrestled his way through, grabbed the lad and hugged him. He couldn't find words, there was such a huge lump in his throat.

■ ■ ■

The team insisted Gilbert come for a drink in the Royal, even though he should have been seeing a doctor. All he wanted was a bottle of water, he told them. He'd been given a shower and fresh clothes in Bristol and plenty to drink, but he was still dehydrated. The rest of them celebrated until Diamond put his arm around the young man and steered him out.

Much of Gilbert's story had been extracted piecemeal in the pub, but not in any connected way. In the sanctuary of Diamond's office, with only the stone carving for company, a more coherent version emerged.

"It's like I was two different people, guv," he explained. "There's what I remember before I was hurt and there's what happened after, with a gap in between that's a total blank. I've been trying to remember, but it won't come back."

"It never will," Diamond said. "It's the way concussion affects you. I had it more than once in my rugby playing days. Could never be sure which thug from the other team knocked me out. Retrograde amnesia. With all the knocks I took, it's a miracle I can remember that. Give me the story in sequence, from when you were up the tree at Nathan Hazael's place."

Gilbert took a swig of water first. "I felt like such a wuss, stuck up there with the dog waiting underneath, but it would have had me. I know those Dobermanns. They don't take prisoners. They go for your throat."

"No one's blaming you for staying where you were."

"But you can blame me for being there. I exceeded orders and what happened was all my stupid fault. If I'd done what I was asked and just checked the state of Ingeborg's car at the dockside, I'd have saved everyone a load of hassle."

Diamond shrugged. The lad had got the message. It didn't need repeating.

Gilbert went on, "I spoke to someone who told me about this video shoot on the *Great Britain* and it was obvious Ingeborg must have been there. I was talking to the local security lads, getting all the information I could, and one of them was on about a bit of a fight nearby involving a blonde and the director of the video. They said he was a local guy called Marcus Tone and it sounded nasty, so I thought I'd better follow it up. But when I spoke to Tone at his house in Clifton I found he'd been doing his best to help her meet the pop star from the video and both women had been snatched and driven off by Nathan Hazael and his thugs." He sighed and shook his head. "I was in a real sweat about her. We all know Nathan's reputation. I thought someone needed to get there fast and report back to you." He rolled his eyes upwards. "I've only just learned she was your under-cover cop and it was all part of her plan to get inside the place. What a mess."

"Not entirely your fault," Diamond said. "I should have briefed you more fully."

"Well, I left my car a short way off and climbed over the wall. I got to about a hundred and fifty yards from the house before the dog found me. I was up that tree like a squirrel, I'm not kidding. After a bit the damn thing stopped barking, but it didn't go away. I can't tell you how useless I felt. I was there most of the night."

"You still had your phone, didn't you?"

"At that time, yes, but after the bollocking you gave me I didn't dare trouble you again. You told me to use my initiative."

Diamond felt a stab of guilt. "I remember."

"I thought the sensible thing was to stay up the tree and wait for the dog to go away. My best chance would be if it was used to being fed in the morning. Nothing much happened, but at one point I saw someone in the moonlight. They were on the roof."

"That was Ingeborg."

"And not long after that the bloody dog started barking again and all hell broke loose. An alarm went off at the house and people came out with guns and started running towards the tree." Gilbert opened his hand. "That's the last thing I remember."

"Lee Li thought you fell from the tree. That's what she was told."

"It's possible."

"But unlikely. Did you have any injuries apart from the head wound? You'd have been badly bruised at the very least."

"Nothing like that."

"My best guess is that they forced you down at gunpoint and clubbed you with a rifle butt. As far as we can tell, you were out to the world for some time after. It appeared you were dead. Then they shoved you into the back of a limo and slammed down the lid. We expected to find a body somewhere in Leigh Woods. The place was searched from end to end. Bristol deserve medals for the efforts they made to find you."

Gilbert put his red, weathered fingers to his mouth. "I know. They told me at the Julian Trust. I'm gutted to have caused so much trouble to everyone."

"Like us, they'll be mightily relieved you were found alive. I'm fascinated to know how it happened."

The young man took a moment to collect his thoughts. "This is the other me, the idiot found wandering the streets of Bristol."

"Is that the first memory?"

"No, when I came to, I was in woodland, feeling terrible. I was cold and sick. Disgusting."

"Any idea where?"

"On the Leigh Woods side of the gorge. They must have dumped me. I don't know if they knew I was alive. I got up and staggered along for a bit. It's amazing I didn't fall right down the side. I have a memory of walking across the suspension bridge."

"Didn't you try and stop a car?"

"I couldn't think of a reason to stop one. I didn't know who I was or how I'd got there. They'd emptied my pockets. My phone had gone. I was filthy. I can't believe any driver would have stopped for me. Eventually I met up with some other rough sleepers. I hung about with them until this afternoon when my head began to clear."

"Something triggered your memory?"

"They got to talking about stone pillows and made some sort of joke about me needing a stone wife, and I remembered this." He leaned over his chair and rested a hand on the *Wife of Bath*. "She's not all bad, guv. Once I got the picture of her in my head, other stuff started to come back as well. I remembered your name and Ingeborg's. I could picture this place. The guys I was with had become friendly by then and they took me to the dosshouse."

"The night shelter."

"Right. The brain was ticking over again and I told the people at the shelter who I was. This was outside the hours they operate but they took me in as a special case and let me take a shower and get into some less disgusting clothes. They'd been told to look out for me as a missing person. I believe they phoned the local police and told them I was alive and basically okay. Then they arranged for one of their outreach people to drive me back here. I won't forget the reception I was given."

"To say we were worried is an understatement."

"Did anyone speak to my mum?"

"She's been away all week. She has no idea."

"I'd forgotten. Thank God for that."

Diamond got up from his chair. "You should get that head wound checked. It seems to have dried up, but it may need some kind of attention. Take the rest of the week off, catch up on some sleep and we'll expect you in on Monday. Oh, and it might be a nice idea to write a letter of thanks to Bristol Central for all the man-hours of searching."

"A bottle of wine?"

"Not unless you can afford twenty cases of the stuff."

32

The motorcade that set out from Manvers Street on Saturday morning didn't, in the end, have outriders, but its status was not in question. At the front, a Land Rover with Avon & Somerset police markings contained Peter Diamond, Denis Doggart, the auctioneer, and George, the driver. They were towing a trailer bearing the *Wife of Bath*, stoutly roped and covered with a tarpaulin. Next, Ingeborg's red Ka, with Keith Halliwell as passenger. And at the rear a white Volvo driven by Erica, Monica's sister. Beside her was Monica, clutching the plastic urn containing John Gildersleeve's ashes.

Diamond had chosen the route: the A39 across country by way of Wells and Glastonbury rather than using the motorway. "No speeding," he told George. "We're on a sensitive mission here. Let's do it with respect."

In his tweed suit and salmon pink tie, Doggart brought some sartorial quality to the occasion. Diamond, even more domineering than usual, had browbeaten the auctioneer into making the trip by insisting over the phone that he was still the custodian of lot 129. Although the Blake Museum at Bridgwater remained the owners, the *Wife of Bath* had been brought to Morton's for a sale that hadn't been completed, so the auctioneers had a duty of care and if they had any doubts they should speak to their insurers. The fact that the carving had been parked for a couple of weeks in the police station was immaterial. Until she was handed back to Bridgwater she was Morton's responsibility. The police were doing them a massive good turn by arranging the transportation. The least Doggart could do was witness the handover.

But a cloud of unease hung over the Land Rover as it cruised across Churchill Bridge and along the Lower Bristol Road. Doggart must have suspected there was more on the agenda than he'd been told. Diamond waited until they joined the Wells Road at Corston before saying any more.

"You didn't tell me you're a Chaucer man yourself."

"I don't know what you mean by that," Doggart said. "My job is to know a bit about everything that comes under the hammer. I can't be much of a Chaucer man. My valuation was well short of the bidding."

"Excusable, isn't it? A sculpture such as that doesn't often come up for sale."

"That I can agree with."

"What I'm getting at," Diamond said, "is that you were the owner of another Chaucer item, a portrait drawing."

The face suddenly turned the colour of the necktie. "I still am. How do you know about that?"

"I'm a detective. You stood to make a six-figure sum from the National Portrait Gallery, but it didn't happen."

A pause for thought. "This was years ago and has nothing to do with the matter you're investigating."

"I'm surprised to hear you say that, Mr. Doggart. We both know there's a connection. Your Chaucer portrait was examined by John Gildersleeve, who downgraded it."

"'Downgraded' isn't a word I recognise. He identified the sitter as Chaucer's son, that's all."

"And knocked a fortune off the value."

"Revaluing is a fact of life in the antiques world. Gildersleeve was the expert and he was right. There was nothing personal in it."

"Except a personal disaster for you."

More red snapper than salmon now, Doggart said, "Oh, I begin to see what this is about. You think I bore a grudge against Gildersleeve. I didn't."

"Did you meet him at the time?"

"I did. I was asked to take my drawing to Reading for his

inspection. It was a civilised meeting over sherry. I left the portrait with him and collected it a few days later."

"When he gave you the bad news?"

"I'd already heard."

"Did he get the sherry out a second time?"

"No. The drawing was left for me to pick up. Can we talk about something else now?"

"Did you meet him again?"

"Not until the day of the auction."

"A blast from the past when he appeared, I should think."

"It wasn't like that at all. I'm a professional. I had a job to do. And I'm not even sure he recognised me, he was so caught up in the auction."

"What do you remember about the incident?"

"Everything in vivid detail. It isn't every day a man is murdered a few feet in front of you."

"By all accounts you were remarkably cool under fire. You handled the arrival of the gunmen rather well."

Alert for anything that smeared him, Doggart took a sharp, outraged breath. "What are you insinuating—that I knew they were coming? I most certainly did not. I didn't panic. When you're at the rostrum, you're in charge. You deal with whatever happens and I did, to the best of my ability."

"Telling three armed men their behaviour was intolerable? That was either foolhardy or exceptionally brave."

"I didn't stop to think."

"What were they like, these three hitmen?"

"How can I answer that? They were disguised in masks."

"I'm hoping for some of that vivid detail you just mentioned."

"Balaclavas with holes for the eyes and mouth. Black T-shirts and jeans. They were brandishing black revolvers. The first of them, the man who interrupted the auction, was the only one who spoke. He shouted, 'Nobody move.' When I protested, he told me to shut up. He said if we all remained where we were no one would get hurt. I said it was intolerable and he told me once again to shut it, as he crudely put it."

"You'd know his voice again, would you?"

"I can hear it now in my head. There was a definite trace of the West Country in the accent."

"Anything memorable about his build?"

Doggart shook his head. "A bit above average in height. Quite slim."

"And the others?"

"Similar."

"You were defiant at the start, but you soft-pedalled soon after. You told the professor to let them be."

"By then I'd seen how real the threat was. I was doing my best to control a dangerous situation—unsuccessfully, as it turned out."

"Was it deliberate, do you think? Was it always their intention to shoot him?"

He hesitated, as if playing the words over. "That has never occurred to me. At the time it seemed very clear that Gildersleeve contributed to his own death by taking them on."

"They panicked?"

"He panicked and so did they."

"Which was why they fled without taking the stone?"

"That was my reading of it."

The stress was showing in the second car as well. Ingeborg had been muttering for some time about being forced to brake repeatedly when they were on an open road with no sign of an obstruction. "This is going to take till the end of the century. If we got out and walked we'd get there quicker. He's got the horsepower. Why doesn't he use it?"

"Don't blame George the driver," Halliwell said. "He'll be under instructions."

"Would the boss kick up if we overtook? We know where we're going. We could be there and get a coffee before they arrive."

"I wouldn't risk it. He was all smiles when we started out. That's worth encouraging."

"I noticed. He hasn't stopped smiling since Paul appeared."

"There's more on his mind, I think."

"Is it because he's finally getting shot of the *Wife of Bath*? She was the bane of his life at one point."

"That's part of it, for sure, but the main thing is he's ready to wrap up the case."

Her voice shrilled in surprise. "Really? Did he tell you?"

Halliwell dug into his pocket and pulled out a pair of handcuffs. "He asked me to bring these."

She took a glance and then a longer look and almost hit the trailer in front. "Who for? Did he say?"

"Likes to keep us in suspense, doesn't he?"

"Denis Doggart?"

"Don't know. It's a bit extreme even by his standards, taking the guy all the way to Bridgwater to pinch him."

"Thinking about it," Ingeborg said, "sitting in the back of the Land Rover with Doggart for an hour or more—"

"At least an hour or more."

"—it's an ideal chance to question him."

"He could do it at the station."

"Not in such a relaxed way."

Halliwell laughed.

"What's so funny?" she asked.

"Would you be relaxed, sitting beside the guv'nor all the way to Bridgwater?"

"Possibly not. I'm stuck with you instead." She watched the two heads through the rear window of the Land Rover. "I'd be surprised if Doggart does get pinched. He's the only suspect we know who *couldn't* have fired the fatal shot."

"That wouldn't have stopped him setting the whole thing up," Halliwell said. "You said he lost a load of money when Gildersleeve rubbished his Chaucer portrait. As the auction-eer, he was better placed than anyone to oversee the hold-up."

"The whole thing was staged, you mean?"

"He would have known the professor was going to be a main bidder. What sweet revenge to watch the prize being snatched away from his enemy just as the bidding was coming to an end."

"So was the shooting staged as well?"

"I don't think so. It all went wrong. But the man who hired the robbers is as guilty as the guy who pulled the trigger."

"And at this minute the boss is teasing the truth out of him?"

"It wouldn't surprise me."

"There could be other factors."

"A history between Doggart and Gildersleeve?"

"If it's there, he'll find it," Ingeborg said. "As a matter of fact, he made sure I brought cuffs as well."

In the Volvo, Erica asked Monica, "Why are we going so slowly?"

"It must be Mr. Diamond's idea of respect."

"What for?"

Monica caressed the side of the urn. "You mean 'Who for?' My poor John, of course."

"This isn't the funeral," Erica said. "We had that. Even hearses go faster than this between towns. We'll be hours getting to Petherton Park at this rate."

"We're making a stop at Bridgwater first, to unload the carving."

"That doesn't show much respect. I thought the purpose of the trip was to scatter the ashes."

"He told me what he planned to do. He's doing me a favour by showing me the site. We have to go through Bridgwater to get to North Petherton."

"We could have stopped there on the way back."

"I don't suppose it will delay us much. Besides, we haven't got to be there at a particular time."

"They ought to have more consideration. It's a sad duty you have to perform and this prolongs it."

"I don't think of it as sad," Monica said. "I'm taking him where he would most like to be, close to Chaucer."

"The last I heard, Chaucer was buried in Westminster Abbey."

"Did he fix a time for the handover at the museum?" Ingeborg asked.

"I expect so. Tomorrow, at the rate we're moving."

"How are we doing? I'm on automatic here."

"Soon be at Wells. Roughly halfway."

"Only as far as that? I'm getting dangerously close to boiling point."

"You're dangerously close to the trailer again. God knows what would happen if we gave it a nudge."

She shook with laughter. "Chunks of old limestone all over the road, that's what, and the guv'nor dodging in and out of the traffic trying to rescue them."

"It doesn't bear thinking about," Halliwell said.

"It's hilarious. And if Monica got out to help and tipped the ashes over . . ."

"Is Monica still with us?" He turned in his seat. "She is. You're going to tell me she and her sister were two of the robbers with their hair tucked into the balaclava masks."

"I have to say I hadn't thought of that."

"Is this what today is all about? Are we nicking Monica and Erica after they finish scattering the ashes?"

"How many pairs of handcuffs did you bring?"

"The building on the right that looks like a church is Chilton Priory," Diamond announced. "It used to be a museum. The *Wife of Bath* was an exhibit there in early Victorian times."

Denis Doggart said in what was plainly meant to be a crushing retort, "It's not unknown to me. I mentioned it in the sale catalogue."

But Diamond rose above it. "So you did. Thought you might not have noticed. It means we're coming into Bridgwater shortly."

Doggart twisted in his seat, unable to contain himself any longer. "What's the real reason I'm here, Mr. Diamond?"

"If you haven't worked it out by now, I'm surprised. But I'll tell you."

33

"Spot on," Diamond said, looking up from his watch.

The museum was at the end of a cul-de-sac in Blake Street and the entire convoy was able to draw up outside. He emerged from the Land Rover as spry as when they'd started, the only traveller free of stress. Everyone else felt as if they'd driven from Inverness.

The building—a converted sixteenth century house named after one of Britain's more successful admirals, said to have been born there in 1598—was closed to visitors outside the summer months, but Diamond had arranged to meet one of the curators.

"This is going to be a doddle," he said, rubbing his hands. "No steps. We can wheel her straight in."

Ingeborg was not so upbeat. "First we have to find some way to lift her off the trailer."

"We need more muscle," Keith Halliwell said. Back at Manvers Street, the heavy work had been done by the team of young constables who had got used to humping the stone in and out of Diamond's office.

"Don't look at me," Denis Doggart said. "I'm not a porter." The shredded nerves were showing.

Nothing would shake Diamond's optimism. "Relax, people. I was promised help at this end. Let's see if anyone's here yet."

As if by his force of will alone, the door opened before he stepped up to it. A meaty and bearded man, who might have passed for Admiral Blake himself, thrust out his hand, "Tank Sherman. We spoke on the phone."

Diamond introduced everyone except John Gildersleeve (in his urn and clasped to Monica's bosom) and they moved into the flagstone entrance hall. Low-ceilinged and with waist-high wainscot panelling, the building left visitors in no uncertainty of its great age. Doors were open to left and right and, ominously for all involved in the heavy work to come, stairs rose to an upper floor.

"Have the volunteers arrived?"

"On their way," Tank said, matching Diamond in conviviality. "We're all volunteers here. The Blake is entirely run on love, loyalty and donations. We get a modest grant from the town council and that's it. Would you care to look round?"

"First, I'd like to see where you want the thing put."

"The good wife? You'll be relieved to learn she's not going upstairs. The floors couldn't take the strain. They're like a switchback as it is. She's to go in the meeting room, on your right here. A temporary stay, we hope. The plan is to sell her to the British Museum as soon as possible. It's a shame, a precious local artefact going to London, but an old building like this needs the occasional face lift."

"Make sure you get a fair price," Doggart said.

"We intend to, believe me."

"Would you like me to value it again? It's worth considerably more than I originally thought."

"Thanks, but we're perfectly capable of working the price out for ourselves," Tank said with a smile that had strength of purpose behind it. "We know how the auction went."

"The auction didn't finish."

"Exactly. The BM can be pushed up appreciably more and with all the publicity the piece must have acquired extra value since then. Believe me, I didn't get my nickname for nothing. I'll be in there with all guns blazing."

Unfortunate turn of phrase. Diamond exchanged a glance with Ingeborg, who had winced when she heard it. But Tank's next suggestion, of coffee in the ground-floor office, was enthusiastically approved by everyone.

"My team will have theirs outside in the street," Diamond said. "Mustn't leave the *Wife of Bath* unguarded."

"Oh, terrific!" Ingeborg said.

Diamond squashed that little insurrection. "And it's the perfect opportunity to brief you on what happens next."

Communication had never been Diamond's strong suit. On the rare occasions he had news to impart, it was worth hearing. So while Monica, Erica and Doggart joined Tank Sherman in the office, the police contingent trooped outside to be instructed on the plan of action. What they heard from their boss was no less than the solution to the case, and it was both surprising and unnerving.

The coffee was the instant kind and the milk was long life, but nobody objected, and there were gingernuts on offer to mask the taste. Diamond joined the others after his impromptu case conference in the street.

"I'd better fill the kettle again," Tank said. "The reinforcements are due shortly. I asked Tim and his brothers, as you suggested, and they were only too pleased to be part of the team."

Diamond explained to Monica, "Tim Carroll is the local historian, the fellow who knows precisely where the Chaucer house once stood. We met last time I was here."

"And will he come with us to Petherton Park?"

"I feel sure he will."

Monica tapped her fingers on the urn. "Does he know what it's about?"

"Not yet. I'll tell him."

With nice timing, at the moment the kettle started to whistle, the local helpers arrived. More introductions. Tim Carroll, in a dark green gilet over a denim shirt hanging loose and black tracksuit pants, looked more than ever as if he had stepped out of a fourteenth century manuscript. His brothers, Wayne and Roger, dressed in workmen's check shirts and blue jeans, were with him. None of them had seen the inside of a hairdresser's for a long time. Wayne Carroll, the oldest, if streaks of grey in the black thatch meant anything, wanted it known that he managed the house clearance business and employed the other two.

"So it's over to the professionals," Tank said. "They'll lift the good lady off the trailer."

"Not without help, we won't," Wayne said, making clear that the bonhomie wasn't going to affect him. "She'll be a fair old weight."

Diamond said they had brought the dolly with them to wheel the stone inside.

"Better get on with it, then," Wayne said. "We haven't got all bloody day."

"Coffee first?" Tank said brightly.

"Coffee after."

Wayne's word was law. Everyone trooped outside again to watch the operation. The parked convoy had been joined by a white van bearing the legend WAYNE CARROLL & CO, HOUSE CLEARANCE, ESTABLISHED FAMILY BUSINESS.

Still in the street, Ingeborg said, "We didn't get our coffee."

"The decision is to have it later," Diamond said without making eye contact. He turned to Wayne. "How many extra hands do you need?"

"Three pairs."

"Looks as if it has to be George the driver, Keith and me." He lifted out the dolly and positioned it on the pavement beside the trailer. "You're the foreman, Wayne. Is this where you want it?"

"It'll do."

They unfurled the tarpaulin and loosened the ropes. The stone wife had completed the journey in better shape than the support team. She looked triumphant seated on her amblere. The pale spring sunshine picked out the chisel marks where the sculptor had cleared the background behind the figure all those centuries ago.

"She's had a wash and brush-up, by the look of her," Tim said.

"Tell you later. It's a long story," Diamond said. "How do we go about this?"

Wayne was definitely in charge. "Shift it to this end of the trailer, where we can let down the side. It's going to be a brute to move, but if we all put our backs into it, we'll cope."

"Then what?"

"I'll tell you."

Four of them prepared to push, two to pull.

For Diamond it brought back memories of being a prop in the front row. He took a firmer hold.

"Careful where you put your hands," Tim piped up in a fit of alarm. "Keep them off the figure. You'll damage her."

Without a word, Diamond readjusted.

"On the count of three," Wayne said.

At the first attempt they succeeded in sliding the stone a couple of inches. The second try was marginally more. It took six hefty shoves to do the job.

"Everyone all right?" Tim asked, as if to show that the Carroll family had a caring side.

"That was the easy part," Wayne said, his dark eyes flicking over the crew for signs of weakness.

"What next?"

"We tip her on to the near edge. Then hold her steady at the point of balance, letting the trailer take the strain. This has to be done in one go. We don't want anyone's fingers squashed. You, mate."

Diamond looked right and left. "Talking to me?"

"Come this side and stand between Roger and me."

More used to giving orders than obeying them, Diamond was having to rein himself in. He squeezed between the brothers and bent over the stone. The others stood at the ends and took a grip as well as they were able.

"I'll count to three again."

On the word they braced and tugged.

Stubborn to the last, the stone wife refused to move.

"Maybe if we slid it a little way over the edge, some of us could get a better grip," Halliwell suggested.

"Who's running this show?" Wayne said. "We do it my way, right?"

Halliwell rolled his eyes.

And the next attempt was successful—except for a yelp of pain from Diamond.

"Trouble, guv?" Ingeborg asked.

"Something went in my back, I think."

Not what anyone wanted to hear. The stone was poised on one edge, just as planned. Most of the weight was now being taken by the trailer, but everyone was needed to hold the delicate balance.

"Keep her steady. Nobody move," Wayne said without a shred of sympathy.

"Are you all right?" Tim asked Diamond.

"I'm not sure. I'm okay in this position. Lifting might be a problem for me."

"We need a stand-in." Tim turned to Denis Doggart. "Could you . . . ?"

"Absolutely not," the auctioneer said. "You need a porter for that."

"Don't look at me," Tank Sherman said. "I get hernias."

Diamond said, "I think I can manage."

"I can do it," Ingeborg offered.

"Don't even think about it." Manfully, he summoned a grin and said, "Let's go."

"If you're certain," Tim said.

Wayne said, "Let her tip this way, but gradual. If we lose control now, all of us are going to end up in hospital. When I say the word, lift her clear and lower her on to the dolly."

Tim added with a look at Diamond, "Bending at the knees, not the back."

The manoeuvre began. The stone tipped slowly at first, and then with more force, off the edge of the trailer and into the arms of the six men. Grunting, bearing the weight, but without any shrieks of pain, they controlled the descent to the dolly. She settled with a satisfying thud.

"Beautiful job," Tim said.

For Diamond, there was double satisfaction. He'd avoided

a slipped disc and he'd had a close look at the back of Wayne's head.

Everyone straightened up, backed away and rubbed hands. Diamond rubbed his back.

"We haven't finished," Wayne said. "She has to be dragged inside."

Roger Carroll, who had not said much until now, said, "I reckon the three of us can manage that."

"Give me a moment to get my breath back," Tim said.

"I can take your place," Halliwell offered. "Then we'll all go for that coffee we were promised."

"Before we do," Diamond said, "I've got a favour to ask of you, Tim. Mrs. Gildersleeve and her sister made the journey especially to scatter the ashes of her late husband at the site of the Chaucer house. You took me to the spot before. Would you mind?"

Monica (with the urn) and Erica waited a few yards away in a dignified stance that was a silent appeal.

Even the hard man Wayne would have found it difficult to refuse. Tim was a softer touch. "No problem," he said.

Diamond thanked him. "I fully intended to join you, but my back's playing up and I don't think I can manage the walk across the field. Ingeborg will take my place."

"Right away?" Ingeborg said.

The sisters were obviously ready to go. Ingeborg, quietly fuming, would never get her coffee. The four got into the Volvo and Erica did a three-point turn and drove them away.

The *Wife of Bath* was trundled into her temporary new home and everyone not actually pulling or pushing headed inside as well—except Diamond and George the driver.

Tim Carroll gave the directions to North Petherton from the back seat.

"It's not far then?" Erica said, at the wheel.

"A couple of miles."

"You're interested in Chaucer, obviously," Monica said to him.

"Through the local connection," Tim said.

"But are you familiar with his poetry?"

"What I know of it, yes."

"In that case, perhaps you'll be kind enough to help with the valediction." She took a sheet of paper from the glove compartment and handed it to him. "A few lines from the Prologue to *The Canterbury Tales.*"

Talk about being put on the spot.

Ingeborg, uncomfortable with this, said to Monica, "I didn't know you were planning a ceremony. Tim agreed to show us the site of Chaucer's house, nothing else."

"He's a Chaucer scholar. It's serendipity that he's with us. He'll do it beautifully."

"If that's really what you want," Tim said. "I'd have worn my suit if I'd known."

"You couldn't have dressed better than you have," Monica said. "What you're wearing is ideal. John would have approved. And it isn't meant to be a ceremony, but just a dignified farewell to my dear husband."

So it was that after they had pulled up at the edge of the field and picked their way across the rutted ground to the area Tim pointed out, the four stood together with lowered heads. From across the field, the drone of motorway traffic was steady, but could almost be ignored in the intensity of the moment. This unmarked patch of ground was where the Chaucer house had once stood, where the *Wife of Bath* had been buried for centuries until the Victorians had unearthed her, and where John Gildersleeve had come with high hopes and been disappointed.

Monica ended the meditation by tugging at the lid of the urn and finding it too tight to open. She turned to Tim and passed the urn across.

"Be an angel, would you?"

He looked uncomfortable.

Ingeborg was thinking this had the potential to be a

disaster, but Tim managed to ease the lid away and keep the urn upright. Not a speck of ash was spilled. He returned it to Monica.

She said, "Now, Tim, if you would."

He took the paper from his pocket and in a low voice started reading Chaucer's words:

"*A Knyght ther was, and that a worthy man,*
That fro the tyme that he first bigan
To ridden out, he loved chivalrie,
Trouthe and honour, freedom and curteisie."

Tim's voice was faltering. He stopped, his eyes welling with tears. "I'm sorry. I can't go on." He thrust the paper into Ingeborg's hand and took several steps away from the little group.

Emotion can get to people on occasions such as this. What could Ingeborg do, except take up the recitation? She intoned in a firmer voice than Tim's:

"*And though that he were worthy, he was wys,*
And of his port as meeke as is a mayde.
He nevere yet no vileynye ne sayde
In all his lyf unto no maner wight.
He was a verray, parfit gentil knight."

She became aware as she was speaking that Monica was walking ahead, tipping the ashes at the same time.

Sister Erica waited for the urn to empty and said, "Amen." It was as good a way as any to bring an end to the proceedings.

Monica said, "Thank you, all of you. What happened to Tim?"

A needless question. In full sight of everyone, Tim was sprinting away across the field, not in the direction of the car, but towards the motorway.

Diamond would have a fit.

"I must stop him," Ingeborg said, kicking off her shoes.

If her innate sense of occasion hadn't browbeaten her into reciting Chaucer, she would have grabbed Tim the moment he stepped away. As it was, he was at least thirty yards off already. And he was quick. Bats and hell came to mind.

So it was a sudden transition from the dignity of the scattering to a cross-country chase. Ingeborg prided herself on her fitness. She could run and now she had to. She could feel Diamond's fury whipping her forward ('You let him escape? Were you sleeping on the job?"). Striding over the ploughed ground, ignoring the pain of the occasional stone under her feet, she went flat out to try and reduce the advantage.

Tim was bolting like a panicking goat, but he wasn't a natural runner. He glanced over his shoulder and the long, brown hair got in the way and he had to drag it against his neck. When he sighted Ingeborg, he lost his line and veered left. Then he almost tripped. He staggered several paces just to stay on his feet.

She cut across the angle and gained yards. Her left heel struck a flint and she cried out with the stab of pain, yet she kept going. Action like this was what she craved in all those dull hours in the office. Even so, she was more of a sprinter than a distance runner and she knew from experience she wouldn't last a long run. She urged herself into another burst of top speed.

Steadily she cut the distance. Tim was ahead.

He was slowing appreciably.

Ten yards.

Five.

Two.

She dived. It wasn't quite a rugby tackle, but she managed to grasp the flapping gilet and halt his by now faltering progress. Tim flung out an arm and she ducked and felt it pass closely over her head. His balance was going. He toppled over and hit the mud and brought Ingeborg with him.

Gasping loudly for air, he tried to fight her off, but she was in the superior position, bearing down on him from behind. She grasped his right arm and yanked it upwards. Then she struck him above the elbow with a karate *shuto*—the knife hand—that she knew would disable him. She grabbed his other wrist, slammed it against the numb one and hand-cuffed him. His resistance hadn't amounted to much and now it was at an end.

She hauled herself up and stood over him. She, too, was panting like a dog.

"On your feet."

Not easy when you are pinioned. He achieved a kneeling posture first, and then forced one exhausted leg forward and levered himself up.

Ingeborg looked across the field to where Monica and her sister were standing open-mouthed at what they had just witnessed.

She told Tim, "Let's go." And the pair of them dragged their aching limbs across the ground to unite the party again.

Erica, a headmistress by temperament if not by appoint-ment, handed Ingeborg her shoes and said, "You both need a good bath after that. What on earth was it about?"

It was too soon after the scattering to go into detail. Inge-borg simply said, "My boss said to make sure we all travelled back together."

While more coffee was being served in the museum office, the next phase of the police operation was under way out-side in Blake Street. George the driver had moved the Land Rover and trailer to a new position at a right angle to the kerb on the far side of the Carroll brothers' van, effectively sealing the street.

As an extra safeguard, Diamond drove a screwdriver through the nearside front tyre of the van and enjoyed the sound of the air escaping. A screwdriver is a versatile tool. He scraped enough paint off the van's bodywork to satisfy himself that it had been sprayed and was originally silver. Then he smashed the side window and let himself in. Finding the murder weapon was too much to hope for, but after a methodical search he located two plastic replica handguns taped against the sides of the seats. Both were Webley revolvers. He showed them to George.

"They're toys, aren't they?" George said.

"Not when a hitman points one at you. You'd take them seriously then. Under the ASBO legislation, it's an offence to carry replicas in public. I'm thinking these were used in the hold-up at the auction."

"Fired, you mean?"

"No. It's likely the killers had one working weapon between them. These were used to back up the threat."

"Where's the murder weapon? Still hidden in the van?"

"They'll have got rid of it unless they're bigger idiots than I take them for."

"You've found your killer, then? Was it Wayne?

"They were in it together. They'll all face a murder rap."

"Why? What was the point? Surely not to steal that old lump of stone?"

"Tell you later," Diamond said. He'd spotted the flashing blues and twos at the end of the street. His request for back-up from Bridgwater police had been answered. It was time to interrupt the coffee drinkers.

Taunton police station with its interview facilities was the setting for Diamond's face to face with Tim Carroll, now mostly cleaned up after the fracas in the field. Ingeborg (fully cleaned) sat beside Diamond. The duty solicitor was on the other side of the table with Tim.

"I don't know about you, but I don't want to make a drama out of this," Diamond said to the prisoner after the preliminaries had been got through. "You've had a stressful time. Joining in the final rites of the man you killed was obviously a step too far. I can understand that." He'd found over the years that if you made an effort from the start to reach out to the suspect and understand his point of view, it helped, whoever you were interviewing.

Tim was admitting nothing, but there was a sign that

he appreciated the show of sympathy. He pressed his lips together, parted them as if about to speak and then appeared to think better of it.

"Let's recap on your first involvement with Professor John Gildersleeve," Diamond went on. "You were a history student at Reading University, right? A first-year, October 1999 intake. I know you were because I've seen the list of undergraduates. You weren't in Gildersleeve's department, but as a historian you were offered a place on the dig at North Petherton he organised in the summer vacation. Good experience, you thought. How am I doing so far?"

Tim glanced at the solicitor, who was there to assist the man under arrest and see that he was treated fairly, but was learning the facts of the case as they unfolded. The lawyer simply raised his eyebrows as if to say that only Tim himself could judge how innocuous the information was.

Diamond didn't wait for a response. "We both know what happened. The dig was no dig at all. It had already been dug. As the days went on and nothing was found, you students got discouraged and bored. Someone—and I suspect it was you—had brought cannabis with him and pretty soon Gildersleeve had a spaced-out team, in no condition to continue. It all ended in recrimination and bad odour. The professor was deeply scarred by the experience, more than any of you realised. He had never been too popular in the senior common room and now he became a laughing stock. As dean of the faculty, he felt entitled to respect."

He paused—an opportunity for Tim to come back at him—but nothing was said. No sweat, he thought. Move on. You haven't yet played your best cards.

"When the new term started, you landed yourself deeply in trouble, dealing in cannabis. You were reported to the dean. This isn't guesswork, Tim. I've checked with the university. It's all documented in their files. You were sent down—for good."

Tim blurted out, "He destroyed me. He didn't give me a chance."

The solicitor was quick to shush him.

Encouraged, Diamond said, "I'm sure it seemed harsh and still does, but you ought to realise the damage you'd already done to Gildersleeve's self-esteem. In his mind, the failure of the Chaucer dig and the misconduct of the students were fused together in the same humiliating episode. Years later, he related it all to his new wife and she repeated it to me. He never forgot you. So when you came before him for dealing in drugs, he couldn't avoid being influenced by what had happened in Somerset. It was a repeat offence as far as he was concerned. He expelled you, and no redress."

Tim's shoulders sagged, but he said nothing, locked in his own unhappy memories.

"To your credit, you came back to Somerset, where you lived, and rebuilt your life. You got a job at the arts centre in Bridgwater. The interest in history hadn't been knocked out of you. You joined the local archaeological society and took an interest in the early history of the area. They thought well of you. Unfortunately, when the economy went belly up you lost your job like everyone else. You worked for your brother instead, clearing houses. You're not going to deny any of this because you told me about it yourself."

"That's true," Tim said. The exchanges were still civil: a good sign.

"And although it was a comedown compared to what you might have achieved as a university graduate, you had one remarkable success. Down in the basement of the arts centre, you found the *Wife of Bath* sculpture and recognised it for what it was. A personal triumph, that, and a sweet revenge, finding a major medieval carving with a direct link to Chaucer that probably had been recovered originally from the Chaucer house in Parker's Field. You were so proud of the find that you took me down there and showed me the empty space where you first spotted the thing."

"You asked to see it," Tim pointed out.

"You're absolutely right. I had an interest. You were very obliging. But let's backtrack to the excitement of that discovery, a terrific boost to your self-confidence. The people in the museum and your archaeological society were impressed. Terrific—until the Blake Museum committee discovered what a valuable asset the stone wife was. They were running the place on a modest grant from the council and donations and now they had a chance to boost their income by thousands of pounds. I don't suppose you approved—"

"I didn't," Tim couldn't resist saying.

"But you understood the economics. You couldn't do anything to stop the sale. And then—to your horror—you learned that your old enemy John Gildersleeve was taking a strong interest and apparently had the funds to bid high at the auction. All the old wounds were opened. The thought that your find was about to fall into his hands was more than you could bear. You had to stop it and you had the means." Diamond paused and watched across the table.

The reaction came, even if it was unspoken. Alarm, if not panic, was all too obvious in Tim's eyes.

"We know that Gildersleeve was shot with a thirty-eight calibre bullet that was typically fired from a Webley—almost an antique in itself. I'm going to make a guess now, and it won't be far out. Working at house clearances, as you do, I'm sure you come across plenty of things tucked away in old places. Some of the generation who served in the war hung on to their service revolvers until they passed on and then the guns lay in the loft or under the floorboards for professionals like you and your brothers to find when you cleared the house. Don't worry. I don't expect to find the murder weapon—if, indeed, the shooting was murder."

"It wasn't," Tim said, keyed up and quick to react.

The solicitor said, "Careful now."

The interview was fast approaching the critical point. "Do you want to explain?" Diamond asked.

Tim hesitated, and then shook his head.

"Three masked gunmen were involved in the attempted hold-up at the auction," Diamond continued, still willing to lay out the facts. "Those balaclava masks worked well.

Fortunately, we had a helpful witness—a Miss Topham, from Brighton, known in the trade as the glass lady—and she was standing behind the one we called the first gunman before he pulled the balaclava on. His head was blocking her view and she noticed a few things about it. He had long dark hair going grey. The hair had refused to grow over a scar on the back of his neck described by Miss Topham as like a little crater on the moon. And there were no lobes to his ears. Now fast forward to this morning. We're lifting the stone off the trailer, I'm next to your brother Wayne, and when he leans over the stone I get a good view of the back of his neck, the hair, the moon crater, the ears."

Tim's attempts to stay aloof from the narrative were losing all conviction. He was trying to stare at the ceiling.

"What's more," Diamond pressed on, "just after I had the twinge in my back and cried out with the pain, Wayne said, 'Nobody move'—the same words he used at the auction. Denis Doggart, the auctioneer, tells me he's certain it was the voice he'd heard before. If Wayne was the spokesman for you three—and he seems to have been—I have to ask myself who fired the fatal shot, and why?"

The solicitor put a restraining hand over Tim's arm. The intricacies of the case must have been difficult to follow, but when a fatal shot is mentioned, you don't want your client uttering a single syllable.

Diamond played his ace. "It could make all the difference to the charge, the question of intent. Did you go to that auction with the clear intention of murdering Gildersleeve?"

"No!" Tim shouted. "Definitely not. It was never in the plan."

The solicitor said to Diamond. "That's enough. I'm stopping this now."

But Tim saw this as his chance to head off the murder charge and he wasn't letting it go by. "I only ever planned to get the stone back, to stop Gildersleeve from owning it. I knew he'd bid really high and he did. I couldn't stomach the thought of it going to him." He swung around to the solicitor who had stood up and spread his arms as if he was herding geese. "Let me have my say, for God's sake. The bastard had messed up my life already, big time. This was more than I could bear. I persuaded my brothers to help me take the stone back. We didn't plan to kill him. We'd have hidden the stone where no one would ever find it. Wayne and Roger wouldn't have agreed to murder anyone. They were carrying plastic guns. I only loaded mine in case I needed to fire a warning shot. He was shot because he went berserk in there. He was trying to grab the stone. I hadn't expected that. He was always this cold, unfeeling guy. I panicked and pulled the trigger. That's the truth of it. One shot and it killed him. How unlucky was that?"

"Thank you," Diamond said. "We've got the picture now."

While Diamond had been interviewing Tim, Keith Halliwell, with a Taunton detective for company, had taken statements from the other two brothers. Nothing said by Wayne or Roger conflicted with Tim's account.

"What happens next?" Halliwell asked Diamond over beer and a sandwich with Ingeborg before they took to the road.

"We transfer them to Bath and go over it all again."

"Is it a murder charge, or what?"

"It's homicide, for sure, and in the course of an attempted robbery."

"Tim on a murder rap and the others as accessories?"

"Plus the driver. There must have been someone waiting in the van. We'll talk to the CPS. My guess is that they'll do Tim for murder and leave the court to decide on any leniency. A nice little earner for the lawyers." Diamond looked across the table at Ingeborg. "How are you feeling?"

"Great," she said, frowning. "Why shouldn't I be?"

"I was thinking about the arrest in the field. I wasn't there, but it sounded quite physical and you were covered in mud."

"It was nothing, guv."

He smiled. Ingeborg was never going to admit to frailty, even if she was covered in bruises. "That's all right, then."

"And you?" she said.

"Me?"

"You gave quite a shout when you were lifting the *Wife of Bath* off the trailer. Were you faking, to distract us all while you looked at the back of Wayne's head?"

"I didn't think of that," Diamond said. "Actually, I did feel something go in my lower back. I don't mind admitting, it's pretty sore."

Halliwell winked at Ingeborg. "That'll be the sting in the tail."

ABOUT THE AUTHOR

Peter Lovesey writes in a garden office he calls his shed, but in reality it's a handsome white shingle-tiled building in the American colonial style. Carpeted, double-glazed and heated, it contains a collection of books on the history of track and field, his other strong interest. As a child in 1948, he was taken to the London Olympic Games and a lifelong enthusiasm was sparked. When, years later, he came across a picture of a Native American named Deerfoot who visited Britain in 1861 and amazed everyone with his running, Peter began a quest to find out more. From this ultimately came his first book, a history of the sport called *The Kings of Distance.*

Encouraged, he entered the 1970 First Crime Novel contest with *Wobble to Death,* based on a Victorian long distance race, and won the £1000 first prize. This launched him as a mystery writer, but he continues his sports research and writing and is a mainstay of the International Society of Olympic Historians.

The Victorian mysteries developed into the Sergeant Cribb series, which really took off when they were televised (leading in UK ratings in the 1980s) and were chosen to launch the PBS *Mystery!* series. One of the Cribb novels, *Waxwork,* was awarded the Silver Dagger of the Crime Writers Association. Peter now has a small armory of such weapons, including the 2000 Cartier Diamond Dagger in recognition of his career. For some twenty years he has been writing the Peter Diamond series, so the honor had an extra cachet.

Peter married Jax, a psychologist he met at university, and she encouraged him to give up his lecturing job and become a full-time writer. As proof of her support, she co-wrote many of the TV episodes, but really she prefers painting and learning foreign languages to writing. While Peter was working on his novels, Jax embarked on a London University degree in Mandarin Chinese. They have a son, Phil, and a daughter, Kathy. Phil is a suspense writer who recently picked up his first Dagger Award for the best short story of the year. Kathy took a different route, moved to America and became a Vice President at JP Morgan Chase.

Continue reading for a sneak preview from the next
Peter Diamond investigation

DOWN AMONG THE DEAD MEN

1

"**A**re you sure this thing works?" Danny asked Mr. Singh, the gizmo man.

"You want demonstration?"

"I'd be a mug if I didn't."

"No problem. Where did you leave car?"

"A little way up the street."

"What make?"

"It's the old white Merc by the lamppost."

"Locking is remote, right?"

Danny dipped his hand in his pocket, opened his palm and showed the key fob with its push button controls.

"Very good," Mr. Singh said. "We can test. Go to car and let yourself in. Step out, lock up and walk back here. I am waiting on street with gizmo."

Danny was alert for trickery. He wasn't parting with sixty-odd pounds for a useless lump of plastic and metal. But if it really did work, he could be quids in. Thousands.

The gizmo, as Mr. Singh called it, looked pretty basic in construction, a pocket-sized black box with two retractable antennas fitted to one end.

No money had changed hands yet, so the guy had nothing to gain by doing a runner. Danny stepped out of the little coffee shop and did exactly as suggested. Walked to the Mercedes, unlocked, got in, closed the door, opened it again, stepped out, locked, using the smart key, and walked back to where Mr. Singh was standing outside the shop with the gizmo in his hands.

"You locked it, right?"

"Sure did," Danny said.

"Where is key?"

"Back in my pocket."

"Excellent. Leave it there. Now go to car and try door."

Danny had walked only a few steps when he saw that the lock pins were showing. Just as promised, the car was unlocked.

He was impressed. To be certain, he opened the door he'd apparently locked a moment ago.

"Good job, eh?" Mr. Singh said when Danny went back to him.

"Nice one. Who makes these things?"

"Made in China."

"Wouldn't you know it?"

"Simple to operate. You want to buy?"

"How does it work?"

"Okay. You know how key fob works?"

"Using a radio signal."

"Right. Sending signal from fob to car. Programmed to connect with your car and no other. But this gizmo is signal jammer. Breaks frequency. You think you lock up, but I zap you with this."

"Let me see."

Danny held the thing and turned it over. "All I have to do is press this?"

"Correct. All about timing. You are catching exact moment when driver is pointing fob at car."

"Hang on. There's always a sound when the locks engage. And the lights flick on and off. If that doesn't happen, the driver will notice."

"Did you notice?"

Danny hesitated. "There was traffic noise and I was thinking of other things."

"So?" Mr. Singh flashed his teeth.

"In a quiet place the driver would notice."

"Don't use in quiet place. Street is better, street with much traffic."

Danny turned the jammer over and looked at the other side, speculating. "How much are you asking?"

"Seventy, battery included."

He made a sound as if he'd been burnt. "Seventy is more than I thought."

"Fully effective up to fifty metres."

Danny handed it back. "I don't suppose it works with the latest models."

"Now I am being honest. Very new cars, possibly no. Manufacturers getting wise. Any car up to last year is good. That gives plenty choice. To you, special offer, not to be repeated. Sixty-five."

Danny took a wad from his back pocket, peeled off three twenties and held them out.

Mr. Singh sighed, took the money and handed over the jammer.

"Before you go," Danny said. "There's something else. This gets me into the car, but it doesn't let me drive it away. I was told you have another little beauty for that."

Mr. Singh's eyes lit up again. "Programmer. Which make? BMW, Mercedes, Audi?"

"I need a different one for each make, do I? How much will it cost me?"

"Two hundred. Maybe two fifty."

Danny whistled. This was getting to be a larger investment than he planned, but he thought about the top-class cars he could steal. "Let's say the Bimmer."

"BMW three or five series I can do for two hundred."

"Is it difficult to operate?"

"Dead easy. All cars now have diagnostic connector port. You plug in and programmer reads key code."

"Then what?"

"Code is transferred from car's computer to microchip in new key. You get five blank keys gratis as well."

"So I can drive off using the new key? Have you tried this yourself?"

"No, no, no, I am supplier only. Supplying is lawful. Driving off with some person's car is not."

"But you can show me how the thing works?"

"You come back with two hundred cash this time tomorrow and for you as special customer I am supplying and demonstrating BMW three series programmer."

Next afternoon special customer Danny drove away from Brighton with the programmer and the pride of a man at the cutting edge of the electronic revolution. In his youth he'd used a wire coat hanger to get into cars. He'd graduated to a slim Jim strip and then a whole collection of lock-picking tools. But the days of hotwiring the ignition were long gone. In recent years anti-theft technology had become so sophisticated that he'd been reduced to touring car parks looking for vehicles left unlocked by their stupid owners. For a man once known as Driveaway Danny it had become humiliating. The Mercedes he was driving was twelve years old. He'd liberated it in July from some idiot in Bognor who'd left it on his driveway with the key in the ignition.

Everything was about to change.

He would shortly be driving a BMW 3 series.

It wasn't easy to nail one. For more than a week he patrolled the streets of the south coast town of Littlehampton (which isn't known for executive cars) with his two gizmos in a Tesco carrier bag. The new technology called for a whole new mindset. He wasn't on the lookout for a parked car, but one that happened to drive up while he was watching. He'd need to make a snap decision when the chance came. *If* the chance came.

Late Sunday evening it did. After a day of no success he was consoling himself with a real ale at his local, the Steam Packet, near the red footbridge over the River Arun. He lived in a one-bedroom flat a few hundred yards away and liked to wind down here at the end of a long day. The pub was said to have existed since 1840, trading under a different name, because the cross-channel ferry that departed from there hadn't come into service until 1863. WELCOME ABOARD THE

STEAM PACKET, announced the large wooden board attached to the front with a profile of a paddle steamer—and in case the maritime message was overlooked, the north side of the pub had a ship's figurehead of a topless blonde (in the best possible taste, with strategically dangling curls) projecting from the wall. With a little imagination when seated in the terrace at the back overlooking River Road and the Arun you could believe yourself afloat. This was a favourite spot of Danny's, nicely placed for seeing spectacular sunsets or watching small boats chugging back from sea trips. But at this moment, alone in the half-light at one of the benches around 9:30 on a September evening, his thoughts were not about sea trips or sunsets. He'd just decided he'd wasted his money on Mr. Singh's gizmos. How ironic then that this was the moment when a silver BMW drove up and came to a halt in the parking space across the street.

Danny almost knocked over his beer reaching for the carrier bag. He tugged out the jammer and extended the antennas. Its first use for real. He couldn't have been better placed, all but hidden by the chest-high terrace wall.

The car's plates weren't visible from this angle. He couldn't tell from the design of the thing which year it had been manufactured, if it was too recent to respond to the jammer. If the trick didn't work, so what? It was worth the try.

The door opened and the driver got out, no more than a youth, slim, in a dark blue hoodie and jeans. He pushed the door shut. He didn't immediately use the key.

Danny's right forefinger was poised over the switch. As Mr. Singh had said, this was all about timing. *You catch exact moment.*

With a springy step and a bit of a swagger, the kid started walking in the direction of the footbridge. No one else was about. He hadn't used the smart key yet. As if in an afterthought, about three paces from the car, he turned his head and glanced back.

Danny's view was masked. All he could see was the youth's back half-turned. It was impossible to tell for sure if the key was in his hand, but reasonable to assume it was. Drivers habitually took a few steps from their vehicle and then turned, pointed the key and pressed.

Now or never. Danny brought his finger down and instinctively ducked out of sight behind the terrace wall.

Nothing happened.

He had to remind himself that the whole point of the jammer was to get a negative result.

When Danny put his head above the wall again, the kid was halfway across the bridge, moving briskly. Danny stowed the jammer in the carrier and hurried out, leaving almost half a glass of real ale behind. On his way through the lounge he raised his free hand in a farewell to the barmaid and stepped out of the building and round the side to where the BMW was parked.

A thousand blessings on Mr. Singh. The pins were up. The car was unlocked, begging to be liberated.

But not yet.

He needed to use the second gizmo, the programmer, to make his own key before he could drive his free gift away.

After checking to make certain no one was about, he stepped round to the driver's side and let himself in. The interior was still warm and smelt faintly of body odour. He left the door open. He dumped the carrier bag on the passenger seat and lifted out the programmer. Now it was a matter of locating the on-board diagnostic system and plugging in the sixteen-pin connector.

Should be simple.

Danny had been given a demonstration by Mr. Singh, who was as wiry as a strip of three-core flex. Danny was overweight. Grovelling under the dashboard of a car wasn't easy. On his knees and breathing hard, he made more room by pushing the seat back to its fullest extent. Just above the pull switch for the bonnet he found the cover with the letters OBD on it. He opened up, plugged in, watched the programmer light up, used the controls to collect the key code and then remembered he would need something else. He reached for the carrier and scrabbled inside for one of the blank fobs, found one and pressed it against the programmer.

All done in under three minutes.

Relieved, he unplugged, extracted himself and stood up. His hands were shaking and his knees were wobbly. He looked towards the footbridge and saw no one.

The next job would be more familiar: driving the thing away to get the registration plates changed. A guy called Stew was the local specialist, always relocating to outwit the fuzz and currently on a trading estate in Chichester, not more than twelve miles away.

Danny got in, slotted in the key and yelped in triumph as the dashboard lit up. The fuel tank was three-quarters full.

Bridge Road, the main road to Chichester, went past the front of the Steam Packet. Danny drove off as sedately as if he was taking his mother shopping. He didn't want to get pulled over for speeding. The good thing was that the young owner was still unaware his car had been driven away and with any luck he wouldn't return for a couple of hours. You couldn't have much sympathy. He was probably some rich kid whose father had bought the thing for him. Dad would shout the odds and then buy him another.

The Bimmer handled well and was a smooth ride. Danny didn't object to driving an automatic. Not much over two years old, he reckoned. No need for a respray when there were so many silver saloon cars out there. Once this had the new plates, he'd dump the old Mercedes. Selling wasn't an option in the stolen car game. But it was all very satisfactory, and for not much outlay so far. Stew would be more expensive than Mr. Singh, but that had to be faced. New plates were essential.

Now that he was clear of the crime scene, so to speak, Danny needed to check with Stew that he was willing to take delivery. The guy had never been known to turn down a job, but he liked to be contacted first. Only reasonable. Generally he was in his workshop until around midnight.

Out in open country, after the A259 had changed its identity from Bridge Lane to Crookthorn Lane to Grevatt's Lane, he found a field entrance with enough room to pull off the road and make the call on a cheap mobile he'd bought specially for this job.

"You working?"

Stew answered and he knew Danny's voice right away. "Yep. Got something to show me?"

"If you got time."

"When were you thinking of?"

"Now if you want. Say twenty minutes."

"See you, then."

Having made the call, Danny wedged the phone under the back wheel of the car so that it would be crushed when he drove off. Technology is a two-edged sword to anyone in a high risk occupation. He was tempted to do the same with the gizmos, but they'd been an expensive buy.

Before leaving, he thought he would also clear the glove compartment of the manual and any documents. It's common sense to remove everything that can reveal the owner's identity. The seats and door panels were free of obvious clutter, which was a help. For a young owner, it was all incredibly tidy. He leaned across and clicked the latch. The flap pushed against his hand.

An avalanche of banknotes tumbled out. Masses of them, mainly twenties.

The thump, thump wasn't the money hitting the floor; it was Danny's heart. Either the young guy who drove this car didn't believe in using banks or he robbed them. There must have been more than a couple of grand here.

Alternately swearing and thanking God, Danny scooped up handfuls and stuffed as many as possible into his pockets. The rest went down his socks. How glad he was that Stew hadn't found this lot.

What a turnaround in his luck. If it wasn't so late in the day he would have bought a lottery ticket.

Fully ten minutes passed before he calmed down enough to drive again. Even then he was mentally spending the money. Good thing the route was obvious. He was through Felpham

and Bognor and onto the Chichester Road without register-
ing that he'd passed anywhere.

Concentrate, he told himself. The job isn't done yet.

The last stretch of the A259 was a dual carriageway leading
to the A27. Two roundabouts and he would be at Stew's. He
could safely go up to seventy here and test the acceleration.
Watch the speedo, but feel the power.

Faintly over the engine sound he heard the twin notes of
a police siren.

Can't be me, he thought. I'm inside the limit.

In the mirror he saw the blue flashing light. Do what any
law-abiding motorist does, he told himself. Pull over and let
them pass.

He eased his foot off the pedal. Hardly anything else was
on the road and they could easily get by, but he did the
decent thing.

Instead of overtaking, they closed in behind him and
flashed their headlights. What now?

He pulled over, braked, lowered the window and switched off.

Bluff this out, he thought. They can't possibly know this
quickly that the car is stolen. It's got to be some minor
infringement like a faulty rear lamp.

He grabbed the bag of gizmos and pushed it out of sight
under the passenger seat.

They were taking their time, probably checking over their
radio that the car wasn't on their list.

Finally a figure appeared at the window. Heavy black moustache. "Evening, sir. Are you the owner of this car?"

"I am."

"Step outside, please."

What was this? The breathalyser? He hadn't finished his pint
of real ale. He'd be well under the limit. "Is something up?"

There was a second officer, a policewoman.

The male cop said, "Place both hands flat against the car
roof and stand with your legs apart. I'm going to search you."

"What for? I've done nothing wrong." As he said the words,
he thought of all the banknotes stuffed inside his pockets.

He did as he was ordered and felt the hands travel down his body. What the fuck was he going to say?

"What's your name, sir?"

"Daniel Stapleton."

"Date of birth, please."

"Ninth of October, 1970."

"Mind if I call you Daniel?"

"Danny will do."

"What's this in your pockets, Danny? Keep your hands exactly where they are."

"Some cash."

"Quite a lot of it, apparently. What's all this money doing in your pockets?"

"I, em, did some business. Cash transaction."

"What sort of business?"

"In Littlehampton. I sold a boat."

"Is that where you came from—Littlehampton?"

"Yes."

"And where are you travelling to?"

"Only Chichester. Bit of a night out."

"Spending all this money?"

"Not all of it."

"You said you own the car. It's been reported as stolen. That's why we stopped you."

"This car? Stolen?" He was able to say the words with genuine disbelief. The young guy had disappeared across the footbridge. He'd been on his way somewhere. He couldn't have returned so soon and got on to the police.

"Do you have any proof of identity? Your licence?"

"That's at home."

The search had been progressing down his body. "Do you normally keep banknotes in your socks?"

The cop didn't seem to expect an answer, so Danny didn't attempt one.

A large amount of cash might be suspicious, but it wasn't necessarily illegal. They hadn't found drugs or a weapon.

They were probably disappointed. Danny was wondering if the comment about the stolen car had been a bluff.

The cop said to his female colleague, "Let's have a look in the boot, shall we?"

Danny heard her open it.

She said, "God help us."

2

"You won't believe this," Jem said.

"Try me," Ella said.

"The Gibbon has gone."

Shrieks of amazement and delight from the group. Miss Gibbon was the most disliked teacher on the staff. Her idea of teaching art was endless exercises in perspective.

"Gone where?" Ella said. Always primed for excitement, she was the perfect foil to Jem, the information gatherer.

"I don't give a toss where. Up her own vanishing point, for all I care. She didn't tell anyone in the staffroom she was going at the end of last term. I expect the head knew, but none of the others did, so there wasn't, like, a leaving present or a farewell drink or anything."

"Who cares? At last they found out she was a crap teacher. I still haven't got the faintest idea what she meant by the golden mean and she never stopped talking about it."

"Golden section."

"Golden balls. Was she kicked out?"

"A scandal? Touching up the year sevens?"

"Not the Gibbon. She was sexless. More like pinching the art funds to go on those cultural cruises she was always on about," Jem said, and her opinion always triumphed. "The thing is, what happens to us in our final A level year? They'll have to bring in someone new."

"That's *all* we need, some new teacher straight out of college."

"Could be a bloke."

More shrieks. Jem, shorter than anyone, had a big

personality. She was like a conductor controlling the highs and lows of excited chatter.

"You wish!"

"Jem, you're joking . . . aren't you?"

Clearly she had more to tell. She waited for the noise to stop. "When I came in I happened to notice a sweet little vintage MG in the staff parking. And then I copped the back view of this tall young guy going into the head's office."

"Get away! What's he like?"

"Like an artist. Dark, wavy hair to his shoulders, bomber jacket and chinos, black shoes with Cuban heels—"

"Stop—I'm getting the hots."

"*You're* getting the hots? Think about the head. He was in with her for twenty minutes."

Everyone was rendered helpless. Even the coy Naseem got a fit of the giggles.

"Did he stagger out all shaky at the knees?" Ella said.

"I waited and waited, but I'd have been late for French conversation."

"Wouldn't it be bang tidy if he was our new art teacher?"

"Please God!"

"Dream on."

"We've only got to wait till third lesson to find out."

Mel, a pale, watchful girl who didn't often trust herself to speak, went to the window and looked out.

Jem saw her move and joined her. "Em, sorry about this, people."

"What? What have you seen?"

"The MG isn't there anymore. Dreamboat has gone."

"Aw, shoot!"

"The head must have put him off."

"She'd put anyone off."

"Or . . ."

"Or what?"

"Or he was only a computer salesman and she was like, 'While you're here, young man, how about checking my software?' and he panicked and legged it fast."

A ripple of amusement, tempered by sighs all round.

"Back to normal, then," Mel said, but she wasn't heard.

The mood was even more subdued in the art room at eleven, when no teacher appeared. Genuine anxiety surfaced about their exam prospects. Some hoped Jem had got it wrong for once, and the boring Miss Gibbon would shortly put her head around the door. She at least knew the syllabus and was capable of getting most of them a grade of some sort.

Naseem said, "We ought to tell someone. We're way down on where we ought to be at this time of the year."

As usual, it was Jem who took the decision. "That's it, then. Why don't you go to the staffroom, Ella, and say we're in urgent need of an art teacher?"

"I knew you'd ask me. Why don't you go yourself?"

"Cos you're always on about your future and that."

"I was hoping, like, someone else would do it."

"I don't mind going," Mel said.

She stood, refastened her hair, and left the room.

"I feel bad," Ella said, "leaving it to Mel."

"Don't," Jem said. "She's a peasant. Let her run the errands."

"You asked me first. Am I a peasant, too?"

"Course not. Your parents pay for you to be here. You're just a pain in the bum."

In under ten seconds Mel was back. "He's coming this way."

"Who is?" Ella asked.

"The new teacher, with the head."

"Dreamboat? Never."

"It's true. His car's back," Jem said, from beside the window.

"Tell me I haven't died and gone to heaven," Ella said.

No time to tidy hair, make-up, anything.

The head entered first, gowned as always, followed by Dreamboat, except he wasn't dressed as Jem had described. He was in a pinstripe suit, white shirt and tie that made him look like a bank clerk, apart from the long hair.

"I have an announcement," the head said, although no

one was looking at her. "Through circumstances beyond my control, your art teacher, Miss Gibbon, has taken an extended break from teaching and left the school. However, Mr. Stand-forth will be taking over. He is an accomplished artist and an experienced teacher who will guide you ably through this critical last year of your A level and I have assured him he will have your total co-operation. Because Miss Gibbon left at short notice, I am not entirely sure how much of the syllabus she covered with you. I am confident you girls will be only too pleased to inform Mr. Standforth, so that he can effect a smooth transition."

That was it. A swish of the gown and they had Dreamboat to themselves. The hush was total.

"Forget the 'Mr. Standforth' stuff. It's Tom," he said, revealing a set of gleaming teeth. "Sorry about the late start. I was here in good time, but stupidly I misjudged the dress code, so I had to nip home and change. Can't say I'm too comfortable in a suit. If nobody minds, I'll take off the jacket."

Take off whatever you want, the dumbstruck class was thinking. Not one of us will object.

His shirt was short-sleeved, revealing muscular forearms and tattoos. He loosened the tie as well and undid the top buttons of his shirt. Thrills in plenty.

"It will help to know your names," he said, perching his breathtakingly cute bum on the front desk. "Can't promise to remember them all right away, but let's make a start. Who are you, for instance?"

His brown eyes were on Ella. She managed to speak her name in a strangled voice.

"And is there any topic that excites you, Ella?"

Now she could only blink like a patient with locked-in syndrome.

"Any topic in art."

Her mind had gone blank. "The golden mean."

The rest of them spluttered.

"Well, that's an answer I didn't expect."

"Golden section, then."

"Still surprising to me. I'm impressed. Can't say I know a huge amount about either, but no doubt you'll all be able to tell me." He raised his hand. "Not now. Who are you, next to Ella?"

"Melanie, sir."

"Leave out the 'sir.' I'll let you know when I get my knighthood. What have you been doing with Miss Gibbon, Melanie, or should I call you Mel?"

Jem muttered, "The smell," and there were sniggers.

"What was that?"

"I said she's Mel," Jem said.

"I expect she can speak for herself. I asked you a question, Mel."

"We did exercises in composition. Lots."

"Composition. Right." He didn't sound thrilled. "The young lady who just spoke, what's your name?"

"Jemima. Everyone calls me Jem."

"So will I, then. I take it you, too, are well up on composition and the golden mean. Has it helped you creatively, Jem?"

"Like in my photography?"

"You're a photographer?"

"I wouldn't say that. I take pictures."

"You don't have to be modest about it. You have a camera, you take pictures, you're a photographer. Jem the shutterbug."

Smiles all round, except for Jem, who wasn't too sure if it was a compliment.

"I expect the rest of you do some snapping with your smartphones, don't you, all in the name of art? I'm joking, but your phone can be a useful aid. You've all got one, I'm sure."

"We're not allowed to get them out in class," Ella said.

"School rule, is it? Well, I'm not going to report anyone I see using hers as a camera. For one thing, you should all keep a record of your work as it develops, and for another you should always be on the lookout for visually stimulating images."

This was becoming unbearable. At the mention of stimulating images sounds like cars starting up came from around the room.

"But here's a warning," he added. "I draw the line at video games. Anyone caught playing Dumb Ways to Die can expect more than just a telling-off. Who's next to give me her name?"

In lunch break, there was only one topic: the man of the hour, the day, the week and probably the year. Eat your heart out, Prince Harry. Everyone agreed Tom Standforth was a perfect ten regardless of how he would shape up as a teacher. The art group were the envy of the school. People who hadn't yet clocked him made sorties to the staff car park to see the red MG.

For a time the art students were incapable of doing anything except replaying the lesson in their minds.

Jem, a good mimic, had his voice already. "'If nobody objects, I'll take off the jacket.'"

Peals of laughter.

"'And is there any topic that excites you, Ella?'"

Ella squeezed her eyes shut and said, "Don't."

"She goes, 'The golden mean.' Anything that excites you, and she's, like, the golden bloody mean."

"It's all I could think of. Oh my God, I wish he'd ask me again."

"'Anyone caught playing Dumb Ways to Die can expect more than just a telling-off.' What did he mean—a spanking? Bags me first."

Naseem had been using her smartphone. She put an end to Jem's miming with, "I've found his website."

Gasps.

"You what? He has a website? Yoiks." They almost bumped heads trying to see.

"They must be his paintings. Cool."

"Genius. Those colours."

"Such energy."

Active fingertips moved Tom's output at speed across the small screen.

"It isn't only abstracts."

"What's that? She's starkers. He paints nudes."

Shrieks.

"Let's see. Hold it higher, Nas. The size of those boobs."

"They look normal to me," Jem said.

"They would . . . to you."

"I'd rather have mine than your pathetic pair. D'you think he paints these from life?"

"Of course he does, pinbrain."

"Is it, like, his girlfriend? Oh, I hope not."

"How would I know? I expect she's just a model. Look, this one's blonde. She's gorgeous."

"They can't all be girlfriends."

"Why not? With his looks he could pull whoever he wants."

Naseem navigated back to the home page and found some pictures of Tom in his studio. The place looked large and cluttered, the walls and easels spattered with colour. "Why does he do teaching when he has his own studio?"

"Maybe he can't sell anything. All the great painters were like that, living in poverty."

"Poverty?" Ella said. "He owns a vintage MG. They're not cheap."

"He's a proper teacher. The head told us."

"And she's in the best position to know." Jem grinned.

"Who, the head? What position's that?"

Amid the laughter, Jem said, "Ask her. I dare you."

By the end of the afternoon, the excitement had scarcely abated. The A level group were watching from an upstairs window when the young man returned to his zippy sports car at the end of the day.

"There's only one question left," Jem said.

"Only one? I can think of hundreds. We know sweet F.A. about him."

"Yeah, but this is the one that counts: who gets to ride in the MG first?"

OTHER TITLES IN THE SOHO CRIME SERIES

Peter Lovesey
(England)
The Circle
The Headhunters
False Inspector Dew
Rough Cider
On the Edge
The Reaper

(Bath, England)
The Last Detective
Diamond Solitaire
The Summons
Bloodhounds
Upon a Dark Night
The Vault
Diamond Dust
The House Sitter
The Secret Hangman
Skeleton Hill
Stagestruck
Cop to Corpse
The Tooth Tattoo
The Stone Wife
Down Among the Dead Men

(London, England)
Wobble to Death
The Detective Wore Silk Drawers
Abracadaver
Mad Hatter's Holiday
The Tick of Death
A Case of Spirits
Swing, Swing Together
Waxwork

Jassy Mackenzie
(South Africa)
Random Violence
Stolen Lives
The Fallen
Pale Horses

Seichō Matsumoto
(Japan)
Inspector Imanishi Investigates

James McClure
(South Africa)
The Steam Pig
The Caterpillar Cop
The Gooseberry Fool
Snake
The Sunday Hangman
The Blood of an Englishman
The Artful Egg
The Song Dog

Magdalen Nabb
(Italy)
Death of an Englishman
Death of a Dutchman
Death in Springtime
Death in Autumn
The Marshal and the Madwoman
The Marshal and the Murderer
The Marshal's Own Case
The Marshal Makes His Report
The Marshal at the Villa Torrini
Property of Blood
Some Bitter Taste
The Innocent
Vita Nuova
The Monster of Florence

Fuminori Nakamura
(Japan)
The Thief
Evil and the Mask
Last Winter, We Parted

Stuart Neville
(Northern Ireland)
The Ghosts of Belfast
Collusion
Stolen Souls
The Final Silence
Those We Left Behind

(Dublin)
Ratlines

Eliot Pattison
(Tibet)
Prayer of the Dragon
The Lord of Death

Rebecca Pawel
(1930s Spain)
Death of a Nationalist
Law of Return
The Watcher in the Pine
The Summer Snow

Kwei Quartey
(Ghana)
Murder at Cape Three Points

Qiu Xiaolong
(China)
Death of a Red Heroine
A Loyal Character Dancer
When Red Is Black

John Straley
(Alaska)
The Woman Who Married a Bear
The Curious Eat Themselves

John Straley cont.
The Big Both Ways
Cold Storage, Alaska

Akimitsu Takagi
(Japan)
The Tattoo Murder Case
Honeymoon to Nowhere
The Informer

Helene Tursten
(Sweden)
Detective Inspector Huss
The Torso
The Glass Devil
Night Rounds
The Golden Calf
The Fire Dance
The Beige Man
The Treacherous Net

Jan Merete Weiss
(Italy)
These Dark Things
A Few Drops of Blood

Janwillem van de Wetering
(Holland)
Outsider in Amsterdam
Tumbleweed
The Corpse on the Dike
Death of a Hawker
The Japanese Corpse
The Blond Baboon
The Maine Massacre
The Mind-Murders
The Streetbird
The Rattle-Rat
Hard Rain
Just a Corpse at Twilight
Hollow-Eyed Angel
The Perfidious Parrot
Amsterdam Cops: Collected Stories

Timothy Williams
(Guadeloupe)
Another Sun
The Honest Folk of Guadeloupe

(Italy)
Converging Parallels
The Puppeteer
Persona Non Grata
Black August
Big Italy

Jacqueline Winspear
(1920s England)
Maisie Dobbs
Birds of a Feather